PRAISE FOR AMY HAGSTROM

"In this atmospheric and propulsive read, Amy Hagstrom masterfully ratchets up the tension not only with bad guys—of both the human and natural kind—but with complex relationships that will keep you feverishly turning pages. Perfect for anyone craving another disaster thrill ride after *Twisters*, *Smoke Season* is a must-read!"

—Brianna Labuskes, bestselling author of *The Lies You Wrote*

"*The Wild Between Us* shows how a suspense novel should be written. The tension ramps up with every scene, starting with the callout through to the shocking resolution. With the authentic description of the search and rescue mission, and the beautifully realized characters and scenery, Amy Hagstrom has created a story that all readers of suspense will relish, an achievement all the more remarkable given it's by a debut author."

—*Authorlink*

"*The Wild Between Us* is an unputdownable novel full of heart-stopping suspense and emotions. I couldn't read fast enough and was blown away by this stellar debut."

—Lyn Liao Butler, Amazon bestselling author of *Someone Else's Life*

"*The Wild Between Us* is a taut, engrossing story about searching for lost people and lost love . . . Part thriller and part tender love story, this novel will find resonance with a wide array of readers."

—Nicole Baart, bestselling author of *Everything We Didn't Say* and *The Long Way Back*

"Revolving between two search and rescue missions fifteen years apart in the Marble Lake wilderness, like two points of gravitational pull, *The Wild Between Us* explores the depths of guilt, secrets, and the unbearable weight of time in the face of tragedy. This immersive thriller had me riveted from the first page. Do not miss Amy Hagstrom's exceptional debut!"

—Mindy Mejia, bestselling author of *Everything You Want Me to Be* and *To Catch a Storm*

"Prepare yourself for *Smoke Season*, where Amy Hagstrom expertly guides you on a white-knuckle ride into the heart of an epic Oregon wildfire. Impossible choices flare up with every turn of the page as Hagstrom forces you to consider how far you'd go to help the ones you love. Consider this your Level 3 warning . . . GO NOW to get this book!

—Tony Wirt, bestselling author of *Just Stay Away*

NOW THAT I KNOW YOU BY HEART

OTHER TITLES BY AMY HAGSTROM

The Wild Between Us

Smoke Season

NOW THAT I KNOW YOU BY HEART

A Novel

AMY HAGSTROM

LAKE UNION
PUBLISHING

This is a work of fiction. Names, characters, organizations, places, events, and incidents are either products of the author's imagination or are used fictitiously. Otherwise, any resemblance to actual persons, living or dead, is purely coincidental.

Published by Lake Union Publishing, Seattle
www.apub.com

Amazon, the Amazon logo, and Lake Union Publishing are trademarks of Amazon.com, Inc., or its affiliates.

EU product safety contact:
Amazon Media EU S. à r.l.
38, avenue John F. Kennedy, L-1855 Luxembourg
amazonpublishing-gpsr@amazon.com

ISBN-13: 9781662535017 (paperback)
ISBN-13: 9781662535000 (digital)

Cover design by Eileen Carey
Cover image: © Tinna widianti / Shutterstock

Printed in the United States of America

For Erika, the wine connoisseur I'm lucky to have alongside me in life.

Chapter 1

The 1 p.m. ferry to Friday Harbor was late.

Shelby Wright waited in the long line of auto traffic, her fingers tapping an impatient staccato beat against the wheel. Overhead, the glow of a No Idling sign blinked through the fog coming off the sound, and she groaned at the irony. She'd found her first forward momentum in a year, only to be delayed at the very edge of the continent, within yards of her goal.

She turned off her engine and rubbed her hands together to stave off the cold. August seemed to have abandoned this far-left corner of Washington State, the low ceiling of the sky folding seamlessly into the flat gray of the bay. Cocooned in her Prius, Shelby felt the entire ferry terminal was complicit in forming an atmosphere of isolation.

Doubt crept in. Could she really make a brand-new life for herself, starting a business venture on San Juan Island? Or would she lose herself further, perched on this one island among the hundreds in the San Juan Islands archipelago? She glanced at her passenger seat, where she'd stuffed several binders' worth of legal papers in her box of ceramics supplies and clay. Uprooting and buying property had required a lot of work, but she wondered whether she should have bothered packing the rest. Who could find artistic motivation in this gloom? Locals said the first winter on-island was the hardest, but . . . *August.* Shelby shivered. It was only August.

Forward motion, she told herself. She'd promised to embrace this opportunity as she'd watched her hometown of Portland, Oregon, shrink in her rearview mirror that morning. She'd promised her son, Alex, that, with his dad's funeral behind them and his affairs finally settled, Shelby would get unstuck. Alex had his own launching to do. She'd promised her grief counselor, Margie, she would make the most of this new chapter, and her colleagues in the art department that she'd find fresh inspiration.

She'd promised Josh.

So many things.

Most of which she hadn't been able to deliver.

The last thought landed like a sucker punch to the gut, and Shelby willed herself not to buckle under the force of it.

"You'll finally . . . do what we've . . . always . . . talked about," her husband had said, each word formed with painstaking effort as he lay in the hospice ward. His voice had slurred even in his increasingly rare lucid moments, but, mercifully, the malignant brain tumor that had changed the trajectory of their whole world had not yet chewed away at too much cerebral hemisphere. He still somehow applied his trademark enthusiasm to every step of this final plan of his.

Mortal fever, the hospice nurses had called it.

"Josh on a Tuesday," Shelby had corrected with a lift of one eyebrow. These strangers couldn't appreciate the drive Josh put into every project, from the simplest contract job to the complexity of his marriage. And they didn't know how long he had dreamed of buying the historic inn. He'd fallen in love with it on their honeymoon twenty years ago, only to have it finally come on the market when he'd become too sick to travel.

So what could Shelby do but grasp his hand with all the medical tape snaking across it, with tubes and leads tethering him to the bladders of fluids over his bed? She'd looked past the oxygen mask that hid half his face and assured him that yes, she'd carry out this last wish of his. She'd use his life insurance payout to make a go of the Captain Merrick

Inn on San Juan Island, despite the fact that neither of them had laid eyes on it in those twenty years they'd been married.

"And you'll find . . . a studio again," he'd pressed. "You'll . . . work on your art."

Yes, she'd nodded, despite her doubt. It was simply what you did for a dying man, she'd later told her best friend, Beth. You yielded to his last requests. What she hadn't said, what she hadn't been able to bring herself to add, no matter how many times she'd tried, was that seeing this dream to fruition felt like penance after the truth bomb she'd dropped on Josh days before his diagnosis.

The bomb that may as well have killed him, her mind told her now, right on cue.

Shelby pushed back this thought with effort. After all, the most-sought-after neurologist at the Pacific Northwest's number one teaching hospital had drawn upon eight years of medical training and four years of residency to tell them that astrocytoma brain tumors "just happen."

"These things are no one's fault," she'd said.

No one's fault, Shelby made herself echo now, eyes closed in the confinement of her car, as the guilt took over, pinning her to her seat like a butterfly to felt. She strained against the agony of it. *No one's fault.*

When she forced her eyes to open, the fog still lay thick as a blanket on the sound. The first—and only other—time Shelby had waited in this line at the Anacortes terminal was with her new husband, and the bay had been a study of brilliant blue on blue, the ocean smooth as blown glass. The Friday Harbor ferry had approached right on time that day, a perfect white dot on the horizon growing in brightness and size until she and Josh had been able to make out the green-stenciled WSDOT lettering stamped along its hull. If conventional wisdom cautioned against committing to a new place until seeing it at its worst, Shelby had inadvertently heeded this advice in the reverse.

Forward motion, she reminded herself. Even if this venture *was* essentially just Josh getting the final word. He had tackled the construction of Shelby's new, second life like it was the most important contract of his celebrated architectural career, each step executed with the care and attention he'd give a foundational cornerstone or a load-bearing pillar. Brand-new career as an innkeeper. *Check.* Change of address, moving from the suburbs of Portland to a remote island. *Check.* Paying homage to their shared history, or establishing herself solo? That, Shelby supposed, was for her to decide.

She'd dragged her heels for a year now, getting Alex off to college, wrapping up her part-time teaching position in the art department, half hoping, half fearing, that by the time she could do right by Josh, the Merrick Inn would be off the market. That she wouldn't be required to circle back to the start of her marriage just when she so desperately needed to move forward.

No matter how good Josh had been to her.

No matter how much she had loved him.

Being the Shelby half of Shelby-and-Josh—always a single, connected phrase coming off the tongue—had left her unsettled. Partnered, yes, but somehow imbalanced. Like running a three-legged race when all she'd wanted to do was cut the rope and find her own stride.

It had taken her years to come to terms with why.

"You can tell me anything," Beth always said, but the words kept getting lodged somewhere between Shelby's head and her heart. How to say it? *News update: Your best friend of fifteen years is gay?* No. *I managed to tell Josh, but then he got sick, and everything went sideways?* Beth would understand. Hell, Beth, with her infectious confidence and quick wit, had been the catalyst to Shelby's self-awareness in the first place, unbeknownst to her. So why the inability to get it out?

Maybe it was the cloak of widowhood still wrapped so snugly around her. Somehow, in the midst of organizing the funeral, dealing with insurance, and consoling herself and Alex, "coming out to family and friends" had failed to get checked off the to-do list. Even now, her entire identity still shouted to the world: Straight! Grieving wife! Platonic friend! Each time the opportunity to come out to Beth presented itself, Shelby's throat closed up, all hope of finally being *seen* by her closest friend melting into a puddle on the floor. It wasn't until Shelby had been asked to head up the newly formed Wright Foundation, providing architectural department scholarships to underserved students in her late husband's name, that she'd finally cashed that life insurance check, quit her teaching position, and driven herself to this ferry dock. She might not know the first thing about innkeeping, but she certainly knew she'd only continue to lose herself entirely if she didn't try. She owed Josh, yes, but there were limits. How could she hope to move forward in Portland if her job description was literally to honor his memory?

"You can't do both?" Alex had asked, youthful optimism carrying all the way from his new dorm room at Vassar.

The guilt had gripped tight again, giving her a good squeeze. Whenever Shelby thought about her son adjusting to so much, so fast, she was left immobile. Unable to confide in Alex any more than in Beth.

"The other partners can run the foundation for now," she'd said, even while wanting to take it back immediately. While wishing she could tell Alex she would stay right where he'd left her, always. A placeholder for his father. A safe haven amid all he'd lost.

Shelby worried her lip, staring out into the fog. Unfinished business had a way of never quite relinquishing its hold, but she couldn't very well turn the car back around now. Even if she wanted to, the travel trailer in front of her and the minivan wedged behind her ensured the impossibility of executing a three-point turn. No, with Josh's affairs finally settled and her Prius packed, change—ready or not—was imminent. She couldn't think about who she'd been back in Portland. Even if she'd been that person just that morning.

As if on cue, a scratchy announcement over the ancient audio system heralded the arrival of the long-awaited MV *Samish*, and Shelby squinted through the windshield glass to glimpse the ferry gliding in through the fog like a ghost ship. Traffic attendants in reflective vests emerged from their heated kiosks to direct the line of vehicles toward the gangway, and Shelby restarted the car.

Fifteen minutes later, she stood on the passenger deck as the foghorn sounded, signaling departure. The floor beneath her feet gave a lurch, and the *Samish* slowly made its way out of Anacortes and into the sound. A breeze stirred the air, and she looked toward the outdoor observation deck, where weak sunlight now gleamed against the glass, dissipating the fog into mist.

For the first time in the year since Josh's death, Shelby felt true motivation beckon. She'd break out of this gloom toward something new, even if she had to contend with Josh's vision for her in the process. She'd embark on this new life, even with the baggage of the past heavy at her feet.

"Time to be your own woman," Beth had said upon Shelby's departure from Portland, not noticing the way Shelby flinched.

Could she? Be her own woman on San Juan Island? Either way, the *Samish* chugged forward into the sunlight, chasing a shared dream that probably should have died with Josh.

Chapter 2

San Juan Island appeared by jagged degrees, the last of the lingering fog along the rocky coastline burning away like paper set on fire, seared at the edges. By the time the *Samish* squeezed itself into the narrow ferry terminal at Friday Harbor, the sky had taken on the dependable dark blue of late summer, and the bank of shop windows and inns hugging the harbor winked at Shelby in welcome, the reflection blinding.

She dug her sunglasses out of her bag, eager to take in the island. It was good to note how little had changed. The same cheery, whitewashed buildings climbed the slope from the ferry terminal: B&Bs with harbor views wedged like puzzle pieces on the backs of fish-and-chips stands and tourist traps selling seashell bric-a-brac, bumper stickers, and overpriced hoodies.

She certainly hoped the Captain Merrick Inn hadn't changed much, either. According to Debbie Phillips, the one-woman show behind the island's most successful real estate operation, the previous owner had generously financed an on-site groundskeeper to "keep up appearances" after his abrupt departure just over a year ago, a service Shelby had verified through Google Street View images. Debbie had still felt compelled to use descriptors such as "needs TLC" and "charmingly rustic" on the listing, but she *also* hadn't balked at Shelby's first and lowest offer, which Beth had found suspect but which Shelby had viewed as the first *good* news she'd heard in a while.

Waiting her turn to disembark, she spread a paper map of the island out on the passenger-side seat of the Prius, having been warned that her cell phone might inadvertently ping the TELUS tower in neighboring Canada, resulting in international fees. Five minutes later, she eased out of the yawning depths of the *Samish* and made her way through town. King's Market, Friday Drugstore, and the Griffin Bay Bookstore all sat waiting along Spring Street as though Shelby had tucked them all in tissue paper for safekeeping two decades ago. She turned inland past the San Juan Historical Museum and almost immediately traded a seascape for countryside dotted with hay fields, the bales already neatly rolled. Dairy cows stood idly beside well-kept red barns, and roadside stands advertised local honey, jams, plums, tomatoes, and corn.

If Shelby recalled correctly, she'd find the Merrick Inn tucked into a tangle of old-growth forest on the northwest end of the island, about thirty minutes from the ferry terminal at Friday Harbor. For at least ten of those minutes, she cruised by more nondescript farmland, until a sign for a local lavender farm caused a memory to rise up in front of her with the unpredictable speed of a jackrabbit darting across the road.

"Just try it." Josh had laughed, waving the spoonful of lavender-infused ice cream under Shelby's nose in the packed-to-the-rafters gift shop on the second day of their honeymoon.

Shelby had already scrunched her nose at the smell of lavender lotion, lavender sachets, and lavender honey. The sharp scent had seemed too aggressive to put on her skin, let alone consume.

"Trust me." Josh's eyes had danced as Shelby's lips closed around the spoon, the taste of cream and vanilla with just the hint of lavender tang meeting her taste buds in a delicious blend of dairy and herb. She'd smiled at him around the plastic tester spoon in her mouth, conceding defeat.

Of course Shelby had trusted Josh. Even for his occasional over-effort. Despite the brownie points he had always been convinced he had to earn in their marriage.

"See, I already know you by heart," he'd told her proudly, a slogan, of sorts, that would become a favorite of his over the years.

If you asked Shelby, it was more that he'd memorized her like material he'd need to pass a test, week after week, year after year. His instincts had been more on target postmortem, actually, this plan with the Merrick Inn at least getting Shelby out of her rut in Portland and on to a new adventure, even if she did have to embark upon it with the label of cis het wife still clinging to her. And without Alex, whose childhood treasures were now packed in a storage unit three hundred miles south.

Without Portland traffic, either, she countered stubbornly, fighting the sudden sadness this induced. Without daily bridge delays and continuously gray skies, thanks to the welcome rain shadow cast by the Olympics.

Without her best friend, whom Shelby probably needed now more than ever.

Forward motion. What else could Shelby do? Being in Beth's company felt uncomfortable now anyway, Shelby's self-awareness prickling like a thin bruise blossoming just under the skin. It was too bad Beth, Portland Police Department's most celebrated forensic detective, couldn't see what Shelby simply couldn't bring herself to say. It would make things a whole lot easier.

With a sigh, she doubled down on her current mission, eyes peeled for her next turn, Mitchell Bay Road. It appeared right on cue, and she allowed herself a moment of victory as she approached the four-way stop. See? She didn't need the street smarts of PPD's rising star. Shelby had this well in hand.

Within a mile or so, the pastures and steep-sloped hay barns were overtaken by dense evergreens, just as Shelby had remembered. The Prius wound through groves of fir, the shoulder of the road carpeted with ferns and moss. She slowed, chancing a look toward her map again while sorely missing the convenience of turn-by-turn directions provided by Apple. Her final right, the one that would take her down Merrick Lane to the inn, had to be close.

It eluded her. Instead of encountering what Debbie had described as a narrow, asphalt drive disappearing into the trees, she came to the abrupt end of Mitchell Bay Road, which deposited her into the heart of a small, working marina. More of Debbie's possibly inaccurate advice echoed in her ear: *If you hit Snug Harbor, you've gone too far.*

With a frustrated sigh, Shelby scanned the marina for any sign of life and came up empty. The only building seemed to be a gas station combined with a bait-and-tackle shop, both of which appeared to be closed, and the few utilitarian boats bobbing on the water sat empty at this time of the afternoon, looking a bit abandoned. Shelby commiserated for a beat before executing a U-turn while avoiding boat trailers and stacks of lobster traps.

She headed back the way she'd come, but the turn off Mitchell Bay Road again failed to reveal itself. Shelby exhaled in frustration. Did this island require a special passcode in order to give up its secrets? She was reminded of the time she and Josh and Beth and her husband, Michael, had attempted an escape room in Portland. Finding the pathway to the magician's lair had turned into an unmitigated disaster, with only Josh meticulously working the clues long after Shelby had admitted defeat and Beth had resorted to strong-arming levers and pulleys into compliance. Michael hadn't even tried in the first place, absorbed in his phone all evening.

A third pass along the road proved equally futile. It probably didn't help that Shelby hadn't eaten since breakfast and it was now well after 4 p.m.; low blood sugar wasn't exactly conducive to concentration. She had just about decided to call Debbie, international data fees be damned, when the road opened up again at a small meadow, at the edge of which sat a large whitewashed barn with a small parking area out front. Spanning out behind this structure up the hill like a trailing cape: a wave of grapevines. Shelby turned in her seat as she passed to read the block-printed sign in thick black paint over the front barn doors: SAN JUAN WINERY.

She'd had no idea San Juan Island had a winery. And vineyards! The sight induced memories from childhood, the rows of her parents' vines like gnarled knuckles under the shadow of Mount Hood.

For kids growing up in Boring, Oregon, like Shelby, the jokes had made themselves. And whenever Shelby's peers went to Portland or Seattle for some culture, it seemed she was pruning vines or crating the fruit her folks sold to local wineries. With her parents perpetually preoccupied by yields and winery associations, Shelby had turned to the school counselor the first time she'd crushed on a girl. It hadn't occurred to her that the fact that the woman was also the wife of the local Baptist pastor might pose a conflict of interest.

Long story short? When Josh, a senior, asked her out, she accepted, lost though she felt.

And still felt, Shelby corrected, though more in the literal sense at this moment. She managed a much smoother U-turn and swung into the narrow parking lot on impulse. Surely someone here could give her directions.

She walked with purpose up the drive, then paused at a set of large, imposing barn doors. Was this the entrance? She pushed experimentally, and the doors slid open partway on metal runners above her head. In some past life of this barn, loads of hay must have been delivered through this door. She stepped hesitantly inside and was . . . delighted. There was no better word to describe the instant warmth that filled Shelby.

The winery's interior was just as pleasantly rustic as the exterior, with a wood-planked floor and whitewashed plank walls. The thick rafters overhead had been strung with soft white lights, and here and there, simple, farm-chic wrought iron chandeliers added to the ambience. The bar was also whitewashed wood, the stools made of the same crude ironwork as the light fixtures. A cluster of high-top tables made from upright wine barrels rounded out the room, and what clearly looked to be local art adorned the walls. Most were vibrantly hued watercolors of sea life ranging from rockfish to sea urchins.

A smattering of customers was responsible for the pleasant murmur of conversation that provided background noise to a musician strumming "Brown-Eyed Girl" in the corner. Several of the high-top tables were occupied by groups of threes and fours, all in various stages of tasting flights, and a couple sat at the far end of the bar, settled in close to one another. Shelby's eye caught on them, lingering discord and regret fraying the edges of her momentary sense of well-being.

Shelby searched for a distraction, her eyes lighting upon a colorful painting of a squid suspended in water, bright ink splashing to the edges of its canvas, which hardly helped. It reminded her of Josh's tumor spreading tentacle-like through brain tissue, and she pivoted on the spot. She couldn't do this. Not right now. Maybe she couldn't handle any of this . . . the move, the running of an inn she couldn't even find . . .

A woman's voice stopped her. "Can I help you?"

Shelby doubted it, but she turned back around anyway.

If the person hadn't called out to her, Shelby would have mistaken the owner of the voice for a man. Or a boy, perhaps. She was young, though not that much younger than Shelby, now that she looked closer, her dark hair cropped very short. Not buzzed to the scalp, but as close as Shelby supposed scissors could get, hence her momentary misidentification. She wore jeans and a tank top that showed off strong, finely muscled arms, and though petite, she gave off an energy that was somehow both masculine and feminine, confident and poised, as she moved to pour the couple Shelby had been staring at their next taste. Shelby found herself unable to look away as the ruby liquid splashed into the glasses.

"Uh, yeah," she managed. She felt wholly unprepared for this reaction to this woman, right here and now. For a second, she wavered between fight and flight before taking a step toward the bar. "Thanks."

The woman smiled. It opened up her whole countenance, adding to that air of boyish good looks. Shelby had never allowed herself to notice good looks in a woman before, not consciously anyway, with the exception, of course, of Beth. The fact that she was doing so now, while on this mission as Josh's widow, for god's sake, felt problematic.

"What can I get you?" the woman asked.

"Directions, actually. I'm looking for the Captain Merrick Inn . . . I'm sure I'm close."

The woman looked at her oddly, almost as if trying to decide whether Shelby was joking. A trio of older ladies sitting at one of the high-top barrel tables in the middle of the room swiveled around in their seats, sudden interest in their eyes.

"That place hasn't been open for guests for quite a while now," the bartender said carefully. "What's the address on your reservation?"

"I'm not a guest," Shelby clarified. "I bought the place."

Now *all* the patrons of the winery turned to openly follow this conversation, their expressions curious but guarded. Shelby shifted uneasily on her feet.

"You bought the Merrick," the bartender repeated slowly. She sounded almost . . . impressed?

Shelby nodded, and the woman's face broke out into a smile again. "No shit."

Yes, Shelby definitely detected a trace of respect in the woman's tone. But why? She felt tired and hungry, and the beginning of a stress headache was toying with the edges of her brain. She was unable to have a headache these days without thinking of Josh, and she shook him from her mind with effort.

"It's a long story," she offered the woman behind the bar, who stuck her hand out.

"Holly Caster," she said. "And I like a woman with a long story."

She delivered this line without guile and while maintaining intense eye contact, which Shelby broke first, feeling herself unexpectedly blush. "Shelby Wright." She mustered a weak smile in return.

"Well, as you thought, you're not far from the Merrick," Holly said more brightly, as though the situation called for solidarity and support. "It's actually the next turn, heading toward Snug, but it's been a while since anyone's maintained the road. Bet the sign's down." She looked down the bar toward the couple. "Bill? You know where I mean. Merrick Lane."

Bill looked wary, like he wasn't entirely sure he wanted to be associated with this conversation, let alone become complicit by handing out directions to the Merrick. Shelby swallowed a wave of apprehension. What could possibly warrant such caution?

After a pointed look from his wife, Bill reluctantly instructed Shelby to watch for a red wooden sign halfway up a fir tree just past the curve after the last fence post of the neighboring sheep farm. Shelby cast a glance about in hopes of finding a pen to write this down as Bill added "Maybe she ought to have company" in a vague tone that clearly conveyed he was not volunteering for the job.

"I'm meeting my Realtor," Shelby offered hastily. The last thing she wanted was an entourage of uncomfortable townsfolk as she stepped across the threshold of her new inn for the first time. She turned to go with a flustered thank-you, making it halfway across the tasting room floor before Holly's voice halted her again.

"Come back to see me once you're settled." When Shelby turned to acknowledge this, she'd lifted one hand up in farewell, adding with a laugh, "It's not every day my musician manages to conjure an actual brown-eyed girl to my bar."

One patron stifled a chuckle while nervous energy continued to radiate from the rest of the tasting room. Bill stared down at his wineglass while his wife wore an expression of outright fascination.

The ladies at the barrel-top table resumed their own conversation, but Shelby wasn't entirely convinced it wasn't about her.

Her footsteps sounded loud on the wooden-plank floor as she made a beeline for the barn doors, trying to convince herself the word *Merrick* had not just triggered a very odd combination of concern and circumspect bemusement in every local in the room.

Chapter 3

Back on Mitchell Bay Road, Shelby scanned the forest line as she drove, looking for the elusive sign to Merrick Lane. Sure enough, she caught a flash of red lettering and braked just in time to glimpse the CAPT of what must be CAPTAIN MERRICK INN on an aging plank of wood half obscured by ferns. Victorious, she eased onto the narrow one-lane road and reduced her speed for the final quarter mile.

When the lane ended, she stopped the car right in the middle of the drive, peering up through the windshield glass. After listening to Bill and Holly, Shelby half expected to see plywood over every window or squirrels and owls making homes in the rafters, but to her relief, the Captain Merrick Inn stood as stately and proud as she remembered it, aside from a few signs of weathering and a couple of sagging steps leading up to the wraparound porch. The cedar planking glowed almost red-gold in the afternoon sunshine, and the second-story gables beckoned just as they had when she and Josh had pulled up for their honeymoon.

Past the porch, thick-paned windows stood sentinel on either side of a wide wooden door, and around the side of the porch, the east wing of the building curved out of sight, giving the Merrick a rather rambling look that still managed to charm. What on earth had elicited such a reaction at the winery?

Shelby parked between a matching cedar-planked annex building she hadn't remembered from before—an addition, perhaps?—and an unattached garage or maintenance building at the end of the turnaround driveway. Retrieving a manila envelope from her overnight bag, she shook out a set of keys and crossed the garden (as well manicured as pictured on Google) on her path to the front door, which was adorned with an ostentatious brass anchor.

It took three tries with two combinations of keys, manipulating several dead bolts to wrest the door open. Once inside, she paused, allowing her eyes to adjust to the sudden lack of sunlight, then took in the wood-paneled walls, planked floorboards, and high, raftered ceilings. Yes, this was the historical architecture Josh had loved, despite the perpetual gloom.

She fought the impulse to cross the vestibule to thrust open the floor-to-ceiling velvet curtains and let in some light. She'd assumed that after sitting empty for so long, the Merrick would convey a sense of abandonment, but only a light layer of dust covered the rolltop desk and lampshade. An ornamental display of lavender sprigs prettied the hall table, and a vase of wildflowers sat on the empty check-in counter. Clearly, someone had been making an effort to keep things cheery. Or in the vicinity of cheery, anyway.

The entryway wasn't much changed, really, from when she and Josh had crossed the threshold together twenty years ago, right down to the scent of cedar and fir that mingled with a distant ocean breeze, just like she remembered. While she'd hoped the inn would not be in disrepair, part of her wished a previous owner had remodeled, or at least redecorated, since her last visit. It had been hard enough seeing Josh's influence in every element of their Portland home—he had designed it, after all—but it was even more jarring to feel his stamp here, too, from the Victorian furniture he'd admired to the tongue-in-groove flooring he'd been determined to replicate at his firm. A desperate need for space of her own, which had often immobilized her with guilt in Portland, clawed at Shelby's throat.

Screw it. She flung open the drapes, dodging particles released into the air as light streamed in, immediately transforming the room.

That was better.

But she still felt a bit claustrophobic. As the dust motes swirled in the wake of her movement, she dutifully attempted the breathing exercises Margie had taught her in their one-on-one sessions, while that scent she'd long associated with this inn—that appealing mix of fir and brine—continued to waft past her nose. In . . . out. In . . .

"Knock, knock!"

Shelby nearly jumped out of her skin, whirling back around to the door. She recognized the voice immediately from phone calls exchanged while still in Portland: Debbie Phillips, real estate agent extraordinaire. And if the sound of another key in the lock was any indication, she had no intention of actually knocking.

"Welcome wagon!"

"In here," Shelby had time to call as Debbie pressed her way inside.

Debbie nearly bumped right into her. "There you are! All arrived and in one piece!" Her booming laugh ended in a coughing fit as she, too, breathed in the displaced dust. "Well, c'mon in then."

She brought a gauzy magenta-colored scarf up to her face as she waved Shelby along with her through the vestibule and into the Merrick proper. The dining area took up most of the ground floor, which creaked a bit ominously under their footfalls. Shelby took in the round oak tables and heavy china hutch as her heart rate returned to normal. Did this room remind her of Josh, too, with its doilies and iron candle centerpieces? It did. His plan for this space, so painstakingly outlined from his hospice bed, might as well be etched directly into the walls.

"We could serve scones and coffee cakes at breakfast," he'd said, trying to grasp Shelby's fingers in a weak show of very real enthusiasm. "That will be simpler than a full hot meal. And in the evenings . . . we can bring in live music . . . violins, maybe, or folk singers."

It was always "we." Josh never said "you." This was common, Shelby had been told by the hospice nurses on the floor, their eyes always sympathetic. Their hands always stronger than Josh's as they'd caught hers and squeezed. Of course, Josh had been trying to make them a "we" from the moment they'd gotten married. And he'd been angling to return to the place where they'd debuted as a couple from the moment they'd checked out.

"Nice, right?" Debbie said now, watching Shelby analyze the space. "So much potential."

Debbie personified met Shelby's imagined visual expectations precisely: late fifties, ample bosom, big hair. She wore an aggressively bejeweled sweatshirt, and her fingers showed off lethally long, ornately polished nails.

Debbie caught her looking. "Like 'em?" she asked, thrusting her fingers toward Shelby for further inspection. "Island Nails is just down the road at Roche Harbor, honey. Ask for Terri. She's the only one who can do design work like this."

Shelby decided she was looking at what were either tiny fuchsia seashells or oddly shaped stars on Debbie's nails. "Those are . . . wow."

Debbie beamed. "Fun, right?" She crossed to the far end of the room, toward an entire row of windows. "At least you've got some nice weather so you can air this place out a bit."

Shelby agreed. "It's not nearly as musty as I thought it would be."

"Oh, well, that would be on account of Ezra, I suppose."

"Ezra?"

"Ezra Peterson, your groundskeeper and gardener? I did mention him, didn't I?" Debbie's hands came up to frame her cheeks as her mouth stretched into a comically wide O.

"Yes, yes, the groundskeeper. Of course. The gardens look lovely," Shelby assured her.

"*So* lovely!" Debbie agreed, resuming her assault on the windows as she hefted the rest of the row open. As more sunlight poured in, the warmer ambience softened the jarring memories of Josh to something closer to nostalgia. She could certainly see why he'd loved *this* part of the inn, with its large fireplace and ornate bar. With some new touches, new accents . . . she studied the thick Persian carpet at her feet, deep russet and emerald competing for dominance on a backdrop of soft cream. Maybe something to complement it . . .

"Well!" Debbie clapped her hands together loudly. "I should show you around. Give you the grand tour!"

Shelby followed her obediently to the Bay Bar, its driftwood slab shined to a polish, its stools lined in mahogany leather. The mirror behind the counter was pockmarked with freckles of rust, and Shelby's eye immediately found what had been their bartender's favorite talking point during their honeymoon: the splinters from an antique bullet hole, its cratered center spiderwebbing toward the bottles carefully displayed on the shelf below. As the story went, Captain Merrick himself had taken a drunken shot at a bottle of Beefeater during a New Year's Eve bash in the late nineteenth century.

Debbie followed Shelby's gaze to the mirror. "I can't deny it adds a bit of local color."

Shelby agreed. She turned to study the rest of the room again. When she and Josh had stayed here, most of the tables had been filled by locals . . . Snug Harbor fishermen and local quilter and crafter groups. Could she regain that cozy patronage? Or would the inn's recent neglect sour the locals on returning? The cool reception she'd received at the winery—with the exception of Holly—hung like an unsettling cloud over her head as she continued her visual inventory.

A rock-walled fireplace dominated a sizable portion of the far end of the room; Shelby and Josh had warmed up in front of it after a morning stroll through the fog, hot tea in hand. But . . .

"I don't remember that being there," Shelby said, gesturing toward a giant wooden ship wheel mounted over the mantel.

Debbie sighed. "That would be another contribution of Ezra's," she said.

"He certainly does a lot around here."

Debbie proceeded cautiously, which didn't strike Shelby as a good sign. "Like I said on the phone, Ezra just sort of comes with the place," she said.

In the caretaker's cottage at the far end of the property. Shelby hadn't loved the idea when Debbie had explained the living situation established by her predecessor, but Beth had breathed a sigh of relief.

"At least you won't be rattling around in that old place all alone."

She hadn't had the energy to argue. In some ways, from the moment she'd left the neurologist's office with Josh's diagnosis ringing in her ears, his tumor had taken up all the real estate in *her* brain as well.

"Well, c'mon then," Debbie said. "We still have lots to see."

Shelby followed Debbie past the fireplace, where French doors led to what she knew would be a wide veranda. She braced herself for more reminders of Josh, because he'd had plans for this part of the inn as well. "We can serve high tea out there," he'd told her, pointing at the feature on the real estate listing. "Like they have up in Victoria."

What did Shelby know about high tea? What did she know, even, about serving any sort of meals to B&B visitors? But she'd only nodded, returning the weak smile that had played about his lips, chapped by days of intubation, at the thought of her making their mark on the Merrick. She stepped out onto the veranda, which was as she remembered it, save for the far end, which was sheeted with construction plastic. She frowned, pointing this out to Debbie.

"Just a small repair job, I'm sure," she said.

"I'm sure," Shelby agreed, not quite as enthusiastically.

The view was dominated by the back gardens, which were as impeccably kept as the front, and beyond, a pocket view of the bay peeked between fir trees. Josh could keep his antique glass and stone fireplaces . . . *This* was Shelby's favorite part of the inn . . . the outdoors. The views. The way nature seemed to encase the entire property in a green embrace. Taking in this view, she warmed to Josh's idea. She could definitely place at least a few tables out here on the veranda during the warmer months, provided there was nothing too worrisome under that plastic tarp.

Back inside, they returned to the vestibule, where Debbie's persistent chatter continued as they passed the old-fashioned rolltop check-in desk to climb the stairs.

"Eight guest rooms up here," Debbie puffed, "and then you've got one suite downstairs, and the annex, too."

The building by the garage. "How many rooms there?"

"Oh, capacity for twelve more guests, I think?" Debbie had to pause at the landing to suck in deep gulps of the still-stale air. "It's three suites, you see."

So about twenty-eight guests total, and Shelby would be at capacity. She ruminated on this as she climbed the rest of the steps. She could handle twenty-eight people, right? With a small staff? Her mind swung to the job postings she'd need to place, the interviews she'd need to conduct. Where should she begin?

"Do you have a reopening plan yet?" Debbie asked, which only added, of course, to the stress rapidly raising Shelby's heart rate.

But at least she had an answer to this question. She'd gone over the math with the firm's lawyer, and then again with Beth, after settling Josh's affairs, purchasing the inn, and declining the offer to head up the foundation. She'd accepted the partners' offer to buy her out of Josh's share in the firm, but all of that had gone directly to Alex's inheritance.

"I'll need to start showing an income from guest stays by December," she said, "in order to stay afloat." That gave her three solid months. Would it be enough? The life insurance settlement had paid for the inn, but the day-to-day costs of running the Merrick, even just living in it, would soon pile up. She'd already begun the process of securing a business loan.

"The overhead at a place like this is nothing to sneeze at," Debbie agreed. "But you're right: Priority number one needs to be getting heads in beds again." She *tsk*ed. "*Also* nothing to sneeze at."

Would it really be such a hurdle? Shelby wanted to ask follow-up questions but wasn't entirely sure she was ready to hear the answers. It reminded her of sitting across from Dr. Kaval in the neurology office all over again. God, toward the end of Josh's life, Shelby had had so many questions. How long until Josh's short-term memory went? How long until he forgot his own son's name? And most haunting of all: Did Josh even remember the most important thing she'd ever told him, triggered by her feelings for Beth?

Not my fault, she reminded herself again. It was a desperate mantra, but it would have to do.

Debbie cleared the stairs, and they poked their heads into the first few rooms—all standard two-person occupancy, Debbie recited—as Shelby took stock of the rather dreary curtains and faded bedspreads. No wonder no one wanted to be here. She could see how badly the Merrick's guest rooms needed a refresh. Ditto for the en suite bathrooms with their pedestal sinks and aging tile. How much would that cost to replace? Shelby worried.

She and Josh had thought the Merrick so elegant when they'd checked in. They'd felt like real adults, staying at their first hotel without a neon sign and freeway exit access. He had been the one to book it, always so eager to rush forward with Shelby to the next chapter of their life together, while she'd always trailed behind, in his wake.

At the end of the hallway, she lingered again, trying to recall which guest room she and Josh had occupied during their honeymoon. Though she couldn't be sure, she thought it might be this one, right on the end. She stared into it for a long moment, taking in the large wooden dresser and queen-size, four-poster bed, half afraid to go in. Instead, she tried to conjure her twentysomething self into the room. The romantic nights Josh had planned hadn't exactly gone smoothly, had they? She took a deep breath, still trying to calm the unsettled feeling in her gut. Signing that marriage certificate had made everything feel so real. Newlywed Shelby had been a deer in headlights, a shell of the mature woman she'd hoped to be.

Not that she was much further along right now. As she trailed Debbie back downstairs, Shelby still felt a sense of incompleteness, a hollowness inside even after coming out to Josh and fulfilling his wish for her to open this inn. She fought the nagging feeling that she was still waiting for something . . . the shading to be filled in, for her sense of depth to be defined.

"I recall you saying your husband loved this place," Debbie said as they reached the bottom step. "And who could blame him!"

Shelby forced a smile. "I think it was the perfect combination of architectural history and romantic togetherness for him," she said.

"It certainly is," Debbie gushed, present tense and all, while Shelby worried: What if this inn, just like everywhere else, was still too filled up with the presence of Josh to make any room for her?

Chapter 4

Back downstairs, Shelby did a second visual inventory of the dining room. This part of the inn, too, would need work. Its doily-topped tables and clunky chairs were outdated and tired, a complete departure, for instance, from the welcoming farm-chic ambience in the winery Shelby had just visited.

Comparing the two reminded Shelby again of the odd reception she'd experienced there. "I know the Merrick's been a bit neglected, but what exactly happened with this place?" she asked Debbie. Beth had urged her to dig up the inn's BBB records before signing on the dotted line, advice Shelby now greatly regretted pushing to the bottom of her daunting to-do list. "Did the previous owner have a change of heart?"

Debbie seemed just as reluctant to discuss the details of the inn as the patrons at the winery, becoming immediately and urgently interested in anything but the question at hand. "How about tea? Could you use a cup?" she asked, unnecessarily, it seemed to Shelby, as the woman was already making a beeline for the large kitchen off the bar, where she seemed right at home opening cupboards until she'd produced a kettle and an old box of herbal tea. Lavender something or other, of course; everything was lavender infused in some way or another on this island. This tea was probably from the same farm Shelby and Josh had toured that long-ago day.

Debbie set water to boil on the massive Viking stove while Shelby's thoughts returned to the task of hiring a kitchen staff and chef. "I could use all the information I can get," she pressed.

"Well," Debbie said carefully, once she'd claimed a stool back at the driftwood Bay Bar. "First this inn was in the Merrick family, of course." Her feet—in bright-red Keds—dangled above the floor, giving her perch on the stool a whimsical, childlike look.

"Established in 1860," Shelby recited from the information she'd gleaned upon applying for the National Register of Historic Places of America plaque Debbie had informed her she was entitled to. This, at least, had been a task she'd relished.

"Mm-hmm," Debbie concurred. "Captain Merrick and his wife lived here until almost the turn of the century, but it wasn't an inn until he died of old age. He left Mrs. Merrick—don't know her first name, come to think of it . . . isn't *that* the way of history, honey—in appalling debt, and she had to earn a living one way or another, or so the story goes. She was a good decade younger than the late captain, and women, well, we just tend to live longer, don't we? Men seem more than willing to croak first."

Debbie laughed loudly at her own joke before flushing with awareness, straightening on her stool. "Ah, damn. I'm sorry, honey. I don't know how I could have forgotten your circumstance." She laid one manicured hand on Shelby's arm and said earnestly, "Please forgive my insensitivity."

"Consider it forgotten," Shelby managed. She was used to this. Not jokes about male life expectancy, exactly—that was new—but the awkwardness that followed Shelby everywhere, once people knew her "circumstance," as Debbie called it. Strangers and acquaintances, even those she would have considered good friends, always seemed at a loss for words.

"Time heals, they say," she added to Debbie, to dispel any lingering weirdness, even though it had been only a year since Josh died. The kettle began to sing, and she escaped to the kitchen to pour two cups of the pale-purple tea. She scrunched her nose again as the scent wafted up around her.

As she'd anticipated, it brought her directly back to Josh and the lavender farm. People said that about smells, didn't they? That they had the power to draw forth memories sharper than anything else. Was this a mistake? She'd known coming back here would be hard, but how was Shelby supposed to be who she was meant to be on this island if Josh was everywhere?

She returned to the bar, where she offered Debbie her cup with a pained smile and renewed determination to get to the bottom of things. Shelby knew why *she* needed a fresh start, but why, exactly, did the Merrick? "So after Mrs. Merrick's reign, the inn stayed in the family for the next few generations?" *Fast-forward to the part where the locals won't look me in the eye.*

"Yes, that's right. Until just past the turn of the millennium, which would have been around the time you paid your visit, right? On your honeymoon?"

Shelby nodded. August 2005.

The night they'd arrived, she and Josh had ordered oysters on the half shell right here at this bar. She could still conjure up the sensation of them sliding down her throat in a slick wash of sea and salt. Despite the disorientation of having Josh so overshadow her today, that inexplicable sense of nostalgia made her chest literally ache. Her younger self, tasting oysters, smiling at her new husband across the table . . . How had she managed to push the knowledge she was gay so far down, she couldn't reach it? A stubborn—and at least partially subconscious—determination to succeed at the life she'd laid out for herself? By the time Shelby had gotten herself out of Boring and into the wider world—with its wider perspectives—to join Josh in Portland, her wedding was already in the works.

Even so, how had she allowed that moment, right here at the bar, and then the next, and then the one after that, to pass without coming to terms with who she was? Unable, for whatever reason, to hit the brakes to stop their lives from careening further forward, right into parenthood and a decades-long partnership? Her mind spun, trying to reckon with this.

Debbie looked at her a bit oddly but mercifully continued her narrative. "Anyway, the inn continued to be quite the pride of the island, right up until the . . . trouble."

Debbie said the word *trouble* like it ought to have traffic cones placed strategically around it. Shelby frowned as she leaned forward in her seat. "What kind of trouble are we talking about, exactly?" Again, she berated herself for going into inn ownership so naively . . . such an amateur mistake.

Debbie squirmed on her chair, her mouth opening and then closing again in hesitation. She resembled the coho salmon that had been mounted on the wall over the *Samish*'s galley as she finally blurted, "Don't tell me you don't know?"

Well, this doesn't sound good. "Don't know *what*?"

Debbie blinked. "Why, about the Merrick being 'haunted,' of course."

She created air quotes around the word with four manicured fingers, but Shelby still heard warning bells going off in her head. "Haunted how?"

Color rose in Debbie's cheeks, hot pink to match her nails. "How? I'll tell you how. 'Haunted' as in 'publicity stunt.'" More air quotes. "'Gimmick.' Which, I will mention, only resulted in a run of terrible PR."

"What happened?"

"That awful owner happened, that's what. Your predecessor, Jack Monroe. Sometime after the pandemic, he came back from a trip to Tombstone or Buffalo Bill–ville or some such place with the notion in his head that ghost stories equal dollar signs. Now, it's true that tourism was down in those days, and most of us business owners were getting creative. But Monroe took it altogether too far. Got right to work concocting a ridiculous story about the Merrick family haunting their old home . . . It was all 'widow walks' this and 'footsteps on the stairs' that. You know . . . Victorian-era black taffeta veils, little girls wailing in wells . . ."

Shelby got the gist. "Surely no one took it seriously," she reasoned. Even with this place filled to the rafters with the gloom of velvet curtains, hurricane lamps, and yellowed doilies.

Debbie sighed. "Not until Ezra took up the story and ran with it."

"Ezra my gardener?"

Debbie nodded. "More like . . . gardener turned pseudocelebrity," she admitted, exhaling sharply through a clenched jaw to send a puff of air upward toward her coiffed bangs. "Though to be fair, the internet made way too much of it all."

Shelby just waited, a pointed look on her face, until Debbie stumbled through the rest.

"Like I said before, Ezra's basically an institution around here. At least as much as a twenty-three-year-old can be," she amended.

"Twenty-three?" Hardly older than Alex, then. Shelby had envisioned Ezra as much, much older.

"My point being," Debbie went right on, "he's harmless as a fly, no question about it. Our Ezra's just had a tough time of it of late, and something in Monroe's story resonated with him, bless his heart. I daresay he got rather infatuated with the idea that the Merrick might harbor spirits." She pinned Shelby with a beseeching look. "He lost a loved one of his own recently. I suppose he just wanted to believe Monroe's yarn."

Shelby nodded cautiously while her gut tightened anew. The last thing she needed was the possibility of a loved one's spirit hanging around.

"Anyway, Ezra jumped right in. Went so far as to concoct a whole ritual of sorts . . . a regular performance arts piece! Monroe wasted no time advertising Ezra's act on message boards and paranormal groups all over kingdom come, leading every conspiracy theorist and kook on the World Wide Web to believe a *ghost* had taken up residence at the Captain Merrick Inn. Or that, at the very least, they'd enjoy some entertaining dinner theater." She clasped Shelby's hand in a sweaty grip. "Believe you me: It brought ghost aficionados here in droves."

Shelby flashed on the looks she had seen on the faces of the winery patrons earlier. "And I take it people around here didn't like that much?"

"What's to like? Just picture it, Shelby, as a reputable business owner: ghost hunters driving up on your lawn, Instagrammers trampling through the garden! Quite the hoopla! And did all these visitors behave like proper tourists, booking rooms and dining in our restaurants? Oh no! They camped right in the ferry terminal and slept in their cars, unable to take a break—even a moment—from their heat sensors and energy vortex wands and whatever other nonsense!"

"But isn't 'any publicity good publicity'?" Shelby hadn't seen even a hint of any of this "hoopla" while scrolling through the Merrick's social media listings.

Debbie puffed herself up in her indignation, her eyebrows reaching her hairline, making her look like a flustered hen. "I should say not! Ezra went entirely too far with his candlelight ghost tour, séance, whatever." She took a bracing swallow of her tea, lips pursed. "We had to clean up after him, reporting all the misleading reviews on Tripadvisor and whatnot."

"What, like contesting the hauntings as false or off topic?" The architectural firm had had to report a few reviews on Yelp over the years.

Debbie nodded. "Respectable folks don't want to think they're going to get *haunted* when they come to the island, honey. The regular tourists, the ones who just want to whale watch and storm watch and buy lavender sachets in peace? They'll go to Orcas instead!"

The next island over. Debbie made it sound like the worst of betrayals.

"We did as much damage control as possible, but we *still* ended up in a top-ten haunted islands list on BuzzFeed. Reservations from regular folks dropped drastically." She made a nosedive motion with one hand. "Whooosh."

That did seem dire. But . . . "who's 'we'?"

Debbie stared down at her hands, curled around her tea mug, as though suddenly fascinated by her nails again. "Oh, you know. The chamber of commerce. Rosemary Simons, the president of the San Juan Islands tourism board. You have to remember, business communities are tight-knit on islands. It's . . . what's the word?" She lifted one finger in triumph as it came to her. "Symbiotic. One business goes down, and the rest suffer. Do you know how many historic buildings we have on San Juan?" Debbie didn't wait for Shelby to guess. "A hundred and twenty-seven! Imagine if Ezra cried ghost in every one of them!" She looked aghast.

Shelby nodded, trying her best to mirror the dismay on Debbie's face.

"He meant no harm," she repeated firmly. "Everyone agrees on that. But Monroe was playing with fire. And look what it got him! A 'for sale' sign in the drive."

"And a listing for you," Shelby pointed out.

Debbie puffed up again, her face heating. "Well, now, if it's best for the island . . ."

She turned doe eyes on Shelby until she nodded again cautiously. "Tight-knit" didn't seem to accurately describe what she'd just stepped into here.

"Once Monroe left, things settled back down," Debbie continued, "but not before Bob Widen's back pasture was trampled to smithereens and the Cassidys' hardware store was looted for electrical tape and metal sheeting. We had *vandalism* on Spring Street, Shelby." She hissed the word like a curse. "Vandalism!"

All this certainly explained the locals' disquiet at the mention of her inn this afternoon. The wary glances and pointed looks suddenly made more sense. No wonder the Merrick had still been for sale when Shelby had finally gotten around to buying it.

Debbie reached across the bar to pat Shelby's hand kindly. "I don't want you to get the wrong idea. We're a friendly bunch. Always happy to help fellow businesses. You know the saying . . . 'A high tide raises all boats.'" She nodded again to herself. "That's us. We take the high road. The only reason we were glad to see the Merrick closed? It put a halt to Ezra's . . ." She leaned in close. *"Stirrings."*

"Is that what he called his rituals?"

Debbie nodded emphatically, then succumbed to a full-body shiver. "Thinking about it still gives me goose bumps, I'll give him that." She chuckled.

Shelby had to be getting punked. This story was some kind of small-town hazing. Right? "But it's all hogwash, as you said." Shelby said this very firmly.

Debbie frowned at the misgiving on Shelby's face. "Oh honey. You're not buying into any of this, are you? I really did think you seemed so much smarter than Mr. Monroe."

"I, uh . . ." Part of Shelby related to Ezra; this inn *did* seem capable of harboring the past in a powerful way, already wrapping memories tightly around her. But the power of the chamber of commerce's influence loomed large as a cautionary tale. "Of course I'm not buying into it," she told Debbie. Her voice rose only one octave as she said it.

Debbie gave her another long look and, once satisfied, wiggled off the barstool and gathered her purse and keys. "Well then. I better skedaddle. Thanks for the tea, and don't you worry. Ezra will be back soon, and he won't be an inconvenience. You'll see."

Debbie cast a look over Shelby's shoulder to where the dining room windows gave way to the gardens, and Shelby followed her gaze to take note, for the first time, of the well-kept outbuilding framed by sunflowers that her newly acquired groundskeeper called home.

"And Monroe told him he could expect to stay on here?" Shelby wasn't entirely sure she wanted him to.

"Having him at your disposal makes him a very valuable employee," Debbie said defensively. "Provided you keep his, you know, *outside interests*, from raising their ugly head. Mr. Monroe told me he worked for under the industry standard, on account of his housing. And this way he's at your disposal 24-7."

Which was precisely what worried Shelby. "And where is he now?"

"Over at ParaPsyCon in Vancouver until Friday." Shelby must have looked blank again, because Debbie added, "You know, the paranormal and psychic convention. Goes every year to sign autographs."

The paranormal what?

"I'll see myself out," Debbie insisted, calling over her shoulder with a parting laugh, "Honey, you should see your face."

Chapter 5

After Debbie got herself back into her neon-blue compact Nissan and disappeared down the drive, Shelby marched directly back out into the lingering August sunshine and crossed the grounds of the Merrick to further inspect the groundskeeper's cottage. Neatly kept and more than cute enough to grace a tiny house Instagram account, the arched white wooden door looked reminiscent of something out of a Beatrix Potter storybook. She knocked just in case, but true to Debbie's word, no one was home.

Turning away from the doorstep, she took in the old-timey cruiser bike leaning against the cottage wall next to a stack of ceramic pots recently filled with dense potting soil. The musty smell of earth and lime tickled her nose. At the windowsill, planter boxes housed clusters of geraniums, their cheerful pink petals bending gently to the afternoon breeze. The entire scene spoke of *Better Homes & Gardens* tranquility. Had Debbie really just been talking exorcisms five minutes ago?

A peek through the double-paned window by the door, however, brought Shelby swiftly back to the realm of *The X-Files*. If the outside of Ezra's cottage painted a picture of pastoral domesticity, the interior screamed conspiracy theorist meets Unabomber. Some sort of old-fashioned recording device—a phonograph?—sat on the only table in the room, its brass Victrola-esque horn reaching out like a cone-shaped appendage toward a dusty collection of wires, a broken motherboard, and what looked like the innards of a Walkman. Shelby read the titles on the spines of the books within view on the shelf over the copper teakettle in the small kitchenette: *Ghost Hunting Washington*, *The Everything Ghost Hunting Book*, *Paranormal Activity for Dummies*, *The Science of the Unexpected and Unexplained*, *Kinetic Energy of the Unknown*.

Holy. Shit. Shelby was a self-help fan herself, but this deep dive into the paranormal was on a whole other level. Was she really expected to live on the same property, alone, with a man whose taste in tiny house decor would creep out Stephen King? She crossed back over the lawn—dammit, it really was impeccably kept—and sank down on the front stoop of the Merrick, trying to think. Maybe she should call Beth and ask her to run a background check on this guy. Could she do that?

She told herself she was overreacting. At least Ezra was away at his convention or whatever. Eye snagging on the sight of her Prius still parked in the drive, she decided what she'd do right now was move in. She dragged her few duffels from the car and hauled them into the large corner bedroom and en suite off the restaurant kitchen Debbie had referenced. As it was not easily accessed from the public spaces of the inn, Shelby decided to take it out of the nightly inventory and claim it as her own. At least no memories of Josh would cling to it.

Other than its generous size, the Merrick Suite, as advertised by the ornate gold lettering over the door, didn't shout "homey." Despite a large window, the wood-paneled walls gave the room a cave-like look, and a series of dark oil paintings in elaborate gilded frames didn't exactly help. Each seafaring scene seemed stormier than the last, masts cracking, sails ripped to shreds. With the hulking wardrobe in the corner and more lace doilies over every flat surface, Shelby had to wonder again whether Ezra had a point: This room absolutely looked like a place that could be haunted.

Her few personal belongings did precious little to make the space feel like her own, and even after the rest of her possessions arrived via Evergreen Moving, this room, like the rest of the inn, would need a serious overhaul.

At some point the Merrick Suite must have been someone's idea of a tribute to Phineas Merrick's sea-captaining days, because the nautical theme didn't end with the gloomy oil paintings. A smaller captain's wheel had been mounted on the side wall, and the quilt over the bed displayed more ships in various states of peril, the delicate stitching understating the violence of each scene. Shelby eyed her own faded but homey down comforter poking out from its box and wondered whether she'd be disrespecting the good captain in his own home if she were to make a switch.

She took a chance, laying the old quilt to rest in the musky, Narnia-esque wardrobe, where she found a collection of random light bulbs and air fresheners instead of a magical land. Since the closet smelled strongly of faux jasmine blossom, she shut it again and busied herself trying to further personalize this decidedly masculine museum to Merrick. She set her framed photos on the antique wooden dresser, then put her toiletries away in the bathroom, which, she was glad to note, housed a deep claw-foot tub. She braved the wardrobe again to deposit her clothes, liberating all the air fresheners and marching them down to the kitchen garbage.

She carried in her box of art supplies, setting them temporarily in the kitchen pantry before unpacking the one box of favorite books she'd brought along in the Prius, lining them up on the single shelf in a veritable parade of self-help. She had them all: books on grief, books on parenting in the wake of grief, books that attempted to explain Josh's brain tumor. She'd picked up several new ones right after Josh announced his determination that she buy the Merrick: one on inn and restaurant ownership and one written specifically on women-owned businesses. Both felt apropos, though after the day Shelby had had, she wondered whether she shouldn't switch subject matter to something more supernatural, like the volumes she'd spied in her caretaker's cottage. *A Woman's Guide to Inheriting a Haunted Hotel*, perhaps? *Paranormal History of the West*? She'd do a Kindle search later.

It was well after 6 p.m. by the time she'd done all she could to Shelby-ize the room. A card of encouragement from Beth now sat on the dresser, the front depicting Thelma and Louise in their convertible, the inside reading *You're my ride or die!* She slid a snapshot of Alex, taken at camp with Beth's son Dillon three summers ago, into one of her new books, then set his framed high school graduation photo by her bed. Next to it, Josh's face smiled at her from the confines of his own frame.

She stood for a long time, comparing the photos, illuminated by the light from the bedside table lamp: Both her son and her late husband had the same strong jaw; sandy, always unkempt hair; and blue eyes, though Alex's were, as was typical, narrowed slightly in thought.

Josh's were squinted in laughter. She'd taken this photo herself with her new DSLR Nikon at the last holiday gala they'd attended together at his architectural firm. The phrase *life of the party* came to mind, swiftly followed by mortification at her own inappropriateness.

The camera had enjoyed only one winter's enthusiastic use before Josh's diagnosis had blindsided the Wright family, colliding like a freight train into a car crossing on the tracks, sending them all skidding, throwing their lives into a new-normal nightmare. Shelby's love of photography had been instantly obliterated, cast aside to join her long-neglected ceramics career and newly discovered self-identity amid the rubble.

In this "before" photo, Josh had been wagging his eyebrows at her, the lens capturing a goofy surprise. Josh had always been the carefree one, Shelby the burdened one. Now, his lighthearted happiness made her wonder: On the day of that party, had the malignant cells that ultimately killed him already been silently doing their damage?

Shelby sighed. What did timelines matter? She'd thought about this a lot in the past year. Surely the bombshell she'd dropped just before Josh had gotten sick would have ended their marriage if his tumor hadn't beaten her to the punch.

Shelby's heartbeat had been deafening in her inner ear the day she'd finally faced her truth, pumping blood with the speed of a piston engine.

Her voice shaking, she'd sat him down on their living room couch and delivered the long-overdue speech she'd rehearsed in her head.

And Josh had said nothing. Nothing! Had he not heard her? He'd just stared, his expression off, somehow . . . even more off than she'd expected it to be after she'd uttered the words that she'd known would devastate him.

She'd cleared her throat. "I said, I think I must be gay."

This moment had, of course, lain dormant but patiently waiting for her for years. It had nudged her every time their marriage had felt off balance, had prodded her every time she'd felt that vague unhappiness she couldn't quite shake. It had finally erupted from that deep and hidden place within her in the most unexpected of ways: Beth, in the midst of one of her many rough patches with her on-again, off-again husband, Michael, had canceled their annual girls' weekend away in Willamette wine country in favor of a "long overdue" romantic trip for two.

Like it was nothing! Shelby had thought, instantly gutted. *Like their girls' getaway wasn't everything!*

The jealousy had burned sharp enough to finally cut away the layers of denial Shelby had padded around her heart for years. It had swept over the landscape of her entire existence in a violent rush of debris, taking her ability to be Josh's wife right along with it.

He still hadn't responded, paralyzed on the couch. "Josh. Say something."

This hadn't been the first time he'd stared at her like this lately, now that Shelby thought about it . . . seeing not seeing, eyes not focusing. "What are you talking about, *gay*?" He'd sounded more baffled than anything. "What is that supposed to mean?"

She'd tried to explain her revelation in a rush: The swift drop of disappointment that had left her stomach in her throat after Beth had canceled their trip. The irrational way she had imagined Michael taking her place on *their* weekend—cozying up with Beth under a blanket in the vineyard to watch the sunset. Beth and Michael toasting the revitalization of their marriage over glasses of pinot noir at the chef table Shelby had booked at Fireside. Listening to Beth's platitudes and promises of rebooking, Shelby had been crushed. Not disappointed. Not concerned about her friend or absorbed in sisterly worry. *Crushed*, like a jilted lover.

"Do you know what I mean?" she'd asked Josh desperately. Josh knew her better than anyone. She had to know: Had he seen this coming? Did any of this resonate?

Josh had still looked disoriented. "Well, sure. That's how I'd feel," he'd reasoned out slowly, "if *you* were with someone else."

"Yes. Exactly." Misery had churned with the clarity in Shelby's gut, fermenting there. It had been hard to watch, that moment when understanding had fully dawned on her husband's face, and she'd looked away.

"You've felt that way for Beth? All this time?"

She'd nodded, unable to dislodge her tongue from the roof of her mouth for a long moment. *She doesn't feel the same,* she wanted to say. *She doesn't even know.* It wasn't really about Beth, as much as it was about the insight Shelby's feelings provided, so what did requisition matter? "I tried not to," she'd breathed. *I tried so hard, for so long, to be who you needed me to be.*

Right up until Beth's cancellation had cracked the truth open for both of them. In the months following the wine weekend, Shelby had stewed in her awareness, the dread of this very conversation looming over her every waking moment. She'd thought of Josh's favorite phrase—*I know you by heart*—and had ached at the irony.

For two decades, the foundation of Shelby's existence had been slowly shifting under her, inch by inch. Just enough to make her wonder whether she'd imagined it. The best thing she could liken it to was when you were stopped at a light, and the car next to you crept forward, and for just a second it felt like *you* were moving backward. *That* feeling. And then, finally, she'd allowed this label—gay, queer, whatever—to mercifully slide into place in her brain, saving her like a swift yank on the emergency brake.

"Say something," she had said to Josh. But a sudden sweat had broken out on his face. His skin had looked clammy and red. And then he'd reached out to grasp the edge of the coffee table, fingers splayed, and missed.

"Josh!"

He'd crumpled to the floor, and as he'd lost consciousness, any chance at finishing their conversation had been severed like a lifeline.

In the awful days that followed, Shelby had tried—god knows she'd tried—to engage him, to remind him of what they'd been discussing before he'd fallen, but between CT scans and hospital overnights, diagnosis and testing, the specialists continually told her: Short-term memory goes first. It was more important to show Josh photos of herself and Alex, to help him recall childhood memories, to let him study the faces of his family. Josh hadn't been able to keep his eyes open for long, let alone follow a conversation, his skull, he'd complained, feeling heavy as a bowling ball on his pillow.

No one's fault, Shelby repeated desperately now, standing alone in the Merrick Suite. What had everyone told her after the funeral? Now was the time to be gentle with herself.

"Take care," Josh's colleagues had told her one by one, grasping her hands as they'd left the service. "It's what Josh would have wanted."

And they were right. He would have. But to take care of herself, Shelby needed to finally feel authentic in her own skin. Centered and grounded. Less like an impostor, married to a man while feeling anything but straight. Had she thought that, by arriving here, any of this would magically change? She looked bleakly at the largest of the oil paintings on her new bedroom wall, depicting a ship dashing upon an outcropping of rocks. *That* stormy sea was as calm as a kiddie pool in comparison to being forced to relive her own inadequacies.

On impulse, she wrested it off the wall, surprised when the heavy frame complied without much struggle, the nail holding it up bending easily to her will. She took this as a sign to rid the suite of the additional seafaring paintings, which she did with vigor. When she was done, only her framed family photos remained, staring back at her from the bedside table. She pinched her eyes shut to stave off tears. The tumor had robbed Shelby of this cheerful, smiling, *coherent* Josh long before the date of his death, and now she would never know: Had he retained the confession she'd uttered to him, the day she'd told him she was gay? On some level, had planning Shelby's new life at the inn been a needed distraction for him, a redirection he could spin to, to bury what he didn't want to—or couldn't—face? Or had he died never remembering her confession?

It made her wonder whether she had failed at coming out not just once, but twice. Here she was, exiled of her own volition to this far corner of the continent, still personifying the het woman she'd always been. Still the grieving widow in the eyes of Beth, of Alex, even of Debbie, and, soon enough, of everyone else on this island. How did she shake that while still honoring her grief? While still missing Josh?

It was too bad ghosts weren't real, despite what Ezra Peterson believed, because Shelby certainly had "unfinished business" with hers.

Chapter 6

The silence in the inn felt even more unsettling as the sun finally went down. Shelby still hadn't eaten anything that day, unless she counted teatime with Debbie, and she realized with a pang that she was starving. The woman at the winery, Holly, had invited her back once she was settled. Would it still be open at this hour?

Seeking escape, she got back in her car to find out, pausing only to unburden the front door of the Merrick of its heavy brass anchor as she locked up. Maybe this long day had unhinged Shelby, but this anchor, like the oil prints, reminded her of too much history. Too much turmoil.

At the intersection of narrow Merrick Lane and Mitchell Bay Road, she eyed the broken sign, too, but let it pass. She'd deal with it another day, after paying a visit to Friday Harbor Hardware for nails, paint, and plywood. She drove the short way to the winery, relieved to find the parking lot still occupied by a few cars. She wasn't sure what exactly drew her to this place, except that it was one location on the island she did not immediately associate with Josh, which gave it a certain appeal. Either this winery hadn't been here twenty years ago or they hadn't stumbled upon it, clouding it with their memories.

When she entered, a new group of women sat at one wine barrel table, sharing a bottle of something white, and a touristy-looking couple had replaced the locals from earlier, their own map of the island spread out on the bar. This, Shelby decided, accounted for all the cars out front. She made her way to the counter and offered a smile to the pair at the other end, pleased with herself that, unlike this afternoon, she hadn't let the sight of happy coupledom throw her.

"The owner will be right back out," the man informed her pleasantly.

The woman added with an air of self-importance, "It was an early harvest season, you know."

Shelby didn't know but had experienced enough of the wine business to know that this fact had nothing to do with the bottle the woman was sampling now. She tried to look agreeable nonetheless, then looked in the direction they indicated as Holly emerged briskly from some back room, looking slightly pink from exertion.

Shelby smiled at her and offered a half wave, which she almost immediately tried to retract, feeling ridiculous. Would this woman even remember her?

But Holly beamed at her. "Welcome back, innkeeper."

Shelby exhaled and returned the smile. "Thanks."

"What can I get for you? Assuming I have you here for more than five minutes this time, that is."

"Well, um . . ." Shelby flushed. Was Holly teasing her for fleeing earlier, or was she genuinely as delighted as she sounded to have her return? Earlier, when she'd made that comment about a brown-eyed girl, she'd almost sounded like she had been flirting. Shelby glanced down at the laminated tasting menu sitting on the bar, furiously trying to keep the color from rising in her cheeks. Until today, she had never pinned hopes of female attention on anyone but Beth, who was as straight as they came, and the instant attraction she felt was a new and somewhat alarming experience.

She forced herself to meet Holly's gaze with what she hoped might pass for nonchalance. "I thought I'd come back in for that glass of wine, actually. And maybe something to eat?"

Holly leaned forward across the counter to flip the tasting menu over, and the blood heated in Shelby's veins again.

"Our full kitchen's only open on the weekends," Holly explained, "but we've got a few small bites I can make you." She indicated a charcuterie plate or a hummus-and-chips option. Shelby's stomach registered a quick flip of hunger at the description of the charcuterie, and she ordered it on the spot.

"Good choice." Holly smiled. "A tasting, too?" She set a water on the counter as she talked, and Shelby studied her, despite her best intentions not to stare. There was something about the way this woman carried herself that fascinated her: strength and grace, intertwined.

"A flight would be great, yes." If meeting Debbie, confronting the memory of Josh, and getting the 411 on the Merrick's haunted history hadn't been enough to earn her a glass of wine, Shelby didn't want to know what *did* qualify.

Holly set a glass on the counter and measured out Shelby's first pour, an estate-grown pinot gris, she said, as the couple at the other end of the bar settled their bill, folded their map, and wandered out. Holly disappeared into the back again as Shelby sipped her pinot, which was decent but not great, returning a few minutes later with a fantastic-looking plate of charcuterie. Shelby's face must have registered her happiness over this sight, because Holly laughed.

"Told you it'd be good." She eyed the remainder of the pinot in Shelby's glass. "What'd you think of the first pour?"

"It's . . . nice," Shelby said carefully, remembering that the man at the bar had identified Holly as the owner of this winery. But to her relief, Holly laughed again. She repossessed the glass and upturned the final swallow into the dump bucket on the counter before Shelby could protest. She flushed again, this time in chagrin. "No, really, it was fine!"

"No, your palate didn't lead you astray. That bottle was from the last case from my predecessor here, and when people know their way around wine, I can't give it away. I have something better for you."

"Oh, okay." Shelby felt flattered, which she suspected wasn't deserved, since all she'd done was offer lukewarm feedback.

Holly poured Shelby something else and set it in front of her with more flourish. "Tell me what you think," she said, then waited, right there against the bar, watching as Shelby brought the glass to her lips.

Her stomach did that little flip again, but she did as she was told, and tasted. A bright note burst on her tongue—apricot, chased by honey. "Oh yes. This is excellent."

Holly beamed. The open, earnest expression made her look boyish again, just for an instant. "So," she said, "am I to assume by your return that you've settled in cozily at the Merrick?"

Shelby had a slice of Gouda halfway to her mouth but made herself pause politely. "I wouldn't say cozily. But I do know a little more about what I'm dealing with, thanks to my Realtor."

Holly nodded, chin in her hand as she leaned over the bar. "Debbie Phillips is a lot of things," she said candidly, "but thankfully, a ghost fanatic is not one of them. Woman's got a good business head on her shoulders."

"Huh." Shelby smiled a bit feebly. "I guess I really am the last to know about any of this." She supposed she shouldn't be surprised, given the thorough scrubbing the tourism board had orchestrated online.

"I'm sorry," Holly said. "It must suck to feel blindsided."

Shelby searched her face for any hint of titillation or gossipy interest in the Merrick Inn controversy, but read nothing in her expression but keen intelligence and genuine concern. "I'm just not sure what to make of it all," she admitted.

She hadn't planned on discussing the Merrick's colorful history with anyone that night, but Holly's refreshing sincerity proved hard to resist. This woman didn't feel like just "anyone." Talking to Holly felt easy and natural. Like Shelby already knew her from some past life. Not that she believed in that stuff. Obviously.

"It was a mess for a while there," Holly said unequivocally. Her no-nonsense tone reminded her of Beth. "If you're looking to turn it around, I suppose the place—or person, rather—to start with is Ezra Peterson."

This *did* surprise Shelby. "Do you know him?"

"Everyone knows Ezra," Holly said. "The general consensus is the guy got in over his head. He didn't know Jack Monroe's media posts would draw such attention to his rituals or whatever."

"Why not?"

Holly leaned forward on the bar, her chin cradled in one palm as she gave this question some thought. "I guess because . . . Ezra just seems to live in his own world. And for a Gen Zer or whatever, he isn't exactly what you'd call tech savvy.

"He acts more like sixty." Holly chuckled. The sound rumbled low in her throat, almost melodic. "Dresses like an old man . . . tweed and suspenders, that sort of thing. The man positively lives for the annual San Juan Historical Society rummage sale. Think steampunk meets historical reenactor."

"Is he a history buff?" Was that why he had so thoroughly embraced Monroe's ghost story? Debbie had made it sound more personal, if she recalled correctly.

Holly nodded. "Ezra does everything vintage . . . still subscribes to the newspaper . . . the print one. Doesn't have a mobile phone . . . just an old rotary still connected to a landline. Rides everywhere on a cruiser bicycle, little wicker basket in front and everything."

"He sounds . . . concerning?"

Holly gave this question, too, the weight it deserved. "No," she decided. "Ezra's harmless. Lifetime residents on the island, they think of him like a son." She frowned, then laughed again. "Or maybe a very young uncle."

Shelby smiled, but added, "Despite exorcising Monroe's made-up ghosts?"

"Oh, he does it quite politely." Holly smiled. "Welcomes the opportunity to commune with them, even. Wherein lies your challenge, Ms. Innkeeper."

"It all seems a bit above my pay grade, to be honest," Shelby admitted.

She must have looked as overwhelmed as she felt, because Holly reached out and touched her hand, still resting loosely around her wineglass, in apology. "Hey, I didn't mean to sound flippant. Like I said, Ezra is what you'd call colorful. But that doesn't mean he doesn't have the best interests of the Merrick at heart. He loves that place."

Debbie had said something similar, hadn't she? That Ezra was like an institution. Shelby nodded, trying to appear more self-assured.

She must not have pulled it off, because Holly offered, "Maybe we can figure out this business-ownership thing together." She slapped her palms on the polished bar. "I bought this place early last year. With the exception of a few white varietals, including what you're tasting right now, my own wine is still in barrel, which is why you've been left to drink the swill of San Juan Winery 1.0."

"You're owner *and* winemaker?" Shelby tried not to sound as impressed as she felt.

Holly nodded toward the wine in Shelby's glass. "This is my first attempt at Madeleine Angevine. Pinot doesn't grow nearly as well here, a scientific fact that the previous winemaker didn't seem willing to let get in his way."

"It's excellent," Shelby told her sincerely. "The Madeleine, I mean. Finished in stainless steel, right?" Wine making was one part creative instinct and two parts chemistry, when it came down to it. She heard herself saying this thought aloud.

Holly approved. "You do know the wine business."

Certainly not compared to her present company. Shelby opted for humility and said this, too, adding only, "My parents were viticulturists in Oregon, but we never made the finished product."

Holly nodded with interest while Shelby finally let herself take her first bite of cheese. She followed this immediately with a thin slice of peppery prosciutto brushed in a vinegary mustard. Either she was even hungrier than she'd thought, or it paired perfectly with the Madeleine, or both, because Shelby practically hummed with satisfaction as it hit her palate, a reaction Holly seemed to enjoy.

"Wait," she said. "This will be even better." She unearthed another bottle from under the bar and then reached to retrieve a new Riedel wineglass from the wooden rack above her head. She poured Shelby a red the color of garnet, if the stone were wrapped in velvet and polished to a shine.

Holly followed her gaze to the glass. "I wanted to call it Heart of Darkness," she confided with a self-conscious laugh that completely contradicted her confident air, "but my partner insisted that was too literary."

Shelby registered the word *partner* with an upward question mark of her eyebrows she couldn't quite curb in time, and Holly added, "Biz partner, chica." She punctuated this information with another, shyer smile, as though pleased Shelby had noted the word and sought clarification. "Full disclosure? He's my dad, but he's a *silent* partner, at least."

"Oh," Shelby said stupidly. Indicating this new pour, she followed up with "And what exactly is Heart of Darkness?"

"My take on a cabernet franc, barreled back at my last place and moved out here on a flatbed, if you can believe it. I shouldn't let you try it directly following the Madeleine, but I just can't help myself. It will go with the prosciutto and salami so well."

"You mad scientist, you."

Wait . . . was *Shelby* the one flirting now? And if so, exactly how fast did wine go to one's head here on San Juan Island? Teasing felt natural and easy, despite having just met this intriguing but rather intimidating woman. Whom Shelby didn't know the first thing about, she reminded herself fervently. She swirled, smelled, and sipped as she'd been taught to do, a peppery tang singing through her mouth in answer to the ham. She closed her eyes for a moment, unable to help herself while savoring the wine. "Wow. Are you kidding me? This is even better."

"With the salami now, and the smoked cheddar," Holly insisted, taking the liberty of creating a tiny charcuterie sandwich for her on the plate. Shelby found she didn't mind the forwardness. Clearly Holly was having fun, and Shelby realized she was, too. She tried this salami-cheddar combination, and the structure of the cab franc shifted subtly, the peppery notes yielding to the salt of the meat and the smoke of the cheese.

"Forget scientist," she told Holly. "You're an alchemist."

Holly's eyes danced. Green eyes, Shelby noted, musing that she'd never really looked into another woman's eyes before, not even Beth's . . . at least not like this. They were pretty. Were all women's eyes this pretty? Yes, Shelby was definitely buzzed. Too many enthusiastic swallows of wine on a nearly empty stomach. She made quick work of several more charcuterie-cracker sandwiches.

Holly worked her backward through the rest of the tasting menu (*just to make sure you get your money's worth,* she said), and by the time she'd poured her predecessor's 2017 merlot (*don't get your hopes up*) the two of them were talking quite easily about Holly's former life in Milwaukee, where she had been grafting vines in a greenhouse near Green Bay. The sky fully darkened outside the windows of the barn, casting shadows across the tasting room floor, and the lights twisting around the rafters twinkled, and for the first time during this very long, tiring day, Shelby felt a sense of—if not homecoming, exactly—at least temporary safe harbor.

She made her way to the restroom at the back of the tasting room, where posters for local bands and advertisements for pet-sitting services and knitting clubs adorned the hallway. When she emerged from the bathroom, she was surprised to note it was already 8 p.m. Somehow over two hours had passed in Holly's company.

Back at the bar, Holly cleared out bottles and stacked dishes and glasses. "I kept you until closing time," Shelby said.

Holly smiled. "We closed an hour ago."

For the first time, Shelby noted she was, indeed, quite alone in the tasting room now. "Oh! I'm sorry."

Holly had slid a sweater over her head; she looked less Peter Pan–like in its wool bulk. "Don't worry about it. Just send me those guests of yours when they arrive at the Merrick."

Guests. A fresh wave of anxiety washed over Shelby. "We don't plan to open, officially anyway, until the holiday season," she said, before cringing inwardly at the use of "we" . . . a long-held habit. She hoped Holly hadn't registered it. As cared for and cozy as she felt here in the winery, she was reluctant to launch into the Josh explanation that was now woven into her life story. Would it be asking too much of the universe to give her just a few more minutes to be the woman she wanted to be right now, before her previous life caught up with her?

"Well then," Holly said, ushering Shelby out the barn doors in front of her, hitting lights as she went. "I guess I'll just get to see more of you, then. Or," she added carefully, "more of you both?"

So Shelby's slip of "we" hadn't been lost on her after all. As observant as Holly had been all night, Shelby had been foolish to hope otherwise. "It's just me," she heard herself say swiftly. "I mean, I'm here on my own."

She waited for loneliness to sideswipe her at this admission. Instead, as she'd hoped, being an "I" felt welcoming on this island. Like Shelby had taken a first but significant step out of Josh's shadow toward a label that fit so much better but had so far proved elusive: single. Unattached. Gay.

Even if no one knew it yet.

"I see," Holly said thoughtfully, though Shelby knew she couldn't possibly.

But the prospect lay there, almost in reach: the idea of someone like Holly getting it right. Understanding her. It filled Shelby with a sudden and unexpected gladness. She opened her mouth to further explain, and then closed it again just as quickly. What on earth would she say? She heard herself settle for, "Thanks."

God, for what? She was glad Holly couldn't see how her face had heated as they parted ways to cross the parking lot. A moment later, a single headlight beam cut through the darkness as a motor revved.

Shelby turned. Of course this impossibly cool and mysterious woman rode a motorcycle.

"See you soon, Shelby Wright," Holly called. Donning a black helmet, she waved once more from atop her bike before disappearing down Mitchell Bay Road.

Chapter 7

Back in her car, Shelby's buzz had worn off, but she still felt pleasantly warm and full as she returned to the Merrick and heaved open the heavy front door. She stood still for a moment, letting her eyes adjust to the gloom permeating the entryway on this moonless night, chastising herself for failing to leave a light on. She had to grope for the switch, the pads of her fingers sliding along the wall as if guided by braille, unfamiliar as she was with the layout of the foyer. When the yellow glow from the old-fashioned wall sconce finally chased away the dark, she exhaled in relief. Not because she'd subconsciously braced for Monroe's ghost to descend the staircase. Not because it was far too easy to imagine how convincing Ezra's (non)exorcisms must be, held here amid the shadowed antiques. A few hours removed from the events of the afternoon, buoyed by companionable conversation with Holly, the idea seemed completely ludicrous, even alone in the dark.

Right?

She left the entry light on anyway and moved through the vestibule toward the bar and kitchen, turning on more lights as she went. It was this unfamiliar place. Surely anyone would feel a bit creeped out walking into this big, old inn at night, alone. Seeing it for the first time after sundown, getting used to the way the shadows of the old-fashioned furniture fell across the rugs and hardwood floors to bend at the middle and stretch up the walls. Shelby just needed time to learn the hum of the Merrick's particular type of quiet, the old building kind that settled over empty dining room chairs and upholstered love seats and side tables like a velvet drape that every so often rustled in a nonexistent breeze.

She poked around the kitchen, taking inventory of any staples on hand that might reduce her grocery list back in town tomorrow. Afterward, she made her way to her bedroom suite and turned on the lights there, too, then circled back to the vestibule to climb the stairs and walk the upstairs hallway. Just to ensure all the guest room windows were closed, things like that.

Squaring her shoulders, she made herself switch back off the lights up there, even though she was half tempted to leave them all on, too. Who *wouldn't* be? Beth came to mind. Shelby tried to channel some of her best friend's fearlessness, which she'd come to regard as Beth's superpower, as she hustled back downstairs. She wished Beth were here right now, but it was a moot point: Beth was no sidekick. She didn't play the supportive role in anyone else's story.

Because Shelby felt less of a need to play the hero, she allowed herself to keep the downstairs hall sconce glowing after she checked the lock on the front door and worked her way back toward her bedroom. She took a shower, unearthed her favorite Merino wool pajamas from a box she hadn't yet emptied, and climbed wearily into bed.

Had it really been only this morning that she'd departed Portland? Only early this afternoon she'd waited for the ferry? It felt like at least a lifetime ago. She stretched in the unfamiliar bed and winced. Her arms ached from carting boxes from the car. Changing one's entire trajectory of life, solo, was exhausting.

She let that word—*solo*—rattle around in her brain again for a bit, haphazard as a pinball in a maze. Now that she wasn't in the welcome distraction of Holly's company, the idea wasn't as comfortable. She should check in with Alex, let him know she'd arrived in one piece. She hit the first contact in her favorites list and listened through two rings.

"Hiya, Mom."

The sound of Alex's voice, even three thousand miles away, brought the comfort she needed. It was late in New York, but background noise buzzed—a dorm scavenger event just underway, he said. "How's the inn? Cool?"

"It's something, all right." She smiled. "I just wanted you to know I'm here, and that I'm thinking of you," she said.

"Yeah, me too." He delivered this in the teenage-boy tone Shelby knew well: happy to hear from her while simultaneously distracted by the whirlwind of his own life.

"You're busy . . . I'll let you go. Call me soon, though, all right? Let me know how your classes are. And Alex—be sure to study."

He laughed, and the sound was so like his dad, Shelby closed her eyes while gripping her phone, just to savor it a bit. Josh hadn't laughed like that at all since . . . well, since he got sick. "Talk soon, Mom."

Shelby bit back the urge to ask Alex to stay on the line. There was more she wanted to say, more Alex deserved to hear, but Shelby couldn't bring herself to come out to him now, while he navigated his first weeks of college life. So she said only, "Talk soon, honey."

Her phone rang again the second she hit *end call*, and she nearly jumped, all self-indulgent rumination vanishing from her head like a candle flame snuffed out by a door slammed shut.

She glanced at the screen: Beth.

"So you made it, I take it," she said by way of greeting. "I was beginning to wonder if the ferry had sunk."

"Cheery thought," Shelby replied. "But, in a way, befitting of the day I've had."

"Oy. What do you mean?" Beth sounded out of breath, and it took Shelby a beat to realize she was on the treadmill. Never mind that Beth had been gifted with a metabolism a supermodel would envy; if she wasn't blithely consuming calories, she was busy burning them, at any and all hours. The woman was simply incapable of standing still. What on earth had made Shelby think she could ever outrun her?

"It's just . . . this place is a little bit creepy at night."

"Why? What's wrong with it? Is it not how you remembered?"

"Not exactly, no." Shelby filled Beth in on her day, from her arrival on the island to meeting Debbie, the haunted history lesson she'd received on the inn, and the state of her new caretaker's cottage. "I've got my work cut out for me, that's for sure."

An electronic beep sounded, and the pounding on the treadmill mercifully subsided. "Let me get this straight. You buy this place sight unseen—against my advice, I might add—but instead of finding out your historic inn has . . . I don't know, termites or mold or something," Beth said slowly, "you're telling me you have *ghosts*?" She laughed.

Shelby tried to laugh along but failed. "Just my luck, right?"

The cop's intuition Beth was famous for kicked in as she picked up on the dejected note in Shelby's voice. "Oh, honey. You aren't kidding. You *have* had a hell of a day."

And Shelby hadn't even gotten to the part about the winery. She conjured the image of Holly pouring her cab franc tonight, comparing her to Beth before she could help herself. Both women had dark hair, but any similarity ended there. For one thing, Beth was shorter, her build less muscular. People continually made the mistake of underestimating the "lady cop" who looked like she might blow over in a stiff wind, when, in fact, Beth would bowl you over like a hurricane. Shelby couldn't imagine *anyone* underestimating tomboyish Holly, so why the comparison?

"It has been a lot," she conceded.

For at least the dozenth time, Shelby wanted to tell Beth everything. She wanted to purge it all, starting with her unrequited but enlightening crush on her, and all the embarrassment and heartache that had arisen along with it. After she'd ripped off that Band-Aid, she could unburden herself of the crushing guilt of coming out to Josh in the way she had, and then she could top it all off with how she had gravitated toward Holly at the winery tonight.

Instead, she pushed it all down, a reaction she'd begun to recognize as a problematic pattern. But her self-realization and subsequent conversation with Josh had become a rolling snowball that neither of them could outrun. What if talking to Beth sent her running, too?

Shelby couldn't risk that. If there was one thing she knew with certainty, it was that she needed Beth in her life, however she could have her.

"I'll be fine," she promised her. "I'm just tired."

"Of course you are. Get some sleep," Beth agreed. "I guarantee everything will look brighter in the morning."

~

Beth was right, per usual. The yellow sunlight streaming through the sheer blinds in the Merrick Suite blinded Shelby promptly at 6:45 a.m., the reflection of the rays bouncing off the full-length mirror of the wardrobe. She groaned, throwing an arm over her eyes. Maybe it was the lumpy bed, but if she didn't know better, she'd say this inn had given her an unwarranted hangover.

She rolled out of bed, reaching for clean clothes from whatever moving box proved closest. She needed coffee and breakfast, stat. Unfortunately, until she went to King's Market, she had neither. Besides, procuring these items every morning had once upon a time been in the purview of Josh, a.k.a. Mr. Morning Sunshine. Even a year later, Shelby woke up half baffled, half disappointed not to smell her favorite Stumptown dark roast brewing.

On the way to the kitchen, she glowered at the hallway lights she'd left glowing all night, an unwelcome reminder of how out of her element she felt here. She found a granola bar in her handbag sitting on the barstool, then made another pot of the not-so-terrible lavender tea, the spicy aroma slowly taking the edge off her mood.

"Talk to your mother at your own risk," Josh had regularly announced cheerily to Alex on school mornings, handling all field trip permission slips and last-minute lunch requests. "She doesn't clock in around here until at least eight."

And yet here it was at . . . Shelby craned her neck to make out the hands on the giant grandfather clock in the dining room . . . 7:22, and she was upright and feeding herself and everything. *Who's a morning person, now?*

Of course, if she was going to get technical about it, it had never been Josh who'd doubted her. About anything. It was *Shelby* who had second-guessed. Josh had believed in her unwaveringly.

"You got this," he had promised, the day she'd accepted her teaching position in the art department, the biggest step Shelby had taken professionally since Alex had been born.

"About time someone took charge over there," he'd said without a beat of hesitation, when she'd joined the board at Alex's charter school.

And, of course, the hardest boost of confidence to hear: "The Merrick Inn won't know what hit it."

Tears pricked, stinging her eyes, and she swiped at them roughly, remembering how fervently he had told her, over and over again, that she could do this. That she could realize this dream of theirs. What had he expected? For her to just pick up where they'd left off twenty years ago? She couldn't. She just couldn't.

But failure wasn't an option, either. Not with Josh's life insurance spent on this inn, money that, had Shelby not been obeying his last wishes, would have gone directly to Alex's education.

She'd worried, in those final days, whether he was coherent enough to be having these conversations. Whether he was clearheaded enough to be insisting on such requests.

He had beseeched her to stay strong. "If not for yourself, then for me, okay?" he'd rasped, while Shelby had shaken her head, trying to get him to see reason.

"Vassar could be paid for," she'd reminded him, only to watch his face cloud over, his certainty faltering. God, did he remember that Alex had gotten accepted? Did he remember *Alex*? Shelby's thoughts had swum in ever-more-frenetic circles, her mind a turbulent sea of doubt. Should she plant Alex by his bedside day and night, so he wouldn't lose sight of what mattered most? Should she pick up where they'd left off during that awful, interrupted conversation on the living room couch and remind him she was gay? Did that negate her obligation to follow through with the inn, or make it all the more important? She didn't know. She didn't know. But she had waited too long, and then it seemed the decision had been made for her. By the time Josh had to be reminded where he was and why he was in his hospice bed, it had almost been a relief to think that most likely, his tumor had chewed through the memory of her coming out and spit it back out. He would die in peace, leaving Shelby with all the culpability.

Now, sitting alone in the Merrick kitchen, she fisted her hands in frustration, nearly spilling her tea. How was it fair that even now it felt like she still owed Josh something?

It had always been this way: Josh overachieving, Shelby withholding, even without meaning to . . . it was just that Shelby's barely-under-the-surface understanding of herself caused Josh's carefully planned date nights to feel over the top. His arm slung around her shoulder in public or his hand outstretched across the table at an expensive restaurant had left Shelby feeling uncomfortably exposed. Even this perfect "second act" plan for his widow had left Shelby seen by the world in the wrong light.

"Wrong how?" Beth had asked time and again, when Josh never forgot an anniversary. When he produced the perfect gift, yet again, or held Shelby close when she wanted to wiggle free. Shelby couldn't blame her . . . how could she understand what felt elusive even to Shelby? "All *I* see is a dedicated husband," Beth had said. "It's as if you wish he'd try *less* hard."

That was it exactly. Shelby could see now that her suppressed secret had pinned her there, in that perpetual cycle of emotional debt.

I know you by heart, my ass. If that had been true, Josh could have saved them both a great deal of misery.

She took a gulp of tea just as a hard knock sounded on the front door, making her jump again. She really needed to get a grip: The dregs in her tea sloshed in her cup, which Shelby almost dropped in her haste to get to the vestibule. Who could be calling at this hour?

She opened the door cautiously to a beaming, once again bejeweled Debbie. This time, the ball cap perched on top of her teased hair spelled out Sweet & Salty in sequins. "Good morning!" she singsonged, while Shelby mutely allowed her entry.

"Beautiful day, isn't it? I have your business license forms, and your welcome packet from the chamber of commerce," she announced, bustling toward the kitchen before pointlessly calling over her shoulder, "Is this a good time?"

"Um, sure." Shelby glanced down at herself, relieved to remember she'd already changed.

"I just knew you'd be an early bird!" Debbie exclaimed. "I could have brought this over next week, I suppose, but after leaving you a bit shell-shocked yesterday, I just said to myself, Deb, you go on over there and get Shelby started off on the right foot, right now." Debbie's bulk pushed past the stool Shelby had pulled out earlier, then abandoned. She cozied right up to the bar with an "Mmm. Tea."

"Let me get you a cup," Shelby said. Now that the shock of hosting Debbie again had begun to wane, the company felt a bit more welcome. At the very least, it got her mind off Josh and any impossible-to-uphold expectations he had harbored . . . for her, or this inn. A moment later, she returned to the bar, tea in hand. "Careful, it's hot."

"You know just what hits the spot." Debbie smiled. She stirred the tea bag around the steaming water, which seemed to suddenly remind her of something. "Oh! I come bearing gifts!" She dug into her cavernous tote bag and produced another mug, this one emblazoned with a mapped outline of the island and SJI's motto: *Inspiration for the senses!* Tucked inside were what looked to be a handful of discount cards and coupons.

"From the chamber of commerce," Debbie explained.

Shelby flipped through the offerings, which entitled her to free appetizers at several area restaurants (with purchase of a cocktail or entrée, not valid during happy hour), 10 percent off at a bakery called

Queen of Tarts, and a complimentary scarf pattern at Baa Baa Black Sheep, presumably a knitting-supply shop.

She tucked the coupons back into the mug. "Do all new business owners get such a welcome?" she asked. "Or is this the 'sorry you have a haunted hotel' special?"

Debbie *tsk*ed at her irreverence, but confirmed: "The chamber and the tourism board are happy to see the Merrick get a fresh start." She brought her mug up to her lips for a sip she seemed to savor while Shelby wondered how difficult it would be to get the bright-red lipstick smudge off the rim later.

"Anyhoo!" Debbie said, setting her cup down. "I'm sure Rosemary will be by—she's with the tourism board, you remember—but in the meanwhile . . ." She dug back into her bag, this time producing a glossy brochure that she set down on the bar with a definitive flourish. Shelby read YOUR SMALL BUSINESS AND YOU! written across the front in an excitable font.

She dutifully unfolded the brochure to be confronted with an attractive, smiling woman in a chef's apron, shaking hands with a jovial-looking banker. The next panel displayed a colorful flow chart entitled PATH TO SUCCESS!

"But why should I expect a visit from this Rosemary?" Shelby asked.

"Oh, you know, just checking in."

Checking in, or checking *up*? Shelby bit back the impulse to ask this out loud, settling for "How thoughtful of her."

"I know I can speak for all of us in the chamber when I say we just want our local small-business owners to be successful, you know, honey?" Debbie pinned Shelby with earnest eyes framed by bright-blue eye shadow.

"Of course." Shelby made a show of placing the brochure on top of the to-do list she'd already drafted for herself. *Finalize business loan* and *hire staff* jumped out at her before becoming mercifully hidden by the glossy smile of the successful businesswoman. More than ever, restoring this inn to its former glory felt more like a homework assignment from beyond the grave. What if she couldn't make a go of it? What if this inn's reputation proved too high a hurdle? "To tell the truth, Debbie, I could use all the help I can get."

She wanted to do right by Josh and certainly didn't want to waste the insurance payout, but also? Shelby wouldn't mind embodying the carefree confidence exhibited by Ms. Business Owner here. If the tourism board wanted to make a not-so-subtle point, she'd listen. If Debbie offered a tutorial in Business Ownership 101, she'd take it.

Chapter 8

For the following three days, Shelby worked dutifully on her checklist and Debbie's flowchart like her life (and sanity) depended on it. She signed the small-business loan paperwork at First Federal in Friday Harbor, where the local bank manager—whose demeanor bore absolutely no resemblance to the smiling man on the brochure cover—claimed the high interest rate had nothing whatsoever to do with the Merrick's recent reputation; took full inventory of the commercial kitchen, down to the last whisk and spatula; and managed to make headway with the mountain of linens, towels, and other hotel supplies stashed haphazardly in closets and cupboards all around the inn. As she was forced to do all of this while continuing to absorb memories of her stay here with Josh, she had more than a few setbacks. He'd so admired the wood paneling in the parlor, citing it as a perfect example of Victorian architecture, but how she wished she could lighten it up a bit! And they'd talked about how quiet it got here in the evenings . . . what *would* it cost to hire local bands to play in the dining room on Friday nights?

On day two of official inn ownership, she opened windows and removed the draperies of the inn, just to get a sense of what she was dealing with, cobweb and dust-wise, but even with more light shed on the situation, the Merrick still looked worn. Tired. Had it looked this dreary on her honeymoon? Maybe young Shelby and Josh had assumed that sophistication was *supposed* to seem stuffy and outdated.

Either way, the old, musty smells lingered like bad mojo. If she hoped to attract new guests, it was time for a thorough scrubbing. Setting aside her daunting to-do list for the afternoon, she tackled the Merrick top to bottom, dusting, vacuuming, polishing antique furniture, and waxing floors until she feared breathing in any more lemon-scented fumes might result in permanent brain damage. No surface evaded her dustrag, Pledge, and mop.

The sheer physical exertion helped, but as she collapsed onto the antique fainting couch in the vestibule, sweaty and spent, her hands cracked from whatever chemicals resided in Comet, she still couldn't seem to shake the feeling that she was only a visitor here, playacting at ownership.

She just wasn't used to her new role, she decided. A little more elbow grease was all she needed for a clean slate. She vowed to clear the gutters next, unearthing a ladder from the maintenance building. Then she dispelled the cobwebs from behind the Viking stove. The annex building needed a thorough cleaning as well, as did all the bathrooms, with their ornate porcelain fixtures that somehow seemed to invite extra rust. *Forward motion,* she reminded herself. What did Josh always used to say when trying to impress new clients? Fake it till you make it.

She faked it until her shoulders ached, until grit collected under her fingernails, until she was messy and hot and hungry. She showered, ate her first proper meal in the Merrick kitchen, and crashed at 8 p.m., sleeping like the dead.

The next morning, with coffee in her mug and a real breakfast in her stomach, Shelby felt like a new woman. Ignoring the odd creaks and groans of the old building, refusing to stop and reminisce as memories trespassed, she sat herself down at the antique desk in the foyer behind the check-in counter, ready to pick up where Jack Monroe had abruptly left off. Armed with Debbie's small-business brochure and an equally vague pamphlet handed to her at the bank, she set to work making sense of the business side of this inn.

Your Small Business and You! suggested starting with any Excel spreadsheets, booking software, and QuickBooks invoicing systems cataloged and saved by a previous owner, but all Shelby found after an inventory of the desk included a dusty ledger of figures that looked positively Dickensian, a sticky note alluding to a wiring issue with a phone number scrawled underneath, and a filing cabinet filled with loose papers ranging from photocopies of random work orders to restaurant supply and landscaping and nursery invoices, none of which seemed chronological or alphabetical. And nothing about the damage to the back porch she'd noted upon arrival.

She emptied the drawer directly onto the floor and began sorting the papers into piles: two bids for what looked like the annex addition, completed six years ago; several photocopies of blank W-4 forms; a work order for the front-entry lights (something to do with the wiring problem?); and a dozen or so invoices from the last few years to ACME Food Supply out of Akron, Ohio. Shelby pulled one from the pile and scanned it. It looked like Jack Monroe had a regular order for meat, cheese, dairy, and produce.

Shelby frowned in confusion. Why ship food thousands of miles when you lived in a farm-to-fork microclimate with local . . . well, *everything* . . . right in your backyard? San Juan Island was hardly a food desert. But maybe this was just how business was done. She made a note to consult her business books.

Next, she called the mystery number on the sticky note.

"Grover Electric."

"Hello, yes, this is Shelby Wright. I'm the new owner of the Merrick Inn just outside Snug—"

"I know the Merrick." The man on the other end of the line sounded more cautious than terse.

"Oh. Well, good. I'm wondering if you could help me. I think I have a work order from your company here. For a lighting issue?"

There was a pause. "You bought the place?"

"Yes?" Shelby cringed; she hadn't meant to make that sound like a question. She cleared her throat. "Yes."

The man let out a low whistle, followed by a sigh. "Good luck, ma'am."

"Well, thank you, but I'm hoping not to need any." Shelby attempted a light laugh, which wasn't returned. "Anyway, I'm playing a bit of catch-up around here. The work order? Do you know if it was fulfilled?"

"Listen, we tried to come out. Several times, actually. But the owner—previous owner, I mean—he *liked* that the lights flickered. And that just isn't up to code. We can't put our reputation on the line for 'paranormal ambience' or whatever. So if you want it fixed for real this time—"

"I do. Definitely."

"I suppose I could try again. I'll arrange it with your maintenance kid."

For a second Shelby didn't know whom he referred to. "Oh, Ezra? Well, he isn't here at present. Maybe we can just go ahead and take care of this ourselves."

A pause followed this suggestion. "Here's the thing. You know how many outdated electric boxes your inn has? How many breakers and in how many nooks and crannies? Yeah, well, me neither. But that kid? Ezra? He knows the Merrick like the back of his own hand. Have him give me a call, and we'll come out and see what we can do."

Since all Shelby could do was agree, she agreed, hanging up with a frown. She tried ACME next, where she was eventually put through to a regional sales manager, who, again, asked for Ezra. Ditto for the Friday Harbor nursery and garden supply store, which was at least local.

"But Ezra knows all the quantities needed for the fertilizer, not to mention what he wants to plant seasonally," the young woman said, audibly perplexed at Shelby's suggestion that they establish a standing order, to save time and cost. "What would I even put on the form?"

She had no idea and was forced to say so. The chimney and fireplace maintenance company wanted to talk to Ezra next, followed by the window washers. She stuffed all the loose papers back into the filing cabinet in defeat, wondering what, exactly, the entrepreneurial Mr. Monroe had been doing all these years, while Ezra Peterson ran his inn.

Your Small Business and You! cautioned against allowing setbacks to win the day, so she pivoted to tasks she could accomplish, even without her ghost-loving groundskeeper. She reactivated the Merrick's Tripadvisor and Yelp pages, glad now that the chamber had taken the initiative to contest most of the old reviews. As promised by Debbie, they had been scrubbed clean of keywords like "haunted" or "paranormal." No grainy photos of unexplained blurs or smudges accompanied the remaining reviews, and none reported anything sinister.

"Like what?" Beth asked, calling to check in. "Inexplicably slammed doors or snuffed-out candles?"

"Yes, exactly like that. Which is why I wouldn't have noticed any red flag even if I *had* done my due diligence back in Portland."

Beth could only *humph* at that, knowing Shelby was right. For once.

Only a few reviews still alluded vaguely to Ezra and Monroe's exorcism act.

This place is a definite must! one guest enthused. *Felt the "vibe" the moment I stepped in the door. Five stars!*

The Merrick is lit! said another reviewer. *Big crowd by the time I got here, and everyone agreed this Ezra dude is the real deal. You gotta see it to believe it!*

At least these reviews were five star, Shelby reasoned. And once she reopened, new reviews would push even these to the bottom of the page. Satisfied, she turned her attention to registering for a Google business listing next. She got stuck again almost immediately, however: She didn't yet have a definitive date for her reopening, couldn't decide on dining room hours until she hired a kitchen staff, and wasn't sure how to organize her various room categories per nightly rate. Josh had envisioned seasonal lodging packages, but what did that mean, exactly?

And would the historic Bay Bar be full service? What about the dining room? Their favorite Penn Cove oysters wouldn't serve themselves on the half shell. She resisted the urge to beat her forehead against the antique desk in defeat. She didn't even know if the inn's current web address worked.

She tried it, and immediately added *hire a web designer* to her ever-growing to-do list. She'd need someone who could widen the margins and add drop-down menus, take some professional photos, and add a feature for online bookings (*Give us a call to inquire!* just wasn't going to cut it).

She experienced a minor victory when she discovered a 2019 Puppies of the Pacific Northwest wall calendar in which someone (Ezra, presumably?) had made note of necessary monthly maintenance tasks. She used this as a reference, updating her own online calendar to alert her when it was time to change all the air filters and the batteries in all the smoke detectors . . . only to realize half the guest rooms didn't even *have* smoke detectors, let alone carbon monoxide detectors and the legally required accessibility features.

By midafternoon, Shelby's to-do list had grown to the length of her arm. Fearing she might be losing the battle against small-business defeat, she abandoned her post at the desk to gaze out the window of the foyer to the garden. Staring down a gigantic sunflower bobbing in the late summer breeze, she fought tears. What on earth had made Josh think she could do this? That she'd even *want* to do this? The only thing she was getting out of agreeing to this unpredictable venture was the possibility of a new start, but how could she hope to redefine herself in this time capsule of shared history?

The antiques and mid-eighteenth-century architecture had been *Josh's* passion; Shelby had much preferred the time they'd spent outside during their honeymoon, kayaking and hiking. The guest room upstairs had left Shelby feeling inadequate and somehow let down; the time spent with other couples downstairs at the bar had felt forced, just one more example of acting out a role she was ill suited for.

The sunflower continued to bob, and Shelby continued to stand there, once again stuck in place, reliving the worry, self-doubt, and heartbreak that had so often undermined her marriage. Surely Josh hadn't been immune? A new thought occurred to her: Had their time at the Merrick been the pinnacle for him? Had it represented a small slice of idealistic coupledom that proved elusive for the rest of their marriage? Maybe he had hoped that by returning to the inn, it would be possible to recapture this. Maybe it was why he'd never stopped talking of buying the Merrick together.

But if so, why send her back here, now, alone? To fix what had been broken here? As a redo? With a frustrated cry of pent-up stress, she grabbed her keys and retreated, escaping to the first place she could think of where she wouldn't feel confronted by the impossible-to-uphold expectations of her late husband. How convenient that San Juan Winery sat only half a mile down the road.

Pulling into the winery parking lot, Shelby felt calmer already. Lighter somehow. She practically floated up the steps, her mood buoyed by the thought of sipping a glass of the excellent Madeleine Angevine she'd sampled earlier that week.

And the wine was indeed on offer, right there on the tasting menu between the '18 pinot gris option, which Shelby now knew to give a respectful berth, and the cab franc Holly had deemed Heart of Darkness. But the mad scientist herself was nowhere in sight. Instant, overwhelming disappointment punctured Shelby's brief optimism like a pin popping a balloon.

"What can I get for you?" an older man asked pleasantly enough, turning with a smile from sliding wine stems into the drying rack above his head.

"Oh, I was hoping to . . . I mean, I was looking for, um . . ." Staring at her menu, Shelby tried to salvage what she could of her shattered hopeful outlook, but it was no use. She looked up bleakly. "Your winery owner had some suggestions for me last time."

"You must mean my daughter." The man either didn't notice, or discreetly overlooked, Shelby's unenthusiastic reaction to his presence behind the bar. He held out his hand. "I'm Dan Caster, Holly's father."

The silent partner. Though he certainly seemed chatty enough. Shelby frowned at herself, baffled by this uncharitable thought, still struggling to make sense of the disappointment coursing through her.

"Holly made a trip to the mainland for some sort of wine seminar, and to pick up some harvest equipment that hadn't shipped with the rest of her pallet," Dan told her. He took the liberty of pouring Shelby a glass of the franc. You must be new around here," he added predictably.

Was there a script all San Juan Island residents followed when they smelled fresh meat? Shelby gave him her usual spiel about buying the inn, and then, before he could beat her to it, she heard herself say defiantly, "And yes, I already know what I'm in for."

One eyebrow lifted. Shelby noted that Dan had Holly's green eyes. Or rather, Holly had Dan's. "Ah, yes. The haunted history."

Just like last time, several additional heads turned at mention of this taboo topic of conversation, but also like before, the Caster behind the bar seemed immune to the stigma sticking to the Merrick. Suddenly, finding Dan at the winery instead of his daughter didn't seem like *quite* as much of a waste of an evening.

"Do you know much about it?"

"I was working doubles here in the tasting room most of last season, while Holly bottled out back," he said. "Had a front row seat to the stream of . . . enthusiasts . . . driving past to gawk at the Merrick. Word has it, Ezra Peterson put on quite the show."

Shelby worried the inside of her lip with her teeth before taking a sip of wine to curb the habit. What awaited her when this man returned from his paranormal conference? An unhinged extremist or antisocial history buff? An unhinged antisocial extremist?

Dan offered an encouraging smile. "At least you don't need to worry about finding good help. I don't know anyone more devoted to their job than Ezra. His work ethic certainly defies the stereotypes you hear about his generation."

She thought immediately of the stream of vendors she'd tried to contact today. "Yes, I've been learning how indispensable he is."

Dan nodded. "Kid's island born and bred. There's no one he doesn't know. And as far as his cuckoo stuff goes, he's had his wrists slapped by the tourism board. They'll keep him in line." He chuckled. "You, too, if they can manage it."

Shelby smiled before circling back to the word *cuckoo*. "You don't think . . . you know, that he truly believes it all, do you?"

Dan finished drying a wineglass with a rag, clearly weighing his answer before speaking. Again, not unlike his daughter. And just like while in Holly's company, Shelby felt a strange urge to confide. *I came here to move on and find myself surrounded by memory instead. I want to start fresh, but my groundskeeper apparently wants to cling to ghosts. If I don't make a success of the Merrick before my business loan runs out, I'll have to sell and retreat, but I have no idea how to be an inn owner.*

"Hard to say what Ezra believes," Dan decided. He eyed Shelby thoughtfully. "But one thing's for sure: For a history buff, he sure got his facts wrong."

"What do you mean?"

"Well, you see, his whole act he does—or *did*, rather—featured the Merrick's nautical antiques. The ship wheel, the oil paintings, the hurricane lamps, the brass anchor . . ."

All the stuff Shelby had pulled off the walls her first night on-island. "So?" She'd better proceed with caution.

"So, I'm a bit of a history nerd myself, and I did a stint as a volunteer over at the San Juan Historical Society. Turns out the esteemed Captain Merrick wasn't a sea captain at all. The guy was a captain in the American army, back when the Americans and the English faced off here on the island for the Pig War, back in . . . oh, eighteen—something." Dan chuckled again. "Apparently, the only casualty of the war was a pig, caught tromping through an officer's wife's garden."

Shelby smiled.

"So," Dan continued, "maybe your inn *is* haunted." He paused, then leaned over the bar, presumably for dramatic effect. "By the pig." He gave Shelby a wink and laughed again.

Shelby laughed lightly in return. "Or Captain Merrick himself, pissed off to have been misrepresented all this time. I actually just took down the anchor over the door and the oil paintings the other night. They were a bit too . . . much . . . for my taste."

"Well, see?" Dan grinned. "You're a natural business owner already. Instincts on point."

"All I need to do now is rename the place the Pig Inn," Shelby agreed. "My ghost will disappear, my employee will behave, and all my problems will be solved."

Dan grinned. "Here to help."

Shelby tipped her glass of perfectly structured wine in his direction in salute. She felt considerably better as she thanked Dan for lending an ear, settled her bill, and saw her way out. The Casters definitely had a knack for lightening her mood.

Chapter 9

Ezra Peterson arrived back at the Merrick late Friday afternoon to promptly eradicate Shelby's many preconceived assumptions about him. Oh, physically, he embodied the picture Holly and Dan had painted: as advertised, Ezra looked like he'd stepped right out of the pages of a Victorian novel. He wore trousers, leather boots, and a wool tweed cap the likes of which Shelby had last seen in the prop room of Alex's high school production of *Newsies*. In one hand, he carried an ancient-looking suitcase Shelby was pretty sure she should refer to as a carpetbag. No wonder Jack Monroe had been inspired to turn the Merrick into a haunted house; Ezra looked born to play the role of the good captain's newest spirit.

"Hallo there," he called as he walked up the drive, doffing his cap.

Shelby hadn't even realized she had the word *doff* at her command until it sprang into her mind at his gentlemanly gesture. She immediately understood why Holly had been hesitant to consider this young man a threat: His face was almost cherubic, with light crinkles around his eyes. He looked more like twenty-three going on fifty.

"Ezra Peterson, I assume?" she asked, even though there was no way he could be anyone other.

He extended his hand as he let the bag drop at his feet. "Yes, ma'am. At your service."

"Shelby Wright. I just bought the place."

Ezra nodded stiffly, whether out of a rigid sense of politeness or because he worried his reputation had preceded him, Shelby wasn't sure. "You're the widow," he observed solemnly.

"Word certainly travels fast." Shelby tried to hide a prickle of annoyance behind a smile. But to her relief, Ezra didn't scroll through the usual follow-up questions and observations: *How did he die? So young! How tragic. You poor thing.* He simply nodded again, and Shelby was surprised to realize she didn't feel any pressing need to fill the pregnant pause that followed. Despite his stilted manner, something about this young man suggested a gentleness she wouldn't have expected in an exorcist. Perhaps his whole ghost routine *was* just an act, after all. For the second time in as many minutes, she felt relief.

He continued to stand in front of her, shifting awkwardly from one leather boot to the other until Shelby said, "We should talk about your hours and pay," at the exact same time Ezra said, "I'm keen to stay on, if you'll have me."

Shelby nodded. "From what I'm told"—Ezra tensed—"you're quite invaluable around here."

He released a pent-up exhale. "I do try to be, ma'am. There's nothing I don't know about the place, I promise you that. In fact, here." He dug into a small satchel Shelby hadn't noticed around his waist and produced a folded piece of paper, which he thrust into Shelby's hands.

Merrick Tasks, August was handwritten at the top, followed by a long list of agenda items. She was pleased to see it already included contacting Grover for a new estimate on the lighting issue, making an appointment with the chimney sweep (which surprised Shelby to learn was still an occupation), and picking up an order at the Friday Harbor nursery. Several more action items followed that Shelby wouldn't have even thought of: arrange pest control (yellow jackets), order hay bales from Pleasant Ridge Farm for fall harvest decor, and obtain holiday lights and decoration permit. It wasn't until Shelby reached the bottom of the list that she felt any prickle of concern.

"What's this?" she asked. *Ad for second and fourth Friday candlelight program* had been written, then crossed off by hand.

Ezra flushed. If possible, it made his face even more angelic looking. "Oh, that's just something I did for Mr. Monroe. After he left, folks would still trickle in for it, from out of town. But Rosemary says open flames are against county regulation or licensing or some such. So I crossed it off."

"Friday candlelight program" must have been code for "séance." "Yes, well, as you know, Ezra, Mr. Monroe's business tactics caused a lot of discomfort for folks around here, and ultimately made it impossible to keep the Merrick open." Shelby cringed at her tone, which sounded a lot like when she had to school Alex on driving too fast or forgetting about his homework. Remembering Ezra's youth softened her somewhat. "I'm committed to making a fresh start of it, realizing something new around here."

It was hard to miss the hint of alarm that colored Ezra's cheeks at the words *fresh* and *new*, which Shelby tried to chalk up to his passion for all things classic.

"Yes, ma'am," he said grudgingly.

"Please, call me Shelby."

"Yes, Ms. Shelby."

Shelby sighed. "Well, come on in. We might as well get your paperwork all up to date. I'll need you to fill out a new W-4, that sort of thing." Luckily, she knew right where to find one.

He followed her toward the front door of the Merrick, only to stop short just shy of the threshold as abruptly as if he'd been yanked back by an invisible chain.

"Ezra?"

His entire demeanor jumped from acute politeness to a high stress level like the readout on a heart monitor spiking. "You took down the anchor," he said. He turned from the door to her face, regarding her so intensely she wondered whether she'd just committed a very serious faux pas.

She eyed him warily, reminding herself again that Holly had called this man harmless. "Yes, it just seemed a bit much."

What remained of Ezra's careful civility abandoned him as he pushed his way past her into the vestibule. Shelby bit back a *Hey!* as he pivoted in a tight circle, performing a rather wobbly pirouette as he took additional inventory. "What else have you changed?"

"What have I . . . what do you mean?"

He visibly tried to regain his composure, drawing in deep breaths. He'd probably noticed Shelby's hesitant step backward. *Harmless,* she repeated to herself firmly. Debbie had called him a "son of the island." And Shelby definitely needed to stay on the locals' good side.

"Aside from the anchor," Ezra asked more calmly, "have you removed anything else?"

"A few things."

"But what *exactly*?" Ezra would have sounded like the possessive or controlling type had genuine fear not arisen in his tone.

Shelby did a quick mental inventory. "A few oil paintings in the Merrick Suite," she said. "A ship wheel, I think. But as it turns out, I learned something new from Dan Caster the other day. You know, over at the winery? Funny story: Captain Merrick wasn't a ship captain at all! So all this nautical stuff? It really doesn't fit the time period or the inn's history."

If she'd hoped to appeal to Ezra's devotion to island lore, she'd clearly miscalculated. His face went from pink to white. "But where are they?"

"The antiques? I think I put most of them in the maintenance shed out by the driveway—"

Ezra turned on his heel right there in the entry, making a beeline for the shed across the drive. She trailed after him at a cautious distance. Forget Holly and Debbie's endorsement: Was this guy as nuts as she'd originally feared?

But a minute later, reassured by the sight of the nautical antiques stacked neatly in the shed, as promised, Ezra looked significantly more composed.

He exhaled and turned back to her, hugging the ship wheel to his chest. "I'm well aware of the inn's history, and with Captain Merrick's contributions during the Pig War. But these pieces *are* historic," he explained primly. "I bequeathed them to the inn personally. They were my grandfather's, who *was* a sea captain, until he passed. Or, rather, a whale-watching captain."

This grandfather . . . he must be the loss Debbie had referred to.

"Mr. Monroe wasn't too concerned with historical accuracy," Ezra continued, "but he was happy enough to have my things here, as they're—or, rather, they *were*—important to my . . . process."

"Your exorcisms, you mean?"

Ezra frowned at the word, which Shelby took as a good sign. "Father Mark, out on Orcas, does *exorcisms*," he said. The face he made confirmed what he thought of Father Mark's practices. "I do stirrings."

"Stirrings," Shelby echoed, remembering how, when Debbie had said the word, it had come out almost as a whisper. Despite herself, Shelby's heart accelerated in her chest. Part of her didn't want to know, but . . . "What is the difference?"

Ezra eyed her cautiously. Because he wasn't used to being taken seriously by San Juan business owners, or because he feared being tattled on for discussing his paranormal activities again? A desire to confide seemed to win out. Shelby could relate.

"An exorcism is an indeterminate act," he said eventually. "Aggressive and unrefined, like an exterminator tenting a house. Or spraying for weeds out in a garden. A stirring is selective. Targeted. It's personal, and therefore it requires a personal touch." When Shelby just continued to look at him expectantly, he added, "To do a stirring, you have to know what holds significance to the person. At least, that's what they say at ParaPsyCon."

Shelby wanted to argue, but hadn't she felt Josh here from the moment she'd arrived? What *wasn't* significant to him in this place?

"After death, people attach themselves to the things they loved in life," Ezra said, while Shelby continued to see alarming parallels. "Master Psychic Prism Jones, at ParaPsy, says it's a kinetic thing."

"And you think it . . . works?" God, Shelby hoped not.

Ezra hesitated, but only for an instant. "With patience and continued efforts, my grandfather will eventually come near. I'll be close to him again, close enough to feel his presence on my skin."

If anyone else had delivered this line, it would have sounded like a gimmick sold to tourists. But Ezra didn't embody the attention-getter Shelby had anticipated, jockeying for his five minutes of fame. He sounded like . . . like he actually believed what he said. All of it.

Which was probably why Holly had warned her she had her work cut out for her. "But like we talked about," she said as gently as she could, "we won't be doing these . . . stirrings . . . anymore."

The flush returned to Ezra's cheeks, but he only muttered another "Yes, ma'am, Ms. Shelby."

Sympathy tugged at Shelby's gut. Maybe it was her maternal instinct kicking in, or maybe it was the unsettling amount that she could relate to this young man, but she heard herself offer, "I suppose the ship wheel can stay, if you want to display it somewhere."

So what if Ezra wanted to hang on to a few keepsakes. Shelby was attached at the hip to this whole damn inn.

"And the paintings?" he asked eagerly.

No way was Shelby going to reinstate these dreary vignettes into the Merrick Suite, even though they, too, clearly meant a great deal to Ezra. But she didn't want to start off on the wrong foot with her only employee, a.k.a. the island's beloved mascot. She needed to collect allies, not enemies.

"Pick your favorite, and we'll keep the rest in the maintenance shed, for now. They'll be safe," she promised.

Ezra selected a heavy oil painting of an outcropping of rocks dashed by a turbulent sea with the care one might reserve for fine china, and Shelby's sympathy faltered.

Allies, she reminded herself. *Beloved mascot.* "Listen," she said, keeping her voice as neutral, but still as gentle, as possible. "I know how hard it is to lose someone." And everyone dealt with it differently, right?

Ezra might be harmless or he might be certifiably insane, but either way, she needed him. "But I also know how much you love the Merrick," she added. "So I hope that you'll help me reopen the place successfully."

Finally, she'd said the right thing. Ezra looked up and nodded, a bit of the gloom leaving his face. She managed to extract some personal information out of him for the required employment forms, wondering as he filled out his W-4 whether she could ask Beth to run Ezra's Social Security number, just in case. *Harmless,* she repeated to herself, while longing for just a pinch of Beth's intuition.

Long after he had excused himself to settle back into the caretaker's cottage, Shelby remained in the vestibule, eyeing the wheel and the oil painting Ezra had rescued from the shed. She then widened her gaze to take in all the architectural touches Josh would cling to, if he were to inhabit the Merrick like Ezra's grandfather. The bay windows off the dining room, with their beveled storm glass, the arched doorways and cedar-planked flooring.

If she did right by him and reopened this inn in the way he envisioned, would the memory of him be appeased? Would he forgive her for the way she'd sprung such a hard truth on him, just as his body had betrayed him?

Forward motion . . . she reminded herself firmly. Wasn't that still her motto? All this talk of hanging on to ghosts was a setback, and Shelby needed to keep pushing forward, checking all the boxes on her to-do list. Once she'd fulfilled Josh's vision for this inn, then, maybe, she'd find the key to navigating her new life. She could only hope that if and when that moment came, Josh would forgive her for turning the lock.

Chapter 10

The next week, with nothing more to clean within the Merrick, Shelby decided it was time to further inspect the damage to the back veranda. Under the tarp, it looked like one section of the wooden floorboards had been singed by fire. Minor, but noticeable, smoke damage trailed up the side of one railing. Ezra worked in the garden, repotting calla lilies, and she waved him over.

He came at a trot, only to slow practically to a crawl once he saw the tarp overturned. Shelby stifled a half-amused, half-annoyed sigh. He reminded her of Alex at age five, trying to slink away from spilled cereal all over the kitchen counter.

"Do you know anything about this?" she asked, wincing anew at how much she sounded like a parent scolding a child. "I'm trying to make heads or tails of it."

Ezra stared down at his soil-stained hands for a beat. "I've been meaning to get on that," he said eventually. "Only, I didn't want to hire the job out, on account of . . . well, um, how it occurred."

Shelby frowned. "And how did it occur?"

If Ezra had looked like a child trying to weasel out of responsibility a moment before, he had now leveled up to "whipped puppy." "It was an accident," he blurted. "And it wasn't for an audience, nothing like that."

"What do you mean . . . not for an audience? Wait: Were you doing another stirring?"

"This was before you got here," he said swiftly. "And it wasn't anything the tourism board could object to! This one was just for myself."

Shelby eyed the smoke and fire damage again, then resumed her study of Ezra. She'd be more angry if he didn't look so miserable. And not only at being caught. He was just . . . *miserable.* "Maybe I don't understand," she ventured, though she feared she might. "Something caught on fire?"

"I use smudge pots," he said, so quietly she had to step toward him, standing below her off the porch, to hear. "They just create smoke . . . incense, you know? Mr. Monroe always encouraged that . . . it helped with the ambience. But they also recommend it at ParaPsyCon, because of the memory-inducing properties. Anyway, it was windy, and I guess . . . well, I get distracted when I am concentrating on bringing my grandfather near. I put the fire out just the second I noticed."

The misery seemed to double, Ezra's face a study of conflict and grief. It tugged at her; Alex had looked just like this during those first awful days and weeks after losing his father. Like he had been set adrift, his anchor pulled right out from under him. She took another step toward Ezra.

"Listen, I get it. But there are other ways to feel connected to those we lose." Just look at Shelby . . . she couldn't stop feeling connected if she tried.

Ezra shook his head swiftly. "No, this is the only way I can reach him. It has to work."

Shelby sat down on the steps and motioned to Ezra to join her. It took him a moment to decide, and then he sank down next to her.

"Tell me about him," she prompted. When he hesitated, she added, "Maybe it will help."

Ezra was quiet long enough for Shelby to wonder whether he'd decline her invitation. "He raised me," he said eventually. "We worked together, from the time I was small, on the *Evergreen Lady*. That was his whale-watching boat," he added. He nodded his head toward the Bay Bar, where he had re-erected the ship wheel. "That's the *Lady*'s." He gave a half-hearted laugh. "That boat made me so seasick. Every weekend, plus Fridays, we'd take groups out from Roche Harbor, and every time I'd lose my lunch."

Shelby smiled. "But you still went?"

Ezra looked at her as though this was an odd question. "Of course. He was my grandfather. And he needed me. Besides, I wanted to see the pods."

"Pods?"

"The orca pods. J, K, and L . . . all the Southern Residents in the sound. My grandfather knew everything about them, right down to which was which. They all have names, you know. And their children and teenagers? They stay with the pod their entire lives."

"I didn't know," Shelby said. "That's amazing. I've never gone out on one of those tours."

At this admission, Ezra's face took on an animated sheen as some of the sadness abated. "They're wonderful . . . if you have the constitution for it. It helps to go out early in the morning, when the sound is flat. Plus, that's when the seagulls are feeding. And the eagles . . . once, when I was eleven, we saw an entire orca pod work together to make a meal out of a harbor seal."

This was perhaps the longest speech Shelby had heard from Ezra. Talking of the departed seemed to energize him. Maybe he was onto something, in a way. Maybe his continual stirring up of the past *was* his way to mourn.

Her glance fell back on the damaged porch. She assumed that if Ezra knew how to fix it, he would already have done so. "You don't know a local contractor who isn't a member of the business chamber, do you?" Because he was right: Shelby certainly didn't need it getting back to the tourism board that Ezra had almost burned the place down in a personal ghost hunt.

He shook his head. "But I can show you where some extra boards are."

She followed him to the maintenance shed, where they dug through some of the exiled antiques and random hotel supplies to unearth a stack of redwood planks. The sharp scent of the wood reminded Shelby of the wine barrels in the tasting room, which made her think: Maybe Holly or Dan knew of someone she could hire. And Shelby was always up for a visit to San Juan Winery.

~

By now she could drive the route practically with her eyes closed. As she made the last few turns through the forested section of the road, she reminded herself that this wasn't a social visit. She needed information and help, and Dan Caster was probably her best source. So what she wouldn't do, she told herself as she approached San Juan Winery's barn, was harbor any unnecessary hope that Holly was back from her trip to the mainland.

And then she pulled into the parking lot, which she immediately scanned for the motorcycle.

Which was nowhere in sight.

Before she could let self-judgment and disappointment simultaneously sink in, however, a fully loaded beat-up pickup truck swung into the drive behind her, circling to the side of the tasting room. Holly hopped down from the cab, lithe as a cat, as though Shelby had somehow managed to conjure her by wishful thinking alone. She turned to grab something out of the truck bed, caught sight of the Prius, and did a humorous little pivot in the gravel, spinning back around with a grin.

"Shelby!" she called, and the fact that Holly still remembered her name instantly filled Shelby with much-needed warmth.

She smiled back. "Do you need some help?"

Holly, in fact, looked like she had it well in hand. Making her way across the parking lot, Shelby slid her gaze to the gravel after catching herself enjoying the view as the winemaker leaned over the side of the truck bed in her Levi's, reaching for whatever she'd hauled here. It was a correction Shelby was well accustomed to making when in Beth's company, too, on the occasions she'd caught herself unintentionally admiring. The feeling had always been chased by a jolt of shame; after all, Shelby's gaze wasn't solicited.

Holly's expression remained welcoming, however, those green eyes shining as she willingly burdened Shelby with two crates she'd hefted from the truck. What sounded like empty wine bottles rattled around inside.

"Your dad said you went to Seattle?" Shelby said.

One eyebrow quirked as Holly reached for a third crate. She paused, balancing it on the tailgate. "I'd signed up for a viticulture course," she supplied. "You met my dad?"

Uncertainty filled Shelby. Had mentioning Holly's father sounded too chummy? Shelby had to remind herself she didn't really know Holly yet. It just felt like she did, for some reason.

But Holly laughed with a grunt as she lifted the crate. Clearly she'd saved the heavy one for herself. "Dan does make it his business to be all up in *my* business," she said with a jovial jut of her chin toward the tasting room. "Literally!"

Shelby smiled in relief while her mind shifted to overdrive. Did that mean Holly considered Shelby "her business"? No, of course it didn't! She flushed at her own foolishness, just like she so often did with Beth, adjusting her grip on the crates so she didn't shatter a couple of dozen bottles as she overthought absolutely everything. She followed Holly's lead toward a side door of the tasting room, flushing a second time as she caught the woman casting a sidelong look at her over the top of her crate.

It meant nothing. Just like it never meant anything with Beth.

Except . . . Holly was different in one important way, wasn't she? Nothing about Holly shouted "straight."

Setting the crates down on a bench just inside the tasting room kitchen, she hastened to explain. "It's why I stopped back in today. To pick his brain about something."

Holly cocked her head. "Oh? Mysterious."

Shelby blushed again like an idiot. Or, more precisely, like a closeted woman who couldn't even brave coming out to her best friend, let alone let such an intimidating and confident woman know she was available.

Was that what Shelby was? Available? It hardly seemed like an apt description. Plus, what did she really know about Holly or *her* availability? Nothing.

Except that she was still standing there, waiting for Shelby's "mystery" to be unfolded. "It's nothing exciting. Just some minor fire and smoke damage I have on my back porch. Collateral damage from one of Ezra's past . . . rituals. I hoped to downplay it, you know, in the community." She made an apologetic face, remembering that Holly and Dan were part of said community. "And more importantly, I hoped he might be able to recommend a contractor for me."

"Ah. I see." Holly beckoned Shelby back out the door. "One more load? I'll buy you a beer."

For god's sake, do not blush. "Sure."

Back at the truck, she accepted a cardboard box filled with some sort of chemicals this time. She watched as Holly rolled a huge oak barrel to the lip of the truck bed before wrapping it in a bear hug to gingerly bring it to the ground. She misread the blatant admiration Shelby hastened to mask in her expression and added, "The beer is optional, of course. In case you're not a beer girl."

"No, I . . . I like beer," she answered weakly. How Shelby longed to confide in this woman! But who was she to make assumptions?

"And I think I can help you out, with the carpentry work you need."

"Oh! You know someone?"

Holly nodded, shaking out her arms before rocking the wine barrel into a vertical position to heft it back off the ground. "Yeah. Me."

Shelby blinked. Even empty, the barrel had to be half of Holly's body weight. "Oh." She regained her composure in time to add, "I had no idea." God, she should never have assumed *Dan* would be the one who could help.

Holly grinned. "I'm not licensed or anything, but I think I'd lose my lesbian card if I didn't know my way around a SKIL saw."

She laughed, while Shelby's face once again went red. This time, it was with envy, even as gladness to have her assumptions confirmed came on its heel. Holly felt comfortable enough in her skin to out herself in a *joke*, while Shelby remained as twisted up and tortured as ever.

Holly misread her flustered silence and backpedaled. "I mean, it sounded like you wanted this job done off the books. So I'd be glad to help, if you want me, that is."

That would be an emphatic, unqualified yes. "Sure, of course," Shelby managed, trotting after her, very glad Holly couldn't see her blushing. The contents of her crate made a racket as they clattered against one another.

Holly eased the barrel down against the outside of the tasting room wall and stretched her arms. "Labor Day weekend will be a zoo on San Juan. I'll need all hands on deck here on Sunday, but by Monday, things should die down, and my dad is already scheduled to run the tasting room. How does that sound?"

Labor Day. Just four days away. Shelby absorbed a jolt of alarm. How had August nearly passed already? She still had so much on her to-do list: a complete staff to hire, minus Ezra; supplies to order; and an opening date to confirm and promote. And none of this could happen until the inn was back in working order.

The veranda wasn't priority number one, she supposed, but it *had* been important to Josh. He'd been so specific, adding this detail to his perfect picture of inn ownership. Maybe if she started with the veranda, the rest would fall into place. "I'd love the help," she told Holly. "And the company, of course." Because there was that, too. There was definitely that.

Holly cast her uninhibited grin in Shelby's direction. "Plus, I owe you that beer."

There was that warmth again, rushing back into Shelby's cheeks. Carpentry and beer . . . circular saws and pickup trucks. What was this life Shelby suddenly found herself living? She almost answered *it's a date* before catching herself just in time.

"After this, I'll owe *you* one," she promised instead.

Chapter 11

September

When Shelby woke up to Labor Day weekend, it seemed that the population of the island had swollen overnight. Driving down Mitchell Bay Road on an ill-timed-but-crucial grocery run, she was slowed by unprecedented traffic, and once she hit Front Street, it was positively bottlenecked by the ferry terminal. Washington State Department of Transportation traffic cops, looking charmingly old-fashioned in their reflective vests and white gloves, directed a seemingly endless line of cars off the ferry and onto the main artery of Spring Street, urging them toward Friday Harbor's public parking lot two blocks up. Pedestrians jaywalked willy-nilly as they souvenir shopped, and even the parking lot at King's Market was full at 8 a.m. Holly had been right: Friday Harbor was a zoo. Shelby made it back to the inn with her two bags of groceries, feeling like she'd just fought her way along I-5 in Seattle at rush hour.

Stopping by for one of her "pop ins" to the inn, which Shelby was definitely beginning to consider more like "checkups," Debbie remained unfazed by Shelby's tales of traffic woes.

"Best just to go with the flow," she said, encouraging Shelby to use the rest of the holiday weekend to play tourist. "Get to know the local attractions; see them in their element," she said. "You'll want to know what to recommend to guests. When you have some, I mean." She patted Shelby on the arm in a gesture she supposed was meant to be comforting. "It's too bad you haven't created new brochures yet," she added, casting a glance around as if a pile might magically appear. "The ferry will be flooded with tourists today."

Debbie was right. Why hadn't she thought of that? She'd be ready to receive guests by the time these current visitors returned to capture all the cranberry-and-fir wreaths and lavender-scented candles in the holiday season markets on Instagram. She hastily scribbled *print flyers* at the bottom of her to-do list, right under *hire staff.* The words swam in front of her eyes as she fought against an ever-encroaching panic; what if she drowned in her own inadequacy?

"I placed an ad for housekeeping and kitchen help, but no one's answered it yet," she admitted, still frowning at the legal pad. "Should I try again on Indeed or something?"

Debbie *pshaw*ed. "Heavens no! I'll spread the word. Folks will just take a little . . . coaxing, given how things were under Monroe's leadership. Don't you worry . . . word will spread. I wouldn't even bother with recruitment until Tuesday. Everyone is either off-island or picking up temp shifts for the long weekend. Even your Ezra."

"Oh?"

"He'll be helping out Captain Mitchell over at Wild Orca Expeditions. On the dock, handing out tickets, on account of his weak stomach, of course."

"Captain Mitchell?" Shelby asked. She indicated out the window. "As in Mitchell Bay Road?"

"That's right, another family that goes way back around here. Mitchell was close to Martin Peterson. Whale-watching compatriots."

Shelby nodded, remembering the whale-watching legacy left by Ezra's grandfather. "Do you think Ezra will ever revitalize the *Evergreen Lady*?" she asked, adding, at Debbie's puzzled expression, "His family's boat?"

"Oh, I know the *Evergreen Lady*," Debbie assured. "But, honey, that vessel has been at the bottom of the harbor for half a decade."

"It sank?" From the way Ezra spoke of it, Shelby had gotten the impression the *Evergreen Lady* had been beloved in the Peterson clan.

"Eventually," Debbie nodded. "After Martin Peterson got Parkinson's, bless his heart, he went downhill fast. Couldn't handle the upkeep or the monthly rent at the slip in Roche Harbor. Ezra—he would be his only living relative, you see—was away for a time. A wood carving apprenticeship or some other old-timey thing. This must have been when he was eighteen or so. By the time he got back on-island, the hull had rotted right on through. The whole boat sank right there, still moored to the pier. Only thing salvageable was the wheel. Not sure if Ezra ever told Martin, come to think of it, before he passed. It would have well near killed him. You know, if he hadn't already been dying, of course." She barked out an awkward laugh.

Shelby attempted an answering smile while aching for Ezra. The lack of closure, the unfinished business . . . it was all so terribly familiar. Was Ezra feeling the same weight of guilt she was? Was he spinning in circles, unable to find forward momentum, as she had been in Portland? As she still was, if she was being honest, as she tried to find her own way with this inn?

After promising to be in touch regarding her hiring requirements, Shelby saw Debbie out, retrieving the bulky set of keys off the pegboard in the vestibule to lock up behind them both. She might as well take her agent's advice and enjoy the early fall weather, which seemed contractually obligated to remain at a perfect 74 degrees for the holiday weekend.

She was still standing there, head bent toward the door, trying to find the right key for the old-fashioned lock, when a soft voice inquired from just over her left shoulder, "Might I enter, before you depart?"

"Oh!" Shelby swiveled on the spot, taking in Ezra's sudden presence at her elbow. He wore a wool tweed cap today, and a black overcoat at least one size too big, which made him look unsettlingly like an undertaker. "You startled me, Ezra."

He snatched the hat off his head and held it awkwardly in front of him in both hands. Sweat beaded on his forehead, undoubtedly due to the seasonally inappropriate headwear. "Apologies, ma'am."

Shelby still felt flustered. "I thought you were headed to the harbor today. And please, call me Shelby."

He took a tentative step toward the entryway, peering into the Merrick as if the interior of the vestibule might be unfamiliar to him. "Yes, I just hoped to check on a few things first. The outlet in the vestibule, the placement of my antiques . . ." His voice trailed out as he looked at her hopefully.

"There's something wrong with the outlet?" Shelby asked.

"It was prudent that I turn off the power at the breaker before cleaning out the cobwebs around the windowsills, ma'am—Ms. Shelby."

"Oh. Well then, of course." She pushed the door wide, allowing him entry, but then hesitated. "I planned to be gone most of the day," she said.

Ezra's gaze made its way slowly back to her face. "I won't dally," he promised, and indeed, he did look like he might have snapped out of whatever trance he'd been in, now making his way purposefully toward the hallway. Maybe he had just been overheated.

"All right then. I'll just have you see yourself back out." Shelby started for the porch steps, then turned one last time. "Ezra? Maybe go ahead and take off your coat?"

She did not get an answer, but by the time she'd started down the drive, she'd successfully shaken off most of the vague sense of unease Ezra had brought with him, which she was now beginning to think he always brought with him. Despite the predicted crowds, she dutifully hit up all the top tourism spots per Debbie's suggestions, keeping notes on which attractions were worthy of recommending in the three-ring guest guide she planned to create for each guest room. She'd already put San Juan Winery, with its cozy barn and friendly appeal, at the top of the list.

The Whale Museum in Friday Harbor also met with her approval, as did the San Juan Islands Museum of Art. She and Josh had visited both museums on their first visit, and she found them charmingly unchanged. In the Whale Museum, Josh had mimicked the deep, warbling song of a humpback as Shelby had bent double in laughter, until a docent had shushed them both. At the art museum, they'd rushed right past the main hall to see a collection of ancient earthenware pottery on loan from the University of British Columbia.

Stopping short at the glass case, Shelby hadn't known it was possible to feel both inspired and defeated at the same time. "I'll never create anything like it," she'd breathed.

"No," Josh had agreed, a hand resting on her shoulder.

Shelby had glanced up at him, brows knitted in surprise. Josh was always her cheerleader. He wasn't supposed to be a realist.

"You'll create something that's all you," he had concluded.

And yet Shelby hadn't, had she? Forgoing a serious ceramics career after Alex was born, she'd crafted what was expected of her at the community college. What was pretty, marketable, and predictable. Her throat swelled a bit painfully. With Josh, too, she'd tried to imitate what was traditional and expected. What was all good, but not hers.

She turned toward the permanent exhibits, which remained comfortably free of hindsight. Beautiful native Salish tapestry hung from the walls of the featured collection gallery, their signature red, black, and white blocks depicting ravens and eagles nested against human forms. Shelby stood gazing at them for a long time, unable to tear her eyes from the geometric symmetry of the fiber art, married so seamlessly with a breath of human spirit. Authenticity practically radiated from each piece, like someone's heart had been sewn, ventricle to vein, into each design. Her chest ached again, wanting to answer that authenticity. Her fingers twitched, wishing they could create something as unique.

On her way out, signage over a secondary building behind the museum caught her eye: SHARED PALETTE, A COMMUNAL SPACE FOR

ARTISTS. This was precisely the kind of art co-op Josh had wanted her to join. Shelby poked her head in.

The small space was as packed with people as everywhere else today. A tie-dye demonstration took up one side of the room, where parents and kids dipped knotted T-shirts into vats of indigo, orange, and sea green. From the sound of it, a drum-making class occupied studio space somewhere past the T-shirt brigade, and right here in front, what looked like a senior citizens' group diligently mixed watercolors in plastic ice cube trays.

A harried college-aged intern in a paint-splattered smock helped Shelby track down the art director, who approached wearing a petulant frown.

"You really should have called ahead," he said, smoothing a hand down his wool-vested front before reluctantly shaking Shelby's extended hand. His manicured fingers were impeccably clean . . . suspiciously clean for an artist. "Today's workshops are quite at capacity."

Shelby wondered whether she was destined to forever be mistaken for a tourist on this island. "I'm not here for a class. I wanted to ask about any available studio space in the co-op? I'm new here," she added, probably unnecessarily, since everyone who lived on-island seemed to infer this.

This guy, however, didn't deem her interesting enough to peg her as a newbie or anything else, waving her off immediately with a vague reference to an "impossibly long" waiting list.

She walked out of the co-op feeling like she'd somehow just embarrassed them both. Back when she'd been creating regularly at the college, as a woman in a male-dominated art form, she'd been second-guessed and talked down to on the daily. Or at least weekly. So why did this sting so much today?

Because it was just one more failure in a string of failures since arriving on San Juan. One more roadblock. Why couldn't Shelby seem to gain a foothold? Nothing came easy on this island. Nothing at all. Except . . .

On impulse, she aborted her sightseeing tour, pointing the Prius back toward Beaverton Valley Road and her side of the island. A minute later she'd left Friday Harbor to cut inland through the now-familiar farmland. Call it surrender, or call it a retreat, but she felt better already as she navigated to San Juan Winery.

~

Debbie wasn't kidding about holiday weekend crowds. The tasting room was so crowded, Shelby had to pull an empty stool from an adjacent four-top and drag it to the end of the bar. She spotted Dan first, then a younger employee washing wineglasses at the sink, and didn't even realize she'd been half holding her breath in anticipation until she saw a blur of energy with cropped hair and a hoodie weaving between tables. She exhaled as she called out, "Holly! Hey."

"Hey yourself." She smiled that dazzling smile, pushing up her sleeves as she slid herself back behind the bar. "What can I get you?"

Shelby settled for a glass of sparkling rosé she knew was on tap. "I can't stay long," she said, explaining her quest to get to know the island.

"Just thought you'd come in for a pick-me-up?"

I just needed to retreat to somewhere I belonged, just for a minute. "Something like that."

"What have been the highlights so far?" Holly leaned forward against the bar as her father rushed past behind her, carting a dripping ice bucket.

Shelby hesitated, not wanting to monopolize Holly's attention, but she didn't seem to be in a hurry to go anywhere, even when some lady called out *Yoo-hoo!* two tables away. She dispatched the dishwasher and said, "Did you hit up the Whale Museum yet?"

"Yes, and the art museum. Both were great. But then I went into Shared Palette . . . you know, the art co-op?" She filled Holly in on her experience.

"Who'd you talk to there?"

Shelby cast about in her head for the art director's name and came up empty. She felt just a bit vindicated, realizing how forgettable *he* was.

"Was it Jackson Polenski? With one of those stupid manscaped beards? Wearing a wool vest and looking like he had a stick up his ass?"

Shelby smiled. "Yeah, that sounds like him."

"Well, that explains it," Holly told her. "I know why he acted like that."

"Why?" Had Shelby committed some sort of faux pas? Was this Jackson Polenski a big deal in the art world?

"You see, Jackson is . . ." Holly beckoned with a crooked finger, leaning in conspiratorially. Her breath brushed Shelby's ear. "A first-rate asshole."

They both laughed. Holly didn't shrink back immediately. Instead, she laid her hand on top of Shelby's, stilling her next reach for her glass. The touch felt significantly intimate instead of simply friendly, and though Shelby must have misread this, her heart pounded weirdly.

"Don't give him another thought," Holly said sternly. "Not one, all right?"

She kept her hand there, lightly covering Shelby's, until she answered, "Jackson who?"

"Atta girl."

Somehow Holly made this encouragement sound sweet, like Shelby had already accomplished something significant. Not at all like she was addressing a dog. It was the consideration she gave Shelby as she said it, she decided. The warmth in her eyes, which always studied Shelby with interest, never with dismissal. Even when Holly turned to clear the empty glasses from the bar next to her, Shelby still somehow felt the warmth of her attention.

Restored, she swallowed the last of her rosé and pushed back from the bar. She still had plenty of daylight left, and no reason not to pick up her island tour where she'd left off. It was probably just her imagination that Holly looked slightly disappointed to see her departing so soon, but even so, Shelby's heart did another quick flip.

She visited the marina next, with its fresh-caught seafood stands and Do Not Feed the Sea Lions signs posted on every other piling, then spotted the San Juan Islands Visitor Center a block up from the water. A quaint bell sounded over the door as she stepped inside to the sight of a full-length mural of a pod of orca whales breaching. A petite, impeccably dressed older woman stationed behind a desk cluttered with flyers and brochures chirped a shrill "Welcome! Can I help you?"

The name tag pinned to the woman's silk scarf read ROSEMARY. Shelby smiled, extending a hand. "Yes, hello. You're actually the perfect person for me to find here."

"Oh?"

"I'm Shelby Wright. I recently bought the Merrick Inn."

"Ohhh."

Luckily, Shelby had gotten used to this response. She pushed forward with extra cheer, and a dash of flattery. "Debbie Phillips mentioned you were invaluable on the tourism board."

Rosemary tilted her head to one side. Her perfectly styled silver-streaked bob followed suit. "I *am* the tourism board." She smiled. "It's just me, plus a few interns in the summer. I work directly with the chamber of commerce, and man—or, woman, rather—the desk here on weekends.

"And I'm glad to meet you," Rosemary continued. "I've been meaning to stop by." As Debbie had warned. "It helps me do my job better, you see, if I know what sort of . . . vibe . . . a business is aiming to embody."

Shelby forced her smile wider. "Well, you're more than welcome anytime. I'm eager to give the Merrick an entirely new start. I'd value your impressions."

"I would be more than happy to help. We'll want to update your listing in our directory," Rosemary said. "New contact information, photos, things like that. We get media inquiries, you know," she added importantly, silver bracelets jangling on her slim wrists as she turned to a massive computer on her desk and began to type. A moment later, the back end of the San Juan Islands tourism page appeared on the screen, *Inspiration for your senses!* leaping out at Shelby in 16-point cursive font. "You can purchase ad space with us, and we can arrange for media visits, influencers, guidebook authors . . ." Rosemary trailed off, one manicured hand to her chin in thought. "Although, we may have had enough media at the Merrick . . ."

"I'm looking to rewrite that story," Shelby heard herself say. She liked how confident her voice sounded. "Start a new chapter."

Rosemary looked pleased. She sent Shelby on her way with a form to fill out for the directory, information on getting into the San Juan Islands tourism brochure, and a list of advertising contacts for regional magazines all over the Pacific Northwest. In other words, more items for her ever-growing to-do list.

She hit up the San Juan Historical Museum next, with its living-history exhibits and pioneer-era schoolhouse open for the last weekend of summer. This location was mercifully unmarred by memory, and she weaved between bonneted docents and families pushing strollers to tour the nineteenth-century farmhouse and sample a slice of peach pie on the museum society lawn.

Thirsty, she popped into Queen of Tarts, the little café in Roche Harbor advertised in Debbie's welcome packet. The owner, who introduced herself as Sandy, brought her iced chai to the table personally, and Shelby exchanged pleasantries, happy to know yet another female business owner in the area. And after eyeing the cinnamon rolls and morning buns tempting her from under the bakery glass, she knew she'd be back, for "research" in addition to the pleasant company.

She made her way back along the coastline toward Snug Harbor, past the sign for Lime Kiln Point Lighthouse, where she and Josh had shared a picnic once, taking in the sunset while whale-watching boats bobbed like specks of chalk set to glow on the darkening blue of the water. She glanced out over Haro Strait as she drove and the sun sank, but today no elusive spouts of water or rare breach of an orca greeted her. Instead, for about a quarter mile, she paralleled the progress of a kayaking tour floating their way home like ducklings following their mother, bobbing on the tide.

She felt ready to head to sanctuary herself and was glad to reach the turn for Mitchell Bay Road. Maybe she'd draw a bath in the claw-foot tub when she got back to the Merrick and crack open one of her new books on business ownership. She pulled into the drive, already feeling more grounded, more comfortable. Even her to-do list seemed less daunting, out of sight for the day.

Which was why it was a rude awakening when she pushed open the heavy oak door to be greeted by a scene out of *The Exorcist*.

Chapter 12

The vestibule was aglow in flickering, low-flame tea lights littering every surface. The antique desk, the heavy velvet drapes, and the wine-colored Persian rug all glowed an eerie, vintage yellow. What might have been a romantic or whimsical ambience was marred by the presence of two large smudge pots in the middle of the floor, emitting a dense, black smoke that wafted toward the ceiling. A cloying scent of something herbal—sage?—seized Shelby immediately. Coughing, she dodged tea lights and furniture in her pursuit of the light switch, only to crash directly into the creator of the chaos.

"Ezra!" One hand rose involuntarily to clutch her chest. Wasn't he supposed to be taking tickets or something? "What is happening here?" Though she knew . . . of course she knew.

"Ma'am!" he exclaimed, equally startled. He still wore the cap and jacket he'd been wearing when she'd departed hours ago, which he had visibly sweat through. An unmistakable look of distress lined his face.

"This has to stop!" She reached for the light. Was something on fire again, like on the veranda?

"Please don't!" he cried, moving to stop her. "I just began again! It might work this time."

Shelby clutched her nose. "Ezra, this smell!" She guided him out of the vestibule and into the dining area of the inn, where the smoke thinned somewhat. "Why are you doing this?"

Now that her eyes had stopped stinging from the smoke, she could see that the oil painting she'd permitted had joined the ship wheel behind the bar.

"You said I could put the wheel back up," he reminded her swiftly.

She *had* said that, but how to explain to Ezra that every time he preserved something here, she lost precious yardage in her battle to move forward and prepare the inn for reopening? "We can't have any more damage done to the inn." At the very least, she couldn't allow him to make a mockery of her promise to Rosemary, Queen of Tourism.

"I know! I won't. I promise!"

Dwarfed by the oversize clothing, he would have conjured the innocence of a child playing dress-up, if he hadn't looked so pitiful. "Maybe you shouldn't be alone?" Shelby ventured.

"I don't feel alone, not when I'm trying to reach him." His voice caught on the word *alone*, wrenching at Shelby's heart. He clenched his jaw tightly, then practically growled, "That's the whole point of this."

Shelby should probably have felt more alarmed than sympathetic, but Ezra's words were not ominously whispered like a ghost story in the dark. He sounded more like Alex used to, when homesick at sleepaway camp. A sheen of vulnerability lay on the surface of Ezra's demeanor, making him seem fragile to the point of cracking.

Shelby couldn't allow him to break into pieces. "All right," she conceded with a sigh. "You can finish . . . just this once, though."

Maybe going through his ritual one last time would give Ezra that oh-so-elusive thing called closure. Margie talked about that a lot. Or maybe it would just make a mess, like he had on the veranda. Either way, Shelby planned to stick around to watch, fire extinguisher on hand.

"Thank you, Ms. Shelby," Ezra breathed. He looked so relieved, her heart ached still further.

"So, how does this start?" she asked.

He looked taken aback. "Oh, I don't need help."

Tough luck. Witnessing this "act" Ezra had put on so many times under Jack Monroe's reign might give Shelby some valued insight into her current PR problem. Besides, if Debbie popped by unannounced again, or worse, Rosemary, *someone*, needed to do damage control.

"It's my inn, Ezra. I won't interfere, but I'm not leaving." She offered an apologetic smile. "Don't take this the wrong way, but you're a bit of an insurance liability."

A hint of an answering smile played about his mouth. "That's fair," he decided.

He began his stirring back in the vestibule, where all his paraphernalia lay strewn about. The candles still flickered, though several stuttered as the wax melted to a shallow puddle at the bottom of their tins. For a long while Ezra simply stood there, eyes closed, as if taking in the ambience of the room.

Shelby shifted impatiently from one foot to the other, reminding herself that she'd just promised to respect the process. Night was falling fast, and she didn't relish the idea of a candlelit vigil in full darkness.

Eventually Ezra cleared his throat and opened his eyes. "I always start with something he loved." He crossed toward the bar, where the surviving seafaring oil painting stared back at them.

Shelby studied it dubiously while subconsciously holding her breath, as Ezra took a deep inhale of incense from the smudge pot closest to them. Grasping the frame of the painting in both hands, he cocked his head to one side, as if waiting to be alerted of something. When nothing seemed to happen, he reluctantly released the painting and took a step farther toward the bar. He touched a stool next, stopping again to listen, then the hurricane lamps that sat by the stemware—lightly this time, at the base, as the glass had to be hot to the touch. Still nothing happened, but Shelby was starting to see why this ritual had been popular to witness. A sense of suspense hung in the air, along with the candle smoke and incense.

Ezra worked his way slowly toward the dining room, Shelby trailing after him, trying to gauge what might be a respectful distance. Every twenty to thirty seconds, he would stop again, or pivot, or lay his hands on something. An antique mirror, foggy and silver at the edges. Another oil painting that had somehow escaped Shelby's scrutiny, this one of a lighthouse on a jagged cliff, in a gilded frame. All the while, silence continued to prevail.

He stood for a long time in front of a gilded nautical map . . . long enough for Shelby to realize, with some chagrin, that she was holding her breath. Eventually he exhaled hard. "Damn."

"What is it?"

"Nothing," Ezra said. "Which is the problem."

"Does it normally . . . do something?" Shelby felt ridiculous asking this; what had she envisioned? The map suddenly growing legs to run amok through the inn like an enchanted piece of furniture from *Beauty and the Beast*?

But Ezra just frowned. "No," he admitted.

He looked so dejected, Shelby forgot she was supposed to remain impartial. "What about the ship in the bottle?" she asked, pointing to the corked bottle on the bar.

Ezra shook his head. "Mr. Monroe picked that up at HomeGoods last year."

At the entrance to the kitchen, he turned in several circles, his wool socks reminding Shelby of the padded paws of a hound on the trail of a scent. He dismissed a utilitarian-looking ceramic vase, the toaster, and the KitchenAid mixer. He contemplated the teakettle for a moment, then moved back out to the bar, where he ran his hand along the polished shelf under the mirror and moved a few bottles around, but mostly, it turned out, just to take inventory.

"You need Jameson and that blue vodka that looks like mouthwash," he told her absently, then paused long enough that Shelby felt compelled to grab her to-do list sitting by the register and write this down.

He returned to the dining room, where he now worked more quickly, or rather, more efficiently, pausing to turn chairs a few degrees in one direction, then the other. Once, ridiculously, he peered under the linen of a tablecloth, like a child playing hide-and-seek. The parlor in the newer wing of the Merrick got a thorough going-over next, where he systematically rejected a porcelain candy dish and a velveteen love seat in favor of a rather beautiful piece of antique scrimshaw. He cradled the carved whalebone with both hands, but this, too, proved reluctant to "speak" to him. Shelby still didn't know what on earth Ezra planned to do if he did actually channel his grandfather through one of these objects, but by now she was well versed in how he reacted when foiled: His shoulders slumped as his face set further and further in stony frustration.

"This makes no sense," he said, as he circled back around to the ship wheel on the bar, touching it again before slumping in defeat. "From everything I've read, I should feel him here."

He fumed silently, staring from the braided rug on the floor to the end of the hallway as though a trail of crumbs might reveal a path.

But to what? Shelby stumbled around in her mind for a way to be of help. "And that's because of these things that were his, from his life?"

"Significant, even."

Shelby thought of her stacks of books by her bed in the Merrick Suite, her framed photos of Josh and Alex, the clothes in her closet . . . she hadn't really brought anything specifically of Josh's with her here. Just herself, of course. Had Ezra wanted to "stir" him, all he'd have to do is touch his widow.

Maybe Ezra *was* attuned to these things. And maybe Josh's "presence" here was taking up all the space in the room, so to speak. That certainly sounded like him.

Or maybe, Shelby told herself firmly, she was just letting her imagination get the better of her. She reminded herself of Alex, testing Josh's and Shelby's parenting skills in the second grade. All three of them had lived through more than their fair share of sleeplessness that year, thanks to a fifteen-second snippet of a horror movie glimpsed at a friend's house.

"It doesn't matter how many times you tell him films like that are just pretend," Josh had insisted after Shelby had spent yet another night lying on Alex's floor, his favorite dinosaur blanket leaving her freezing below the knees. "As long as Alex thinks those ghosts are real, they're real. You have to fight fire with fire."

He'd perched on the end of Alex's bed, inviting their son to address his ghosts directly. "Have yourself a little heart-to-heart," he'd said, "and just ask them to leave." Josh had chosen to acknowledge the reality their son had conjured rather than convince him of fact. He had been like that: willing to suspend disbelief. Happy to meet the people he loved wherever they struggled.

Had he done that with Shelby, too? When she'd confessed them, had he considered her feelings for Beth just another monster under the bed, something he'd indulge or ignore until it dissipated?

I'll never know. Josh's diagnosis had been like the scratch of a record as the needle jumped the groove. Again, she wondered: In absence of a tumor snatching his short-term memory, toying with each synapse, would he have handled Shelby coming out to him differently? This was the merry-go-round she couldn't get off, the vicious circle of doubt that kept her pinned in the current of him, unable to fully break free.

For a long moment she stewed in her own pain and fear, while Ezra stewed in his, his mouth set in a hard, flat line. His now-familiar misery lay bare on his face, more palpable—and far more relatable—than Shelby wanted to admit. It pressed in close, humming as though with the very kinetic energy endorsed so enthusiastically on Tripadvisor.

"I'm sorry, Ezra," she said, "that you can't find what you're looking for."

Ezra was quite possibly the only person to whom Shelby might be able to talk candidly about losing Josh the way she had, but his instability ran too deep. Debbie's warning about indulging him at the risk of her business success rang in her ears. "But right now we need to clean all this up," she added. Before someone walked in and the Merrick's reputation took yet another hit.

He acknowledged this with a stoic nod, and they worked together in silence, blowing out candles, snuffing out incense, and opening windows to air the place out. As Ezra picked his way through the dark, back across the gardens to his cottage, a smudge pot under each arm, Shelby turned the lights in the vestibule back on, one by one. *Forward motion,* she resolved anew. She would leave the ship wheel in place as promised, but as of tomorrow, every last one of the oil paintings would be relocated to the shed or Ezra's cottage. No more nautical antiques bouncing back into the Merrick like eighteenth-century boomerangs.

No, it was time to fix the veranda, hire her housekeeping team, and create that brochure that would bring in new guests. And unlike Ezra, she wouldn't have to go it alone. She had Holly's promise to be at her side, starting with that porch.

Chapter 13

Labor Day Monday dawned cool and clear. Not that Shelby had much time to savor it. An engine rumble on Merrick Lane announced Holly's arrival just after 7 a.m., sending Shelby into a quick flurry to throw on jeans and rake a brush through her hair before the San Juan Winery work truck came to a stop by the front door.

Holly slammed the door as she hopped down from the cab. "I'm ridiculously early," she said, handing over a cardboard box marked with the Queen of Tarts stamp and two paper cups of steaming Fog Town Roasters coffee. "But trust me on this: We had to get our hands on Sandy's blackberry scones before the tourists bombarded the place. No one will be on the ferry home until at least nine a.m." She flashed a smile. "I simply couldn't risk it."

"Oh! Thanks." Shelby inhaled the scent of berries and butter and coffee while juggling the box in her free hand. "They smell divine."

Holly followed her into the dining area, glancing around as she went. "I haven't been in here in ages."

"You and everyone else," Shelby said. "Islanders, I mean."

"Monroe's antics did put a bad taste in folks' mouths," Holly acknowledged. She seemed to note the sudden wave of uncertainty Shelby wished she could hide, and added, "Time to change that, I would say."

"Yes. Definitely." But where to start?

With these scones, at least for now. They sat at one of the dining room tables and tucked in, Holly passing over a paper napkin and Shelby handing back over one coffee in a seamless exchange, like they shared breakfast every morning.

One bite, and Shelby sank in her chair, moaning in satisfaction. "Oh my god. These taste even better than they smell." Holly's bemused expression, partly obscured by the rim of her coffee cup, had her straightening back up. "What? You disagree?"

"On the contrary"—she smiled—"I've always appreciated a woman who knows how to properly savor a good meal."

Shelby flashed back on the first meal Holly had watched her consume, the charcuterie at the winery. She had been so hungry that first night on-island. "Well, you *have* fed me well so far."

Holly laughed outright, then took her own healthy bite of scone, washing it down with coffee. They ate in companionable silence until all that remained on the table was an empty paper bakery bag and a scattering of crumbs. "I got this," Shelby said, while Holly said, "Let's see what exactly we need to DIY today."

She swept up the trash and led the way to the back porch, where Holly surveyed the wreckage left by Ezra's smudge pots. "He really did a number on this, didn't he?" she said, rocking back and forth on her heels.

"Is it really bad?"

"Just superficial damage," she said, bending to survey the singed boards. "Should be easy enough."

But just like everything else about the Merrick, it wasn't. When Holly returned from retrieving her tools from the truck, they pried back the boards to reveal rot underneath, a common problem, according to Holly, with redwood. "Add the permanent damp of island living, and it's a terrible combination."

"But it's fixable, right?" Shelby asked.

"Sure." But Holly had begun rocking on her heels again, her brow furrowed in thought. "Ezra said he had replacement boards somewhere?"

"We left them in the maintenance shed," Shelby remembered. She led the way again, adding, "They're buried behind all the oil paintings."

At Holly's questioning quirk of one eyebrow, Shelby explained her impulse to take the depressing seafaring images down from the walls of the Merrick Suite her first night, and the reason for Ezra's strong reaction.

"So *that's* why he did his stirrings," Holly said, pausing to study the paintings in the shed. "I wondered what could be important enough for him to put the Merrick at risk like that. He didn't seem the type to be Monroe's lackey."

Shelby debated telling Holly she'd indulged Ezra in an encore just last night, then decided against it. She was enjoying the feeling of being simply herself in Holly's company too much to explain why Ezra's pleas had swayed her.

They uncovered the stack of replacement boards and carted them back to the porch, where they pried up more rotted wood before Holly set Shelby to work pulling out rusted nails while she measured and cut the replacements. What had seemed like a straightforward-enough task soon had sweat dripping from Shelby's forehead, her hands damp inside the heavy leather gloves Holly had lent her. Each nail seemed more reluctant than the last to release its grip on the veranda floor. A sudden whir cut through the air, and she glanced up to the sight of Holly in safety goggles, wielding her circular saw.

Holly was stripped down to her signature tank top, her finely honed biceps straining as she guided the saw through the new wood. Sawdust flew, and Shelby swallowed hard before training her attention back down at the veranda and her next stubborn nail.

The sun rose high, and they worked through lunchtime, but even so, by their third water break, they'd made their way through only the first few feet of flooring. This was what Holly described as a simple project? Shelby was about to suggest scrounging up some food when she heard "Ah, damn . . . would you look at that. Shit."

She rose to her knees to peer over Holly's shoulder, but whatever she'd seen eluded her. "What?"

Holly waved her closer and pointed down into a small abyss she'd created with her saw. "It's the foundation," she said with a hard sigh, peeling back another floorboard. "It's rotted, too."

Shelby's heart sank. "That can't be good," she ventured.

The dismal look on Holly's face confirmed this diagnosis. "No," she said. She wiped her brow with a gloved hand, leaving a smudge of dirt behind. "Goddamn it." She peeled the gloves off, flung them to the ground, and then exhaled again. "Sorry."

"Can we pull up the foundation, too?" Shelby asked, already suspecting the answer.

Holly bent to pick up the gloves. "I'm afraid to mess with that, because those planks connect with the ones through the dining room floor, too. I'm really sorry, Shelby," she repeated. "I thought I could help you fix this, but I'm in over my head."

If *Holly* was in over her head, Shelby would full-on drown if she tried to persevere on her own. Defeat sapped the last of her energy, and she sat down hard onto the (probably rotted) porch step. She wanted to throw something, too, but lacked the stamina. "Why is this so, so hard?"

It was a rhetorical question, of course, but when no answer was forthcoming, tears rushed with a sudden intensity to the back of Shelby's eyes. She stared hard out into the garden, battling them fiercely but losing in an instant when Holly sat down beside her, one hand applying soft pressure on her back.

"Oh, hey, it's okay," Holly said, rubbing now in slow circles against her spine. "We'll have to eighty-six the porch, but we can build new steps out of the replacement boards, so guests can still access the garden from the back door. You'll see, it'll be fine."

But it wouldn't be, because without this veranda, how the hell was Shelby supposed to serve tea alfresco, like Josh had envisioned? How was she supposed to check this off her to-do list, getting her one step closer toward settling the score? Shelby cried harder, embarrassment only fueling her misery.

"It's just . . . that . . . every single damned thing has . . . gone . . . so . . . wrong," she gasped between sobs. "Why can't even one thing be easy? Why?"

She'd arrived on this island so determined, only to encounter obstacle after obstacle. The Merrick's reputation was questionable at best, her only hired help was probably certifiably insane, she couldn't make heads or tails of the mess of paperwork and purchase orders she'd inherited from Monroe, and all the while, Josh was *everywhere*, in every corner and rotted board, reminding her of everything she'd done wrong by him. "It's just . . . it's just . . . I have an inn that's fucking haunted!" she cried.

Holly let out a guffaw of a laugh. She tried to immediately stifle it, a hand over her mouth, but it bubbled up in that way her laugh always seemed to, flowing over Shelby like a balm. She laughed, too. She couldn't help it. She was both laughing and crying, a blubbering, sobbing, hiccuping mess.

"*Allegedly* haunted," Holly corrected between gasps. "But that's a bigger problem than rotted floorboards, I'll grant you that."

"But the floorboards *are* the problem," Shelby breathed. Holly didn't get it.

Holly sobered as she saw Shelby was serious. "Why are you so determined to salvage them?"

Suddenly Shelby wanted her to understand, wanted to be exposed to this woman, even if explaining the twisted logic behind this mental breakdown burst the very welcome bubble she found herself in while in Holly's presence. Ever since arriving on this island, she'd felt pulled like an elastic band: wanting to forge a brand-new life for herself one minute, desperately trying to fulfill Josh's vision the next.

"I have to fix the porch," she said slowly, each word pulled painfully to the surface from somewhere deep inside her, "because I promised my late husband that I would serve scones and tea out here." God, that sounded ridiculous! "You have to understand, buying this inn was his dying wish."

There. She'd said it. As pitiful as it sounded. Shelby cringed. She didn't ever want to seem pitiful to this strong, confident woman.

But Holly didn't look as surprised as Shelby had expected. Or even as disappointed in how weak she must seem, bossed around by what she had essentially just described as a ghost.

"I'm very sorry for your loss," Holly said. Her hand remained on Shelby's back, the weight and warmth of it welcome.

"It's probably weird I didn't mention him sooner. Why I was here, I mean."

Holly didn't answer right away. When Shelby chanced a glance up at her, she scrunched her face into an apology. "It's a small island," she said. "And . . . I may have asked around about you."

Oh. Shelby wanted to take this as a compliment, but hadn't *she* asked around about Ezra? Shelby probably came across as just as concerning to Holly.

"I must seem pretty pathetic to you."

"Not at all." Holly removed her hand from Shelby's back to tilt her chin up until she faced her again. "I mean it."

Shelby nodded, then drew away, staring out again at the gardens, and then beyond, at the evergreens blanketing the slope all the way down to Snug Harbor. Somewhere past them, the coastline dropped away into Haro Strait, flat and blue. And somewhere to their backs, past Friday Harbor and across the sound, the jagged spine of the Olympic range rose through the perpetual fog of the mainland peninsula. Shelby had the sense of being very insignificant in this moment, sitting here on this porch, trying to make sense of her tiny corner of the universe.

"Talk to me," Holly said.

Shelby deliberated. The bubble had burst, yes, but some sense of self-preservation remained. If she told Holly everything, starting with the fact that she'd failed to come to terms with her sexuality a full twenty years into her marriage, she'd also have to explain how guilty she felt for the way she'd come out to Josh . . . so much so that she'd allowed Ezra to do another stirring. Holly would think she wasn't moving forward at all. She would see just how much Josh still toyed with Shelby's emotions, and she'd realize how stuck she was. And then, at best, this pleasant hum of electricity Shelby knew she wasn't imagining between them would vanish. At worst, Holly would run for the hills. Who wouldn't?

"I'm just exhausted." She sighed.

That was true enough, but Shelby didn't feel as relieved as she thought she would, having dodged a more authentic conversation. She didn't miss the brief flash of disappointment on Holly's face, either, before she pushed herself off from the porch step and held out a hand.

"C'mon, then. We need a break, and I, for one, am starving."

Shelby accepted the proffered hand. "You do owe me a beer," she remembered with a light laugh, "although after today . . ."

Holly pulled her to her feet. "After today? I'm good for a proper cocktail instead."

Shelby felt lighter as they locked up the Merrick and headed to the truck, relieved she hadn't revealed anything alarming enough to cause Holly to cut their day short. Even though the veranda was a bust. Even though Shelby had turned into a blubbering mess. As long as she got to spend the evening, too, in Holly's company, all was not lost.

Chapter 14

Shelby assumed Holly would take the left back toward Roche or even Friday Harbor, but she turned the pickup truck toward Snug instead, driving past this smaller harbor to climb up the coastline on the west side of the island. They passed the state park where Shelby had taken in the view of the whale-watching boats the other night, then sped right by the island's most expensive restaurant, the Flying Fish, perched impressively on the edge of a bluff with endless views of the strait. Shelby was glad; she and Josh had splurged on a meal there on their honeymoon, only to share a bowl of clam chowder on the way back to the Merrick, still hungry after six courses of what they'd dubbed "nettles and weeds."

Holly cut inland just before False Bay, veering into the heart of the island before turning down a dirt drive next to a sheep farm. Just as Shelby started to wonder whether they were lost, a stone cottage emerged, lavender bushes spilling out around the sides of the wide patio, ivy climbing up to the slate roof.

"This is adorable," Shelby said.

Holly smiled in what looked like satisfaction. "So I take it you haven't stumbled upon Stone Soup yet?"

Sure enough, the sign carved into a weathered board hanging over the rounded front door read STONE SOUP, CULINARY ALCHEMY AND LIBATIONS.

"Everything here is seasonal, and the mixologist infuses his own spirits with foraged herbs, wild berries, local honey, you name it."

"Sounds amazing."

It was nearing dusk, and Holly slid a plaid flannel shirt over her tank top before hopping out of the cab. "You going to be warm enough?" she asked. "I think I may have something else in here somewhere." Though she looked dubious.

"No worries." Shelby already felt overheated in her T-shirt. "I'll be fine."

And she was: As they stepped into the cheery dining room, warm lighting cast by sconces in the stone walls washed over Shelby, illuminating swags of sage and mulberry. Mason jars filled with wild rosemary and thyme graced each small table. They bellied up to the bar opposite from Stone Soup's cavernous fireplace, which was lit with flickering tea lights instead of logs. It reminded Shelby only a little bit of Ezra's stirring.

"Oh look! They have your Madeleine Angevine on the wine list," she noted in happy surprise.

Holly's eyes twinkled, but she shook her head. "Don't get me wrong, I'm glad you're a fan, but at least *look* at the cocktail list first."

Shelby immediately got lost in the offerings, hibiscus simple syrup this and lavender bitters that marching across the page in a whimsical typewriter font. The bartender eventually saved her, recommending a muddled strawberry-basil gimlet.

"Two, please, Brandon," Holly said.

Five minutes later, Shelby sipped appreciatively, feeling herself relax amid the eclectic, cozy ambience of Stone Soup's bar. She certainly hadn't felt so contented amid the almost-sterile minimalism of Flying Fish. She and Josh had sat at a table for two by the floor-to-ceiling window, the sunlight blinding. As usual, his hand on hers atop the tablecloth had made her squirm inside. It had overshadowed her enjoyment of the evening. Of his company. It had made her glad for the excuse to withdraw her arm when the bread arrived. They'd been married exactly five days.

It hurt to remember, but the feeling didn't linger, chewing at Shelby's insides the way most of her memories did, in the Merrick and around the island. She suspected this had less to do with Stone Soup and more to do with Holly at her side. Maybe no one here understood who they were to each other—Shelby certainly didn't—but at least no one was clocking Shelby as straight, simply by the company she kept. She glimpsed two men sharing a bottle of wine at a quiet table across the room, their eyes locked on each other's, and smiled. She used to look away: All happy-looking duos seemed to trigger her, but gay couples were always hardest for her to witness. It happened all the time in Portland, while out on date night with Josh, while walking the waterfront trail, while enjoying a family day at the Saturday Market under Burnside Bridge: Other couples' open, comfortable queerness jolted her into remembering she was off kilter. She was mismatched. She was unseen.

But tonight at Stone Soup, her heart didn't ache with a longing she couldn't name. For once, she didn't feel the awful combination of envy and misplaced anger such observations had induced in her for decades.

Maybe this was just what Shelby needed: more time away from the inn, exploring the island on her own terms. Making memories somewhere her past with Josh couldn't reach her. She waited for the stab of guilt this wish would send through her, but again, here with Holly, it wasn't forthcoming.

She turned her attention back to the bar to see she was being studied. "So, why *didn't* you ever mention Josh before today?" Holly asked.

A healthy portion of Shelby's newfound Zen abandoned her. That queer envy she had momentarily shed returned. *Because I didn't want you to think I'm straight.* What if Shelby said that, and Holly didn't believe her? What if, as far as Holly was concerned, a past marriage to a man precluded any right to authenticity now?

She swallowed the trite "you never asked" along with a healthy sip of her cocktail. "I guess I didn't want to arrive here carting a lot of baggage," she said with a self-conscious laugh.

"We *all* have baggage," Holly answered.

But mine is mislabeled. I'd at least like to trade it out.

On the other hand, she hadn't liked denying Josh. It felt better to be honest with Holly, at least this much. "We visited the Merrick on our honeymoon," she said. "A million years ago. He fell head over heels in love."

"And you?"

The intensity in Holly's expression made her rush to clarify. "I meant, with the inn."

Holly smiled. "I know."

Shelby felt herself blush. "Oh. Well, I liked the Merrick, too."

Holly cocked her head to one side, cradling her chin in her palm. "Past tense?"

Shelby hadn't even realized she'd done that. "I guess I don't know exactly how I feel about it yet, now. I love the island, but . . ."

"What?"

Could she explain? "It was just . . . Josh was so *all in*. That was his personality. Mr. Enthusiastic. But for me . . ."

That feeling of impostor syndrome returned with a vengeance. How had it taken Shelby two decades of marriage and friendship to come to terms with herself? Who gets it *that* wrong?

She felt like a poser. Like a fraud.

Fuck it. Holly would either run or she would stay, but right this second, Shelby couldn't bear even one more second of misidentification. "The thing is, now that I'm here—"

"Holly Caster? Girl, is that *you*?"

Shelby turned, startled. They had been interrupted, it appeared, by a tall, curvy woman in a fedora currently waving from the end of the bar.

Holly's eyes remained on Shelby a moment longer, a slight frown creasing her forehead, before she looked over her shoulder and rose from her stool.

"Monique! It's great to see you." And it looked like it really was. Holly had turned that brilliant smile Shelby enjoyed, the one that gave her such appealing boyish impishness, in this Monique person's direction. "Can I get you another gin and tonic?"

Holly leaned over the bar, talking to the bartender again while Shelby stared down at the dregs of her gimlet. Holly knew this woman's drink? Monique said something to make Holly laugh, and there it was again: that damned smile that had a way of temporarily overriding Holly's general air of badassery.

Wait. Was Monique some past girlfriend? God . . . a current one?

Something shot through Shelby she couldn't immediately identify. Dismay? Discomfort? Or simply garden-variety jealousy. It was similar to how she'd felt each time Beth reunited with Michael, but she'd known Holly for such a short time.

Holly returned to her seat, bringing this woman-girlfriend-date-whoever-she-was with her. Shelby numbly shook Monique's proffered hand, scooting her stool over to accommodate her, obsessing all the while. Was she someone important to Holly? Was she not? When Shelby had pressed Holly that first night about her "partner," she'd been swift to clarify and hadn't mentioned anyone else significant in her life.

The hypocrisy of it all loomed large. Hadn't Shelby just revealed an as-yet-undisclosed marriage?

"Another, Shelby?" Holly indicated her glass. "And we need some food, for sure."

Half of Shelby wished she could crawl under the bar, but the other half had already risen from her stool. "Actually, I was just thinking maybe I should get going."

"What? No." Holly looked taken aback. She leaned in, the collar of her flannel shirt brushing Shelby's arm. "Please stay." She grabbed a food menu, turning that killer smile on Shelby. "Plus, I'm your ride."

Monique pushed back from her stool instead, polishing off the remainder of her drink in one swallow. "It's me who's gotta run, sadly, but I'll swing by the winery, Holly. End of the week, at the latest." She waved again, wagged her fingers at the bartender, and saw her own way out.

"Monique is my wine distributor," Holly explained immediately, sliding the empty stool back out of the way. "She's responsible for my Angevine making an appearance on the wine list here, so I have to play nice. Lucky for me, she has a fondness for Beefeater . . . and beefy Brandon here."

The bartender interjected "Oh, please" while looking quite pleased indeed.

Shelby's immediate relief was most definitely too palpable. Her entire body felt oddly light, in fact. The gimlet must have made its way into her bloodstream. She felt bad now, having been so petty about a person who was clearly helping Holly with her business. So much for supporting fellow professional women. Some feminist Shelby had turned out to be.

"So," Holly said. "Let's talk appetizers." She raised an eyebrow at her. "Unless you're still in a sudden hurry?" The way she said this left no room for misinterpretation: Shelby had just been read like a book.

They ordered food as Brandon set to work on another round of gimlets, but their conversation stalled in the wake of their second drinks, like they were a half stride out of step. Had Shelby weirded Holly out, discussing her former marriage? Was Holly waiting for her to finish what she'd been trying to say when Monique interrupted them?

"Listen, I—"

"I wanted to ask—"

Shelby smiled self-consciously. "You first."

Holly raked a hand through her cropped hair, leaving it momentarily standing on end before she smoothed it back down. "Well, we had to get the grapes off the vine early this year—an August frost hit us below the belt—and the last of the fruit will be in by Tuesday. I planned to use the slow midweek period to stem and sort. To play mad scientist, as you called it." Holly paused for the briefest of moments before tipping her head almost imperceptibly to the side; if Shelby hadn't been paying such attention to her body language, she would have missed it. "Since I remember you saying you have some experience with grapes, I wondered if you might want to stop by and help me out."

Help Holly with the actual wine-making process? This proposition pleased Shelby more than she could say, especially in light of her recent disclosure about Josh. After today, she felt like she actually had a friend here. Someone other than Debbie. "I'd like that," she told Holly. "But are you sure? I fear I don't know as much about the process as you think I do."

"Am I sure about free labor? Yes." Holly's eyes twinkled again. For the umpteenth time, Shelby noticed their near-emerald shade. She couldn't quite get over them, contrasting against her cropped hair and dark lashes. For a moment she had a hard time looking away.

Their food arrived at the bar, and they hastened to clear more space. "It's win-win for me," Holly said, as Shelby stabbed a stuffed mushroom. "Pretty soon you'll have guests—"

"Well, I hope so, anyway," Shelby couldn't seem to help throwing in self-deprecatingly.

"You will," Holly repeated firmly. "And when you do, I want you knowing what to recommend." She almost, but not quite, blushed. "If I can be so bold as to assume you'll recommend my winery, that is."

Shelby laughed. "I think that's safe to say." No need to disclose that Holly already enjoyed top billing in her recently researched binder of local businesses. Holly didn't strike her as someone who needed an ego boost, though this conversation was the first time Shelby had detected anything resembling hesitancy in her voice. "I'd love to come by," she promised. "What do you think? Wednesday?"

Holly nodded. "What else do you have going on this week? Debbie keeping you busy with her *New Business and You* checklist?"

Shelby laughed. "You got one of those, too?"

"Stop by the chamber: Check! Register with the BBB: Check! Call the food inspector and get that liquor license: Check and check!" Holly straightened on her barstool to give an imaginary Debbie a crisp military salute.

They talked for another hour, the fireplace warming Shelby's back, the twinkling lights—and her slowly abating buzz—giving reality a soft glow around the edges. She told Holly about Alex and his studies at Vassar, then a bit more about Josh, navigating around any land mines to stick to random, happy memories. Holly gave her space to say more, she paused in all the right places, she nodded and observed and didn't allow any more interruptions, but Shelby still couldn't articulate what she really, desperately, fervently wanted to say. Josh's silence in the wake of his illness and Shelby's inability to come out to Beth had bottlenecked the words somewhere in her chest.

Help, she wanted to say. *You see it, right? Even if I can't yet say?* Instead, after they'd waved down the check and settled the bill, she answered Holly's "You good?" with a simple nod.

Clarity with Holly would have to wait. Shelby let *be true to my identity* once again slide down on her mental to-do list. She had an inn to get off the ground, a porch demolition to finish, and, apparently, grapes to process and ferment. In the meantime she'd simply have to get comfortable living with her own ghost at the Merrick, assuming Ezra didn't burn any more of it to the ground.

Chapter 15

Shelby slept blissfully late, waking to a morning of utter silence and stillness. The wind chime by the eave outside her bedroom window hung without stirring, and she couldn't detect so much as a single car out on Mitchell Bay Road. It was as though the island had shaken herself of the tourists that had scurried from shore to shore since Saturday.

She had interviews with several potential employees scheduled for today. She also fully intended to enlist Ezra's help demoing the rest of the rotted veranda before an appointment with the chimney-cleaning company. She dressed on autopilot, then worked on taming her long hair for several distracted minutes before deciding the situation was hopeless. Another day, another ponytail.

Her first potential employee was the quite-formidable Mrs. Sanderson, who came highly recommended by Debbie for the role of head housekeeper; she let Shelby know she'd arrive every morning at eight and leave every day at precisely two, as she checked in on her aging mother in the afternoons over near False Bay. Shelby blinked: Mrs. Sanderson herself looked not a day under seventy. How old must her mother be? No matter: She was clearly competent and had already recommended a local high school girl eager for a part-time job to assist her.

So far, so good, she thought, dusting her hands as she saw Mrs. Sanderson out. Unfortunately, staffing her kitchen proved harder. Josh had always envisioned a full-service dining room, breakfast through dinner. How many times, when he and Shelby had been out to eat in Portland, had he made note of items he'd add to his imaginary Merrick menu? The cedar-planked king salmon at the Heathman had made the cut, and the wild-mushroom-and-shallot risotto at the Pearl. The seared halibut at that wine bar downtown, and . . . the list went on.

But it became immediately apparent that the head chefs Debbie scrounged up were way out of Shelby's budget. And the Merrick's previous kitchen help, culled from a list Ezra had put together for her, proved as gun-shy as the rest of the island. The waitress Monroe had hired hadn't returned any of Shelby's calls, and the busboy assured her he was doing far better on OnlyFans than he ever had washing dishes. The previous cook was the most candid of all.

"If I wanted to do dinner theater, I'd apply to the Can Can Culinary Cabaret over in Seattle."

No amount of assurances of the Merrick's new direction would sway her. And with plenty of other restaurants with a less dramatic history on the island, Shelby held none of the bargaining power.

"The Merrick is isolated," Josh had said more than once. "You *need* to serve meals, because there's nothing in walking distance, like at Friday Harbor, and no one will want to get back in their cars to find food each evening."

But wasn't that one of Shelby's favorite things about San Juan? Exploring the island was half the fun. You could be tucked away from it all one moment, then at a Michelin-worthy restaurant the next. At least a dozen popular eating establishments could be reached in under half an hour. Why compete?

She interviewed new candidates all day Tuesday anyway, ruling out a French Laundry sous-chef who demanded weekly prop plane flights home to San Francisco on his days off, a rising star anxious to relocate from the Los Angeles food scene after an "unfounded allegation," and a recent Food Network finalist who "didn't do anything but Oceanic-Pacific fusion cuisine," whatever that was.

Shelby connected only with Anthony, a young, heavily tattooed and pierced and refreshingly down-to-earth guy who didn't come recommended by a prestigious kitchen. His enthusiasm was catching, his smile was genuine, and he'd graduated from a culinary institute even Shelby had heard of.

"But I create menus for the farm-to-fork nonprofit over on Lopez Island Monday through Friday," he explained. "Debbie encouraged me to apply anyway, in case you needed help on weekends."

"I'm afraid weekends just won't be enough," she told him with true regret. Shelby couldn't possibly run a full kitchen on her own five days a week.

She and Ezra spent the better part of the afternoon with crowbars, attempting to dismantle the remainder of the rotted veranda planking. With each awkward yank, he winced, muttering apologies to the boards he splintered.

"Ezra. Think of them as weeds in your garden." Honestly. She could do without the dramatics.

"Sorry, Ms. Shelby," he said, before swinging his crowbar downward in another awkward swipe at the veranda. "I'm a nurturer, see. It's why I'm good with the flowers."

Shelby sighed, releasing him from duty as soon as the chimney guy showed up. Ezra set his crowbar gingerly on the porch step and made a hasty retreat. "Sorry I couldn't be of more help!" he called back.

Not that Shelby fared better solo. With each yank, the term *pulling teeth* came to mind. It didn't help that with each upward thrust of the crowbar, she was breaking apart another chunk of Josh's vision for this veranda.

Sweaty and dirty after tossing the last board toward the growing stack, she stomped back into the Merrick just in time to rescue Ezra from the clutches of Rosemary, who had stopped by as promised, and was now grilling her groundskeeper for intel.

"I hear you're doing some work to the back veranda," she said, adding that little chin tilt that was starting to get on Shelby's nerves.

"Just some cosmetic updates," she said breezily, hoping Ezra hadn't already said too much.

It was hard to tell, because Rosemary just pursed her lips while Ezra beat a hasty retreat back to where the chimney sweep stood by the Bay Bar, writing up an estimate.

"Do you have an opening date yet?" Rosemary asked. "I could add it to my press releases."

"No later than December," she hedged. How could she possibly know a precise date, when her list of tasks continually grew?

Rosemary nodded, heavy beads on her neck clanging. Today, she wore a perfectly ironed, impossibly white blouse and crisp slacks. Standing next to her in stained jeans and a T-shirt, Shelby felt her sense of inadequacy double. Time to get Rosemary on her way.

She mercifully left after one more studied glare over her shoulder at the few tea candles still clustered on the rolltop desk, and one more gaze across the gardens toward the wreckage of the veranda. After seeing her to her car, Shelby walked back inside to be told that the chimney would require something called a "full flush," which would cost an extra $450.

"And Grover Electric called back," Ezra told her. "They can't get out here to deal with the wiring issue until next month."

"Next *month*?" Was there some sort of electric emergency she didn't know about?

"I have the inkling they just don't want to come calling on us," Ezra said carefully, which Shelby took to be old-timey talk for "They said, screw you." She sank down on a dining room chair, head in her hands.

After a long, hot shower and a quick dinner, she called Beth. She was still at the precinct, which Shelby intuited by the general level of chaos in the background. "Either that or you're watching one of your cop shows again," she said.

"I'm here till midnight, waiting on a witness. What's up?"

Where to start? With the veranda? Or with the fruitless kitchen interviews, the wiring issue, the increasing pressure from Rosemary of the tourism board, Ezra's eccentricities, or the problematic reputation of the inn? She groaned. "I don't know if I can do this, Beth."

Silence met this statement, followed by "Just a sec."

The muffled background noise gradually decreased as Beth exited whatever space she'd been occupying. "Okay, I'm back. What do you mean you can't do it? You *have* to do it, Shelby."

Resentment arose, hot and sharp. On its heels, the ever-present sense of debt, burning through this like acid. "I don't *have* to do anything," she said sharply.

"But it was Josh's dream."

"Well, every goddamn thing is going wrong," Shelby said. "Maybe it's just not meant to be."

Now Beth sounded almost angry. "What are you saying? You're going to just sell it? Cut and run?"

Beth wasn't here. How could Beth judge? And yet, at the same time: "I know it was Josh's dream, all right? No one knows that better than me."

What about *her* dreams? *Her* wishes? Didn't they figure in at all?

"All right, sorry. Listen, I just want to help," Beth said. "But you have to give it a chance, you know?"

Beth, always the go-getter. Always the one to dig in, fight the good fight. What if Shelby would rather surrender, for once?

"Fine," she promised weakly, already longing for her bed and another heavy night's sleep. "I'll keep trying."

But for whom?

~

True to her word, Shelby doubled down on her efforts the next morning, setting up a new reservation system she'd bought in anticipation of updating her website. A friend of a friend back in Portland had offered web design at a discount—Josh had done her Cannon Beach remodel—and promised mock-ups of a new home page within the week. She just needed photos, so Shelby wandered the inn for the next hour, taking and retaking shots of the dining room, entrance, guest rooms, and exterior. No matter how she worked the camera angle or changed the filters to make the inn look spacious and bright, however, the new images of the Merrick looked anything but.

Dammit. The outside shots looked great, but how was she to capture the charm and beauty of the interior amid all this heavy furniture and tired decor? Even without most of Ezra's nautical touches, the old-fashioned rolltop check-in desk looked imposing and stern, the way it took over the whole entryway, and even wide open, the heavy dining room drapes cast all the breakfast tables in shadow. She didn't want to erase the inn's history, but the gloom had to go.

Cleaning and polishing every surface clearly hadn't been enough. Neither had ridding the Merrick of the oil paintings. Josh would be the first to say the "bones" of the inn weren't the problem, but how could she make it look fresh without making drastic structural changes that she couldn't afford and he would have hated?

It was a relief when it was time to go help Holly at the winery. And she wouldn't feel bad about escaping to her happy place, Shelby told herself, even as the guilt returned, predictable as the tide. She pushed back against it as she gathered her keys and let Ezra know when she'd be back, along with a stern reminder about incense and open flames. By the time she'd reached the junction at Mitchell Bay Road, her desire to see Holly had drowned out any lingering remorse, and by a healthy margin. She resolutely pressed her foot down on the accelerator, arriving at the parking lot in a record four minutes.

The tasting room was closed midweek now that summer was officially over, so after she'd parked, she walked around back to find the crush pad. She ended up walking right across it without realizing it, as it was just a concrete slab with some workstations and agricultural-looking crates and a forklift. She wasn't sure what she'd been imagining . . . something out of a postcard for a vacation to Tuscany, Shelby supposed.

She spotted Holly in the smaller industrial building tucked between the pad and the barn. This warehouse sported similar concrete flooring framed by sheet metal for walls and a ceiling. Stainless steel tanks rose like sentinel giants along one wall, as though guarding the neat tower of oak barrels behind them. Holly aimed an industrial-size hose at a stream of red liquid that slowly made its way toward a massive drain in the floor.

"Looks like I'm just in time to help you cover up a murder," Shelby called, adding a wave in case her voice had been drowned out by the pressure on the hose.

"Hey!" Holly called. She smiled, her gaze lingering on Shelby for a beat. She felt the woman's appreciation wash over her, an unexpected but not unwelcome feeling. It felt almost like . . . yes, Shelby felt reasonably sure she'd just been checked out. She found she didn't mind at all, in contrast to when strange men had turned their heads from time to time.

Holly had refocused her attention on her water hose. "No one died, I promise," she called. "But if I *was* cleaning up a crime scene, something tells me you'd be just the woman to have at my side."

"Is that right?" Shelby bantered. Just like during their previous interactions, she found Holly easy to talk to. After meeting so many new people and feeling so constantly on edge of late, perpetually worried about disappointing the memory of Josh, spending time in this woman's company felt like easing into a warm bath.

This warehouse, however, was *not* bathtub temperature. She folded her arms across her chest, the chill intense. She should have worn a jacket.

"You *are* just in time, though," Holly said, turning off the water. Despite wearing only yet another white muscle tee, she added "You need this?" and tossed Shelby a gray hooded sweatshirt that had been lying on the cluttered counter by the tanks, University of Wisconsin Badgers emblazoned in crimson lettering.

She pulled it over her head gratefully, breathing in a musk of yeast and dust followed by an inviting tang of something sweeter—citrus and sweat? Shelby absorbed another jolt of the juxtaposition that seemed to cling to this woman. Combing her fingers through her long hair to tame it after donning the sweatshirt, she permitted herself another studied look at Holly, finding the same appealingly discordant characteristics as each time before: almost masculine mannerisms that seemed to protect a distinctly feminine core. A sharp wit accompanied by a sincere smile. Corded muscle, and yet soft swells where her tee clung snugly to her chest. Shelby cleared her throat.

"In time for . . . ?" she stammered.

"Making the must." Holly reached overhead for a large plastic tray on the shelf over the counter while Shelby tried not to stare again at how toned her biceps looked in that top. Something about it reminded Shelby that it had been over a year—no, far longer, with Josh's sickness—since . . . well . . . She shifted uncomfortably from one foot to the other, looking away from Holly to take in the barrel room again.

Holly beckoned her over to the tray, which she set on the counter. Shelby could now see it was filled with clusters of red grapes. "We have the first of our harvest in, which will eventually be my cabernet sauvignon. So since that's a red wine, we're stemming before processing, but leaving the skins intact. Let's take it all outside, where it's warmer."

She carried the tray out the door to the crush pad while Shelby trailed after her. Blinking in the sunshine that had chased away the typical morning island fog, Holly indicated a big steel drum, where she'd obviously already begun tossing stemmed grapes. "Go for it."

First, Shelby peered at the next drum over, which she'd walked right by before. They held green grapes, still in clusters, stems and all, like she used to package them as a teen. But these looked like they'd been smooshed, for lack of a better word, into green grape soup. "What about those stems?"

"That'll be my Marsanne–Roussanne blend, so those stems stay on, for white wine, and the juice is extracted from the fruit with all the clusters intact." She turned back to the tray of red grapes and gave Shelby a demo, pulling a cluster off their stems and tossing them into the red drum one by one, where they made no sound as they joined the layer of fruit already deposited there. "Easy, yeah?"

"Well, yeah. And I remember . . . I'm here for manual labor." Shelby smiled.

"And your charming company, don't forget about that." Holly laughed. Shelby liked the sound of it. It seemed to bounce all around the concrete and steel drums. She realized that laughter, too, was something she'd been lacking in the last few months.

They got into a steady rhythm, grabbing grapes off the tray and stemming. Shelby was about to observe that they'd be done in minutes when Holly produced another large tray, then a third.

"You don't do that thing with the stomping? You know . . . with bare feet?" she asked.

Holly laughed again. "Don't tell, but no one actually crushes anymore. We still call it a crush pad," she said, nodding back down at the concrete at their feet, "because that rolls off the tongue better than 'wine-processing area.' But we just press the whole grapes. I'll show you, once we have this drum full. It's less romantic, I suppose, than squishing fruit through your bare toes, but far more efficient."

"And sanitary." Shelby laughed. She rolled a red grape, plump but small, between her thumb and forefinger, both of which were already stained red. She popped it into her mouth, just to have tart juice explode across her tongue. She made a face. "I guess I've forgotten these aren't table grapes." She laughed. "But the sugar and acid levels are balanced. You were right to harvest early. Not that I need to tell you that," she added quickly.

But Holly looked pleased to have someone to nerd out with about her grapes. "We were looking for 18 to 24 Brix, depending on varietal, of course, and what we're trying to achieve for each one. For this cab, for instance, we want the max . . . 24."

Shelby nodded. "Most people don't realize there's so much science to it." She swallowed to get the sour taste of the grape out of her mouth. "And you've got the feel for it, for sure."

They moved on to the next tray, and the rhythmic motion of reaching, grabbing, stemming, and tossing quickly warmed Shelby's muscles. She paused to pull the sweatshirt back off, feeling oddly self-conscious when her T-shirt rode up and briefly bared her midriff. When she glanced up, however, Holly's eyes were still on her face.

"So, how's it going with the veranda demo?" Holly asked.

Shelby made a face.

"That good, huh?" Holly reached for more grapes.

"It's done, at least." Crossed off her list.

"Guess it's a good thing you're around to keep Ezra in line now."

"The veranda was just collateral damage," Shelby said, before biting her tongue. She hadn't meant to get into the details. Too late: She'd piqued Holly's interest.

"What do you mean?"

"It's like I said before . . . Ezra's anchor, the ship wheel, all his nautical antiques are the focus for his stirrings. The veranda just happened to be the setting that day, I guess."

"I see," Holly said slowly. "So he inadvertently targeted an object important to *you*."

Shelby glanced up in surprise. "Me? How so?"

"The veranda. *Josh's* veranda," Holly clarified.

Shelby wasn't sure she liked being compared to Ezra. "I suppose that really, it was Phineas Merrick's veranda, when it comes right down to it," she quipped.

Holly didn't respond for a moment. Just grabbed another tray of fruit. "Some people," she said eventually, "do seem to cling to a place. In life, I mean. Even more than to people. Was Josh a place person?"

Shelby shook her head. *Josh, the life of the party,* Beth always said. "Josh was definitely a people person," she said slowly. He had a way of filling every room. "I want the inn to be *my* place," she realized, "but how can it be, with Josh's legacy or whatever at stake?"

She must have looked as distressed as she felt, because Holly set her tray aside and rested a hand on Shelby's knee. "That does sound really hard."

And Holly didn't know the half of it. "It's not just the veranda. Josh had this whole vision for the place," she said. "But every time I try to check something off the list, it's one step forward to two steps backward."

Holly ruminated on this for a moment. "Maybe," she said eventually, "that's because you're trying to follow *his* plan. Instead of your own."

"But the Merrick was all *his* dream." Shelby stared out at the vineyard climbing the slope past the crush pad, then surprised herself by adding, "Like I said, he loved it far more than I did."

He could have his "old bones." Didn't Shelby gravitate toward the outdoors? The fresh air? The open space she'd always craved?

"Well, how do you think you could make it *your* dream?"

Not feeling awful every time I turn around to be confronted with all Josh's hopes and dreams for us.

"I guess," she managed, "it would help if the Merrick wasn't so steeped in the past."

Holly smiled slightly. "Well, it *is* a historic inn."

"*My* past, I mean." Cast right back to the start of her marriage, forced to relive all the ways she hadn't been true to herself for two decades.

Holly's brows furrowed again, just briefly. "I know."

She left it at that, leaving Shelby with a nagging sense of wanting to correct something she was pretty sure had just been misconstrued. Or worse, perfectly construed.

"What I mean is, how do I honor Josh's wishes for the inn, when at the same time, *I* need something different now?" She tried to channel some of Beth's bravery and looked at Holly directly. "Different than I had with him."

It wasn't the whole truth or anywhere near it, and something deep inside Shelby registered low protest, a settling of frustration that worked its way through her like grains of sand too coarse to flow smoothly through a sieve. She still felt like such a terrible fraud, letting yet another opportunity to be fully real with Holly pass her by. She stared back down at the concrete pad miserably.

"*Why* do you need to honor him?" Holly asked.

Shelby glanced back up, surprised. That wasn't the angle she'd expected her to take. "Because I should be loyal?" She hadn't meant it to come out as a question, but she felt like she was picking through a minefield . . . of her own making. Again, she longed to tell Holly the truth . . . the whole truth. But how could she, when she still lacked the guts to come out to her best friend and her son? Surely, Beth, at least, deserved to know first.

Again, she settled for the safe explanation. "Because he died before he could realize this dream. I should be happy for any little piece of him I can still have with me."

Holly regarded her. "He's not a souvenir."

Shelby thought of the collection of snow globes that had sat on Alex's dresser right up until college, each orb neatly containing a perfectly portioned sample of the best and brightest of a place. Had Shelby thought she could do the same with Josh? Isolate his essence like a keepsake, perfectly contained and safe?

Holly leaned in closer. "Let me ask you this: How is preserving the veranda any different than Ezra hanging on to his antiques?"

Shelby froze. "I don't know," she breathed. God, how did Holly see right through her so effortlessly? It took her breath away. It was like she had thought during Ezra's stirring: Josh, the people person, was clinging to *Shelby*. And she was letting him, by insisting on fulfilling all his wishes. This revelation would feel far more satisfying if she had any idea what to do about it.

Holly frowned in thought. "What you need," she said, "is your *own* vision. A fresh look somehow in that time capsule of an inn." She looked at Shelby seriously. "Do you think you're up for that?"

Now, Shelby supposed, wasn't the time to admit she had just called Beth and threatened to quit. But whereas Beth's reaction had made Shelby defensive, for some reason, Holly's gave her strength.

"I'm trying, but nothing is quite clicking yet," Shelby said, thinking of Anthony's weekend schedule availability and the live music concept. She'd assumed both were dead ends, but maybe that was precisely the problem. She wasn't thinking outside the box. It was why she couldn't seem to complete any tasks. Why she couldn't even fill out her Google listing, continually paralyzed with indecision. Why the musty, dark interior of the inn still bothered her. Still looked so uninspiring in the photos she'd taken that morning.

Holly was right: She needed to detour from Josh's plans just as thoroughly as she'd deviated from her own truth so many years before. She kept hitting snags because she wasn't following her own instincts and vision. She'd start by daring to reenvision the food-and-beverage side of operations.

Holly leaned forward with a smile, offering up a grape between thumb and forefinger, raising it in the air for a mock toast. She paused comically until Shelby followed suit. "To making your own mark," she said, "in the Merrick."

"To making my mark," Shelby echoed, touching her grape to Holly's. It sounded good to her ear, and to her surprise, this second grape went down her throat without a bitter aftertaste.

Chapter 16

With Holly's encouragement in her ear, Shelby attempted to shake herself loose from the tethers of Josh's vision. She sat back down at the rolltop desk, reopened her incomplete Google business listing, and set to work drafting *her* goals for the inn's operations. With the help of two of her business books, Debbie's small-business guide, and about a dozen comparative Booking.com listings, she solidified her nightly room rates, cancellation policy, and several discount packages she hoped to offer upon opening. The first included a fireplace suite in the annex building and wine tastings for two at San Juan Winery. She made a mental note to ask Holly about partnering with her on this, then called Anthony back, who sounded surprised to be offered a position.

"But I can't work weekdays, remember?" he stuttered.

"The Merrick dining room will only be open on weekends for full service," she told him confidently. Continental breakfast would work just fine Monday through Friday, especially if Shelby made her list of island dining and activity recommendations available in every room. The bar, she decided, would be fully stocked with an honor system. Beth had described something similar after a swanky trip with Michael, and if it worked for the five-star New Moon Resort on the west coast of Vancouver Island, it would work for her.

Next, she surveyed the interior of the Merrick with a mercilessly critical eye. It wasn't enough to distance herself from Josh's plans. There was also the inn's recent reputation to combat. Even after her thorough cleaning efforts, it looked like a museum in here, at best, and every bit like the haunted house Monroe had envisioned, at worst. She didn't have the capital for a full renovation, but it was time to get more aggressive.

She pulled down the heavy drapes, then decided the gloomy oil lamps needed to go, too, to be replaced by bright LED light fixtures. The Victorian love seats were treasures, but that didn't mean Shelby couldn't reposition them to the lesser-used parlor off the dining room to make way for a more open floor plan in the front vestibule. The dining room was iconic—she'd just found a postcard in Friday Harbor depicting it in a 1930s ink sketch—but the outdated tablecloths and doilies could and should be a thing of the past.

She made these changes but still stared down her inn in frustration. The air continued to feel stale, the vestibule stuffy. If she hoped to fully shed the Merrick's haunted history, Shelby needed the entire place to exhale, breathing in the vibrant essence of San Juan Island.

But how?

"Invite the locals back in," Beth suggested, calling as she'd returned from her morning run. "If the island business community is as interconnected as you say, once the inn is considered part of the network again, they'll promote it organically, and the visitors will follow."

Like the quilters' groups that used to congregate in the dining room, Shelby remembered. *Used to* being the key phrase. "People are still wary of the place," she said. "No one but ghost-hunting teams and morbid lookie-loos have visited in ages." Hadn't Holly just commented on how long it had been since she'd been inside? "And then it sat empty for a year."

"There must be some way to entice them back."

From her perch on the annex steps, Shelby stared out over the cheery gardens and sloping lawn, trying to draw inspiration from the care Ezra put into them. No matter how much cleaning and purging she did, the interior didn't look this fresh. This vibrant. She sighed and changed the subject.

"Anyway. How's it going with Michael these days?"

Beth hesitated. She'd probably set her phone down while she fished into her sports bra for her house key. Shelby had never understood how she could stand to stash it there. Finally, she said, "I don't want to talk about it."

"Are you sure?" Beth had proved remarkably resilient as she'd bumped and scraped her way past every one of Michael's habitual affairs, but for whenever she needed a reprieve from the hero act, Shelby had invoked a rule: "Call mercy when you need it, Beth, and I'll be there. Every time. No questions asked."

They'd used this as a code word of sorts, back and forth, ever since. When Josh had been diagnosed with his tumor: mercy. When Dillon had been caught at school with that joint: mercy. In the overwhelming, numbing angst of funeral planning and insurance payouts: mercy, mercy, mercy.

Shelby could evoke the mercy rule right now. She could confide in Beth, tell her that she and Josh hadn't been perfect together, either, despite how hard they had tried. She could finally tell her why. "Beth, I—"

"You were so lucky to have Josh," Beth said softly.

And there it was, right on cue . . . the guilt Shelby had almost thought she'd shed. It felt more like resentment today, in the San Juan Island sunshine, no longer molding to her body in the same way it had in the early days after Josh's death. "Yes." She sighed. "Yes, I know."

Josh the hero, Beth had laughed once, when he'd produced a bag of their favorite road trip snacks at just the right moment on a shared family vacation. Alex and Dillon, in the back of the van, had cheered.

Here comes Josh, riding in on his white horse, Beth had announced with a whoop and a high five, when he'd raced back into the airport terminal with the passports Shelby had left on the kitchen counter just in time to board their flight to Cabo. Michael would never have done that. He and Beth would have spent enough time laying blame on one another for their plane to depart without them five times over.

"You know I'd give a limb to have someone care about me for five minutes as much as Josh cared about you for twenty solid years," Beth said.

There was a brittle quality in her voice that Shelby hadn't noted in a long while. That guilt-resentment combo persisted. From Beth's vantage point, Shelby had squandered the perfect marriage that had so eluded her. How could she come out to Beth now and admit such a thing? She couldn't. She couldn't.

And so she redirected the conversation back to her inn, and her challenge of rebranding. The first step to making the locals comfortable: keeping Ezra in check. "You should see the way he lurks around," she said. "Always worrying about his antiques, always poking at things and peering around corners. How am I supposed to make this place appealing to *normal* people?"

"Well . . . it's like with a crime scene," Beth decided.

"Oh, great," Shelby interjected. But Beth's customary *I got this* tone had returned, which was a relief. The odd, vulnerable pang Shelby had detected before had disappeared.

"What I mean," Beth said, "is that when there's an off vibe about a place, people's natural tendency is to give it a wide berth. Like when a building has crime tape around it. But that only stigmatizes it further, you know?"

"You're saying my inn is the creepy Boo Radley house on the block?"

Beth laughed. "I'm saying you just need to take away the stigma. Give the locals something different to associate it with."

As if it were that easy, with Ezra reminding everyone to proceed with caution. With Josh seeming larger than life, taking up all the oxygen. *Mercy,* she wanted to say again, but she couldn't get that one single word out, let alone the whole story she so desperately needed to purge. It brought that tense, taut feeling back into Shelby's gut. Beth, like Josh, made Shelby feel constructed of elastic. Wanting to bend, more likely to snap.

Sooner or later, the tension would have to give.

~

An hour later, she'd retreated to the booth she'd begun to consider her own at Queen of Tarts, where she attempted to soothe her soul with her now-favorite blackberry scone and a steaming mug of mulled apple cider. Her conversation with Beth played on a loop in her head despite the Joni Mitchell melody in the background, and she tried to focus on the part of it she could make actionable.

Invite them in, Beth had said, and though Shelby still didn't know how, exactly, to do this, she knew what Beth meant. Hadn't Shelby felt a sense of warm invitation every time she'd set foot in San Juan Winery? And how about this bakery? Queen of Tarts was a perfect example of what she aimed for, she thought, looking around: cozy, authentic, and artsy, with just the right touch of whimsy.

How had Sandy, owner and baker extraordinaire, managed it? There was something for everyone in Sandy's eclectic bakery: local art on the walls, just like at the winery; comfy couches draped with Sherpa blankets and patchwork quilts; live music when Sandy's angsty, feminist-anthem playlist wasn't on repeat.

Shelby had finished her scone and brought her mug up to the counter to pay when a display offering something called Bee's Knees Honey caught her eye. Picking up one of the amber jars, she turned it over in her hands, doing a mental pivot.

"Sandy," she called, bringing her from the kitchen to the register, "where is this honey from? Is it local?"

"Of course. Just down Mitchell Bay Road." Sandy wiped her floury hands on her apron front, adding, "People here, we're nuts about buying local. We like to think it's our pioneering spirit, but probably it's just because it's so expensive to drive off this rock." She laughed.

"Yeah," Shelby agreed, her mind quickly calculating. "Buy . . . local," she repeated slowly. She might spend more in the long run by forgoing the Costco in Seattle, but if the Merrick gained that local appeal that had eluded her, it was worth the investment. And it would show the chamber of commerce that, under its new ownership, the Merrick Inn had truly turned over a new leaf. What had Debbie called it, when the small businesses on this island worked together? Symbiotic.

"Do you think Bee's Knees would sell to me in bulk?"

Sandy jotted down a name—Byron—and phone number on the back of a business card and slid it over the counter. "Sure they will, if they have the inventory. And if you're looking for more local suppliers, we get our coffee from Fog Town Roasters, over on Orcas," she added, "and our cider from Alton's Orchard by English Camp. And you already know about the island's famous lavender tea."

Shelby nodded. "Thank you." She thought of something else, and added, "What about you? Would you ever consider a standing delivery order? I'd love to treat my guests to Queen of Tarts pastries as part of their daily continental breakfast."

Sandy beamed at her, then bellowed into the kitchen behind her to inform her teenage daughter that she'd have to set her alarm an hour earlier once she started making this new morning delivery. She and Shelby both laughed at the answering groan from the back room.

Filled with new purpose and direction, she headed for the door. This was it! This was the concept Shelby had been looking for, that special *something* the Merrick had been lacking. She could go beyond the nightly packages she wanted to offer and bring the local flavor of the island into the Merrick's problematic aesthetic at the same time. The inn needed to reflect the San Juan Islanders of today, not just its history. And when local artisans and suppliers and cooks saw their own unique mark on the Merrick, they might feel at home there again.

A quick search of the San Juan business directory, followed by a phone call to Debbie, revealed additional local sourcing. As she'd thought, there were farm-to-table entrepreneurs galore, from jam and jelly makers to sustainable-catch seafood suppliers to kombucha brewers. Friday Harbor alone boasted half a dozen cheese artisans. She canceled her standing ACME Food Supply delivery on the spot.

"And don't forget about our fiber crafters and visual artists," Holly reminded her, when Shelby swung by the winery to check on the progress of their new varietals and fill her favorite winemaker in on her newly defined direction. "If you're giving the Merrick a locally sourced refresh, you *have* to stop by Jolene's place."

Holly said her "woman friend" (Shelby ruminated on that description for a bit) owned an alpaca farm at the far southern tip of the island, just past American Camp. "Wool blankets, rugs, mats . . . you name it, Jolene weaves it."

"Cool. Thanks." Shelby settled herself onto an upturned wine barrel, surveying the increasingly familiar landscape of the crush pad . . . and the crush pad's resident winemaker. Holly wore men's Carhartt work pants today and a trucker hat that dwarfed her petite head, adding to that endearingly childlike look. She caught Shelby watching her unravel the industrial hose and flushed slightly under the fluorescent glare of the overhead lights. The answering spike in Shelby's heart rate prompted her to blurt, "You know this alpaca weaver how?"

"We run in the same circles," Holly said evenly. She looked like she might say more, then decided otherwise.

This wasn't the first time Shelby had gotten the feeling that Holly had just tiptoed around something, reluctant to let her all the way in. It felt worse each time, and Shelby experienced a little thrill run through her as she decided, on impulse, to nip this in the bud.

"So, you know *my* story," she blurted. "But—"

"Oh, I suspect I haven't yet scratched the surface," Holly interjected drolly. But she smiled. "But go ahead. Ask."

You feel this attraction between us, right? And you're into me, even if just a little? I'm not misreading these signs that rise up and explode like fireworks every time we're together, am I? It's not just wishful thinking?

"I mean, what brought *you* to San Juan?"

Holly eyed her from under the brim of her hat with something like mild disappointment, then offered, "Well, as I said, I'm a transplant, too. Though I didn't move here under such rough circumstances," she added swiftly. She focused on her water hose for a moment, then explained, "I wanted to get out of the greenhouses in Wisconsin, try to make a name for myself somewhere grapes could actually grow, but my girlfriend wouldn't leave her job."

Out of Holly's mouth, the word *girlfriend* landed lightly, honoring her identity as effortlessly as the SKIL saw comment had. Shelby burrowed even more deeply into her internal frustration and impotence. What kind of queer woman couldn't even come out to another?

Holly made it seem so easy, but then again, it *was* harder for Shelby. The burden of proof clearly lay with her, the recently widowed.

Holly indicated the sweatshirt she'd lent Shelby when they'd stemmed the grapes, which now hung from a post by the door. "She's tenured back in Madison," she continued, "my ex, I mean. So I get it. And, well, she and I had run our course. We both knew it, so I came out here alone."

Shelby swallowed. For some reason, the word *alone* sounded even more loaded than *girlfriend*, coming from Holly.

"Doesn't make it less hard," she acknowledged, and Holly gave her a grateful half smile.

"It was a good decision," she said. "I love it here, and I've met some great people." She finished coiling the hose and looked back over at Shelby just long enough for her to dare hope it was her that she meant, until she added, "Which reminds me, when you stop by Jolene's, be sure to tell her I said 'hey.'"

"'Hey,'" Shelby repeated slowly. Was this gay-woman's speak for something more loaded? Or was Shelby being ridiculous? She forced a smile. "You got it."

But she stood there a beat, staring at the concrete floor, trying to put a label on the unpleasant feeling that had taken hold of her. She had no claim on Holly, she reminded herself fiercely. They were nothing more than friends, no matter how many weighted looks seemed to pass between them. At best, Holly probably saw Shelby as a mentee she'd taken under her wing. At worst, she pitied her . . . the questioning woman who was clearly unwilling or unable to come out. *No,* Shelby amended with an internal groan. At worst, she saw Shelby as a straight ally, despite the chemistry Shelby felt sure wasn't just in her head.

When she looked up, Holly had removed her hat and was worrying the bill between her hands. "Listen, Shelby," she said, "I'm really enjoying getting to know you. Hanging out together. Here, and around the island . . ." She cast an arm vaguely in the direction of the pastoral landscape beyond the winery.

"Me too." God, was Shelby about to get dumped, without ever having been anything of substance in the first place? How humiliating.

Holly offered a half smile. "Good. I'm glad. I just wanted to check in, you know? Because I hope I can continue to see more of you."

Relief flooded Shelby with such intensity, she was glad she'd already found a seat on the wine barrel. "Me too," she repeated stupidly. For something to do, she bounced off the barrel to accept Jolene the alpaca lady's phone number, which Holly had scribbled onto a San Juan Winery napkin. She then made her exit before she could do anything rash, like clasp both of Holly's hands in hers and beg her to explain what they were to each other—or what this was becoming—before she lost her mind.

Chapter 17

Once the ball was rolling, ideas for the Captain Merrick Inn 2.0 came fast and furious. With her newfound vision firmly in place, Shelby made good use of her newly acquired business loan, crisscrossing the island nearly nonstop to call on artists, beekeepers, butchers, and bakers. She scribbled inspiration on scraps of paper and sticky notes in the Merrick kitchen and left herself voice memos while driving as her new concept began to take shape. Instead of dispelling ghost stories, she'd focus her energy on making room for something new at the inn . . . opportunities for the island's many talents to shine.

She called on the lavender farm first, its rolling ribbons of purple greeting her with their spicy, sharp scent as she pulled into the drive. She sampled more tea and ice cream and hand lotion than future guests could possibly need, and though the owners seemed aloof upon Shelby's introduction, they warmed up considerably once she'd placed a purchase order large enough to supply all the Merrick's guest rooms with sachets, creams, and lotions, in addition to tea for her breakfast service.

Next, she arranged for an ongoing order of locally produced soap and sugar scrubs at a store called Island Suds, and then tasted salt and vinegar for the dining room tables at San Juan Sundries. The girl behind the counter there had to call her manager from the back at the mere mention of the Merrick, but Shelby turned on the charm, and her enthusiasm for buying local won the woman over. She gave her a hot tip on a local candlemaker, and she headed down the street to Melting

Pot, where she placed an obscene order for a case of beeswax creations that would look amazing on all the dining room tables.

A Snug Harbor linen and garment artist explained how she could use her own natural dyes to adorn all the dining room tables with new tablecloths, and a weaver *she* knew used Lopez Island lambswool to create doormats Shelby couldn't fathom wiping her boots on. They would, however, serve as excellent mats at the floor of each guest bed.

The butcher at King's Market in town knew where she'd find the best organic, local farms for beef, eggs, chicken, and dairy, then drew her a map. He also invited her to hear his band play at Cove Brewing on Friday night with "We can grab a drink after." Even though Shelby gently declined, he let her in on the secret to sourcing the best fresh salmon. The fishing co-op she wanted was based in Port Townsend, on the peninsula, he confided, an easy Puget Sound Express boat ride from Friday Harbor. And the guy she needed to speak to to get on the rotation was a buddy of his in his bowling league. Did Shelby like to bowl?

She made a show of looking at her watch before thanking him as sincerely as she could, relieved to have ducked two dates in as many minutes. Heading back out of town, she found her new biodynamic farm lead tucked behind Stone Soup.

The manager, a college intern wearing Salmon Sisters rubber work boots coated in what Shelby hoped was mud, gave her a lead on the best cheese maker on the island. Her boyfriend had worked all summer as a wrangler for the Dancing Goat, where the rosemary-infused chèvre was to die for. To Shelby's surprise, she found the Dancing Goat just beyond Snug Harbor, by the turn for the winery. The abundance of quality provisions in her own backyard surpassed all expectations. Her decision to cancel Monroe's standing order with ACME seemed wiser every minute.

She returned to the Merrick in time to sink in utter exhaustion on the fainting couch that mercifully still sat in the entryway. It had been a long week, but she had one more thing to do: Call Brandon over at Stone Soup.

She'd had another idea: What if, in addition to live music on certain nights, she hired Brandon to teach a mixology class to her overnight guests?

It's not what Josh had envisioned, a voice in her head protested.

No, Shelby shot back. *It's better.*

She should not, and would not, sacrifice her forward motion feeling guilty. For the entirety of the next week, she made room in the Merrick for her new acquisitions. The outdated decor, accent pieces, and adornments she had previously targeted for another round of cleaning, she was now hell-bent on purging. Ezra took the news better than she'd feared, an initial look of panic giving way to fatalistic acceptance as she reassured him that his ship wheel over the fireplace and favorite oil painting were safe from evacuation.

Apart from these Peterson family heirlooms, Shelby was ruthless, dragging old rugs and braided mats out to the driveway and freeing the dining room tables of their old linens. She stacked the heavy draperies she'd already freed from the windows on the porch, blinking at the assault of sunlight whenever she cracked open the door to deposit another armload.

If Josh could see her now, would he side with Ezra, or would he see the value in Shelby's new vision? Looking up at the gabled rooms with their sloped, cedar-shingled rooftops and evergreen shutters, she assured herself that what he'd loved most about the inn couldn't be carted out or thrown away. The "bones," as he liked to say, were solid. The foundation secure.

At the same time, that *Shelby-and-Josh* construct, and their togetherness here, was crumbling more every day. The more people witnessed Shelby becoming her own entity, embarking on this venture solo, the less that identity could sting.

Ezra hovered around the inn throughout the liquidation process, always at the ready to assist with a screwdriver or extra pair of hands, even if Shelby suspected it was only to get first dibs on items she'd rejected. These he squirreled away with the rest of his ostracized possessions, carefully tucking a whalebone candlestick into his overcoat pocket and carting away an additional oil painting that had escaped Shelby's scrutiny in the upstairs hallway. This acquisition joined the other paintings in the shed, which he checked on periodically, counting the frames before draping the lot of them with old bedsheets in a show of solemn decorum.

"It looks like a funeral in here." Shelby smiled, hoping to crack the grim set of his mouth. The attempt proved unsuccessful.

By the time her new, locally-produced-and-sourced items began to arrive by way of various business delivery vans and couriers, what amounted to the makings of an estate sale had accumulated on the back lawn. The odd assortment of lamps, vases, chairs, and rugs that hadn't passed muster sat in a reject pile awaiting the Goodwill truck.

"Pardon me, Ms. Shelby, but may I have this as well, if you plan to dispose of it?" Ezra asked primly, taking a break from his inventory of oil paintings long enough to unearth a wooden birdcage from its resting place between two dust-choked velvet pillows. He spoke as congenially as usual, but his eyes were dark, his lips still set in a frown.

"Uh, sure." Shelby studied him from the porch while leaning against a white wicker chair that had survived the Great Purge. She folded her arms across her chest; autumn was fully upon them now. "And I've told you, Ezra, please just call me Shelby."

He nodded, still looking distracted and lost. "Yes, ma'am, Ms. Shelby."

Shelby sighed. "Lots of change, right?" she observed. How much emotion was he concealing from her, witnessing the Merrick's previous contents spilled out onto the lawn like candy from a piñata?

He still clutched the wooden cage. "Change can be cathartic," he said carefully, but the sentiment didn't quite reach his eyes, which still looked guarded. His gaze returned for a moment to Shelby's large pile of discarded items. "But none of these things seem to be the problem," he added.

"Problem?"

"With reaching my grandfather."

Ah. She'd been so busy pouring herself into the Merrick, she hadn't thought about his failed stirring in days.

He held up the birdcage to admire it further. "This, I just like," he said with satisfied conviction. "If I hang it outside, guests will see the gardens through the slats."

"Good idea." Shelby paused. "You know, Ezra, change is necessary, right? To make space for new memories, new . . . energy."

He frowned. "People are always so ready to move forward."

There's ready, and then there's able. Shelby, of all people, knew how hard it could be to get unstuck. "I know you prefer the past," she acknowledged.

It was the understatement of the week. Look at the way he squirreled his antiques away. Look at his outfits, for crying out loud. She studied today's attire: a pair of clamdiggers, knee-high socks, and a cardigan. If Shelby didn't know he lived right here in her cottage, she might have been just as willing to believe he popped out of a burrow in the ground every day to go about his work. Or arrived in a time machine.

Something occurred to her. "Ezra," she asked, "are those your grandfather's clothes?"

He looked at her with surprise . . . and gratification. It must feel good to be seen. To be understood, in this small way. "The sweater is, yes," he said, running a hand down its smooth wooden buttons. "But I found these pants at Vintage Treasures on Orcas. I think they pair nicely."

Shelby smiled. At least today's ensemble fit better than the overcoat he had been wearing the day of his failed stirring, but he still looked like he might need to fish a pair of suspenders out of the pile next.

"I know you miss him very much," she said.

Ezra nodded. He blinked and glanced away, but not before Shelby recognized the deep-seated grief in his eyes. "I wasn't there when he needed me," he said tightly.

He meant the Parkinson's. And the way the *Evergreen Lady* rotted away in Snug Harbor while Ezra was busy with his own life. But because he may not appreciate Debbie sharing these details with her, Shelby only said, "It's a special sort of hell, having things left unsaid or undone."

He looked up sharply. "You lost someone, too," he remembered. "Your husband."

And myself, for decades.

"Do you wish he were with you, still?"

Shelby looked out over her pile of Merrick antiques to where the inn proper stood strong and tall in the September sunshine. She wished he were still alive, healthy and whole, of course. She wished it for Josh himself. For Alex. But *her* life would have taken a different path, regardless. She would have lost him either way. Sometimes the crater this reality left in her life, despite her instigating it, left her breathless. She chose her words carefully, finally settling on one thing she knew was true. "Letting go is a complicated process."

As Holly had pointed out, trying to make a new life for herself in the precise place her late husband had harbored so many memories and pinned so many hopes didn't exactly lend itself to healing.

He's not a souvenir, she reminded herself. Still, she'd felt locked in a groove for so long, fighting friction. Could this same place actually become a new, unmarred canvas, helping her finally gain some traction?

Watching a delivery driver cart in a bright pile of fluffy new linens gave her hope. But Ezra frowned.

"We should hang on to what we can."

"We should only hang on to what serves us," Shelby recited. It was a favorite line of Margie's. It had never really resonated until now, looking at Ezra's distress while he stood over the antiques, wearing his grandfather's clothing. She changed the subject to something less loaded.

"Growing up here with your grandfather, you must have gone to Friday Harbor High," she guessed.

He nodded. "But I did more tinkering on my own than book learning."

Tinkering? Book learning? Shelby smiled again, even as a faint trill of warning ran through her.

Now that she'd removed the rest of the old, dusty stuff from the inn, no barricade of antique wardrobes and side tables and oil paintings would serve as a distraction in Ezra's mission. It would just be his own grief, staring him in the face.

She hadn't intended to strip the inn completely of Ezra's comfort items, and for a moment regret gripped her. She forced herself to shake it off. She couldn't let her soft spot for Ezra derail her rebranding. If he started dabbling in ghost seeking again, Shelby would lose any credibility she'd gained with Debbie and the chamber faster than she could say *The Shining*.

Chapter 18

On a chilly morning two weeks after Labor Day, Shelby drove back across the pastoral heart of the island, winding along one-lane roads until she reached a farm calling itself the Happy Alpaca.

Holly's friend Jolene had turned out to be a bit of a recluse, but after a somewhat awkward phone conversation during which Shelby explained twice who she was and how she'd come by her number, she was given directions and a date and time to meet. Fog lay in wisps over the asphalt as Shelby eased up to the locked gate and texted as instructed. A moment later a woman emerged through the gloom in Carhartt coveralls and a trucker hat. Two long braids trailed down her back. They were dashed with gray, but even so Shelby could tell Jolene had once been the proud bearer of luscious raven locks.

"You Holly's girl?" She gave Shelby a once-over that struck her as unnecessarily aggressive, her frown accentuating deep lines across her brow and around her eyes. Under the brim of the hat, high, strong cheekbones framed a straight, almost-regal nose. Shelby fidgeted in her seat, ridiculously second-guessing everything about herself. Did she look capable enough to be an inn owner? Did she stand out as a mainlander? Where had this sudden insecurity come from?

"I'm Shelby," she reminded her. "I run the Merrick Inn."

"Well, c'mon in," Jolene said eventually, swinging the gate wide. Shelby eased the Prius up the dirt drive to a neat double-wide trailer. Behind it, a barn loomed large, surrounded by orderly paddocks cornered off by metal stockade fencing. One by one, small, fluffy heads popped over the edge of the fencing, each alpaca's oddly cheery, startled face registering an almost-humorous curiosity.

"They're adorable." Shelby laughed, gravitating to the alpacas instantly.

Jolene warmed up at Shelby's admiration, her smile briefly transforming those stern wrinkles into laugh lines. She introduced Shelby to each animal and explained in far more detail than necessary the benefits of alpaca wool versus sheep wool, the abysmal eco-by-products of the wool industry, and the difficulties she'd had keeping her alfalfa bales dry with all this fog.

She nodded her chin past the paddocks, where Shelby now noticed several circular, canvas-sided yurts standing sentinel. "A bio-dome company over on Orcas sells those in kits," she said. "All you need is an elevated platform, and you've got yourself a waterproof shelter for just about anything. I use 'em to stash the feed and meds . . . dewormer, that sort of thing."

Shelby tried to look interested in dewormer while studying the yurts more closely. She'd seen similar structures at wilderness eco-resorts, and these looked whimsically out of place, perched above the pastures.

"Holly told me you had blankets for sale," Shelby probed, hoping to steer the conversation back to the business at hand. She had done her research, spending over an hour on Jolene's website and Etsy page.

"Yeah? You spending time together?" Jolene sounded slightly amused while scratching a particularly friendly alpaca's forehead.

"Me and Holly? I guess so, yes," Shelby said. "She said to say 'hey,' by the way." She heard herself blurt out a laugh; relaying this message sounded twice as silly after discussing the alpacas' food supply. Jolene just studied her intensely again, so Shelby sobered and added, "I'm sure you know her better than I do."

This did seem to pacify Jolene, who nodded briskly. Shelby ruminated a bit too long on why, exactly, this confirmation had her feeling oddly left out, then redirected with "I hoped to replace all the bedding and toiletries in the guest rooms of the Merrick with local products, and I'd love to talk to you about a bulk order."

Jolene regarded her from under the brim of her trucker hat, which Shelby now realized read, WE ARE ON INDIGENOUS LAND. "Well, let's talk shop. How many you need?"

"I'd love to start with three dozen . . . enough for each guest room with a rotation of extras for when we need to launder one."

This information prompted another long soliloquy on the care of the blankets. Jolene had a manner of speaking that managed to be both drawling and brusque, and by the time they finally walked over to the house to check out the actual inventory, Shelby's fingers had nearly frozen to the fence slats in the chill air.

The inside of Jolene's place was as utilitarian yet imposing as Jolene herself. To Shelby's delight, however, most of her wool blankets featured the intricate, native designs she'd admired at the art museum. Following the black, red, and white color scheme as strictly as the blankets she'd seen on display there, the wool twisted around eagle eyes and tree trunks and stretched over the arched backs of king salmon. One blanket depicted what looked like a child who'd sprouted raven wings, his birdlike thighs captured in mid-quiver before taking flight.

"These are incredible," Shelby said.

"They're Salish," Jolene said. "I learned from my mother."

"Amazing." And it was . . . all of it. The entirety of Jolene's living room was awash in red, black, and white. Any space not covered with wool blankets had been dedicated to thick spools of yarn. Across from the couch, where most people would situate a television, a huge wooden loom dominated. Stretched across the shaft was the red-and-black outline of a woman, heavily pregnant, against a circle of cream and a black sliver of moon.

"Ayita," Jolene noted, following Shelby's gaze.

Shelby glanced back at her, trying to decide whether Jolene construed her interest as nosiness. But keen interest shone in her brown eyes, so she chanced a step closer to the creation. "She certainly looks ready to have that baby," she observed. How well Shelby remembered the feeling, heavy and lead footed during those final weeks before Alex's birth.

Jolene smiled but shook her head. "She's not pregnant. At least, that's not how my mother told the story, though as with all oral tradition, she could have gotten it wrong. Other than the fiber arts, she, like so many of us, was not taught much of our traditional heritage growing up." Jolene trailed a finger around the orb of the woman's belly. "The way my mom told it, Ayita is carrying the weight of all her people."

"Oh." Shelby rearranged her expression into one of solemn contemplation. What else did one say when confronted with such a statement?

Jolene's smile disappeared again. "Supposedly Ayita had been left behind by her tribe. She wandered to the edge of the ocean, where she gathered stones in memory of all the sons, husbands, and fathers her tribal sisters had ever loved. Each stone reflected a man: boulders for the chiefs, smooth, sea-polished pebbles for the baby boys."

"And she . . . ingested them?"

"Once she had a tall cairn of stones, she consumed them all, yes. One by one."

Shelby pictured Ayita laying these stones like pills on the back of her tongue, swallowing them whole. Would she have felt the scrape of each rock in her throat, long after she'd coaxed it down? Would they have tasted like mineral and rust, or of salt and algae and decomposing sea life? She tried to picture being so thoroughly bound and anchored to her people's importance. Grounded and rooted by her men and boys. Filled beyond capacity. She thought she might know, just a bit, how that might be.

Jolene fingered the hem of the blanket on the loom. "Ayita was well sated by her memories. But when the tide came in, she was too heavy to outswim it."

"She . . . drowned?" Shelby had envisioned Ayita triumphing, she realized. Gaining strength from her memories. She didn't want to think women could become this immobilized by them. Shelby had logged enough hours in grief groups as it was.

Jolene shrugged as if to imply "maybe, maybe not." "She joined her men, ending her lineage. It's a Salish obsolescence story."

When Shelby looked at her in question, Jolene explained, "As opposed to a creation or origin story. See, the Coastal Salish were once called the Cowichan; before European genocide wiped them out to such a small number, they banded with nearby confederations. My grandmother, for instance, was of the Cowichan line, which doesn't exist now. We're all just considered Salish."

Shelby mimicked Jolene's caress of the fabric, touching the edge of the blanket on the loom. The wool felt impossibly soft. The loom itself, intricately carved, was a work of art. "Do you ever show other people how to use this?" She'd love to learn. And then Shelby bit her tongue, worried she'd asked for something that, as a representative of that European group, she didn't have a right to.

But the question was the correct one. Jolene smiled again without reservation, like she had when Shelby had admired her alpacas, her dark eyes squinting with appreciation.

"Maybe one day," she said.

She walked Shelby out to her car, then trotted down the drive with surprising spryness for a woman of her age, unlatching the gate with a final wave. Sharing her Salish story—or perhaps Shelby's genuine appreciation of it—seemed to take the stern edge off Jolene's sun-worn face. It made Shelby think of her own neglected artwork, gathering dust in boxes since the move. Something about the obvious love and devotion Jolene put into her fiber arts moved Shelby to create in a way she hadn't felt since college.

Forget Shared Palette and Mr. Stick Up His Ass. Why couldn't Shelby make space for a ceramics studio right at the Merrick? The storage shed by the parking area was the obvious choice, but after hefting open the creaking double doors back at the inn, one look around the dark interior had her reconsidering. She needed natural light and the influence of nature to get the creative juices flowing, not this jumble of tools and junk.

She spied the pile of boards she'd re-stashed in here after demolishing the veranda, and an idea took hold. Holly had cautioned against rebuilding, out of fear of compromising the foundation, but most of the boards were still usable, and she could get more from Friday Harbor Hardware. What if she built an entirely new structure . . . a platform like the ones she'd seen as yurt foundations at Jolene's?

This thought inspired another, quick on its heels: She would ask Jolene for the yurt supplier's information, and erect one herself, out in the gardens past the inn proper. Right where Ezra's sunflowers flirted with the tree line, she would have shade in the summer and protection from the elements in winter. Her yurt would be her new art studio, but so much more. What if she held workshops for her guests? She could teach ceramics, and maybe she could entice Jolene to lead a weaving class, or a demonstration, at least. Surely some of the other artisans she'd met recently would welcome the extra income and ability to showcase their work, too. *Invite them in,* Beth had said. This was the natural next step, wasn't it?

She hauled all the unused boards back out of the shed and into the sunshine, depositing the pile on the lawn by the back garden. She'd task Ezra with hiring someone for a quick construction job. She'd far rather ask Holly, but didn't want to be begging a favor every time she talked to her. Anyway, Shelby kind of liked the idea of surprising her with this new vision. Hadn't Holly been the one to tell her it was okay to change course? To essentially let the veranda, and its potential as a breakfast dining space, die with Josh?

A familiar feeling of unease accompanied this thought, but she pushed it back, distracting herself by retrieving her boxes of art supplies from the Merrick Suite, inspired to take inventory. *Forward motion.* Rollers, hooks, and shred tools came out one by one, followed by the two large canisters of sculpting putty she'd brought from Portland. The lids to the latter had fused shut tight as a drum, caked with tiny grains of dried clay.

God, when had she last held these tools? Standing at the workstation of the Merrick's kitchen, she turned a blade over in her palm, the familiar grip drawing her instantly back to her art studio at the college, the swampy smell of slop buckets, and the sulfurous fumes wafting from freshly mixed glaze. She'd been told she had what it took to make her mark in the art world. When, exactly, had she lost her confidence? When Alex had been born, and she'd scaled back her hours in the studio? Later, when Josh's career had taken priority and she'd turned to teaching instead of creating?

No, those had only been excuses, yet another example of the whitewashing of her true self she had been so good at, for so long. Shelby had been all in at the studio until she'd met Catherine, the mentor who'd taken a shine to her. And vice versa.

Shelby had told herself it was just admiration for Catherine's talent that had kept her staying late. That inspired her to put in more hours, to mold her clay with such devotion. And when that didn't work, and the door she'd so firmly and carefully shut when she started dating Josh risked opening, she told herself that Alex needed her. It was too late, the stakes too high. She'd been with Josh since high school. Navigating back to where she'd taken that detour, now that she was so far out to sea, had felt impossible.

Could she do it now? Was that a gift Josh had, unwittingly and perhaps unwillingly, given her by burdening her with this inn?

She found a screwdriver in her supply kit and wedged the flat end against the lid of her clay to pop it open, breathing in the concentrated scent of earth and synthetics. She told herself it didn't matter whether Josh's passing had "granted" her this opportunity. Rediscovering her art didn't have to feel like a consolation prize.

Just like her new ideas for the Merrick didn't have to feel like a betrayal. If she kept moving forward, if she kept redefining his vision for this inn, could she finally honor Josh's memory without it feeling like a penance? Would the Merrick stop feeling like purgatory?

She sank her hands into the clay, kneading it a bit roughly, determined to push through the immobility her debt to Josh always induced. She rolled a small ball of clay between her fingers, remembering the feel of it, hoping intuition would guide her. Start anywhere, talented, beautiful Catherine used to tell her, and let the work lead you.

She closed her eyes. The cool give of the clay transported her to the sensation of the grapes between her fingers at the winery, working with Holly on the crush pad. Had Holly gotten the stemmed grapes all liquefied yet? Was the Marsanne–Roussanne blend already in its stainless steel tank? How had it turned out?

The chemistry behind blending the grapes was Holly's own form of artistic creativity. Shelby began working, forming a few asymmetrical orbs she squashed between her palms before finding her groove, rolling out perfect wine grapes without conscious effort as she thought about the crushed grape juice awaiting fermentation.

Her clay grapes formed one cluster, then two. They would look amazing once fired, she thought, before remembering she had no access to a kiln. She paused a moment, considering. Who said she couldn't create a traditional firing pit outside her new yurt? She'd studied raku firing in college, and though decidedly tricky, the results were fabulous.

Smiling, Shelby resumed careful strokes to each grape stem with her small file and plane, then added holes to each grape center to avoid creating what Catherine used to call a kiln bomb. Next: leaves. Once in the groove, thinking solely of wine and grapes and Holly, it only took her a matter of minutes. A few more hours, and Shelby thought she could have an entire, albeit simple, series of pieces done. A small token, perhaps, to thank Holly for letting her help with the grape crushing.

A collection of centerpieces for the wine barrel tables in the tasting room, maybe.

Imagining her work on display there, further beautifying Holly's space, warmed Shelby enough to chase out the lingering fog of indebtedness she still felt too often toward Josh. It made her feel just a bit more able to break away.

Chapter 19

By the end of September, locally made tablecloths adorned all the dining room tables. Tapered candle holders from a shop called By Firelight stood proudly as the centerpiece of each. The kitchen was stocked with local coffee, tea, honey, jam, sea salt, and wine; the guest rooms smelled of lavender and thyme; each bed had been dressed in colorful alpaca wool blankets; and on each bedside table sat a guest journal bound by a hobbyist papermaker Shelby had found right here in Snug Harbor. On the first few pages of each, she'd inserted her personally curated island directory of tour operators, restaurants, bars, and stores. San Juan Winery, Stone Soup, and Queen of Tarts received top billing.

The Merrick's hallways, parlor, front entry, and dining room now shone with the aid of smart lighting, and the newly framed photos and paintings depicting the sea, forests, and pastoral fields of San Juan Island adorning the walls well represented a wide range of local talent. Ezra continued to stew about his salvaged antiques' new place of rest in the shed, but for the most part Shelby tried to grow accustomed to what she decided to spin as his "eccentricities."

She had called the business on Orcas Island to inquire about procuring her own bio-dome yurt, which turned out to be the first nearly effortless transaction she'd tackled since arriving at the Merrick. Holly, she supposed, would tell her this was because she'd ventured in her own, unique direction.

"We can deliver it on the ferry," the distributor told her. "You'll just need to haul the kit from Friday Harbor, and then you'll need a team of at least three to four folks to erect it."

"There are directions included?" Shelby tried to sound less intimidated by this than she felt.

"A child could do it," the guy promised. "Well, three or four children, like I mentioned."

Well, she'd cross that particular bridge when she came to it. That evening around dusk, Shelby settled onto the new back porch steps with a glass of Holly's wine, a baguette from Queen of Tarts, and a wedge of Dancing Goat cheese. She'd thrown a new, handcrafted quilt over her shoulders to ward off the chill. For a long moment blissful silence filled her ears before her phone rudely interrupted.

One glance at her screen, however, and all was forgiven. "Hey, kiddo," she greeted Alex.

"Just calling to make sure you're still alive, Mom." The innocent statement resounded like a gong between them, and he instantly added, "Jeez. Sorry. I didn't mean that."

Over a year after Josh's death, and these little turns of phrase still had this kind of power. Immediately, Shelby felt exhausted. What few people realized about mourning: Part of the battle was simply getting over the fatigue of constantly walking on eggshells. "Don't worry about it, honey," she told him, casting around for a change of subject. The simple dinner in her lap inspired her to say, "You wouldn't believe how many farms and restaurants there are out here."

She launched into an account of her week chasing down artisan cheese, free-range eggs, grass-fed beef, and foraged mushrooms, until Alex stopped her, laughing. "You're making me hungry!"

"You're always hungry," Shelby reminded him, but Alex had just given her an idea. What good did it do to fill the Merrick with local inventory if locals had no reason to stop in and see it on display? She had to do more than arrange for a handful of artists to teach workshops.

"What if I had an event of some sort," she asked slowly, "for the residents here? I could serve all their local foods and wine."

"Sure, I guess so," Alex agreed.

Or maybe a seated dinner? A picnic? A party? "Oh, I wish you could come out for something like this!" she said, before biting her tongue. Alex must have felt unmoored enough, losing his dad and leaving his childhood home. He needed all the time he could get, establishing himself in college. She shifted gears, filled Alex in on the rest of the local goods she'd acquired, though she could feel his attention waning sometime around "hand-dipped candles." To spare him, she shelved the half a dozen follow-up thoughts that continued to percolate and changed the subject to Alex's East Asian Media Studies class.

"I like it even better than Beginning Russian," he supplied, instantly reenergized.

Shelby felt a rush of affection for him in his enthusiasm, despite the fact that she had trouble picturing when he'd actually *use* Russian. "Dad would be so proud of you, taking such interesting courses," she said. Proud was an understatement. Ever the cheerleader, Josh would have been ecstatic. "And I am, too," she added. "Only your first semester in college, and you sound so much more mature already."

He really did. It made her think that maybe, right this moment, she could confide in him. That he could handle hearing her truth in a way he might not have been able to just months ago. She took a breath, readying herself.

"I miss him, Mom," Alex said, and the sound of his pain instantly dropped her back into the crater of loss they both knew so well.

She changed course on the spot. "I know you do, baby."

"Remember how he used to tease that he'd hide in my duffel and come to college with me?" Alex had always reacted in embarrassed horror in response to this suggestion, but now he sounded almost wistful.

"Yes." Shelby smiled. She'd been pretty sure Josh half meant it.

"He never even saw me start at Vassar."

"I know." Though maybe it was a gift for her son to start over in a place with no reminders or memories of his father. No crater reminding him of the empty space left behind. Vassar provided a fresh canvas, no renovation needed. But the defeat, reminiscent of childlike disappointment, in her son's voice cut deep. Did he feel as untethered as she feared? Should Shelby have encouraged him to attend college in Washington State, where he could visit her every weekend, like Ezra now staying near where his grandfather had lived?

"Sometimes I think I feel your dad here, at the Merrick," she offered carefully. Maybe this would comfort her son more than it comforted her.

"Really?" Alex answered in a way that made Shelby's heart ache. "That sounds nice."

So much for new, unmarred space making the grief more bearable. She thought of Jolene's Salish story again, and Ayita's reaction to the death of her people. Why did Josh seem to fill, consume, and live alongside Shelby, and yet leave Alex unsated?

"I'm sorry, honey," she told him gently.

She tried to feed him some memories instead: reminding him how genuinely hard Josh used to laugh at Alex's brutally original knock-knock jokes as a kid, how he had blindly championed every effort Alex had ever made toward any goal.

"Remember when he tried to coax Butters through that maze with bits of Lunchables?" Alex laughed.

"I remember." Alex's pet rat hadn't won them a ribbon at the science fair that year, but the sight of Josh's and Alex's heads together, plotting Butters's route through the maze, had been all the prize Shelby had needed.

"Remember when he coached Little League that one year, then let Dillon pitch instead of me, because he didn't want to show favoritism?"

Alex sounded a bit put out now.

"Are you still bitter about that?" Shelby laughed. "I think you can forgive Dad by now."

Alex's voice faltered. "Remember how excited he was to take me to that college fair thing, and I blew him off to check out that new skate park?"

"You can forgive yourself, too, Alex."

She bit down on her lip, eyes suddenly stinging at the hypocrisy. How could she, Shelby Wright, possibly coach anyone in self-exoneration?

They reminisced a few more minutes until Alex gently begged off, citing a study group meeting.

If this had been Beth's Dillon, the mischievous one, the thrill seeker, Shelby would have rolled her eyes and said, *Study group . . . sure*, but Alex was no doubt headed directly to the library. She made him assure her he'd do something fun afterward, then let him go.

Sad and worried and yet still buzzing about this newest idea for the inn that needed fleshing out, she called Beth immediately after hanging up with Alex, hoping her friend's attention span might prove longer than an eighteen-year-old's when it came to artisanal bread and dairy goats.

"I found a way to bring the locals into the Merrick," she said without preamble, when Beth answered on the second ring. "I have art and food and there will be some kind of party, but I don't know what exactly yet."

"Whoa, whoa." Beth laughed. "Start at the beginning."

Shelby backtracked, describing all her purchases, procurements, and adventures, from the odd but interesting Jolene and her alpacas to the narrow miss of a bowling date. She even described the art studio yurt concept, with lessons and workshops on offer. "With all the new things in the inn, that stigma you talked about will *have* to change, don't you think?"

"I do," Beth agreed. "This sounds amazing, Shelby. See? I told you it was possible to make this happen."

Shelby grinned into the phone. It felt so good to feel wind in her sails. With so much forward momentum, Josh's expectations—and

Shelby's self-condemnation—had no choice but to yield. And then the inn might finally feel like hers.

"I'm going to open early," she told Beth impulsively. She had made such progress last week; what was she waiting on?

"How early?"

"I don't know . . . Thanksgiving?" She had her new look in place. She had her housekeeping team. She could easily adjust her reservations software, and Anthony could start anytime. "There's an amazing farm-to-fork culinary scene here, Beth. And everything is so close by, since this island's about as big as a postage stamp."

In an instant, the idea that had been swimming around the edges of her brain came into sharp focus. "I think I'll put together a progressive dinner. I'll invite all my local vendors, Rosemary from the tourism board, my Realtor Debbie, and the folks from the chamber of commerce. The guests will go from place to place—you know, farms, businesses, restaurants—with the tour culminating at the Merrick for a sneak-peek reopening."

As soon as Shelby articulated the idea, she embraced it wholeheartedly. Who didn't love a party? And if it worked, she could sell the concept as a Thanksgiving package for guests next year. She paused, giving this idea a moment to settle in her gut. No self-condemnation churned there. No guilt. Forward motion on her own unique path was the key. She smiled, feeling gratifyingly powerful.

"You're going to open at Thanksgiving?" Beth clarified.

"It's the perfect way to send a little more love to the local businesses that have contributed to the Merrick." Yes, she'd made good use of her business Visa credit line, but Shelby suspected that in more than a few cases, she had Holly's good word or Debbie's connections to thank for the generous discounts she'd received. And more love might just rewin the locals' trust.

"I'll invite some bloggers, too," she decided, remembering Rosemary's professional connections. "Of the travel variety, not the ghost-hunting variety."

"And Instagrammers," Beth added. "What do they call themselves? Influencers? You'll have to pay them, Shelby."

"And I can offer them rooms," she decided. "They can be my first guests, for a soft launch of sorts." She would take Rosemary up on her offer to contact them, and she'd ask the locals to post photos on their social accounts and tag one another, as well. Debbie was always talking up the symbiotic relationship on this island, wasn't she?

She'd ask for a meeting with the tourism board and the business chamber, so they could all coordinate efforts. And she'd get Holly to help. "The winery would be a natural stop, for charcuterie and their late-harvest Riesling," she said, brainstorming aloud, "and maybe the butcher could smoke turkeys in the outdoor barbecue at Stone Soup."

Anthony could oversee the culinary program, working with restaurants to create a menu that flowed well from one business to the next. That was right in his wheelhouse. And Queen of Tarts could provide desserts. The only problem: Thanksgiving still felt like a very long time away. Shelby needed momentum. Momentum, momentum, momentum.

"Then give yourself a kick in the ass and do it for *Canadian* Thanksgiving," Beth suggested. "You're practically an honorary Canadian citizen that far north anyway, and this way your soft launch could take place in just a matter of weeks. Any issues that arise, you'll have time to smooth out before the holiday season starts in earnest."

"What, you mean mid-October?"

"Yeah." She waited while Beth consulted a calendar. "Canadian Thanksgiving is the second Monday of October, so . . . the thirteenth this year."

Could Shelby really pull this all off in under two weeks? She worried her lip between her teeth while she debated. "I can make this happen on one condition," she decided.

"What?"

"That you'll come and help me out."

She needed Beth here. From the moment they'd met, simultaneously attempting to spy through the classroom window on Alex's and Dillon's first day of preschool, Beth had been at Shelby's side. It had been Beth who had jump-started that part of herself Shelby had pushed down since marrying Josh, Beth who had eventually reawakened her. Beth who had helped her get Alex off to college and had helped Shelby pack her bags. Hell, just last month, Beth had told her, unequivocally, she was not allowed to quit and come home.

Beth: Shelby's forward-motion generator. Her ideal woman.

Until I met Holly.

This thought came easily, because it had absorbed into her body days, maybe weeks ago, hadn't it, embedding under Shelby's skin to settle amid muscle and tendon. All the time spent with Holly these past days, Shelby had felt contented in a way she'd never achieved with Josh *or* Beth. Sitting across the table from her at Stone Soup, her honeymoon memories had landed lightly. Exploring the islands with her, bellying up to the bar at San Juan Winery, shooting the breeze in the barreling room . . . these moments had felt effortless in a way Shelby had never experienced with anyone before. Even Beth.

She'd been trying to downplay and deny the chemistry between herself and Holly since that very first day in the tasting room, hadn't she? Contenting herself with simple proximity. Shelby still wasn't sure what this all added up to, but it was more than just flirtation. More than just an easy friendship. And she might never find out what it *could* be, if she didn't lay her cards on the table. *Finally.*

"Beth, I gotta go."

"What? Hold on, I'm trying to look at my work schedule, see if I can swing the grand reopening or whatever."

Shelby waited, her foot tapping out a rapid beat on the hardwood floor. She glanced at her watch. It was getting late, but the winery should still be open for another hour. And if Holly was already closing up? Shelby would help. Shelby would be there for her, like Beth had always been.

"All right, I have you penciled in," Beth said. "Not gonna make it official just yet, in case you start talking about cutting your losses again."

Shelby smiled. "Not going to happen."

Starting now, she was moving full steam ahead.

Chapter 20

Shelby sped down Merrick Lane and turned onto Mitchell Bay Road, only to come to a grinding halt when she remembered San Juan Winery was closed on Sunday nights. She eased into the gravel lot anyway, intending to turn back around, before noting with surprise that the lights did indeed glow in the tasting room. Instantly her disappointment lifted. Maybe Holly had come in on her day off to finish stemming the fruit or restock the refrigerator cases uninterrupted. Wait: Maybe Holly wanted to *stay* uninterrupted. Maybe Shelby was reading all the signs wrong. She had no point of reference for any of this. No benchmark at all. Maybe she was just too consumed with this woman, simply because of the novelty. Shelby had just come out to herself . . . maybe she was just a tad . . . enthusiastic. Her hand moved to put her car in reverse, but then she hesitated, letting it sit there on the gearshift. Holly was the first *right* thing in Shelby's life in such a long while. So what if she enjoyed floating along in the pull of this tide for once? Everything else in Shelby's life was such a constant struggle.

Her Prius was still purring in neutral in the parking lot when the tasting room door opened a crack. Holly emerged, peering through the darkness as though to make out the vehicle whose headlights shone into her tasting room. When recognition dawned, she lifted an arm in greeting.

That decided it. Shelby couldn't very well leave now that she'd been spotted. She turned off her engine and exited her car, calling out, "I forgot you were closed."

Holly smiled, leaning more casually now against the doorframe. She wore a pair of her boyfriend-cut jeans that sat low on her hips and one of her signature white tank tops, even though they were now solidly into autumn weather. She folded her arms across her chest, and Shelby realized with an embarrassed jolt that Holly might have adopted the defensive posture because she'd been staring.

She immediately dropped her gaze to the dark gravel of the parking lot, the light from the tasting room burning in her retinas. "Uh, if you're working, I'd be happy to help."

When she looked up, a bemused expression had settled on Holly's face. "I'm not working." There was a moment's hesitation, which Shelby noted with a lurch of her gut—was she about to be sent packing?—and then Holly added with what seemed like sincerity, "You're welcome to join us."

Us? Only then did Shelby register the presence of three other cars in the parking lot, down at the far end, by the crush pad. She eyed them as she made her way toward the door, stashing her car key in her jacket pocket.

"We were having a little barbecue earlier . . . kind of a weekly get-together. But now we're just shooting the shit."

A get-together? Shelby hesitated, reluctant to insert herself into what was clearly an invite-only social event, even as a swell of hurt consumed her, to have been left out. She knew she wasn't entitled to this feeling; despite her possibly delusional sense of connection to Holly, they'd only just met, really.

Her expression must have betrayed her, because Holly said, "I wanted to invite you last week, actually, but . . . well, to tell you the truth, I haven't been able to fully make up my mind whether it's your thing."

"If what's my thing?"

For a brief moment Holly wore the same unsure, almost pained expression she'd displayed a few days ago at her crush pad. Then that smile Shelby so enjoyed flitted back across her face. "Just come on in, Shelby."

Four women crowded around one of the high-top wine barrel tables. Shelby recognized Jolene, looking as dignified as ever, even in a well-worn thermal shirt and manure-crusted boots, her salt-and-pepper hair in a neat braid down her back. Across from her, a pleasantly plump woman about Shelby's age set down her wineglass to offer a wave; in an oversize V-neck tee and sneakers, she reminded Shelby of Debbie, but without the flair for fashion, makeup, or ornate nails. Next to her, a pretty brunette with a cute pixie cut and jean jacket flashed her a friendly smile. The fourth, much younger, woman sported an asymmetrical haircut even shorter than Holly's on one side; the other side, which fell over her forehead, was dyed blue. She wore an Indigo Girls tee with the question AMY OR EMILY? stamped across the chest, though Shelby doubted the girl had even been born when the musical duo had toured their first college campuses.

"Ladies, this is Shelby Wright," Holly said, dragging around another stool from the bar. "Shelby's the new owner of the Captain Merrick Inn." She gestured toward the group at the table. "Shelby, you know Jolene." Shelby nodded a hello, receiving a regal nod of acknowledgment in return.

"You get ahold of Orcas Bio-Dome?"

"Oh," Shelby said, surprised Jolene had remembered. "Yes, I did. Thank you again."

Holly resumed her introductions around the table. "And this is Dee"—the Debbie-like woman smiled widely—"and her wife, Alice." Alice's brown eyes twinkled warmly. "And this is Adrienne."

The youngest woman gave Shelby a casual nod hello while brushing her hair back from her face; putting multiple ear piercings on display.

Shelby looked from one woman to the next, to the next, trying to piece this new information together. Since Holly was gay, and she'd implied that Jolene was, too—hadn't she?—and these two middle-aged women were married . . . this young woman was most likely queer, too. Was this . . . some sort of lesbian gathering? Her heart rate picked up, though whether in thrill or nerves, Shelby couldn't decide. She darted a glance to Holly, her face a question mark, but before she could read any answers on her face, Dee waved her toward the table.

"Sit, sit!" She grinned back up at Holly. "Woman, where the hell have you been hiding this one?"

In answer, Holly said wryly, "As you can see, Shelby, we're well into our second bottle."

"You'll just have to catch up, honey," Dee said, scooting to make room, leaning over the barrel top in her reach for a clean wineglass to offer. Her entire chest seemed to spill over the lip of the table, giving everyone a generous eyeful of bosom. Alice made a joke of trying to wrestle the wineglass out of her wife's hand "for the safety of innocent bystanders" while Jolene snorted, assumedly at the reference to "innocents."

Shelby blinked, trying to accept the proffered wineglass while not staring at Dee's chest and flinging another glance toward Holly.

"So, we're the San Juan Sisters," Dee announced, once she'd straightened and resettled on her stool, while Jolene interjected, "We didn't all agree on that insipid name."

Dee blithely ignored her, swilling her wine. She tilted her gaze upon Shelby, looking askance at her as if fully taking her in for the first time. "You a sister, honey?"

"Um . . . well, I mean . . ." Somewhere deep in Shelby, a resounding *yes* was building, but caution and doubt prevailed. These women couldn't possibly accept her, in the closet as she was. Could they? What if they didn't? Shelby shifted from one foot to the other, hard pressed to remember the last time she'd felt so much like a fish out of water. She regretted not setting Holly straight—shit, no pun intended—from the start. What if Shelby's discomfort about her own in-limbo identity caused these women to see her as a fraud?

"Let's just let the woman settle in," Holly said smoothly, filling Shelby's glass with ruby-tinted liquid from a bottle with no label.

"We'll allow for a guest pass," Dee agreed with a laugh, "but just this once," she joked to Holly.

Holly sat, mouthing *Okay?* in Shelby's direction. Shelby nodded mutely. She caught a whiff of her lotion—that citrusy scent—and a hint of the musk of alcohol and yeast that always seemed to cling to Holly's trademark tank tops as she leaned in to explain, "What we have here is completely new territory."

It took Shelby a beat to realize Holly was referring to the wine she'd just poured.

"We've decided to barrel test our most recent pinot noir," she clarified.

"Siphoned it right out of the oak with a turkey baster." Dee laughed. "Kind of like how I knocked up Alice . . . right, love?" She gave her wife a playful nudge.

"Gross," Adrienne interjected, while Alice chuckled and Holly narrated, "Dee and Alice have a two-year-old. Cutest little boy you've ever seen."

"It's why we look so tired." Alice smiled.

"Oh no, you don't look tired," Shelby replied automatically, though now that Alice mentioned it, she'd know that parent-worn look anywhere.

"You have kids?" Dee asked Shelby.

"Ah, yeah. I have a son also," Shelby said, glad to grasp hold of a topic of conversation she felt confident she could execute. "He's grown though. Well, eighteen."

"Eighteen! Holy shit!"

"Dee!"

"What? She doesn't look a day over thirty!"

"I'm definitely not thirty," Shelby interjected. "But . . . thank you?" She didn't know Dee well enough to know whether she should feel flattered. "I guess I just got an early start, on the baby thing." Alex hadn't exactly been planned, though they'd made it work, hadn't they?

"Happens all the time, in our tribe," Dee noted with a thoughtful nod. "Kids have a tendency of coming along before we've had a chance to find ourselves, haven't they?" She paused, while Shelby tried to decipher the shadow that had fallen over her cheerful face. Did Dee assume Shelby had come out earlier in life, then parented Alex alone?

Alice reached over and squeezed her wife's hand, but no words were exchanged between them. Dee took a bracing breath and added more brightly, "Then there's the route to parenthood Alice and I took. God, the donor registries, the doctors, the injections . . ." She smiled at Alice as she said all this, though, then declared, "Guess there's no easy way!"

"I, well . . ." Even though it felt good to have her identity so effortlessly assumed in the correct manner for a change, the impostor feeling doubled, chased by a hefty dose of remorse. Shelby couldn't erase Josh, no matter how good it felt to fit into this group for this one, perfect moment. She couldn't brush aside twenty years of partnership. "I didn't have to do it solo," she mustered. "My late husband and I raised him together."

There. Band-Aid ripped off. Silence fell on the room, just like it always did when Shelby had to drop this wet blanket onto a conversation. Tonight, however, as Shelby had predicted, the word *husband* seemed to land as heavily as *late*. Mercifully, Dee was the first to shake it off.

"Oh," she said slowly. Then, if possible, she released an even more pronounced "Ohhh. I'm so sorry." She glanced over at Holly, a question of her own in the furrowed arc of her brow, and that fear—that terror—of being misunderstood rose back up in Shelby like bile.

"I realized I needed something different a bit late in life," she blurted with a nervous laugh. This correction wasn't enough—it wasn't a coming out, exactly—but at least it placed an asterisk by the word *husband*.

Next to her, a rigidity in Holly's shoulders relaxed. Shelby hadn't consciously noted her tension until it had passed. Dee looked back at Shelby and smiled again. "Well, you're here now," she decided, giving her hand a quick pat. "And we're glad to have you."

Were they? Or had Shelby just committed the ultimate faux pas, crashing this gay women's get-together and mentioning a husband in the first thirty seconds? Despite Dee's assurance, she wasn't convinced she was entirely welcome. Jolene eyed her a bit warily, and she was sure Adrienne had just barely restrained from rolling her eyes. The look on her face reminded Shelby of Alex's a few years back, when he'd been in a thankfully brief bratty adolescent phase. Alice's expression remained as warm as before, however, and Holly had relaxed even more visibly beside her.

Their shoulders brushed as she moved aside the bottle to make room for her wineglass, jolting Shelby from her anxiety back to the women seated around the table.

"It's what brought Shelby to us here on SJI," Holly was explaining. "For a fresh start. Right?" She touched her glass to Shelby's with a deliberate *clink*, raising one eyebrow at her.

Shelby shifted uncomfortably on her stool as a second, rather intriguing take on *fresh start*, the sort this group obviously offered, caused blood to rise in her cheeks. Was it just more wishful thinking that Holly's body heat practically radiated from her, sitting so close? Shelby was blushing, for god's sake. What was she, a teenage girl? Her face flushed even brighter as everyone stared at her.

She nodded to let Holly know she'd gotten the reference to their grape toast, while still a little warm under the collar. "Right." She took her first tentative taste of the experimental pinot noir, her ongoing awareness of Holly's proximity causing the sip to go down more like a shot of whiskey.

Holly looked at her a tad quizzically, something more shining through those green eyes than just curiosity . . . an understanding, an acknowledgment of some sort. *Mercy,* Shelby thought, her mind flitting to Beth. That was what Holly offered. Hopefully with a dash of grace.

Thankfully the conversation resumed around her—something about a new client of Jolene's who appreciated her Salish weaving, then Holly's harvest. Next, Alice prodded Adrienne to go for her yogi teaching certification at the community college in Anacortes, and everyone piled on their agreement. They'd chip in for a ferry pass if she registered by the deadline.

"She teaches yoga classes on the beach at English Camp in the summer," Dee explained for Shelby's benefit. "But if she gets legit, she could get hired at Lakedale year-round."

Politeness dictated Shelby address Adrienne directly, despite body language radiating "don't you dare." "I miss my yoga classes in Portland," she said. "What type do you teach?"

"Vinyasa is my favorite." A flicker of appreciation passed across Adrienne's features before she remembered to be moody again. "Or whatever people will pay me for." She shrugged.

Jolene grunted in annoyance before launching into a story about George, who had been extremely testy lately, on account of losing his lady love. The group at large agreed this was, indeed, a hardship, while Shelby prided herself on realizing George was an alpaca only two minutes into the anecdote.

This launched Dee into a story of her own about their cat, and through her whole first glass of wine, Shelby listened to all this as though from an echo chamber, her mind still churning. Holly looked at her askance more than once, those green eyes continuing to scan her profile as if to determine Shelby's present state of mind, which she perhaps correctly deduced was all over the place. But then a second glass was poured for her, and Alice popped into the kitchen for more snacks, and slowly Shelby felt herself relax.

Holly's presence warmed her. She felt a buzz of energy humming along her arm every time her body brushed close. Shelby flushed again as that second glass of wine allowed her to experiment with leaning into this welcome proximity, with touching Holly's arm as she spoke to her. With holding eye contact for what she would have, just yesterday, deemed an inappropriate length of time. Something about being in the presence of this group bore witness to what had previously been building in a vacuum.

She hid her face behind her wineglass, grateful the rest of the room couldn't pluck these thoughts out of her head. Tuning out a humorous story of Adrienne's about a first date gone wrong, she attempted to draw calming, deep breaths into her lungs. This felt surreal . . . all of it. Who was this stranger, embracing such new and dangerous feelings? Shelby wasn't entirely sure she could handle this right now. Her list for the Merrick ran a mile long, and her personal to-do list was even more daunting.

Healing.

Self-forgiveness.

Closure.

A fresh start.

In that order? Shouldn't starting over come first? She clued back into the conversation in time to hear Adrienne declare "And that's the first and last time I ever operated a chain saw" to a chorus of laughter. As Holly's bright smile lit the room, introspection went out the window. Shelby swallowed a mouthful of wine and tipped her glass to gulp another.

The women turned their attention back to Shelby, asking what she'd done in Portland, and then wanting to know all about the ceramic classes she had taught. She shared her vision for the newly ordered yurt art studio, almost spilling the beans about the wine grape creation she'd begun work on. She stopped herself just in time with a grin at Holly she refused to explain. Holly grinned back, and Adrienne rolled her eyes again.

Dee invited Shelby to weigh in on all things parenting, explaining she and Alice were currently trying to potty train their son.

"*Trying* being the operative word," Alice contributed.

"Tell Alice it's normal for boys to prefer to run around in their own shit," Dee requested of Shelby.

"I just don't understand." Alice laughed. "I've tried sticker charts, treat jars, toddler autonomy strategies . . . even the chance to earn an extra ten minutes of *Guppy Gus* doesn't motivate him."

"His favorite educational show," Dee interpreted. She smiled at her wife, shaking her head. "You've got to toss those parenting books."

"Boys *can* be difficult," Shelby contributed, while Dee nodded. Dillon, for example, had been perfectly content to run around in dirty pants, though not Alex, who'd always been a logical and methodical thinker. Bribery had been right up his alley. "But moms have the right to overanalyze," she assured Alice, who nudged Dee.

"See? There's hope!"

Thinking of Alex made Shelby think of Josh and their family life in Portland, and that impostor feeling returned, flickering at the edges of this evening that had started so rocky but had turned out to be so fun. So easy to slide right into, once she'd let herself. She excused herself to use the restroom, where she splashed cold water on her flushed face and told her reflection: *Just enjoy yourself. What's wrong with you?*

When she came back into the tasting room, Holly and Adrienne had left the table, and Jolene was busing wineglasses to the counter. She said something about putting her alpacas into the barn before it got too late, then departed with a vague, lukewarm wave. Dee and Alice still sat together over refilled glasses of wine, but the scene seemed more intimate now. "We want to get our money's worth out of the sitter," Alice confided, and Shelby smiled.

"Hide out for as long as you can," she agreed. Wanting to give their conversation some privacy, she turned toward the tasting room kitchen behind the bar, where she could hear glasses clanging. Maybe she could help with the dishes.

Just before she could push open the swinging door, however, Adrienne's voice on the other side stopped her. "I can't believe you're doing this," she hissed. "You know the result will be *so* predictable."

Shelby froze, hand on the door. What was she about to interrupt?

"The result of what?" she heard Holly sigh. The sound of dishes being loaded into the industrial washer prevailed momentarily, and then, "No, by all means, please impart your wisdom on me. What is it, exactly, that you think I'm doing?"

"Falling for a straight woman," Adrienne shot back.

Shelby's heart gave a little lurch. Did Adrienne mean *her*? Her face warmed yet again in embarrassment. She knew she should stop eavesdropping, but before she could make her feet move in retreat, Holly volleyed back, "No one's *falling* for anyone." The clang of stemware colliding made Shelby flinch. "Jesus. Could you be more dramatic?"

"*Me?*" Adrienne answered fiercely. Emotion lifted her voice an octave, easily overheard. "You tell me how you won't be there to pick up the pieces after all my breakups, because I ignore every bit of advice you ever give me, and then you go and make googly eyes all night at this Shelby chick? Nuh-uh. No way."

The sound of her name dropped in confirmation sent a shock through Shelby, chasing out any noble intention of easing away from the door. She thought of Holly's numerous gazes over the rim of her wineglass throughout the course of the night; Adrienne had a point.

"You know this can only end one way, don't you?" Adrienne demanded. "You're pathetic."

Shelby couldn't imagine Holly taking that insult well, and she was proved right. "*Nothing* is happening, and so therefore, nothing can end!" More dishes crashed. If Adrienne had a retort, Shelby couldn't make it out. "And you don't *know* that she's straight," Holly added. "You shouldn't make assumptions, especially when you don't know what you're talking about." Almost under her breath she added, "My gaydar isn't *that* far off."

Shelby scarcely dared to breathe. At this point she couldn't have moved a muscle if a snake had slithered across her shoes.

"Please," Adrienne dismissed. "She was like a deer in headlights tonight . . . when she wasn't throwing herself at you."

"Well, which was she? Terrified, or flirting?" Holly shot back.

"Both!"

Shelby appreciated Holly's solidarity, but Adrienne's venom stung. It threatened to poison the brief moments of acceptance she had felt while sharing wine tonight, making Shelby feel the burn of her "guest pass" status all over again. Doubt flushed back through her brain as she continued to stand there like an idiot, paralyzed with confusion. Had she given Holly the wrong idea tonight? It was so hard to know, especially after several awkward conversations and interrupted attempts at transparency. Had she led her on?

Shelby rewound the evening in her mind, frame by frame, trying to decide whether she had, indeed, laid some sort of claim on an identity that was not hers. But no . . . leaning into the brush of Holly's shoulder as she'd settled in next to her at the table had felt right. Holding her gaze when she'd caught her eye had felt authentic. Sure, she had warmed up nicely to the idea of this evening, and okay, yes . . . maybe she'd flirted a bit, even, but so what? Holly herself had implied—no, had outright told her—that she'd hoped to see more of her.

Right?

Her face heated again as her hormones gave her brain a run for its money; she felt every ounce and inch of the inexperienced, late-blooming woman she was.

She pivoted in place, retreating from the kitchen door before she could overhear anything else that hadn't been intended for her ears. Making a beeline to where she'd left her coat and keys, she scooped them up while offering a mumbled apology and goodbye to Dee and Alice. They looked up, startled at her swift exit, as she slipped out the door and into the cool night air.

Chapter 21

Shelby drove with her hands tightly gripping the wheel at ten and two, eyes forward in fierce concentration on the dark ribbon of road before her. Fog already rose up in wispy tendrils to dance in the beam of her headlights, and she rolled down her window as she turned onto Mitchell Bay Road, hoping the cold wind that rushed in would flush out the confusing tangle of emotions that battled within her. She wasn't *straight*, no matter what Adrienne said! Who did she think she was, playing judge and jury on Shelby's self-identity? Adrienne was a *child.* If Shelby wanted to while away the evening sipping wine with a lesbian social group, she damn well would.

Dee had acknowledged her for who she was, and Holly had invited her in, so *there.*

The wind rushing into the car, stinging Shelby's cheeks, could not stifle the memory of Holly's inviting presence, sitting next to her tonight, however, or the way her breath had warmed the nape of Shelby's neck when she'd leaned in close. It failed to banish Holly's smile, which warmed Shelby from head to toe when turned in her direction. And now Adrienne's immaturity threatened to make a mockery out of it all. To make Shelby nothing more than a cliché.

She practically skidded onto Merrick Lane, tires churning into the gravel as she came to an abrupt stop in her parking space by the storage shed. She'd forgotten to set the new smart lighting system she'd had installed when she left earlier that evening, and the Merrick now looked imposingly dark. Only one light glowed on the property, across the lawn, at Ezra's cottage. She let her gaze linger there. Was he still agonizing over the changes she had made? He'd been hopeless at installing the smart lighting hub. Was he spending his Sunday night communing with his grandfather's possessions, caught in the same grief- and guilt-induced inertia Shelby knew so well? For a moment she considered crossing the lawn and knocking on the door, before squelching this maternal instinct. Ezra was a grown man. He deserved his privacy.

On the front steps, she struggled with the front door lock, still shaking with adrenaline, then with the still-unfamiliar smart pad in the vestibule.

"Goddamn it." She dug her phone out of her pocket to shine a light at the keypad before trying again.

Upon granting herself entry, she decided what she needed was a cup of tea, but in the kitchen, her new LED lighting immediately illuminated her clay wine grape sculptures, set aside by the pantry while still awaiting a place to be fired. It now seemed like ages ago, when she'd been rolling clay between her fingers, forming wine grapes into clusters. So much for creative inspiration . . . her new interest in the intricacies of the wine-making process now only reminded Shelby that Holly had been warned about her. That she was a risk, someone to be avoided.

Would Holly avoid her now? The fear of this possibility far outweighed her embarrassment of the conversation she'd overheard. Would she ever be accepted by people like this sisterhood? Or did twenty years of marriage to a man negate any truth she might articulate now?

This question was why she'd let Adrienne rattle her so. For two decades, Shelby had been one half of "Shelby and Josh." She didn't want to spend the *next* two decades being the *surviving* half. Now that this door that had been closed for so long was finally opening for her, why couldn't she be the woman who enjoyed a little rush in the pit of her stomach at the touch of another woman's hand on hers? Why couldn't she feel free to laugh a little too loudly at another woman's jokes?

Unless she wasn't permitted a seat at the table.

She threw herself into tea making, avoiding letting her gaze fall again on her unfinished clay creations. Once she had a steaming mug in hand, she retreated to the Merrick Suite, where, instead of sanctuary, she was met with Josh's framed photo confronting her from the dresser. Again, the unanswered questions pressed in close: What would he think of her new direction for the Merrick, and what on earth would he make of her magnetic attraction to Holly?

No matter how far Shelby detoured from Josh's vision for her life here on San Juan Island, answers continued to elude her. She sank down on the bed, breathing deeply through her nose. She listened for a while to the silence of the Merrick, punctured only by the steady tick-tick-tick of the antique clock in the hall and, just beyond that, the polite purr of her new dishwasher finishing a cycle. The sound brought Shelby right back to the tasting room kitchen, however, overhearing Adrienne and Holly, and she groaned again as the feeling of idiocy returned. Joining the group at the barrel table like she belonged there? Enjoying every minute of it? *Was* she, in fact, a fraud?

Not if you just come out already.

So why was she denying herself?

"I just need a fresh start," she told Josh's image, stealing Holly's words. "Something new," she added, even while grasping his picture frame tightly. Only to remember this was exactly what Ezra did, clutching his possessions during his stirring. She set it down.

New may have been the key word, but it was *need* that had tugged at Shelby in the winery. It was what tugged still. Whatever mess of emotions this night had stirred up like mud kicked from a lake bottom, *need* lay at the heart of it. *Need* felt like the molten core, smoldering beneath the surface. Of course, *want* was right there on its heels, a close second.

But to pursue either, Shelby needed to finally have the conversation she'd been dancing around with Beth. She called her right then and there, before she could lose her nerve. Not that it worked: Her stomach flipped when Beth picked up on the first ring.

"Hey."

Something about Beth's tone felt off, but she pushed forward anyway. "Can we talk?"

"Sure. I'm just getting home from visiting Dillon."

Shelby asked how he was doing at the University of Washington, adding, "You and Michael are so lucky to have him within driving distance."

There was a pause. "Yeah. Michael and me . . . lucky. *That's* the adjective."

The sarcasm was impossible to miss, and Shelby winced. "Bad day?"

But Beth, uncharacteristically, still had little to say. "You wouldn't understand," she said finally. "You and Josh were so perfect, you made it look so easy. And I'm a horrible person, Shelby, because even given all you lost, you and Alex and Josh, I envy you. At least you had a lot to lose!"

"I *did* have a lot to lose," Shelby agreed slowly. She sank back down on the bed. "But Beth? We weren't perfect. In fact . . ." It almost felt like an out-of-body experience, seeing this window of opportunity and leaping through it. "Josh and I, we weren't going to make it, even before he got sick," she said.

"What? What do you mean?"

"I needed something different," Shelby heard herself continue. Her own advice echoed in her head. If she wanted to be accepted, if she wanted to own her authentic experience, she *had* to come out. "I've been wanting to tell you, Beth. Josh, he was so great . . . so wonderful . . . but I . . ."

"Did you *cheat* on him?" Beth sounded appalled. More than appalled. Instantly furious. Shelby couldn't blame her, knowing Michael's track record, but:

"No, god, no, I—"

"Because I know he would never have cheated on *you*. Not the way he felt about you."

Once again, a conversation with Beth had gone sideways. Coming-out fail number four, by Shelby's count. "I'm gay," she blurted, before there could be a fifth. "That was the problem."

She waited, stomach clenched, while Beth processed this in weighted silence. And then a soft "You *are*?"

"Yes." Shelby released the word on an exhale that felt like a very, very long time coming.

"Shelby! Why didn't you tell me?" Beth may have aimed for kind and supportive, but she landed somewhere closer to peeved.

Because if it hadn't been for you, I never would have unearthed my long-buried sexuality. "I wanted to tell you for a long time, but I just . . . I don't know," she admitted. Confessing this to Beth would only taint their friendship, right? "Every time I tried, it was just . . . complicated. I always made a mess of it somehow."

"Well, you didn't think I'd disapprove, did you?"

Again, Shelby supposed this sentiment was meant in a positive way, but there was still an edge to Beth's voice . . . a tension Shelby couldn't find a reason for. Her stomach churned again. Was it as she'd feared? Despite Beth claiming to be supportive, would this news irrevocably damage their friendship?

"I *hope* you don't disapprove."

Beth exhaled on a slightly embittered laugh. "No, I'm just thinking of the waste of it all," she said. "You caught one of the good ones, and yet you were willing to toss him back out to sea."

Shelby inhaled sharply, the bite underneath Beth's quip cutting deep. Did she think Shelby didn't know what she'd given up?

She tried to be fair. There were so many things Shelby had taken for granted in her marriage that Beth had never had in hers: the little notes Josh had left on the kitchen counter, just to tell Shelby to have a good day. The texts he would send before heading home from work each evening: On my way! It all added up to form a solid layer of support that had been yanked out from under her. A form of support Beth had never had.

All of which she'd risked losing by telling Josh the truth. "And thanks to his tumor, I'll never know whether it would have been Josh or me who would have ultimately pulled the plug," she admitted.

"I guess you had no choice," Beth conceded. She still sounded peeved, but she attempted to soften the blow. "I just want you to be happy," she added. "Obviously."

What about you, Beth? Are you *happy, underneath this obvious resentment?* And what about Josh, for that matter? Would he have found happiness again, had he lived? At least he would have had his chance to be.

Shelby's mind spun with the myriad possibilities. This coming out, long overdue, hadn't gone at all the way she had planned. But at least she'd done it. At least it was out there.

"You're sure we're okay?" she asked Beth, just before saying goodbye.

Beth's "Why wouldn't we be?" came too quick, a knee-jerk reaction covering some wound she wouldn't—or couldn't—reveal. It didn't sit right with Shelby, but she let it go. She'd kept her own issues to herself for so long. Could she blame Beth for holding her cards tight to her chest? They were both entitled to their secrets. She rose slowly after saying good night, methodically turning off the foyer lights before readying herself for bed. As she locked up, the isolation seemed to double in on itself, engulfing her.

~

She slept fitfully, alternatively hugging and discarding the extra pillow on what would have been Josh's side of the bed. By the time she gave up sometime after dawn, it had been relegated to the hardwood floor, squished between the antique chest and the leg of the bed. Shelby stared up at the ceiling for a beat, not quite ready to tackle another day if it was going to prove as exhausting as the last.

Eventually, she rose with a groan, making a beeline for the kitchen for coffee before consulting her to-do list. A distraction . . . that was what she needed. She grabbed her camera from the Merrick Suite and went room to room, taking photos of each guest room and public space.

These photos told a new story for the good Captain Merrick: artisanal touches, bright lighting, cheery bedspreads, and fresh flowers. A few nautical accent pieces no one but Ezra would notice, and plenty of open space that enhanced the Merrick's sense of whimsy and historical architecture. Shelby smiled in satisfaction. These images would be far better than her previous batch for her new website and social media pages. She'd send the best to the tourism board, a.k.a. Rosemary, too.

No longer would the inn's online presence draw ghost hunters to tromp through it like a theme park attraction, with their energy monitors and heat sensors and morbid curiosity. She uploaded these new hotel photos to her Tripadvisor and Google listings, where she double-checked that her business was properly indexed. Doing so brought her to the Google Street View page, which reminded her: She still hadn't fixed the sign, the illegible one out on Mitchell Bay Road.

Hammer and nails and a small tin of white paint in hand, she walked up the narrow lane toward the road, the daylight and sunshine of the morning refreshing her senses, resetting her internal mood after her restless night.

She had just wrested the weatherworn sign from its askew angle on a pine tree at the turnoff to Mitchell Bay Road when she heard the whine of a V-twin engine gaining intensity. She turned around to glance down the curve of asphalt as an Indian motorcycle approached and slowed. She didn't have to wait until the rider had stopped and flipped her kickstand in the gravel to know who it was.

"Just the woman I was looking for," Holly said, tugging her black helmet off. She combed through her hair, which currently stood on end, with her fingers and then smiled while all of Shelby's confusion rushed right back up to the surface of her brain like a high tide.

She swallowed a flutter of panic. "Me? Why?"

Holly looked at her steadily, her helmet cradled in her lap. "You left last night without saying goodbye," she said with a directness Shelby wasn't accustomed to from a woman. As those green eyes settled on her unblinkingly, it seemed clear they were done sidestepping. "Was it something I did?"

"No, of course not," Shelby said carefully. Did Holly suspect her argument with Adrienne had been overheard? If so, why was Shelby the one left feeling awkward and apologetic? Holly and Adrienne had been the ones talking about *her*. "I just felt like a fish out of water, I guess. I'm sorry I left so abruptly."

Holly tilted her head slightly, as if a new angle was required to read properly between the lines. "I'm sorry if I made you feel unwelcome in any way," she probed.

"No," she said. She certainly hadn't been made to feel unwelcome. At least not by Holly. She glanced down at the hammer in her hands, turning it over in her palm as if this object were suddenly foreign to her. She caught herself at this, and let it fall to hang limply from two fingers. A truck eased around the turn on Mitchell Bay Road, drifting chivalrously into the opposite lane to give the two of them and the bike plenty of space on the shoulder. As the sound of the rumbling engine faded, Shelby wanted to blurt *If you can't tell, I have no idea what I'm doing, where I belong . . . any of it.* But her desire to appear pulled together and, well, *whole*, especially after losing it on the steps of the veranda, prevailed, even if inside a dozen shards of self-doubt stabbed.

Holly studied Shelby for another long moment, her expression a mixture of frustration and uncertainty. Then she exhaled, like something had been decided. "You know what?" she said, patting the seat behind her. "Hop on."

"What, on that?" Shelby swung her hammer vaguely in the direction of the motorcycle.

Holly held out her helmet in offering. "I'll take you on a little ride. Maybe it will make up for letting you walk into the winery to be ambushed by a gang of lesbians without warning."

Shelby blanched at her forthrightness, but Holly grinned, and that wildly appealing smile broke through their stilted conversation like a knife through butter. She found herself accepting the helmet, which was heavier than she'd thought it would be. The hammer fell gracelessly from her fingers, and she scooped it out of the gravel to set it against the tree by the neglected sign.

When she straightened, Holly offered further incentive, promising, "You haven't seen the island until you've seen it from the back of a bike."

"I've never been on one before." Shelby wouldn't even know where to put her feet or hands.

Wordlessly, Holly shifted up on the seat, making more room. She looked back at Shelby, who fumbled with the chin strap of the helmet. Her eyes burned right through her again. "There's a first time for everything, girl."

Shelby swallowed and glanced away, back toward where Merrick Lane disappeared between the trees. "Mm-hmm," she murmured noncommittally. "I guess."

She mounted the bike behind Holly, swinging one booted leg around the back of the seat in what she hoped was one fluid, agile movement. The whole machine lurched alarmingly at the addition of her weight, and Shelby sucked in a breath, but Holly steadied them immediately, one foot in the gravel. "Ready?"

"No!" Not in the slightest. Shelby groped for a handhold on the seat, finding nothing.

"You should really hang on," Holly noted dryly.

"Where?" Shelby's panic sounded muffled to her ear, thanks to the well-padded helmet.

Holly chuckled and reached back to guide Shelby's hands around her waist. "I'm told I'm a pretty safe bet."

Shelby had to concur, given her experience with Holly thus far, so she encircled her arms around her, hanging on timidly as Holly eased smoothly out in the gravel, launching them onto the highway.

Chapter 22

Holly had been right: San Juan Island looked fantastic from the back of the Indian. The engine's muffled roar in Shelby's ears left little room for thought as the pastoral scenery flew by; all of her became fully engaged with the road. Eyes, brain, skin . . . every inch of Shelby felt acutely alive, down to the cellular level: her hands tingling with anxiety or maybe cold, her core tight and tense, the bike's vibrations bleeding through the leather seat and her jeans to sing along her thighs.

It had taken only the first two slightly terrifying turns along Mitchell Bay Road for Shelby to lose all respect for polite personal space; she'd pressed herself flush against Holly's back, her arms locked around her in a vise grip. The wind rushed by, raising goose bumps along her skin through her sweatshirt. Holly's bare biceps flexed with each practiced twist of her wrist as she manipulated the throttle, her hips under Shelby's palms shifting left and then right as she leaned with the movement of the bike. Shelby started to feel dizzy and trained her eyes on the narrowed point of view available to her through the visor of the helmet: a slice of the road before them, the edge of one handlebar, and the curve of Holly's shoulder.

They bypassed Snug Harbor in favor of West Side Road, which wound wildly for at least a mile, the pavement dappled with pockmarked sunlight filtered through dense forest. As they drove, this light bounced off the fenders of the bike, dazzling as if reflected from a disco ball. When they popped out at the coast at Sunset Point, Shelby blinked into the sudden, solid blueness. Azure sky dominated, broken up only by rust-red cliffside and foam-streaked, cadet blue sea. The road straightened out a bit, and she relaxed her hold, ready to fully appreciate this unexpected ride. They passed the turnout for the scenic viewpoint at San Juan County Park without slowing, then Lime Kiln Point State Park, where Shelby had run into Ezra that recent afternoon. Bit by bit, she let the sunshine, Holly's solid form, and the purr of the engine against her body lull her into a state of security.

Holly turned to look briefly back at her. "Good?"

Shelby had to read her lips, the word lost instantly to the wind. She nodded, catching the briefest flash of mischief in Holly's smile before she opened up the throttle, sending the Indian into a new gear.

So much for feeling secure. Shelby lurched forward, redoubling her grip on Holly's waist, chest pressed hard against her back to fight the sudden pull of g-force. Hanging on so desperately, it took her a second or two to realize that this must have been the motivation for Holly's sudden *Fast & Furious* act. A laugh rumbled through Shelby while she tried to decide whether to feel flattered or well played.

She realized she didn't care. Holly could have her ulterior motives. Shelby loved this. She leaned into both the ride and the company, allowing herself to simply feel, not analyze: air, road, bike, Holly. Ocean on the right, as far as Shelby could see. Farms and farmhouses darting by on the left with the clipped efficiency of slides in a View-Master. She did know one thing: She wasn't going to make the mistake of releasing her full-body hold again anytime soon.

They didn't stop for almost another twenty minutes, Holly eventually guiding them back inland near the south end of the island to connect with a narrow lane called Bailer Hill. They passed an art studio where Shelby had recently signed a purchase order for new tableware and mugs, then a trio of small ponds that advertised trout fishing. The bike finally eased to a stop on the shoulder of the road overlooking a rolling slope of lawn ending in a meadow, at the distant base of which sat a tidy Victorian-era homestead with white paint and green trim.

The windows looked boarded up, but a wooden sign dangling at the entrance of the long driveway identified it as Windchime Cottage.

Holly swung out the kickstand and killed the engine before effortlessly sliding off the bike. Her feet rooted on terra firma, she held out a hand to Shelby, who dismounted much more stiffly. She could still feel the hum of the engine between her thighs. Unbuckling the helmet and tugging it from her head, she ran a hand through her hair, as she'd seen Holly do, but as Shelby's was much longer, she almost immediately gave up on taming it, embracing the helmet-hair look. She asked, "What's this?"

Holly tracked Shelby's gaze toward the cottage, squinted into the sunshine, and said, "Just one of the dozens of B&Bs on the island. But I like the view just over this hill."

She continued to lead, dipping momentarily below Shelby's sight line as she made her way down the hill. Once they'd hiked down the slope away from the road by a good fifty yards or so, Holly sat, stretching out on the grass. Now that they weren't moving at sixty miles per hour, the fall air felt nice, the day definitely warming up. Shelby eased down next to Holly, the muscles in her legs still giving her the Jell-O treatment. She felt tender, like the thumping bass of some song still pulsed through her body.

She set the helmet onto the ground next to her, and Holly said, "Oh! You could have left that with the bike."

Shelby hadn't quite realized she was still holding on to it. She frowned at the light reflecting off the sphere of the shiny black shell, then offered a distracted smile. "Whoops."

Holly smiled back with a shake of her head, then leaned back, resting her weight on her palms braced on the grass behind her. "So listen," she said, eyes now trained forward on the cottage in the distance.

A tremor of anxiety had its way with Shelby, making her tense despite the early-October sunshine on her upturned face. Holly could be so direct, she immediately feared where this "listen" would lead. She exhaled, imagining her nerves hitching a ride on the blood cells making their oxygenated journey through her limbs, diluting somewhat before beating a path back up to her heart.

"Adrienne is very young," Holly continued carefully. "She can't help that, of course. But young people see in black and white, don't they? They actually believe that who they are *now* is who they will forever be, world without end, amen."

Shelby studied a blade of meadow grass curtseying in the breeze to some earth beat she couldn't hear. She breathed in the scent of the soil, alluding to the existence of unseen roots weaving their webs through the ground beneath them. She had compared Adrienne to Alex, but now she thought of Dillon, who'd begun his freshman year with all kinds of declarations. He was a socialist now, he'd informed Beth. And a vegan. Shelby had had to remind an unindulgent Beth that her son was just too young to know what they both knew: that the inevitability of change was really the only consistency in life.

Surely Holly was right; Adrienne was no different in this regard. "In other words," Shelby said to her hands, "Adrienne doesn't think it's possible for me to have been married to a man, and now be . . ." She trailed off before borrowing a line from her own stream-of-conscious thought. "Enjoying your company."

Relief flowed over her upon articulating this aloud, and she looked up to offer Holly a somewhat chagrined smile. The trace of tension she'd felt when she'd come out to Beth had been replaced by a quiet sort of rightness. Shelby felt like the blade of grass at her knee, yielding gently to something greater. She waited for Holly to react, and when she said nothing, the worry did spike in Shelby's veins again, the accompanying adrenaline providing a quick influx of bravery. She heard herself demand, "What do *you* think?"

Holly answered softly, "I think it's good to find your voice. To know your mind."

Josh's favorite line—*I know you by heart*—sprang to mind uninvited, rattling Shelby's brain as if the words shook the bars of some cage. "I found my voice before now," she heard herself blurt. "At least with Josh. I came out to him before he died."

The whole story poured out of her, purged in the way she'd wished she could have purged herself completely with Beth last night: how after years of self-denial, her too-intense-for-friendship feelings for her best friend had been the catalyst she'd needed. How she'd told the truth to Josh just to have him succumb to his tumor. And how she'd finally come out to Beth just last night, only to face the minefield of her friend's resentment. "Like I hadn't deserved his love or something. Like it was wasted on me."

Was it? Maybe it was.

Holly was uncharacteristically lacking in words of wisdom for a moment. Her mouth opened, then closed, and then she shook her head slightly and said, "That's a lot." She looked over, and the sympathy shone on her face. "All this, plus the inn and the move . . . you've been dealing with so much."

And Shelby had left out how daunting it felt, to try to start anew in the Merrick, in particular, ground zero of Josh-and-Shelby memories. She looked out over the slope of meadow for a moment, and then back at Holly's profile as she, in turn, shifted her gaze toward Windchime Cottage. Her cheekbones stood out in pronounced relief, giving her an almost-fragile appearance. It unnerved Shelby; Holly usually exuded such capability. When she turned her head back toward Shelby, for a second, Shelby's breath caught. Those eyes might be the death of her.

"You know," she said, "my own story actually reinforces Adrienne's worldview . . . I knew I was queer from the time I was ten years old. Just didn't have a name to put on it yet. For quite some time, all I knew for sure was that in the company of men, I felt a sort of dissonance. With women, I felt harmony. And so I've loved women—only women—since I started dating."

"Oh."

"But that hasn't been true for most of the women I've loved. Or known. Or met. Or checked out from the back of my bike." Shelby raised her eyebrows, and Holly smiled again, but this time more to herself. "Yeah, I've been around the block enough times to have figured out what Adrienne will eventually learn: Everybody's life is on an arc. It's never a direct line, so to speak. It's more like a trajectory. X and Y gets plotted on an axis, and off you go."

Shelby liked this analogy. It allowed for her decades with Josh to remain as authentic as her new path was now. It didn't discredit who she'd been with him, as Beth had seemed eager to do. "And where your arc starts . . . is it arbitrary?" she asked. Why had she picked Josh then, and why did she want something else now?

"I don't know. But arcs intersect. People meet. And sometimes it works. Sometimes not, and you have to start over, find a new X and Y."

"Or sometimes XX?"

Holly let out a light laugh of surprised pleasure. "Touché." She leaned forward, touching one hand to the top of Shelby's, braced against the earth. Her fingertips lightly brushed her skin. "May I?"

Shelby sat up straighter and tentatively offered her hand, Holly's touch instantly cushioning the buzz of adrenaline and fear this conversation induced under a hum of something warmer and softer. She slid her fingers through Shelby's slowly, threading them together to marry at the knuckles. The appeal of it twisted through her gut, finally chasing away the lingering anxiety.

"Here's all I know about this," Holly said, lifting their connected hands slightly to indicate the "this." She locked her eyes on Shelby, who couldn't seem to tug herself from their gaze. "When you look at me—and yes, you look—I think you like what you see." Her fingers shifted slightly in Shelby's hand so her thumb could trace a light path across the inside of Shelby's palm. Shelby shuddered. Was there a pressure point there? Because the simple caress sent her center of gravity completely off-keel. "And here's what *you* already know," Holly continued. Her eyes didn't relinquish their hold. "I definitely like what *I* see."

Shelby could kiss her. Right now. This thought registered with only a soft plunk, a pebble into a pond. Not a boulder, like Alex or

Dillon might haul to the bank of some lake to make the biggest splash they could.

But despite its delicacy, the ripples of this idea made their way with slow precision to lap at Shelby's psyche. Shelby *wanted* to kiss her. Holly's face was only inches away, her eyes holding Shelby's steadily, waiting for Shelby to decide. Offering without asking. *She* wanted it, too. Of this Shelby was sure.

Still, she hesitated, as though permission needed to come from within. Her thoughts tilted from Holly to Josh as if Shelby were the apex of some emotional teeter-totter, her equilibrium swaying like the little fishing boats in Snug Harbor rocked by the cradle of the tide. Had the moment leading up to her first kiss with Josh felt like this? So easily within reach? As effortless as the breeze blowing the blades of grass?

It hadn't. It hadn't. That kiss had felt intimidating to Shelby; before she'd taken the plunge, she'd had to steel herself, as though leaping into white water.

Holly continued to pin her with that intense gaze. "Only if you want to," she breathed.

"I want to." Shelby leaned forward, and her lips met Holly's in a soft brush of contact.

If Josh's first kiss had made her feel swallowed by a current, this one felt like sinking into a bath. Shelby let the warmth enfold her as Holly let her acclimate. Where was the panicky sensation of drowning? Where was the white-capped turmoil? It was as though with this kiss, Shelby had finally found the path of least resistance. She let it carry her, flotsam idly floating, the heat of Holly's mouth consuming her, the pull of desire sending soft swells of awareness to flood through her. They washed up everywhere: across Shelby's chest, making her breasts ache; in her belly, low and deep; between her legs, as if she were still riding the bike. Jesus Christ, was this how kissing *her* had felt to Josh all those years? Could Shelby be that presumptuous?

She pulled back from Holly slightly, breathing hard through her nose. Holly's hand reached up to curl around the back of Shelby's neck, softly kneading. She held her close, but not too close, her forehead coming to rest against Shelby's. "Nice?" she asked softly. Her breath stirred the tiny hairs by Shelby's temple.

She offered a wobbly smile.

Holly turned her head to place a soft kiss to Shelby's cheek, then leaned back. "You look a little drunk," she observed.

Shelby *felt* a little drunk. "I don't know quite what to think," she admitted slowly. Experimentally, she reached up and brushed her fingers through Holly's cropped hair. This felt nice, too, but . . . maybe it was the way their kiss had swept away Shelby's defenses, exposing the sediment of richer feelings underneath, but her thoughts now pivoted to Beth.

Another tip of her apex. Unlike the soft ripples of warmth Holly induced, thinking of Beth now, of all times, sent unpleasant shock waves through her. In her dreams, when she'd allowed herself to have them, it had always been Beth sitting in Holly's place. She shook her head in disbelief at this, now.

Why had she been so blind, for so long? And then so afraid?

She looked at Holly, and she felt that tug again. It caused her to free her hand to trail her fingertips experimentally across Holly's scalp, watching as Holly closed her eyes to the touch. There was a rightness and ease to it, to everything, actually, in Holly's presence, that she'd never felt with Beth.

She crooked a finger under Holly's chin to tip her face back toward hers. Holly opened her eyes. "Can we do it again?" Shelby asked. The request seemed greedy, but she needed to access this experience—kissing this woman—without having to process the newness of it this time.

Holly gave her an empirical look, but indulgence won out. "I really am an idiot, like Adrienne said," she mumbled, before guiding Shelby back to her, her hand returning to the nape of her neck to massage it gently as their mouths met again. Shelby reached up to caress the side of Holly's jaw as her mouth opened to hers, and then they were kissing in earnest, in that can't-catch-your-breath, don't-come-up-for-air way

Shelby had witnessed in a hundred movies but had never quite known how to replicate at home.

The floating feeling returned, and she wavered in the balance again, feeling dangerously upended, but only for a moment. Holly pulled her closer against her body, and Shelby felt herself careening toward the dizzying pleasure of her lips, her mouth, the hard rise of her nipple brushing her chest through the thin cotton of her shirt.

Her heart rate picked up, her pulse crashing in her ears as Holly continued to kiss her. A headier, wilder lust took hold, flooding Shelby in places the first kiss, she knew now, had only partially sated. *This* kiss was rain on parched earth. *This* kiss sent beads of a new, fiercer desire to form rivulets to erode stubborn, long-held lies.

She risked drowning in this second kiss, but when it ebbed, what remained left behind, exposed in the wrecked path of Holly's tide, was still that persistent sense of regret, for having denied herself this for so long.

She pulled back amid the debris, dizzy and raw and not yet satisfied.

"I'm sorry. Wait," she managed, aghast that she was impeding this woman from kissing her further. "Sorry," she repeated, between gulps she realized were sobs. Tears spilled.

"Oh," Holly breathed. "Hey. It's okay." Her hands slid from Shelby's face to her shoulders, and she held her steady there on the grass until she could breathe normally again. When she dared a look up at Holly's expression, it was sympathetic but guarded. "Is this too soon? Does it make you think of your husband?" she guessed. A thin sheen of sorrow lay on each word, like the mist that, on warm days, burned off over the sea by midmorning. Shelby imagined Holly didn't enjoy thinking that perhaps Adrienne, and maybe her own better judgment, had won the day.

"No," Shelby said quickly. "That's not it." And it truly wasn't, though it somewhat surprised her to realize this, given the sheer weight of years she'd had with Josh. By whichever means she had lost him—death or otherwise—she *had* lost him, her partner of twenty years. And this loss left a hole she could not deny. The question was, could she bridge it?

She looked at Holly helplessly. Truly, that was the thought that echoed through her brain. *Help.*

"Is it the friend, then?" Holly guessed. Her jaw clenched and then unclenched. "And here Adrienne accused *me* of falling for the straight chick," she added tightly.

Shelby looked miserably down at the blades of grass, still bending to the breeze. "It's not that, either. Not like Adrienne thinks."

Holly retook her hand, brushing the top of it softly with the pad of her thumb.

"Then tell me what it *is* like," she said eventually.

Shelby dug down for honesty, but it felt evasive, slippery as the sand crabs that darted between your fingers near the harbor. "I thought coming out to Beth would feel good, but instead, she made me realize how much time I wasted, pining away for her—yes, I did, it's embarrassing—when I should have been owning up to my feelings. When I should have been *doing* something about them." Another wave of remorse shook her. "And if I'd come out sooner, Josh could have still had time. To live a life that would have been truer to him. Everything wouldn't have been such a . . . waste." Wasn't that the word Beth had used?

"Past relationships are never a waste," Holly said slowly. "Everyone has their own timing. And as for Beth, sometimes we place our crushes where they feel safe. Do you know what I mean?"

Shelby shook her head. Her brain was still mostly filled with kiss-induced white noise.

"All the time you two spent together, you pining away, as you call it, subconsciously and then consciously, you knew nothing could come of it." Holly nudged Shelby gently to force her to look at her. "It was a safe space for you to experiment with your feelings, when you weren't yet ready to come out to your husband."

"Do you think she and I will ever be able to get past this? Be close friends again?"

Holly frowned. "I can't know that," she said. "I'm sorry."

"No, *I'm* sorry," Shelby said again, swiping at tears that stubbornly lingered. Of course Holly didn't want to sit here and talk about Beth. Or Josh. Why couldn't Shelby put all that angst out of her head and just enjoy what was on offer right in front of her? The half-disappointed, half-questioning look on Holly's face told her she was not the only one thinking this.

She didn't push, though, and after a while of silence, she exhaled and squeezed Shelby's hand. Lifting herself off the grass with a grunt, she said, "C'mon."

"Where are we going?"

She smiled. In comfort? Apology? "I think there's been enough excitement for one day. I'm taking you home."

The word *home* sent conflicting emotions through Shelby: dismay chased by, yes, it had to be admitted, a slight sense of reprieve. Maybe she *had* had enough excitement. That kiss, all these coming outs, left Shelby breathless and disoriented, like too much of something very rich had flooded her bloodstream.

She followed Holly back to the bike, her legs feeling like rubber after sitting in the grass for so long. She probably looked like a brand-new foal as she stumbled up the slope. When invited, she straddled the bike and prepared to hang on, primly at first, her hands barely grazing Holly's waist. She didn't want to further confuse the jumbled issue of their obvious attraction to one another.

"Oh, c'mon, just hold on tight," Holly said. Her tone held a trace of impatience, but mostly sympathy. "You'll fly right off."

Shelby scooted up the seat, rewrapping her arms around Holly's firm torso. The bike roared to life beneath her, and they were off.

Holly took the direct route back, cutting inland instead of following the coastline north. The ride was just as exhilarating this time as the road dipped and rose beneath them, but for different reasons. Shelby no longer felt like she was speeding toward something, or even simply joyriding now. She actually felt a little sick.

Holly delivered her directly to the front door of the Merrick, where she lingered for a moment after Shelby returned her helmet. She cleared her throat. "You okay?"

Shelby tried her best to rally. "Listen, I appreciate you . . ." What? Humoring her? Letting her test-drive the bike and, well, other things? "What I mean is, I'm sorry I wasn't quite able to, you know . . ." God, what *was* stopping her? Guilt? Fear? Inexperience? All of the above. The answer was definitely all of the above. Shelby bit her lip, feeling her inadequacy down to the core. "I want to lean in," she admitted. "You know?"

Holly ran a hand over the handlebars of the Indian. "Yeah, it seems counterintuitive, but when you're riding pillion on this baby, it's crucial to shift *into* the curves life throws at you." She offered a little demo, leaning a hip coyly into Shelby's.

Shelby smiled. "I didn't mean the Indian."

"You don't say." Holly returned the smile, then let go of the bike to give Shelby's hand a quick squeeze. "Hey. Don't worry. I knew what I signed up for."

"Which was?"

"A hot mess, at best." Holly grinned. "I promise I can withstand any potential damage to my ego."

She indeed looked like she could, commanding her bike like that, her unique one-two punch of strength and vulnerability manifesting itself in the way she cradled the Indian between her thighs, hands casual now on the handlebar. The sight had Shelby yearning for another make-out session, this time on the Indian.

Stop! Holly deserved better. But what did one do with oneself upon the discovery of the most intoxicating chemistry ever experienced with another person, right at the moment of complete emotional unavailability?

"I enjoyed the ride, *and* the morning together. For what it's worth," Shelby promised. "I mean, I *really* enjoyed it."

"Oh, I know." Holly winked, and her green eyes sparkled. Maybe her ego was indeed a big girl, but clearly, the boost didn't hurt.

"So what now?" Shelby didn't know whether she meant between her and Holly, or just in general. Really, she was just trying to delay the inevitable, which was Holly peeling out of her driveway, leaving her alone. She didn't want to be done with this outing. She didn't want this day with Holly to end. She eyed the entry of the Merrick dismally.

"Well, the San Juan Sisters are meeting again this weekend," Holly said simply. "On Saturday at Jolene's place this time." She donned the helmet and fastened the strap under her chin. "I know her alpacas are the only thing warm and fuzzy about her, but all of us will be there, so . . . you know. Be there."

Shelby nodded gratefully, warming at the sound of "us." The pain of admitting her hang-up on Beth still rattled around in her, brittle and sharp, but it couldn't quite puncture the sense of belonging Holly offered.

Shelby would take it, she promised herself. To Holly, she confirmed, "I'll be there."

Holly started the bike, one boot already braced on the foot peg. "I do plan to kiss and tell, though," she called over the roar of the engine. She laughed at Shelby's surprised expression as she worked out whether she'd heard her right. "We can't have Adrienne thinking she was right about you, now can we?"

Shelby felt the hint of a smile tug her lips. "No," she shouted back to Holly. "We can't have that."

Chapter 23

October

The San Juan Sisters had all arrived at Jolene's by the time Shelby turned up her dirt drive on Saturday. The gate had been left open this time, and she pulled through to park next to a beat-up SUV, a late-model minivan, and Holly's bike. The sight of it threw her for a second as she reacted to the memory of their ride together, and she hesitated as nerves danced in her belly. It had been one thing to crash these women's party last week, happening upon it unawares. But it was entirely another to show up deliberately, as though Shelby were actually part of the group. *Was* she? Or would the "sisters" expect some sort of proof of membership she couldn't yet provide?

She shook her head at her own ridiculousness. Holly had invited her, she reminded herself, and that would have to be proof enough. She turned toward the front door, stuffing her hands into the pockets of her wool coat. Sometime in the past few days, the weather had turned decidedly toward true fall. Before she could raise her hand to knock, however, Alice popped out the door, chasing after a brown-haired little boy who ducked under her arm and then around Shelby's legs, making a beeline toward the alpaca corrals. Alice trailed after, waving to Shelby as she ran by.

"Sitter bailed on us!" she called over her shoulder.

Before Shelby could properly react to this, Jolene appeared at the door, urging her inside with a stern "You're letting all the heat out."

Shelby stepped through obediently, closing the door and shrugging out of her coat. Most of the alpaca blankets had been shifted to one side of the couch, and Shelby noted that Jolene's weaving materials had been stashed somewhere, probably to remain out of reach of curious toddler hands. She was sorry, though: She'd hoped for another glimpse of that Salish woman, the one who'd swallowed all her tribe's troubles.

Without further greeting, Jolene retreated to the small kitchen off the entryway, where Shelby could see Alice's wife, Dee, checking on something in a slow cooker. Whatever it was smelled divine. Across the small entryway, Holly and Adrienne sat on opposite sides of the couch, a humongous cat nestled on Adrienne's lap. Today, the young woman sported a T-shirt bearing the slogan A WOMAN'S PLACE IS IN THE HOUSE . . . AND THE SENATE.

Holly looked up and smiled, patting the couch next to her. "Shelby! Come. Sit."

The last thing Shelby wanted to do was wedge herself between Adrienne and Holly, so she perched awkwardly on the far arm of the couch as the cat leaped off Adrienne's lap to come check out the newcomer. Shelby scratched the cat between the ears as Adrienne stood abruptly.

"I need a beer," she declared, offering in Holly's direction, "Can I get anyone anything?"

"Oh! Have Shelby try the sangria," Holly suggested.

Shelby waited for the request to produce a glower on the young woman's face, but she headed to the kitchen benignly enough. Once they were alone, Holly raised both eyebrows in Shelby's direction before offering a wry smile.

"Do I smell today or something?"

Shelby sheepishly slid onto the couch and closer to Holly. Adrienne returned, carrying a heavy glass pitcher of ruby-red liquid. Chunks of pomegranate and blackberries floated in half-muddled stages of fermentation at the top.

"I use what's left in my barrels for a table wine base and add a hint of cloves to give it an autumn-y flavor," Holly explained, taking the pitcher from Adrienne and pouring Shelby a generous cup.

She took a cautious sip. She wasn't one for messing with a good thing, and she considered even the dregs of Holly's wine too good to waste on what she'd always considered overhyped spiked punch. But like everything else about Holly, the sangria surprised her.

"This is fantastic."

It did indeed taste like fall, embodying that fresh, clean taste you could find only in a locally sourced cocktail. Shelby compared it to the gimlet she'd had in Stone Soup and added, "If you ever get tired of wine making, you could be a mixologist."

Adrienne agreed but said she'd stick to her beer, adding with a sly smile, "It's all about KISS."

Shelby swallowed a second mouthful of sangria too fast, fighting an urge to fling an accusatory glance toward Holly, who quickly arranged her expression into the picture of innocence.

Adrienne's eyes danced wickedly. "What? You haven't heard 'Keep It Simple, Stupid'?"

"Oh. Yeah."

Holly tried and failed to hide a smirk. "Better drink up, chica"—she grinned—"or this will be a long night for you."

Adrienne pushed a bowl of chips and hummus toward Shelby, too. "And *eat* up. Dee makes her hummus from scratch, by the vat full. We've never managed to polish it off in one sitting yet, so it's nice to have reinforcements."

A conditional welcome from Adrienne, but Shelby would take it. She accepted the offering, scooping a generous amount of hummus on a chip while chiding herself for making such effort to stay on Adrienne's good side. Since when did she care what a twenty-two-year-old thought of her? Adrienne acted younger than Alex.

Dee called in from the kitchen, "Is that Shelby? Did she meet Jasper?"

"Not formally," Shelby said, swallowing the hummus. "But a whirlwind of little boy did race by me as I came in."

"Jasper Malcolm Bonepart, light of our lives." Dee laughed, joining them in the living room. "Alice drew the short straw tonight, so she's on petting zoo duty until dinner. Jaz is nuts about Jolene's alpaca residents."

"He's gorgeous," Shelby offered. "Jasper, I mean," she added with a laugh. At least what she'd glimpsed of him as he dashed by.

"We all just call him 'the Blur,'" Holly contributed, as Dee laughed, digging a chip into the tub of hummus. Jolene returned from the kitchen to settle herself in the rocking chair in the corner of the room, and they all talked easily for a while, catching up on one another's lives since last week. Adrienne had gotten yet another moving violation ticket from Officer Bob, the most enthusiastic traffic cop in town, apparently, at the speed trap on Roche Harbor Road. She planned to contest it in court . . . again.

"Every time?" Dee asked incredulously.

"Gotta stick it to the man," Adrienne retorted. "It's a patriarchy out there, if you haven't noticed."

Jolene scoffed. "Oh, for fuck's sake, just pay your damned fees. I need that traffic light put in over by Lakedale, where I get my alpaca feed."

Dee guffawed. "See? By paying up, you'd be supporting a woman-owned business, Adrienne!"

Adrienne sank back into the couch cushions in a pout. "I swear," she mumbled, "you all have lost sight of the big picture." She flung an arm toward the doorway. "Alice didn't even go to the Seattle women's march this year!"

"She had already signed up for her Saturday-morning spin class," Dee countered with a shrug. "You know you still get charged if you cancel."

"Unbelievable." Adrienne rolled her eyes in a manner Shelby had seen Alex and Dillon perfect in high school.

Jolene rose to Dee and Alice's defense, giving Adrienne a run for her money in the bent-out-of-shape category. "It's all I can do to relearn pronouns," she grumped.

Adrienne came to the bait with immediate and earnest enthusiasm. "That's rich, coming from someone who insists we add a fucking *y* to *women*," she countered hotly, "or some other exclusionary bullshit."

Dee and Holly laughed and whooped, and Shelby stared back and forth between the young woman and the older ones, attempting to follow all this back-and-forth like a tennis match. Pronouns, she understood. But *y*'s? The look on her face prompted Holly to translate. "See, Adrienne rejects the queer politics of the past generations—you know, your mama's feminism . . . bra burning, Roxane Gay, *her*story—in favor of a gender-neutral stance that is more inclusive, and which she thinks will be more effective in eradicating the concept of the patriarchy."

"And the matriarchy along with it, if you're not careful. Respect your elders, girl," Jolene shot at Adrienne, who now sat stonily, her arms folded across her chest. "We paved the way for baby dykes like you. Your coming out was what? A group text to your friends with a rainbow emoji? Everyone already knew and no one cared."

"Now, hold up," Holly interjected. "We all know it's not like that for everyone, even today."

Dee and Alice nodded, and Jolene acknowledged this with an affirmative grunt but added, "Well, *I* was a homeless teen after I was outed. And how about Dee? Her husband took her for everything, including her kid."

Shelby froze, chip midway to her mouth. Dee had another child? And an ex-husband? She glanced Dee's way to see the humor on her face had faded. She caught Shelby's shocked expression and said softly, "He's almost sixteen now. Lives with his dad."

"Do you see him?" Shelby couldn't fathom not being in Alex's life every day, watching her son grow up.

"I used to get him on holidays, plus some of the summer." Dee exhaled, her shoulders collapsing like she hoped to shift a heavy weight that rested there, if only for a moment. "But his father's family is religious. They have opinions they don't hold back. He was still my little man for a while, but . . . well, he doesn't take my calls anymore."

Shelby's throat constricted, and she felt a swift kick of shame. She'd been so focused on how these women would treat her and accept her, she hadn't given a moment's thought to how *they* might have been treated over the years. How they viewed the world, and how that impacted who they invited into theirs. To her surprise, Adrienne unfolded herself from the couch to wrap her arms around Dee's ample midsection.

"I'm sorry, Dee," she said into her stomach. "That's some messed-up shit."

Dee patted Adrienne's head like she was a misbehaving but beloved puppy. "Oh, go on with you and your Gen Z feminist ways, girl. Shake things up in the name of us old, tired shrews, all right?"

Adrienne released her hold on Dee long enough to raise one militant fist in the air.

~

They converged on Jolene's tiny kitchen for dinner, crowding around her Formica table. Dee dished up bowls of chicken curry and rice soup—apparently a specialty of hers for when the weather finally turned—and sourdough biscuits. Holly's sangria recirculated among the group. Alice had coaxed Jasper back inside, and he sat there with them, happily rolling his biscuit into the shape of a doughy sword that he wielded at Adrienne.

"And so it begins," she muttered darkly, while Alice tried to redirect.

"How about it's a wand instead, Jaz?" she coaxed. "A magic wand that shoots rainbows and unicorns that make Auntie Adrienne less angry."

They all laughed. Shelby joined in, marveling at the way she seemed to melt into this group dynamic, folded in as easily as butter into her bread. Jolene told another of her Salish stories, this one just as bleak as the last. Another woman marched herself into the sea, this time after letting the weight of the whole damned world hitch a ride on her back. She'd turned into a sea turtle at the end, however, though Shelby suspected Jolene had amended the tale for Jasper, half listening while coating Dee's arm in a buttery finger painting.

Whether or not Holly had indeed filled the others in on what had passed between them as she'd half threatened, half promised, no one seemed to question Shelby's place here. They were all satisfied, it seemed, with allowing her to self-identify.

Jasper lifted his sword-wand again in her direction, and she smiled at him, admiring his dark eyes and long lashes that any woman would envy. Dee fussed over him, trying to get him to eat a bite of soup, while Alice dug into her bag on the floor to produce a package of organic gummy snacks. Dee frowned as Jasper gobbled these up in place of the nutritious meal he'd pushed fussily aside, and Shelby smiled again, watching the exchange. Whatever the particulars of Jasper's biological parentage, it was clear that these two were his mamas. She thought of Dee's older son, somewhere out there in the world, being taught to hate, and mourned for him, even while feeling lucky to be sitting here witnessing the restorative power of second chances playing out.

She dipped her own biscuit into her soup, tasting how delicious it all was for the first time. She complimented Dee, adding, "Is this bread from Queen of Tarts?"

Holly nodded. "How's it going, by the way, with all the pastries you ordered? Sandy treating you right over there?"

Shelby gave her an update on her progress at the Merrick, then filled the others in on her rebranding strategy, explaining her need to give it, along with herself, a fresh start here on the island.

A fresh start was something all these women seemed to understand. "So all the old antiques are gone?" Jolene asked. She leaned forward with interest.

"Not all of them," Shelby explained. "Mostly, I just stripped out the seafaring decor to make space for more local products, like your wool." She'd just processed Jolene's invoice for the alpaca bedspreads and floor rugs.

"Good for you," Adrienne said. "Kick that old captain to the curb." But she smiled as she said it, willing, it seemed now, to poke a little fun at herself.

"When does the yurt arrive?" Jolene asked, which kicked off a flurry of follow-up questions from the others.

"I want the Merrick to feel like a community space," Shelby said, after explaining her idea of using the yurt as an art studio and workshop. She looked hopefully at Jolene. "I wondered if you'd consider teaching fiber arts, and Adrienne, what if you held yoga there for my guests? I'd pay you," she added quickly, in anticipation of pushback.

But none was forthcoming. Adrienne actually looked at her with, if not outright acceptance, at least grudging appreciation, and Jolene nodded solemnly in consideration.

"We'll need to do a yurt raising!" Dee decided, to a chorus of agreement from Holly and Alice. Jasper bounced around the kitchen, punctuating each lap with "Yerp! Yerp! Yerp!"

Alice eventually corralled him in her arms as Dee started on the dishes. "The yurt is scheduled on Monday's ferry," Shelby said, "and help would be amazing. Something tells me Ezra and I would fail dismally on our own."

Laughter ensued, and Shelby basked in the warmth of it, caught up in the spirit of everyone's support and enthusiasm. "Can I put something else on your calendars, too?"

Everyone turned to look at her. From her position at the sink, Dee glanced over her shoulder. Shelby felt a flutter of nerves, now that all eyes were on her. She had only lost the interest of Jasper, who had wiggled away from Alice to stalk the cat around the living room.

She took a deep breath. Asking to monopolize even more of the group's time felt like the verbal definition of a trust fall. Would these women catch her? "I plan to host a Thanksgiving progressive dinner," she announced, "and you're all invited."

"A Thanksgiving what?" Alice asked, while Holly swiveled in her chair to face Shelby with even keener interest.

"What can we do to help?"

Relief washed over Shelby. She sat back down, eager to describe the idea in detail. "It will kick off my opening of the inn . . . a sort of soft launch," she explained. "Everyone on the island who's contributed to the Merrick will be invited, as a way for me to showcase all the local products that have become part of the new look. I'll put in a call to travel bloggers and Instagrammers, too."

"What do you mean 'progressive,' though?" Adrienne asked. "Like 'ahead of your time'?"

Shelby stifled a smile. "No, not exactly. Imagine a five-course dinner, each course at a different location. To start, I'm thinking cheese hors d'oeuvres and cocktails at the Dancing Goat in Roche Harbor, followed by charcuterie and wine at San Juan Winery."

She looked hopefully at Holly, who nodded. "Everyone loves a party."

And maybe this island would accept Shelby as one of their own if she threw the best one all year. "Then some sort of soup course," she continued, "and maybe Penn Cove oysters or Port Townsend salmon—they've been so good to me—and the main course at Stone Soup. We'll end the evening at the Merrick, of course, for dessert from Queen of Tarts." She glanced around the table, nervous again, for the collective reaction. "You all can have a room and stay the night . . . as test guinea pigs for me, so to speak."

"A staycation at the inn?" Dee whooped immediately. "You said the magic words, girl. Alice? Book the sitter *now*! Lock her in; I'm not even kidding!"

Holly and Jolene both grinned, and even Adrienne looked intrigued.

"You'll help?" Shelby confirmed more softly to Holly. "I can't do this without you."

Holly reached out and squeezed her hand. The touch felt comforting and certainly inviting, but not demanding. "You couldn't keep me out of this if you tried." She stood, taking her plate to Dee. "And at least we have plenty of time to plan."

"Well, um," Shelby hedged. "I was thinking, in order to set myself up with buzz and new reviews well before the holiday season, I'd do the launch for *Canadian* Thanksgiving, not American. That way, no conflicts for the venues or the guests."

Holly nearly dropped her plate. "That gives us . . ." She did some quick mental math. "Just over a week to plan this thing!"

"I've already done a lot of the legwork," Shelby assured them. Since talking to Beth, Shelby had drafted invites using her Canva Pro account and contacted the businesses she hoped would participate. "And I couldn't keep you out of this if I tried, right?" Shelby lifted an eyebrow, aiming for friendly flirtation but landing closer to shamelessness.

Holly laughed, hands up in defeat. "You got me, chica." She returned Shelby's look with far better effect. "Use me as you will."

Shelby flushed at the clearly intended double entendre, even while feeling the weight of this offering. It tasted as spicy and bold as Holly's sangria on her tongue, but she found herself grinning back at Holly anyway, enjoying the warmth that spread anew through her bones.

~

An hour later, Alice and Dee departed with a sleeping Jasper hefted on Dee's shoulder, Alice laden down with the diaper bag and dishware. Adrienne walked out to the cars with them, starting up her beat-up SUV with a loud roar. Holly sidled up to Shelby in the small second bedroom of Jolene's house, where they collected their coats off the bed.

"You seemed to have a good time," she noted without guile, digging her leather jacket from the pile.

"I did," Shelby agreed emphatically. "Thank you for inviting me, Holly." She paused. "It was generous of you, considering . . ." She trailed off, unsure how to address the way they'd left things, after their bike ride. "Anyway, I owe you one." Again.

Holly looked pensive for a moment, then shook her head. "You owe me nothing," she said, while Shelby felt a second swell of gratitude rush over her. She tried not to show it: Shelby's insecurities often led the conversation back around to Josh. And she had noticed: Josh's name on her lips sometimes caused Holly to cross her arms across her chest, or change the subject, or deflect with a joke.

Though sometimes this happened anyway, despite Shelby's best efforts.

"Save your gratitude for after I single-handedly make your Canadian Thanksgiving Progressive Dinner Hotel Launch Party the best this island's ever seen," Holly added now, giving Shelby a soft nudge of an elbow. "The *only* one it's ever seen, of course, but you catch my drift."

Shelby played along. "This island won't know what hit it."

Holly looked at her a tad too long again over the coat pile before agreeing softly, "That's for sure." She cleared her throat. "And listen, I'm the one who should apologize, if I overstepped the other day."

"What? No, you didn't." *Please don't take it all back.*

Holly exhaled. "Okay, good." She released a shaky laugh. "Sometimes I swear I'm almost jealous of heteronormative dating rituals."

"How so?" Had Shelby presumed something incorrectly? She was so new to all this.

But Holly smiled. "Nothing is quite as straightforward when two women are involved."

"No pun intended?" Shelby risked pointing out with a return smile.

Holly grinned, then added "You'll see" a tad ominously. "In the queer space, we have to flag a bit and test out the waters and gauge the temperature and eventually leap, steeling ourselves to get burned."

Lean into the curves, Shelby recalled. She appreciated the "we" that implied membership in the group, but had to ask: "Did you feel burned? The other day? Because I didn't."

Holly sat down on the bed and exhaled through her nose. "Yeah?" She looked cautiously optimistic, which would have been adorable if the reason for her caution hadn't been Shelby herself. Everything about her probably screamed "heteronormative," as Holly had put it, despite her best attempts at the contrary.

Holly regarded her for a long moment, then seemed to decide something. "Why don't you come by the winery next Friday night? If you can break away from planning your relaunch, of course. It's inventory week, so I plan to close early."

Shelby's interest piqued and then dipped slightly: Inventory didn't sound very fun, but she'd help however she could, given all the support coming her way. No doubt all the sisters would show. Shelby was just thankful to be included in their number.

"Sounds great," she said.

The room was dim; no one had bothered to turn on the lights in here as they'd retrieved their coats, but even in the gathering darkness, she could see the quick uplift of Holly's lips.

"Great," she repeated softly.

Something in Holly's tone—vulnerability? Hope?—signaled yet more caution, but she looked pleased, and Shelby liked pleasing Holly. She wanted her to know she could be counted upon, and vice versa. It felt like the trust fall exercise all over again.

It was time, as Holly had said, to leap. Shelby would just have to brace for the eventual burn.

Chapter 24

Leap, leap, leap. With no time to waste, Shelby tackled Monday morning with full enthusiasm, calling on Rosemary at the visitors' center first thing.

"One week is awfully short notice," she said fretting, her perfectly glossed lips forming a comical O of shock.

But once Shelby explained the benefits of her plan, her expression cleared. Island vendors and venues couldn't possibly accommodate Shelby on the traditional American holiday, but the second Monday night of October was wide open.

"You have a good business head on your shoulders," Rosemary declared with more surprise than Shelby would have liked. "And lucky for us, San Juan Island is in high demand with bloggers."

She produced a short list of influencers who had requested a visit via the media tab on the tourism website, and within an hour, they had worked out a simple blog tour itinerary that included a Sunday-afternoon arrival, a tour of the Merrick and dinner in town, followed by overnight accommodations and the launch event next Monday.

"You'll eat the cost, of course," Rosemary made sure to clarify, "but I've seen this play out time and again . . . it's always worth the up-front investment."

Shelby agreed, returning to the Merrick to craft her very first press release with the heading HISTORIC CAPTAIN MERRICK INN HOSTS ISLAND-WIDE PROGRESSIVE DINNER AND REOPENING OCTOBER 13.

She emailed every travel influencer on Rosemary's list individually to avoid ending up in spam folders, and, following her advice, put "Timely: Hosted Media Invite" in each subject line. She hit "Send," pleased when none of her invites immediately bounced back.

Her brand-new yurt arrived at the Friday Harbor ferry terminal in three humongous boxes, and she and Holly loaded them into the bed of her pickup truck that same afternoon. "Building the platform shouldn't take long," Holly noted on the drive back to the Merrick, "since we have all the boards from the veranda, but you'll need to level the ground first. Do you think you and Ezra can handle it?" Her expression clouded in uncertainty. "I have to work the evening shift at the winery."

Shelby flexed her arms in reply, which seemed to do little to convince Holly of her competence. "I'll send Dan over," she said with a smile.

But as it turned out, leveling the ground out by the garden proved cathartic, Shelby's shovel digging into the earth upon each thrust with relative ease.

"It's the soil here," Ezra explained, digging alongside her. "Everything is so moist, it stays spongy."

And grows mold, Shelby added silently. Otherwise she would have been able to salvage Josh's veranda.

But it was just as well. Shelby didn't have to fight that boxed-in feeling out here, in the garden. She'd been forced for so long to keep her life compartmentalized—her unease in her marriage locked behind one door, her worrisome feelings for Beth behind another, as she'd performed the roles of wife and best friend. And her actual true *self* . . . well, real Shelby had been tucked away on the shelf for far too long.

"Relax, will you?" Josh had said so many times. Out at dinner, with Beth and Michael. At Alex's Back to School night, despite the fact that all his teachers sang his praises. Anywhere Shelby felt in danger of being pigeonholed.

"I *am* relaxed," she'd tell him. "This is me, relaxed."

Because there had been no way to explain: The tension wasn't external. It came from within. It was stuffed into all those little boxes, the pressure building.

She paused in her digging, breathing in the scent of soil and moss and salt air and decay.

"Exerting yourself too much?" Ezra asked formally.

Shelby shook her head. "Not at all." It was nice to feel relief, as each box cracked open. It was wonderful to have all this open air, the evergreens and ferns and ivy and leaves all working together to offer her fresh oxygen in spades.

The San Juan Sisters converged on the inn promptly at daybreak on Tuesday, starting with Dee and Alice.

"Happy Yurt Raising Day!" Alice called out, walking up the drive loaded down with a huge thermos and a pink bakery box. "We brought doughnuts!"

"No scones today?" Shelby laughed.

"I adore Sandy, but we thought you might be all *Tart*ed out." Dee snorted. Jasper sat on her hip, eyes still at half-mast, sporting pajamas paired with bright-yellow rain boots.

Alice set the provisions down in the kitchen, snagged herself a rainbow sprinkle, and headed back to the car for "the cooler and lunch stuff."

"You will not go hungry at a lesbian function, Shelby," Dee promised (threatened?) very seriously.

Adrienne arrived next, looking even less pulled together than Jaz. An oversize trucker hat did a poor job of hiding a serious case of bedhead, and today's shirt read SOUNDS GAY . . . I'M IN.

"It's ironic," she mumbled on her way to the coffee carafe. A moment later, she was opening cupboard doors in a quest for a mug.

Shelby produced one just as Holly and Jolene stepped into the kitchen, wearing Carhartt work pants and jean overalls, respectively. Both sported steel-toed work boots.

"If it isn't Carpenter Barbie and Farmer Barbie," Dee observed, tugging Jasper's arms through the sleeves of a puffy jacket.

"Barbie is a social construct based on capitalism, toxic gender roles, and female complicity," Adrienne said.

"Until Margot Robbie changed the narrative," Dee defended.

Holly laughed. "She's not wrong."

Jolene wandered out to the dining room, where Shelby found her studying the new beeswax tapers and tablecloths and nodding appreciatively. "I like the changes," she told her.

"Want to see the rest?"

In reply, Jolene produced a shrill whistle out of the corner of her mouth, and the whole crew emerged from the kitchen for a tour of the new Merrick. Shelby felt proud, leading the charge, showing off the efforts that had cost her so much in blood, sweat, and tears the past several weeks.

"It's fantastic," Alice said, admiring the handcrafted guest notebooks and ceramic vases that would soon host locally sourced flower arrangements by each bedside.

Jolene turned in a circle. "I bet Ezra isn't all too happy, though."

She said this as bluntly as Jolene said everything, but Shelby ventured, "How well do you know him?"

Jolene had the same answer Holly had given. "About as well as anyone, which is to say, hardly at all." She ran her hand over one of her alpaca blankets on the bed. "But that young man has a very strong energy. And he sure loves his antiques."

"Yes," Shelby said slowly. "I'm actually hoping that, with the changes I've made, he'll feel less temptation to conduct his 'stirrings' at the inn." If these women knew she'd already indulged him, or how the veranda had been damaged, would they feel obligated to tattle on her to Rosemary? Adrienne might out of spite. Or as leverage to get out of her pending speeding ticket.

But instead she said, "I've caught his act. Super cool."

A protective feeling for the Merrick—and, to Shelby's surprise, for Ezra, too—swept over Shelby, swift and strong. "It's going to be different now. No more gimmicks." She spoke more harshly than she'd intended, and Adrienne's face closed back down, enthusiasm dashed.

Jolene said, "Who's to say it's a gimmick? Maybe he does sense something tangible."

"Yeah," Adrienne piled on. "Maybe the Merrick *is* haunted."

"Hey, now," Holly interjected. She set a hand on Shelby's arm, which had gone rigid by her side. "This is Shelby's livelihood we're talking about here. You know what a mess all that ghost stuff made of the Merrick. Go easy with the speculation."

Dee nodded. "Anyway, we're lesbians, Adrienne, not Wiccans."

"Terese Yates is Wiccan," Alice mused. "And *she's* gay."

"Nuh-uh," Adrienne countered. "She broke up with that kayaking guide chick of hers and moved in with a dude."

"Dude," Alice deadpanned. "Nooo."

"That guide was too young for her, anyway," Holly interjected, and the group was off and running again, discussing the merits and pitfalls of dating millennials slash outdoorsy types slash Wiccans versus dating men. Shelby was left in the conversation's wake, feeling unsettled again for the first time in days. Communing with the sisters was supposed to hone her newfound confidence in her place in this world, not remind her of all she couldn't seem to outrun.

They reassembled outside, where Holly started cutting boards to size and Dee and Alice schlepped them over to Jolene and Shelby, who hammered them into place to form the new platform. Adrienne drew the first Jasper duty shift, wandering around behind him as he explored the gardens, a bored expression on her face.

Ezra emerged from the cottage and joined the fray, unboxing the yurt components. As the white canvas unrolled to billow across the lawn, he frowned. "It looks like a sail."

Adrienne sidled up to him, a hand on his shoulder. "We should christen her the *Evergreen Studio*, in memory of your grandfather and his boat," she said, to Ezra's instant and obvious appreciation, before Jasper dashed off with a hammer and she took off in pursuit.

They broke for lunch—Dee and Alice had carted an entire slow cooker of chili over—and then the skeleton structure of the yurt began to take shape, each pillar of the circumference erected under the guidance of Holly and Jolene, each panel of lattice wrap and canvas forming a section until the circle was complete. It was almost dusk by the time Shelby climbed a sixteen-foot ladder to fit the plexiglass skylight at the very top of the canvas ceiling, to much applauding, whoops, and another piercing whistle from Jolene.

Ezra, to Shelby's surprise, clapped the hardest.

They collapsed right there on the darkening lawn until they registered the cold on their sweaty skin, and then someone said, "Do we dare try to install the electrical wiring?" and someone else groaned, "Tomorrow . . ."

Jasper, still in his pj's, entered the yurt and danced with a headlamp around the empty circular room, his shadow throwing undulating images upon the canvas.

"It looks like a puppet theater," Ezra exclaimed, and Shelby turned to see him beaming in the ambient glow of the headlamp. Had she ever seen him smile like this before?

Holly took it upon herself to order a pizza, and Dee and Alice had brought six-packs of beer, and Ezra ran to his cottage to retrieve two large kerosene lanterns.

"Careful," Shelby and Holly both said simultaneously, as he hung them from the yurt rafters.

They cracked open the beers (and an apple juice box for Jasper) and toasted to the new studio—"Evergreen Studio!" Holly announced, her beer held high, to a chorus of approval. They ate pizza right there on the floor of the yurt, under the glow of the lantern light, until the stars shone brightly enough to appear through the skylight.

"We camping here?" Jasper asked, happily cocooned between Holly and Shelby. "'Cause I just need my milk and my SnugSnug."

This was, of course, his parents' cue to rally, and Dee pushed herself off from the floor with an *umph* to hold one hand out to her wife. "Next time," Shelby promised Jasper, lifting him into her arms to carry him to the car. Ezra collected their slow cooker and thermos.

When Shelby returned to the yurt, Jolene was saying her goodbyes. "I'll have to feed the pack by headlamp as it is."

"Wait," Adrienne called. "Gimme a ride home after, and I'll help."

Shelby saw them out, thanking everyone again every chance she got. Ezra retreated to his sanctuary with his lanterns, and watching him go, Holly remarked, "He had a good day, today."

"Yes," Shelby agreed. It was good for him to be among the living. It was good for him to see that second chances made themselves known when you least expect them to, making it possible to honor a legacy like his grandfather's.

"I had a good day, too," Shelby said softly, turning to catch Holly looking at her.

"Good," she said. Then again. "Good."

~

True to their word, the sisters returned to complete the wiring the next morning, and Shelby spent the rest of the day carting her art supplies into the Evergreen Studio. She worked in the bright, airy space happily all afternoon, finishing her clay grape clusters and even erecting the traditional raku firing pit she'd envisioned out of cinder blocks she unearthed in the storage shed. She built the low, octagonal chimney on the east side of the yurt, away from the tree line and garden, pleased that it took her only about an hour. Maybe adding this rather dramatic element to her studio was overkill, but the only times on this island Shelby felt this free was when she reimagined what the Merrick could offer. When she let go from the cord that tethered her to Josh. And, of course, when she explored how she felt in Holly's company.

She heard the mellow rumble of the Indian just after 4 p.m., and had just enough time to stash her clay creations in a box before Holly poked her head into the yurt.

"Whatcha doing?"

"It's a surprise." Shelby grinned.

Holly looked pleased at this, which in turn pleased Shelby to no end. She loved pleasing Holly.

"And what, pray tell, is this out here? Ohh, a pizza oven?"

"No." Shelby laughed, explaining the basics of raku firing. "I essentially created my own kiln," she said with perhaps a trace of pride. "I'll rapid fire, then let the ceramics smolder instead of cooling them quickly. When you starve the pot of oxygen, you get very vibrant colors."

Holly eyed the pile of kindling and old newspaper Shelby had gathered to keep her fire going, once she was ready to place the grape clusters in. "Is this safe?" She lifted one eyebrow. "Or will the chamber of commerce assume you're communing with more ghosts?"

"No more ghosts," Shelby said with confidence. Not when she was diverting from Josh's path, anyway. Not out here in the sunshine, with her new kiln and new vision. "But even Ezra will love it," she added. "This is a method that dates back to the sixteenth century."

Holly smiled. "Well, you've got me sold." She sat down by the kiln, legs stretched out in the grass. "So, today's Wednesday, and your bloggers arrive Sunday, which means we've got three days left to pull this together. Where do you want me to start? Invites? Logistics? Menu?"

Shelby braced to feel overwhelmed, but with Holly here, she didn't have to face off with her never-ending to-do list solo. "I'm delegating menu suggestions to Anthony, and Rosemary and I are following up with the bloggers." She paused in thought. "But logistics could use some work. Maybe we can check in on the venues together, make sure no one has last-minute questions?"

Holly nodded. "Tomorrow?"

It occurred to Shelby that, once again, Holly had stopped by unannounced. It felt good, knowing she felt comfortable enough to just drop in, no agenda needed. Or maybe, she mused, the agenda had been to get something else on the agenda. The possibility put a smile on her face. "Sure. Tomorrow is good."

"So," Holly said, "you planning to invite anyone from the mainland to this shindig?"

Shelby did her best to pretend she didn't know exactly who Holly meant. "Like who?"

Holly rolled her eyes. "Oh, I don't know . . . like maybe your friend Beth? I'd like to thank her for inadvertently dragging you out of the closet."

Shelby laughed this off, trying not to appear as exposed as she felt. Her feelings for Beth had been such a private thing, protected at the core of her being for so long, it felt instinctual to harbor them. Alex had once found a baby chick and kept it tucked under his jacket for an entire day, pressed close to his heart. It was like that.

"I mentioned it to her," she said, "but don't get your hopes up. After our last conversation . . . well, I haven't heard definitively whether she'll come."

It saddened her, but there it was.

Holly nodded, looking out over the lawn. "And Ezra? What role will he have in the relaunch?"

"I'm not sure." He'd promised no more stirrings, but Shelby could see his singing bowls stacked neatly by the cottage door, as if staged for reentry. And though he'd embraced the yurt raising yesterday, he'd ensconced himself among his heirlooms all day today, pleading a head cold.

"I'm still worried about him," she admitted. She understood all too well the inherent desire to hold on to someone while simultaneously enjoying the freedom of letting go.

"Maybe keep him busy," Holly suggested, following Shelby's gaze toward the cottage. "Give him purpose . . . something that honors the history of the inn."

Something that gives him purpose. Something that honors our history. Shelby mulled this over the rest of the evening, while following up on email responses from influencers, while setting the smart pad to schedule the lights and alarm for the inn, while finally drawing a well-deserved bath in the claw-foot tub.

Right before crawling into bed, after texting Beth and invoking their mercy rule—you'll be here, right?—it came to her. The day of the relaunch, she would put Ezra in charge of leading a tour of the Merrick for the bloggers. Hell, he already looked the part of a historical docent, and he knew the story of Captain Merrick, his army career at American Camp, and the Pig War. He could date and describe all the antiques still in the dining area and vestibule, and if he wanted to close his talk with a spiel about the ship wheel and his grandfather's legacy on the island, so be it.

She fell asleep quickly, already crafting Ezra's tour script in her head.

Chapter 25

Thursday flew by in a blur. Shelby had so much to do to prepare for the progressive dinner, she forced herself to set aside her concern over Ezra's still-erratic moods. She'd thought he'd embrace the role of historical tour guide, but he'd so far exhibited a commitment to procrastination Shelby had previously only admired in Dillon, faced with senior year calculus. Instead of helping her craft a basic script, he continually found other chores demanding his attention, from weeding what seemed to be a bed of empty dirt to recleaning the garden shed. When he did cooperate, he followed Shelby around the inn morosely, enthusiastic only when it came to his grandfather's ship wheel affixed above the fireplace.

"Ezra, when we have guests again, think of all the people who will get to admire your grandfather's heirloom," she pointed out.

"When we have guests again, the Merrick will be too crowded for him to reach out to me," he said. "I cannot talk to him if I can't stir him, Ms. Shelby."

She looked at him, at a loss. "What is it you want me to do, Ezra?"

He looked confused by this question. Unprepared, like when Josh used to shoot SAT questions Alex's way without warning.

He eventually shrugged, turning to look out the window to study the fog with a frown. The weather had turned steely gray and humid, which locals assured Shelby was par for the course in mid-fall, but which still made her fret over the possibility of rain for the relaunch.

Holly drove her all over the island on her bike, wanting to get as much use out of it as possible before winter while helping Shelby finalize her various venues for each course of her Thanksgiving dinner.

Shelby found she was becoming rather adept at riding on the back of the Indian, leaning with Holly through the now-familiar curves above Lime Kiln and along Roche Harbor Road. En route to a U-pick berry patch to secure blueberries, she even found herself closing her eyes out of enjoyment rather than fear.

By the time they finished their rounds, Monday's itinerary had been finalized. The first course would be held at Dancing Goat in Friday Harbor, followed by sparkling rosé and late-harvest Riesling at San Juan Winery, followed by crab and salmon cakes and oysters hosted at the gallery outside Snug Harbor that displayed Jolene's alpaca wool. The main course would be at Stone Soup, as Shelby had hoped, and they'd end the evening at the Merrick for a mouthwatering array of cheesecakes and torten Sandy promised from Queen of Tarts.

"It's coming together," Shelby ventured cautiously, as they slowed to a crawl on Merrick Lane.

"*Coming* together? I can already taste the crab cakes," Holly said, leaning back to assure her. "Now all we have to tackle are the local invites." Shelby had procured postcards for the occasion from the island's resident papermaker, which she planned to hand deliver due to the time crunch, but Holly also wanted to put a notice into something called the Whale Song, SJI's virtual community bulletin board.

She hopped off the Indian and held out a hand to Shelby. Shelby took it, despite having become so much more proficient at keeping her feet on the dismount. "So, hey," Holly said. "You're still good for Friday night, right?"

Holly's winery thing. In the flurry of activity this week, she'd momentarily forgotten. "Definitely." She released Holly's grip as she got her "sea legs" back. Her gaze caught on her raku kiln, still awaiting its virgin firing. She decided she would use the bulk of the day to finish her project; she could already envision the grapes gracing the wine barrel tables at the winery, and how great would it be if they were finished in time for the progressive dinner?

She spotted Ezra, finally out and about, by the garden beds, and she indicated for Holly to follow her as she cut across the lawn toward him. "Hey, Ezra!"

"Hallo," he answered, with a dip of his head. "Hallo, Ms. Holly. I'm just putting the garden to bed." He indicated the loose straw and mulch he'd been pitching on top of the leaf-strewn soil.

"How's it going with your Merrick tour?" Holly asked cheerfully, already knowing the answer.

"Ah, well . . ." Ezra stared off in the direction of his cottage and left it at that.

Holly cleared her throat. "I'm sure it will be fabulous." Walking back to her bike, she added in an undertone to Shelby, "What do you think his deal is?"

He doesn't want the Merrick to move on. He can't bear to lose whatever tenuous connection he still feels to his grandfather. He's holding on with both fists.

She felt secure enough with Holly now to tell her about witnessing his attempted stirring, the physicality of it, the tactile rituals that tied his memories to the objects in the inn. His palm curling around the ship wheel. His fingers grazing the gilded frames of his oil paintings. She described how agitated he became when, even before she'd made so many changes, he felt the loss of what he used to be able to find in the Merrick.

"It's like he lost his grandfather all over again," Shelby said. "Maybe I was wrong to indulge him, or maybe I hoped empathy would get me further with him. He's lost someone, I've lost someone, but . . ."

She turned to catch a look of subtle discomfort on Holly's face, which, for a second, she almost didn't recognize. In Holly's easy presence, Shelby tended to forget how talk of grief could make people squirm. She shook off a quick and unexpected ripple of disappointment—et tu, Holly?—and added quickly, "Maybe it's nothing. I guess with the relaunch, I'm just feeling on edge."

This was an understatement. Every day closer to the date, Shelby felt more tense, like gears in her head were slowly but steadily ratcheting. They tightened further every time Ezra protested a change, which only served to remind her that Josh would have probably protested it, too. And, of course, they tightened every time she thought about Holly, which was all too often.

"I think everyone has to figure these things out for themselves," Holly ventured.

Shelby smiled sadly. "The question is, how can we ensure he figures it out by Monday?"

~

Friday morning, Shelby delivered her personalized invitations to individual business owners across the island, though she figured this was mostly a formality—between Rosemary and Debbie, word had surely spread. Thanks to her many rides with Holly, she knew all the country lane shortcuts and how to avoid the traffic near the ferry terminal; it was hard to believe that just a matter of weeks ago, she had been lost on Mitchell Bay Road, unable to even find the Merrick.

A delegation of six of Rosemary's vetted and approved bloggers RSVP'd yes to Shelby's email, requiring rooms Sunday after Ezra's tour as well as Monday night, following the launch.

"Plus, you'll have Kurt on hand," Rosemary told her—the sole travel and leisure reporter for the *Friday Harbor Gazette*—"and two local Instagrammers from Lopez and Orcas. That'll make nine. They'll come for the tour and the dinner and depart on the last ferry of the evening. You'll cover those expenses, too, won't you, Shelby?"

Shelby would. Free rooms and the round-trip ferry fee seemed a small price to pay for a shiny new reputation. Especially on such short notice.

Speaking of which, she finally got a text from Beth, confirming a Sunday-morning arrival on the ferry. *Mercy,* Shelby thought. She would be very glad to see her, but . . . nothing like waiting until the very last minute.

The rest of the day, she devoted herself to her kiln as she'd promised herself, working in the heat until fifteen intricately detailed grape cluster sculptures lined the table in the yurt in a perfect pottery harvest. Yes, they might look better if she could get them professionally fired, but she took deep satisfaction in not returning to the co-op to beg for space. The color would continue to deepen over the weekend, and they would look rustically elegant in time for her Canadian Thanksgiving launch on Monday.

In her enthusiasm for her art, she lost track of time, and it was far later than she had expected by the time she got out of the shower to stand in front of the Merrick Suite mirror, bemoaning her wardrobe choices for Holly's winery thing. She'd neglected the laundry, which left her with an assortment of tees, a pair of work jeans, and a plaid flannel shirt. She'd look like a farmhand when she showed up to the winery. On the other hand, for all Shelby knew, a farmhand was precisely what Holly needed for whatever was on the agenda tonight.

It would have to do. She had tugged a brush through her hair and pulled it up into a messy bun and was halfway out the door when she remembered she had offered to lend Adrienne her how-to book on women-owned businesses. Maybe it would motivate her to go back to school for that yoga certification. She did an about-face, dashing back into the Merrick Suite to dig around through her bookcase, trying to find the right book.

Debbie's *Your Small Business and You!* brochure went flying, followed by *Inn Ownership for Dummies*, which crashed to the floor at her feet. *Understanding Grief* followed in its wake, but then there it was, *Wonder Women and Badasses: A Guide for Today's Entrepreneurial Woman.* Shelby smiled. This was perfect for Adrienne.

She bent to hastily scoop up the other books and return them to the shelf, and then paused, one hand still holding *Dummies* in midair. A sheet of paper had slipped out of the book, and she plucked it from the floor in curiosity. She hadn't even cracked *Inn Ownership for Dummies* open yet, which probably explained the dozens of setbacks she'd experienced since August.

She unfolded the piece of paper, then gasped sharply as all the air in the room seemed to evaporate at once. The paper was a letter, and the handwriting was Josh's.

Well, almost Josh's. Shelby recognized his neat, sharply slanted cursive immediately upon reading the first two words—*Dear Shelby*—but also several uncharacteristic dips in some of the letters, like the pen had slipped from his hand. Josh's tremors. The shakes, he'd called them. They had plagued him the last month of his fight against the tumor.

Which meant . . . he'd written this letter after he'd gotten sick. After Shelby had come out to him.

She froze there, afraid to move. Definitely afraid to read, her stomach one huge knot of apprehension. How many times had she longed to get inside his head, in the days and weeks following his diagnosis? How often, upon arriving to this island, had the threat of *what would Josh think?* hung over her like the fog that clung to the sound?

Was she about to find out?

She chanced a glance at the first line.

By now, you are on your way to a life without me.

The guilt from her early days of mourning slammed back into her, and she let herself sink with a groan onto her bed. You reach out *now*, Josh? Really? She was already late to the winery. Would the other sisters have already arrived? The usual longing to go warred with the need to stay. She could feel the clash of it all in her gut, which churned viciously.

She had been hungry only minutes before, but now she thought she might lose whatever might be left of her lunch.

She turned to look at the bedside clock: 6:30. Then stared again at this letter that she had somehow missed in her possessions all this time. Josh must have placed it in this book right after she'd bought it, his excitement for her evident even while unable to sit up fully in his hospital bed.

With wary resignation, she picked it up again. It was time to finally finish the conversation she'd started before he got sick. It was *past* time.

> What I can't work out, is why you worked so hard to disappear.

Reading his words, at first, Shelby thought he meant here at the Merrick, where she had burrowed with such struggle into this new life. But then she read on.

> Why you molded yourself into someone you weren't, for the sake of us. Was our marriage really that good, that it was worth fading for? Or was it that terrible?

Oh, Josh. Another wave of misery churned within her while she berated herself for her inability to find her own voice for so long.

> I wish you had been honest with me from the start. At the same time, I wish you had never told me the truth.

Shelby sighed. No wonder her marriage had always felt precariously imbalanced and out of sync. Josh had been every bit as tangled up as she was, in the cord that had tethered them together for so long. The question that had burned—did Josh remember what she'd told him?—had finally been answered for her, but what good did it do her? It was the living who had to deal with the unfinished business left behind, cutting and slashing a path through the aftermath.

> I only know this: I want what is best for you. I always have. I'm sorry that I used to think I knew what that was.

This last line felt like it landed in every cell of Shelby's body. Her hands felt clammy, clutching the letter. "I never meant to deceive you," she blurted in the general vicinity of the creased paper. Would Josh have believed her, had she been able to tell him this before he died? Would he have understood?

Tears pricked as she thought of all the lies she had inadvertently told herself and Josh over the years.

She looked again at the time, then back at the letter. A big part of her longed to go immerse herself in the cheery ambience and warm company at the winery—this was what she needed right now, more than anything—but another, more deeply embedded part of herself had slipped back in Josh's familiar orbit, the centrifugal force of him pinning her to the bed, robbing her of forward motion. She hadn't felt immobilized like this in weeks. Certainly not since reimagining the inn and keeping company with Holly. She glanced again at the clock. Almost 7 p.m. now.

What was she missing with the sisters? Another potluck? A work party? *Go,* she thought. *Just go.* When she finally yanked herself up off the bed, it was an act of self-rescue, nothing less. It took nearly everything she had. She scrubbed her face clean of tear tracks and threw an old ball cap over her messy hair.

Hopefully her tardiness wouldn't be noticed amid whatever activity Holly had organized. And Shelby wouldn't worry about the grunge look she sported; she'd noticed that fashion wasn't quite the priority among the San Juan Sisters as it had been for girls' nights out back in Portland.

At San Juan Winery, the parking lot was empty, which seemed odd. A second oddity: The outdoor flood light was on, but the winery tasting room was dark. "Holly?" she called out, fishing for her phone to shine a light across the floor. If she didn't pick the right path, those wine barrel tables would leave a mark. "Jolene? Dee?"

There was no answer for a moment, and then, from the kitchen, Holly's voice sounded somewhat flat: "Just come on back."

Shelby pushed open the swinging doors to find her leaning against the industrial sink, arms crossed over her chest. Her posture wasn't angry, but it did seem . . . what was it? Protective. In front of her, in the center of the kitchen, a single table was set for two. Shelby did inventory in one swift glance: tablecloth. Candles. Wineglasses. Chilled bottle. Oh, god. Was this . . . had this been a *date*?

"Are you all right?" Holly asked. "Did something happen?"

Regret flooded Shelby. "No, I . . . I got delayed, and I just thought . . . I'm so sorry. I thought this was—you know—something with the sisters group."

Holly's face drained of color, and then just as quickly, it flooded red. "Oh." She spun away, like she suddenly needed to scrub something in the sink. "Yeah, I should have said . . ." She turned back around. "It was a mistake, that's all it was. *My* mistake," she clarified. "It was stupid." She turned away to clear the table of the wineglasses in one sweep.

"Holly, wait—"

"No, it's just that you were so late, I worried. That's all. I called but . . ."

Had she? Shelby pulled her phone from her pocket and forced herself to activate the screen. Holly *had* called. Twice, actually. She took a step toward Holly, wanting to stop her from continuing to yank things from the table. The wine bottle was the next to go, the melting ice in the bucket sloshing as Holly extracted a white varietal. The movement was too swift for Shelby to read the label.

"I'm so sorry," she repeated. "I got caught up in something."

Holly took a bracing breath. "It's fine. I'm sure it was important, whatever it was."

Despair seized Shelby. It was the look on Holly's face. The hollow note to her voice. It was not fine. There was nothing fine about this. She wanted desperately to make it right, to fix this all on the spot. And yet she couldn't explain without making everything worse.

No, she corrected herself. There was nothing *to* explain. She had just stood up this amazing woman for nothing that couldn't wait. That had in fact *already* waited, tucked away and forgotten in a book for months.

"Holly," she tried, "I was so looking forward to this evening. I just didn't realize . . ." She grappled desperately for words that wouldn't cooperate. The truth was, if she *had* realized what this was, Shelby would have been all the more excited to be here, and yet she was making it sound like she would have been less so. She was ruining this even further.

"It's fine," Holly reiterated. For the first time, an uncharacteristic harshness entered her voice. "Like I said, I knew what I signed up for."

Another sucker punch to the gut. And unlike with Beth, this one was well deserved. She took another step toward Holly, still leaning against the sink. "I have a lot happening right now," she said. "A lot of . . . I don't know . . . things to work through."

"Definitely," Holly agreed swiftly. She drew in a breath and seemed to center herself. She was so good at that; so little seemed to faze this woman. And yet . . . this had. Shelby had.

"I'm so sorry." She longed to feel Holly's arms around her, longed to lay her head against her shoulder and weep, but she had just forfeited the right to lean into Holly's strength. Shelby recognized this fact immediately as her loss. Holly's shoulders were positively made to be leaned on.

Holly pushed herself off the sink and finally took a tentative step toward Shelby. "Listen, I misread the situation, that's all. Remember that thing I said about leaping?" She pinned Shelby with a look, then offered a pinched smile. "Well, I crashed and burned tonight."

"You didn't! You—"

Holly held up a hand. "I should have known you weren't ready."

"I am. Truly. Let's just . . ." Shelby cast a glance toward the half-cleared table. "Can we eat?"

The pinched look returned to Holly's face. "Not tonight."

Tears swelled in Shelby's eyes, and though she tried to curb them—she didn't want to be a blubbering baby on top of everything else—they still insisted on falling down her cheeks.

Holly's rigid stance softened at the sight and she added, "Here's what you can do for me. Ready?"

Shelby nodded miserably.

Holly placed her request slowly and deliberately. "Tell me when you're free. All right?" She pinned Shelby with one of her looks that demanded the receiver rise to the occasion. "That's it. Just tell me when you're free."

Shelby had to stifle every impulse in her that wanted to repeat immediately, *I'm free! Right now! I promise!* She wanted to be, to the very core of her being. But she wasn't. Not yet. And she knew it.

"Okay," she promised instead, the single word making her feel as though she might wither and die right then and there, the disappointment of this evening so profound. She stood there a moment longer, wanting to apologize again, and then finally turned to retrace her steps through the empty tasting room toward her car in the dark parking lot.

Chapter 26

Tell me when you're free. Tell me when you're free.

Holly's request ran in a loop through Shelby's brain for the remainder of the weekend, while her stomach churned in a perpetual knot at the memory of hurting her the way she had. No matter what distraction she found—helping Mrs. Sanderson prep the guest rooms in anticipation of the bloggers' overnight stays on Sunday, refilling all the dried wildflower arrangements in the new artisan vases—she couldn't stop seeing the moment she'd walked into the winery kitchen to see the evidence of the date night she'd ruined. Couldn't stop hearing the injured note in Holly's voice.

She assumed she'd be out in the cold, as far as her favorite winemaker was concerned. She was both right and wrong: Holly didn't make any attempt to reach out to her personally again the entire weekend, but she also didn't miss a beat in her continued support of the Merrick's relaunch. She recruited Dee to create centerpieces for the tables and greased the wheels for Shelby at the chamber when it became apparent at the last minute that extra invites to the progressive dinner had been requested by curious locals. When Adrienne came around bearing cheesecakes from Queen of Tarts to store in the Merrick's walk-in freezer, she didn't shoot Shelby the death glare she deserved, so clearly Holly hadn't said a word about having been stood up.

The extent of the grace proffered only reinforced for Shelby the weight of her mistake. It didn't help that the weather had turned in earnest toward mid-fall, the perpetually overcast skies delivering a continuous cold drizzle. She found Ezra fretting about the possibility of a late-harvest frost, and though she offered to help lay the thick sheets of gardening plastic over the planters and around the roots, he mumbled excuses for finishing the task solo. He looked every bit as tortured as Shelby, moving back and forth between his gardens and his cottage, his face screwed up in concentration and angst.

She picked up her phone to call Holly half a dozen times that day, wanting to make it right, but stopped herself from connecting each time. What could she offer, except more apologies? Holly had asked Shelby to tell her when she was free . . . without having any idea just how much disentangling Shelby still needed to do.

She did, at least, have an idea of where to start. Glancing at her watch early Saturday evening, she did the Pacific-to-Eastern-time-zone math and decided Alex would still be awake.

Awake, and still out for the night, if the background noise was any indication. But Shelby forced herself to stay on task. She'd let *come out to Alex* remain unfinished business for too long. She began by recounting all the truths he already knew . . . how much he meant to her, how devoted she and Josh had been to giving him the best childhood they could, how much she had cherished their time in Portland as a family.

Only once she'd laid this foundation had she falteringly walked Alex through what he *hadn't* known, couldn't have known, about his mother for all these years. And then she'd stopped talking altogether, waiting for Alex to say something—anything—while her heart thudded in her chest.

"Wow, Mom," he began, "as a college freshman, I thought *I* was supposed to be the one on the path to self-discovery or whatever," which broke the tension beautifully. "But . . ."

"Ask me anything, Alex." Shelby promised herself she would answer him honestly.

"Well, I guess I'm wondering . . . did you love Dad?" His voice was reminiscent of the boy he'd been just years—maybe months—before. "Or was it, I don't know, not like that or something?"

Shelby exhaled. "Oh honey, it was *because* I loved him that I hid from myself for years. Your childhood, our family, that was all too precious for me to mess up. And I thought I would. Mess it up."

What she realized she was actually asking was, *Have I?*

She hadn't, Alex assured her. Not in so many words, but Shelby gleaned this in the way that their usual banter remained intact for the rest of their short conversation. By the fact that he still looked forward to visiting her for the holidays. Shelby's thoughts turned briefly to Dee's fractured relationship with her older son, and her heart broke for her all over again even as it swelled with gratitude for Alex.

When she hung up after insisting he get some sleep, she looked out the window over the Merrick's perfectly manicured garden in the twilight haze, Ezra's cottage cast in shadow beyond it. He, too, had felt like a son of late. And he, too, would probably be burning the late-night oil . . . probably literally, knowing Ezra's fondness for old-fashioned hurricane lamps.

Shelby frowned. Ezra was counting down to the launch with just as many conflicting emotions as she was, and she wished she could offer him the comfort Alex had just granted her. She wished she knew what Ezra needed to feel at peace. To feel fully ready, just like Shelby needed to be, for this next chapter.

~

The rain continued until, by some miracle, Sunday dawned clear. T-minus one day to Canadian Thanksgiving. Though the temperature gauge did indeed show a frost warning, making Shelby glance again toward the tucked-away garden beds, the sight of a blue sky was welcome after a week of cloud cover.

At 7 a.m., she texted Beth instructions in anticipation of her arrival; remembering how hard the Merrick had been for Shelby to find, she told Beth to meet her right off the ferry ramp, at the turnaround just before the loading and unloading zone. Shelby could wait there, then lead the way across the island to the inn.

By 8 a.m., she had showered and dressed, checked that all the bloggers were confirmed on the 3 p.m. ferry, and printed off the final notes for Ezra's tour, which would commence around 4 p.m. Nervous energy still coursing through her, she double-checked all the guest rooms upstairs, despite trusting in Mrs. Sanderson's abilities. Everything looked perfect, each room staged with Jolene's alpaca wool blankets and rugs, new curtains, toiletries from Island Apothecary (a recent find), and lavender potpourri.

Back in the kitchen, she eyed a bottle of wine she'd bought from Holly over a week ago. She'd imagined sharing it with her after the chaos of the launch was behind them, maybe in the Merrick kitchen, maybe out in the yurt studio. Now it sat there, looking all significant, and she glowered at it, the hopeful note it implied a reminder of the date Shelby had so badly botched. She stashed it in the fridge to chill anyway. Maybe Beth would like it.

She did a lap of the grounds for good measure, plucking weeds here and there, and stashing Ezra's hedge trimmer and shovel back into the maintenance shed. By ten, it was mercifully time to go get Beth, due on the 10:25 a.m. MV *Hyak*. Ezra emerged from his cottage to see her off with a solemn wave of farewell, decked out in his favorite *Newsies* cap and dungarees. At least, Shelby decided, he'd look the part while educating the bloggers on the island's history, even if he neglected his script.

She had to squint against the sun dancing off the windshield as she drove south along Roche Harbor Road, and in town, parking was scarce. It took her a few loops around the block before she found a spot in the agreed-upon location by the ferry queue, right where Front Street paralleled the sea. Leaning against the hood of the Prius, she shivered at the feel of the sun on the back of her neck when she lifted her hair to tug it into a ponytail, frowning in the direction of the bright bay.

So much hinged on today and tomorrow; if she couldn't pull off this rebranding, her new vision for the Merrick would fail. And if the Merrick failed, what did that say about *Shelby's* rebranding? She fidgeted, shifting from foot to foot, trying to settle her stomach with a few deep breaths.

For a while, a WSDOT traffic manager she'd met once at King's Market chatted with her as she waited, and while it made for a good distraction, she was glad when his radio squawked, directing him back to his station. It meant Shelby could expect the 10:25 to appear on the horizon.

She watched the ferry grow as it gained access to the dock, starting as a speck and looming slowly larger, until she could make out its rust-streaked white hull. As it came to port, its horn sounded one long, low blast over the water, like whale song. It seemed to take forever to fully dock, for the car ramp to be lowered on its grinding chain, for the traffic controllers to position themselves in their reflective vests at the cavernous opening and along the ferry road.

Finally, the cars emerged out of the gaping mouth of the MV *Hyak* in an organized stream of three rows across, starboard and port. They eased past Shelby along Front Street before merging onto the roundabout to climb one by one up Spring Street, ushered by the island's white-gloved WSDOT traffic attendants. No Beth in her blue Honda CR-V, however. Shelby continued to watch anyway, following the path of the cars as they inched their way past her up the street. It was almost like watching a time-lapse video, how quickly the ferry dock emptied again after the last delivery truck lurched up the hill past her.

She checked her watch. Scanned the road for the CR-V again. Frowned.

Had Shelby missed her, somehow? Had Beth failed to spot the Prius and pull over? She spun around to stare up the street above her, where the last of the ferry occupants now turned up 1st to head toward Beaverton Valley Road. No, Beth could not possibly have driven right past her, undetected. Not the way Shelby had scrutinized each vehicle.

She checked her phone: no text from Beth explaining her absence on the ferry.

For a long moment Shelby simply stood there, trying to decide whether to feel irritated, inconvenienced, or concerned. It wasn't like Beth to flake out; had something happened? She texted her again, to no response. Called her, only to be sent directly to voicemail. Beth's phone had either been turned off or had gone dead.

She called Dillon next, and when his phone went to voicemail, too, full-on worry set in, sparring with a deeper sense of hurt. Maybe Beth had simply decided not to come after all. What had she said to Shelby, during their last rocky phone call? That she would have given anything to have what Shelby had with Josh. Could that have been enough to cause her to ghost her like this?

She thought about what Holly had said, about Beth being a safe place for Shelby. Was the universe yanking away that safety net? Was Beth? Maybe, after their phone call, she had played back too much of their history together and had pieced together how Shelby had crushed on her.

Humiliation momentarily chased away the hurt and worry, until self-righteous anger joined the fray. Her feelings for Beth had been real, yes, but they'd been a placeholder, part of Shelby's process of redefining herself. Shelby's crush had been on the potential Beth had represented, and nothing more. If Beth had just shown up, she could have explained all that.

"Hey!"

Shelby pivoted toward the familiar female voice, instantly on alert, only to deflate at the sight of Adrienne rolling up on one of the electric scooters the tourism board—or, rather, Rosemary—had installed in strategic stations across downtown.

"Who are you waiting on?" she asked, braking by the car. She squinted toward the ferry dock, where the *Hyak* had already begun its return voyage across the sound.

"Um, my friend Beth," Shelby said. Adrienne must have been on her way to teach a class. She carried a yoga mat under one arm like a football, and today's tee featured a rainbow-hued human silhouette performing downward dog with the slogan GET YOUR OM ON.

"She promised to be here for the dinner, but I guess she missed the ferry."

"Oh. Well. *We* got you." Adrienne unexpectedly offered a fist bump, which Shelby awkwardly returned before Adrienne throttled and took off with a distracted wave and a parting "I'm sure it'll all work out for the best!"

Shelby stood there with a sharp retort on the tip of her tongue. It was *for the best* that her best friend was a no-show?

Adrienne had sounded annoyingly like Josh had in his letter, with his *I want what is best for you. I always have.* Even after he'd pushed for her to relocate to San Juan Island. Even as Shelby had clawed her way to each and every change she'd made in the Merrick.

Suddenly it hit her: All this time, Shelby had been fighting against what she'd perceived as Josh's plan for her at the inn, thinking he had wanted to re-create—or immortalize—the life they'd shared together. For the Merrick to live on as a culmination of *them*. When all along, according to his letter, he had known she needed to start fresh.

I know you by heart, he'd always said.

And as it turned out, he had. He really had.

Shelby was no different from Jolene's Salish women, internalizing so much familial responsibility they were both left stranded by their burdens, too bloated to dodge the tide, too heavy to swim into its flow. *Just let go!* Shelby had wanted to shout to those women. *What are you doing? Save yourself!*

Save yourself, she repeated to herself now. It was okay to let go. To empty her arms like ancient Ayïta into the sea. And so she tried to isolate that part of her, deep inside, that still harbored Josh. The memories she thought she'd processed with Margie and mourned with Alex. The shared meals. The late-night talks on long drives, the laughter and the jokes and the togetherness. All the things for which she had traded her own authenticity for years. These were precious parts, embedded in Shelby so long they'd been polished to a shine in her soul. She understood now why Ayita had opted to perish instead of release them.

Heed the warning, she told herself. *Let them go. Live.*

Hadn't she already willingly sacrificed what Beth had deemed "precious and rare" when she came out to Josh? It was time to finish what she had started. It wasn't too late to actualize the life she had fought so hard for. And she didn't mean the Merrick. It was time—past time—to do right by Holly.

She started the Prius. She still had a dozen things to do for the progressive dinner before the bloggers arrived, and she wasn't willing to waste even one more second. She swung a U-turn right there on Spring Street, determined to drive directly to the winery. Maybe Shelby had already completely blown it with Holly, but she had to find out.

Chapter 27

Be there. Be there. Be there. Shelby was so focused on speeding toward San Juan Winery, the sound of her ringtone at first didn't register. And when she did glance at her screen, seeing Incoming Call: Holly C disoriented her further. What was Holly doing, calling *her*? It was Shelby who had so much she needed to say.

"Hey," she answered, wincing at the casual greeting. What she should be confessing instead: *I adore you and you deserve all of me and please give me the chance to show you I am ready to leap.*

But Holly didn't give her a chance. "Where are you?" she asked immediately.

"I'm just . . . I'm headed to you, actually." Disorientation prevailed, nearly causing Shelby to miss the turn onto Mitchell Bay Road.

"No, listen. You need to get back to the Merrick, right now."

"Why?"

"Just get here."

Here? What was Holly doing at the Merrick? Shelby performed her second U-turn in nearly as many minutes, skidding out onto the gravel of the winery driveway before doubling back toward Merrick Lane. She pressed on the accelerator hard enough to leave a dust cloud in her wake along the lane, eyes straining for her first glimpse of the inn. What could be wrong?

Nothing, it would seem, at first glance. Dee and Alice's minivan was parked out front, as well as Holly's Indian, but the gardens and grounds looked undisturbed. Then the inn came into full view, and Shelby's eyes widened.

The Merrick . . . the Merrick was . . . smoking. There was no other way to describe it. It wasn't on fire. Not exactly. But as Shelby threw the Prius into park, the front door opened, and a thick, dark cloud wafted out like the mouth of a grotesque cartoon character puffing on a cigar. More smoke rose from the single open window Shelby could detect from the second floor and trailed in a lazy but unnatural sort of spiral from the chimney above the Bay Bar.

Her thoughts were wrenched from Holly, accelerating to a brand-new gear of so many revolutions per minute, her brain screamed. Had something caught fire inside? Leaping out of the Prius, she ran directly for the smoky doorway.

Someone caught her by the arm as she tried to fling the door back open.

"Shelby! Wait!"

Holly turned her by the shoulders to face her. "It's Ezra," she said. "He won't listen to us, and he won't stop."

Shelby glanced inside the vestibule, where the air was thick with the scent of sage. A huge incense pot, even larger than the bowls Ezra usually used for his stirrings, smoldered on the rolltop desk. A heavy smudge of smoke clouded the air above it, drifting toward the kitchen and the stairwell to the guest rooms.

Shit. "Ezra!" Shelby yelled out. "I got this," she told Holly, who released her grip on her arm with an expletive of her own.

"Careful, Shelby!"

She followed the worst of the smoke up the stairs, coughing as she went, tugging her shirt up over her face as she took the steps two at a time. She should have seen this coming, despite Ezra's warming to the rebranding of the Merrick. His fear of change and mourning for his grandfather ran too deep. And Shelby *would* have seen it coming, had she not been so wholly consumed by Holly, and Josh's letter, and Beth's no-show.

And now, just as she had freed herself from the weight of Josh's disapproval, just as she'd given herself permission to truly live her best life, the inn—*her* Merrick—was in danger of going up in smoke.

Just as an entourage of influencers were due to arrive.

Double shit.

On the upstairs landing, the scent of incense and smoke was so thick, she sputtered and gasped, her body recoiling from the air her lungs screamed for after she'd run up the stairs. The smoke lay like a blanket up here, hovering near the ceiling of the hallway with no way to exit the Merrick except for a single open window at the far end.

"Ezra!" she shouted again. She turned blindly into a guest room, just to realize she'd stumbled into the suite she and Josh had shared as newlyweds. She ran to the window and yanked it open, trying to give all this cloying smoke somewhere to go.

Ezra sat on the floor, his grandfather's ship wheel, wrenched, apparently, from the mantel downstairs, at his side. Another bowl of burning incense sat cradled between his knees. He would have reminded her of Alex in kindergarten, sitting crisscross-applesauce on the reading rug waiting for story hour to start, except for the tension radiating off him as he rocked violently back and forth. And except for the fact that he was attempting to summon the dead, of course.

She had to shake his shoulder several times before he seemed to emerge from his trance—or his lack of oxygen—and acknowledge her. "Don't!" he told her desperately. "Don't make me stop!"

She tried to take the bowl from his hands anyway, but he gripped it tighter.

"Ezra! Please!" She couldn't allow him to sabotage this day, not when she'd come so far. Not when, finally, *her* vision—not Josh's, not Debbie's or Rosemary's or Monroe's, but *her* vision—for the Merrick felt so close she could practically squeeze it to her chest.

What if the bloggers arrived mid-stirring? The inn's fresh start would go the way of the smoke, wafting right out the windows to dissipate in the cold autumn air. She yanked the bowl out from under Ezra's nose, sending it scattering, the whole smoldering mess dumping out on the hardwood floor. She stomped on it spastically, while simultaneously holding on to Ezra's shirt, trying to keep him at bay.

He let out a sharp cry of protest. "Shit, sorry!" Shelby said, letting go. But the moment Shelby did so, Ezra lurched for the upturned bowl on the floor like he could pick back up where he'd left off, and Shelby tackled him. She couldn't have used more force if that bowl had been the Merrick itself and Ezra had been the hand of God ready to snuff it out.

"No!" he yelled. The single syllable ended on a gasping sob. "It *has* to be today. Today's my last chance to try to reach him . . . before the inn is open again."

He scrambled on hands and knees back toward the incense pot, trying to set it upright. Shelby didn't move to stop him this time, lungs and throat burning, but his movements were clumsy, and he failed on two attempts. Ash stained his fingers.

She grasped his wrist lightly. "Ezra, what is it you want to tell him so badly?"

Ezra swiped at his eyes, which watered in the smoke. He said something inaudible, ending on a sob. His pain seemed to suck up all the oxygen in the room, leaving nothing for him to offer anyone else.

"What?"

"I need . . . to tell him . . . that it was my fault." Tears now poured. "All my fault."

Shelby absorbed the pain in Ezra's confession, each word penetrating as surely as the smoke through the pores of her skin, into her cells, all the way into her soul. She knew all about being at fault.

She shook her head to clear it somewhat of the smoke and the cloying incense. Martin Peterson had died of Parkinson's. There was nothing Ezra could have done. And if Josh's letter and her recent revelation had taught her anything, it was that it was okay to embrace the one precious life you still had.

Tell me when you're free, Holly had said. *Leap.*

Confidence and certainty filled Shelby, settling into the places guilt and remorse had taken up residence just minutes ago. "It wasn't your fault, Ezra." Shelby would remind him however many times necessary as she sat adjacent to him on the smudged floor, his hands now kind of cradled in her own.

"But I wasn't here. The *Evergreen Lady* sunk. Do you think he knew I let it sink?"

Shelby shook her head. "I don't know." Did Josh know, wherever he was now, that she was finally giving herself permission to live? It wasn't the *Evergreen Lady* Ezra needed to let go of, but his own culpability.

Could she do for Ezra what Josh and Holly and the San Juan Sisters, and even Beth, in a roundabout way, had done for her? "The boat is gone, Ezra," she said, "but you're not. Whale watching was *his* best life. He'd want you to live yours." Martin Peterson wouldn't commune with his grandson in the form of his old ship wheel. Ezra had always been miserably sick on that boat. "Where do you feel the most at peace? The most like *you*?"

He sat stock still for a moment, pinned in place on the floor like a shank of steel, and Shelby could tell he was, indeed, thinking. "The gardens," he said slowly. "The soil." The molten truth of this seemed to fill the whole hollow mold of him; he smiled in relief, nodding slightly. "Yes. The gardens here, at the Merrick."

"Earth, not sea," she agreed softly. "That's where you need to be rooted, Ezra. You've been looking for answers in the wrong place."

He relaxed further by degrees, his head slowly nodding. "Yes," he said, in that oddly formal way of his. Then more quietly, more fervently. "Yes." He closed his eyes, in some private, inward act of contrition, but then they blinked open in alarm. "But my tour! The bloggers! They'll see all this mess!"

Yes, they certainly would. Shelby looked at her watch: 3:10 p.m. They were due here by 3:30, at the latest, after disembarking from the 3:00 p.m. ferry. "We have less than twenty minutes, at best."

Shelby grabbed the smudge pot and Ezra gathered up the singing bowls and ship wheel, and together they ran back down the stairs, tidying scattered decor and remounting the wheel. For the first time they were truly working in tandem for the greater good of the Merrick. Shelby called outside to Holly, who was, thankfully, still stationed by the front door, pacing slightly in an almost comically serious manner. Dee appeared with a broom and dustpan, Holly snuffed out tea lights, and Shelby ran from guest room to guest room, wrenching windows open wide.

As fresh air flooded in, optimism stirred, until hope was a maelstrom within Shelby, making her giddy as she ran around, opening more windows, bringing in more fresh air. It was as if with each window blind, another cord was cut, untethering her from Josh, from the expectations of their old life, from her guilt and regret and mistakes. She imagined him finally set loose, just like her, somewhere, somehow, free to drift upward into whatever came next.

Chapter 28

Shelby had just finished restaging rooms, and Holly was still brushing the soot and ash from the windowsills and tablecloths, Dee prepping the Bay Bar and kitchen when the small entourage of influencers pulled up, driven by Rosemary in her San Juan Island tourism van. Debbie arrived right behind them in her blue Nissan, then flitted around nervously, manicured hands gesturing wildly as she talked a mile a minute.

Rosemary's eyes narrowed slightly at Shelby's sweaty, rumpled appearance, then scrunched her nose in distaste at the lingering smell of incense upon crossing the threshold of the Merrick. She tensed, darting a weighted look at Shelby, but then Ezra appeared right on cue at the foot of the stairs, having changed into a fresh pair of dungarees and his best tweed cap, and her suspicions seemed to wane.

"Oh! A historic reenactor!" one of the influencers, a young hipster with a carefully trimmed beard and cross-body man purse exclaimed. "Are you here to escort us back to the golden era of this hotel, sir?"

Ezra blinked at him awkwardly for a second or two that felt more like a full minute to Shelby, and then he turned on the charm, doffing his cap with a slight bow. "At your service," he said, as eight iPhones and one DSLR, in the hands of Kurt, from the *Gazette*, simultaneously rose to capture him on social media and, eventually, in print.

He led them all through the ground floor of the newly imagined Merrick, detailing the history of the inn from the army days of the good captain all the way to present, where he paused by his grandfather's ship wheel to describe the unparalleled whale-watching opportunities and other outdoor pursuits of the San Juan Islands. They toured the guest rooms next, where Shelby interjected information here and there, pointing out the many local contributions to the Merrick's decor and ambience while the tour group took notes, asked for social handles for the various businesses, and had her repeat and spell artists' names.

"That's Jolene K'wattlee," Shelby said, as an influencer in a crop top with a site called Travels & Trends with Tiff admired one of the woolen Salish blankets on a guest bed. "K-apostrophe-w-a-t-t-l-e-e. She works out of her farm studio just a few miles from where we're standing now."

It took forever for the group to move to the next room, everyone wanting to pose with the bright red, black, and white woven blanket. Observing the bloggers' enthusiasm filled Shelby with pride on Jolene's behalf. And it wasn't just the blanket. Watching them gush over all the new additions to each room, enjoying Ezra's schtick, absorbing the Merrick's historic role on the island, Shelby thought, *I'm actually doing it. I'm opening the Merrick.* She could scarcely believe it. *Me. Not Josh. Me, and Ezra, and Holly, and the San Juan Sisters, and this whole creative, talented island.* Jolene's Salish tale returned to mind: Consuming her past had been Ayita's downfall. Shelby, instead, would devour her future.

The influencers were full of questions: Where could their readers find more information on San Juan's seasonal activities and dining scene? Where could their viewers order their own custom blankets, watercolor paintings, leather-bound notebooks, and beeswax candles? Did Shelby have any lodging specials coming up? Any special rates or packages on offer? Rosemary positively beamed, furtively taking photos of the photographers to add to a case study she was compiling for the next Washington State tourism conference, and Debbie kept flustering Ezra by blurting out what everyone could expect from each next stop on the tour.

It was almost 5 p.m. by the time they'd reconvened in the vestibule for Shelby to hand out keys to the rooms. The influencers all had time to freshen up, Rosemary said, and then she'd be back with the van to take them all out to Friday Harbor for the best fish-and-chips on the island.

"*Only* fish-and-chips stand open today," Ezra corrected loudly, as Debbie elbowed him.

When they had all dispersed with their luggage, Shelby collapsed right there on the fainting couch, which now seemed very aptly named. Letting go was a lot more work than it seemed, she thought hazily. Embracing what was next took so much energy. And there was still so much to do for tomorrow . . . dispatch Anthony to the various venues to help with the food, decorate the dining area, help Holly prep the winery . . .

Where *was* Holly? Shelby went in search of her, hoping she hadn't left with Alice and Dee during the tour. Gladness instantly filled her when she found her in the kitchen, trying to make more room in the large fridge. "We still have another Queen of Tarts delivery," she explained, "and there are entirely too many types of cheese in here."

"Holly. Listen, I want to tell you—"

"Hellllooo? Shelby?"

Holly emerged from the depths of the freezer just as Shelby pivoted at the sound of a very familiar voice. Beth Donahue, Portland Police Department's finest, stood in the Merrick kitchen, a bag slung over each shoulder, hair still windblown, presumably from the ferry.

"Beth! What the heck?" In all the excitement of the past few hours, Shelby had momentarily forgotten she'd been a no-show. Evidently she'd caught a later ferry and found her own way from the terminal to the inn. Shelby felt bad about this for precisely two seconds before remembering she was supposed to be feeling hurt. "Is everything all right? I worried when you didn't show. *Or* call."

Beth let the bags fall to the floor with two dramatic thumps, then crossed the kitchen to envelop Shelby in a tight hug. "Oh, Shelby, Shelby, I'm sorry." She half laughed, half sighed into Shelby's shirt collar. "I missed the morning ferry, forgot to update you, then lost my phone . . . but you won't stay mad at me, because I've done a thing!"

Shelby pulled back to regard Beth at arm's length, eyes narrowing. "What did you do?" She was in no mood for more surprises.

Beth just grinned. "Boys!" she called over Shelby's shoulder, and then Shelby heard muffled laughter, followed by the galloping footsteps of size 12 feet.

"Oh my god! Alex! Dillon!"

Shelby practically flew across the room to wrap her arms around both of them at once. She squeezed their lanky teenage bodies, laugh-crying to Beth, "You're responsible for this? How?" A day ago, Alex had been three thousand miles away.

Beth looked quite pleased with herself. "We wanted to surprise you. It's why it took me a while to lock down a plan. And then your kid's flight was delayed into SeaTac, which made us late—"

"Beth got a speeding ticket in Anacortes!" Alex contributed.

"And then I left my phone behind, somehow, on the curb by the terminal—"

"And we had to eat lunch out of a vending machine on the late-afternoon ferry!" Dillon finished.

"Are you surprised, Mom?" Alex grinned. "I thought for *sure* my cover was blown when you called me at the airport last night!"

"When I . . ." Shelby shook her head, laughing. "I'm so surprised! So happy." She still hadn't let go of Alex's waist.

Beth laughed again in self-satisfied delight, then said, "Oh! Hi!"

Shelby released Alex and spun back to Holly. "I'm so sorry! I forgot introductions."

Beth extended a hand to Holly, who shook it, saying, "You must be the infamous Beth."

"Infamous!" Beth slid Shelby a look, but she was still smiling like an idiot. "I kind of like the sound of that!"

"Holly, meet the toughest cop in Portland." Shelby laughed. "Beth, meet the most badass winemaker in Washington State."

"And Holly, this is Alex," Shelby said, squeezing her son's shoulder, "and Beth's son, Dillon."

Holly nodded and smiled at each of the boys. "It's really good to meet you," she said.

"Is that your motorcycle outside?" Dillon asked. "It's dope."

"Don't get any ideas," Beth told him. "Not when you still practically need training wheels on your bicycle."

"Dillon crashed his bike into a parked car once," Alex supplied, for Holly's benefit. "And a mailbox."

"And a parking meter," Beth added.

"And that was all just last year," Shelby contributed.

Holly laughed. "I'd better take temptation away, then," she said, gathering her keys and helmet.

"Oh! Stay!" Shelby said. The idea of her departing now deflated Shelby's joy at seeing the boys like the pop of a balloon. "We'll open some wine."

Holly smiled, but declined so politely, it made Shelby wince. "I should let you all get caught up, but I'll be back tomorrow to help, don't worry."

"That's not it—" But Shelby was talking to her back.

After a wave in her direction, Dillon immediately resumed his narration of their travel adventures while Alex asked something about food, but Shelby barely heard them, the vacuum of Holly's absence a screaming static in her ears. She lasted only half a minute before bolting after her.

"Holly, wait!"

She felt ridiculously out of breath even though she'd run only about twenty steps from the kitchen to the porch. Holly pivoted with a look of slight alarm. There was a tenseness to her shoulders that made her look vulnerable despite the unflappable vibe her flannel-over-muscle-tee style usually conveyed. It reminded Shelby painfully of the night of their disastrous nondate. She swore to herself right then and there: Never again would she be that person who had hurt her.

"I'm ready," she blurted, half afraid Holly would make a break for the Indian before she could speak. "I mean I'm free," she explained.

"Ready to leap, like you said. I wanted to tell you hours ago, but . . . well, you know."

Had she completely blown it already, with her emotional unavailability and uncertainty? How had Holly described her? A hot mess. An apt description.

But Holly's eyes snapped immediately to Shelby's face. "Are you sure?" she breathed.

Shelby could only nod, her breath still caught around the hard knot in her throat.

Holly took a hesitant step toward her, then another, as the hint of a smile played at the edges of her mouth, like she really wanted to grin outright at this news, but her need to play it cool prevailed. It was good to see that assured swagger back with gusto. "Well then," she told Shelby, "if you really are ready to leap, I suppose you've been properly initiated into the gay dating scene."

Shelby tilted her head, regarding Holly from an angle. She decided to push the envelope. "Have I, though?" she asked innocently.

Holly did grin then, her face lighting up in that expression of startled, happy surprise that Shelby seemed capable of inducing in her.

"Good god, chica," she muttered, "you'll be the death of me yet."

But she finally closed the distance between them, tugging Shelby around the corner and out of direct view from the kitchen windows. She let Shelby's hand intertwine with hers, then pulled her still closer, bringing them toe-to-toe, torso-to-torso. That enticing citrus scent that always clung to Holly's shirts wafted past Shelby's nose, and she tried not to inhale, for fear it would undo her.

She was still trying to keep it together when the kiss Holly planted on her surprised mouth cast her right back to the grassy hillside after their exhilarating ride on the bike, except this time it was the porch floorboards that threatened to shift under her feet.

It hardly mattered, because Shelby was floating on air, despite Holly's strong arms encircling her waist, her palms spanning her hips. It seemed like a very long time before she released her with a final squeeze and a whispered "*to be continued*," but then, entirely too quickly, they were standing by Holly's Indian.

Holly tugged on her helmet, and the bike revved to life. Shelby had already turned back toward the Merrick when she called out over the noise of the engine, "Shelby?"

She turned to see Holly's chin jut toward the inn standing behind her.

"You did it."

Shelby's throat closed up all over again. She walked back into the Merrick a tad sheepishly, her face still warm, but only Beth glanced her way with raised eyebrows as Alex rummaged through the cupboards and Dillon glimpsed the Indian disappear down the lane wistfully.

~

By the time the sun had set, the influencers had departed for dinner. Dillon and Alex took Beth's car to explore the "Friday Harbor scene," as they called it, and Shelby and Beth settled in by the fireplace at the Bay Bar to share the bottle of San Juan Winery Madeleine Angevine she had bought in the hope of drinking it with its creator.

Drinking it with Beth, however, came in a close second.

"To the Captain Merrick Inn," Beth said ceremonially, clinking her wineglass to Shelby's.

"To the Merrick," Shelby echoed. Holly's *you did it* echoed in her head as she took in the warm ambience of the dining room.

"I will admit," she added, after her first appreciative sip, "when you missed the morning ferry, I worried you were still mad at me."

"What would I have to be mad about?" Beth asked, but she looked down a bit guiltily as she said this.

Shelby eyed her over the rim of her wineglass. "You know . . . because I had 'taken one of the good ones, and then tossed him back to sea,' as you put it."

Beth grimaced. "Oh, Shelby. I'm sorry I'm such a bitter old shrew." She reached over and squeezed Shelby's hand. "You really should stop listening to my rants."

Shelby studied her. The dark circles under her eyes hadn't been there in August. The frown lines around her mouth were more deeply entrenched as well. "There's something more, isn't there?" she intuited. "Something you're not telling me."

Beth sighed. "I didn't want to put a damper on your big day, but yeah. Michael and I are done. For real this time."

"Oh, Beth. I'm so sorry."

Beth waved this sentiment away half-heartedly. "Oh come on, you and I both know this was a long time coming."

A stranger might misinterpret the dismissal in Beth's voice as more bitterness or even disgust, but Shelby heard it for what it was: defeat. Had the unstoppable Beth Donahue finally been bested?

"I'm done hitting my head against a wall," she said flatly. "It's impossible for us; we're impossible. I'm done trying to rationalize my way around his flat-out inability to be loyal."

Shelby nodded. Beth deserved so much better than Michael. Someone like Josh, actually, wholly devoted. And he'd deserved someone like Beth, loyal as a bulldog. Beth had a point about the wasted potential of it all. Shelby was about to say as much when Beth added in frustration, "What is it about me, Shelby, that makes it just *not* work?"

Wasn't this the same question Shelby had asked herself over the years, despite Josh trying so hard in ways Michael never would? It made her ache. For both of them.

"Something I've learned here is to stop taking on blame that isn't mine. Like a boat taking on water, we only sink." She leveled a look at Beth. "You know you gave him every chance."

Too many chances. Beth's marriage was the only arena in which Shelby had ever seen her capitulate. Why?

"You're right," Beth agreed after a beat. She took another sip of wine—a generous sip, if Shelby was being honest—and decided, "I don't think it had as much to do with wanting Michael as it did with . . . not wanting to admit failure."

"You? Fail?" Shelby caught Beth's eye, and they both laughed. But then Shelby sobered. "Was it bad? When you finally ended it?"

"It was bad. But they say it's like ripping off a Band-Aid, right? Finally leaving your good-for-nothing, cheating husband once and for all?"

"Sure." Shelby smiled. "Just like redefining your whole life after coming out to your husband and then watching him die is just a piece of cake."

"Easy as pie."

"Like riding a bike."

"And getting back up on that horse."

They grinned at each other and clinked glasses again. Shelby took a long sip from hers, letting the crisp citrus notes of Holly's wine envelop her taste buds and then warm her from the inside out. She exhaled slowly as all the pent-up anxiety she'd had coiled inside her since leaving Portland finally released its hold. The events of the day, followed by the cathartic acts of finally making things right with Holly and reconnecting with Beth, left her feeling a little stoned, loose limbed and heavy. The tension had finally been released on that rubber band inside her.

She let her eyes wander to the bank of windows reflecting the darkness outside. She thought of the yurt sitting just beyond the gardens, the forest and sea beyond that. She thought of all the friends she'd made on this island, all the people now invested in her inn, in small ways and large.

Beth followed her gaze. "It's all so splendid," she said. "This whole island."

"I made it mine," Shelby said with satisfaction. "But oh, Beth, I felt so stuck here for so long. I was just doing penance, you know?" She described the guilt that had clung, so stubbornly, as she had slowly diverted from Josh's plan. As she had basked in Holly's company and gained confidence in her own business direction. She told Beth about his letter, and her epiphany on Spring Street. "It's a little humbling to realize how long it took me to find closure," she said.

Beth gave a soft snort. "No one is ever guaranteed closure, Shelby. Why does everyone consider it their God-given right? You made the move here, as he wished, but you weren't ready to live fully as yourself yet. So you clung to the familiar."

Shelby turned this theory over in her mind, examining it from angles she hadn't seen before. She had indeed kept herself in check, first with her safe crush on Beth, and then with her reliance on Josh, twin pillars erected to keep her foundation secure.

"But you pushed forward," Beth said, "one step at a time. One day at a time. You. *You* did the hard work. And eventually you found your own foundation. You stood on your own two feet. My point is, Shelby, we make our own closure."

This resonated. Shelby sank deeper into her chair by the fire, thinking of the San Juan Sisters, and how their support, too, now buoyed her. She thought of Holly, always Holly, and the magnetic attraction that had seized Shelby from the start.

The color she felt heating her cheeks must have telegraphed her thoughts, because Beth switched gears instantly. "So," she said, leaning forward urgently enough to risk upsetting her wine. "Tell me about your hog-riding, wine-making love interest. And no dancing around the good stuff. Don't think I didn't notice you bolting outside to say your goodbyes. So spill."

"It was really more like a hello," Shelby confessed with a shy smile. *To be continued,* indeed.

It felt good, she noted with some surprise, to spill as instructed, to share the details of her heart without feeling guarded or inauthentic.

She described how effortless it had felt, kissing Holly for the first time on the grassy slope. How satisfying it had been to finally place her affection where it felt natural, instead of forced or rejected.

"I'm pretty far gone, honestly," she admitted when she finally drew breath between sentences. What had Holly called it, when it worked between two people? Harmony. Shelby and Beth had high notes and low notes, crashing cymbals and even beautiful, linear melody, but not harmony. Harmony, Shelby hoped, had been reserved for Holly.

She and Beth sat in companionable silence for a while, until Shelby's stomach grumbled loudly. Beth insisted she continue to relax while she whipped up her one specialty: grilled cheese sandwiches.

"One day, you really should learn to cook like a grown-up," Shelby noted. This made her think of the menu she and Anthony had dreamed up for the progressive dinner, which she described to Beth in detail.

She laughed when, around a mouthful of grilled cheese, Beth said, "Stop. You're making me hungry."

After dinner, she gave Beth the grand tour she had missed earlier. Outside the annex building, she gazed through the darkness across the gardens toward the caretaker's cottage, where lights glowed, and said, "I'd like to check in on him."

"Ezra? Can I meet him?"

Shelby wasn't sure how well he'd take to yet another new face today, but she nodded, setting out across the lawn. At the cottage, Ezra answered her knock with a polite "One moment, please."

When he came to the door, he registered Beth's presence with a slight twitch along his jaw Shelby wasn't sure many people would notice, but otherwise embodied his usual gentlemanly self, such an odd yet delightful contrast to his earnest and open adolescent face.

"I just wanted to thank you again for leading such a great tour today," Shelby said. "Truly, employee of the year."

Ezra glanced down at his feet shyly, while Shelby indicated Beth at her side.

"This is my friend Beth Donahue," she added. "Beth, meet Ezra Peterson."

Ezra raised his eyes long enough to offer a formal handshake, his entrenched decorum throwing Beth off her game. Normally she'd be full of invasive questions, but tonight she said, "Why don't I give you two a minute."

She stepped away in a show of admiring the dormant vegetable and herb garden beds in the dark, and Ezra invited Shelby inside. She barely curbed a *Really?* before accepting.

The space was small, of course—just a studio with a kitchenette and a desk pushed against the far wall—but Ezra had stacked Martin Peterson's oil painting collection neatly in one corner, and the book he'd left out on the table was not one of his ghost-hunting guides, though Shelby did glimpse the word *clairvoyance* along the spine.

Ezra shuffled from foot to foot, perhaps regretting his offer to welcome Shelby inside. "I would be remiss if I failed to tell you how sorry I am for disregarding your wishes by conducting that stirring. Again." He glanced back down at the floor, practically squirming in discomfort and what Shelby hoped wasn't outright shame.

"I just hope you're feeling better about things now, Ezra," she told him. She thought about what Beth had just said about closure, regretting that she was every bit as incapable of granting it to Ezra as Josh has been to her.

"I thought about what you said, about my grandfather never expecting me to suddenly grow sea legs," he said.

Had that been what Shelby said? She curbed a retort and just listened.

"And I decided I'm going to donate his paintings to the San Juan Historical Museum," he continued. "He'd want them there, and that way I won't be tempted to try to talk to him in the Merrick."

"If you think that would help," Shelby agreed cautiously.

"And if you don't need the other nautical antiques, I could sell them and use the money for something that might honor him. Some are worth quite a pretty penny."

Shelby nodded. "I'd be happy to help, if I can."

Ezra flushed slightly. "Actually, ma'am—Ms. Shelby—I got an idea while we were building your yurt. It will be for art classes, won't it?"

"Sometimes, sure," Shelby said.

"Well, I wondered . . . what if I were to create a children's garden just beside it, where the kids could play. Guest kids at the inn," he added, "and kids here for the art, with their parents. I thought perhaps . . . perhaps Ms. Holly could help me build a wooden boat. An *Evergreen Lady* for the children to play on, imagining they're on a whale watch, or a captain at sea. We could add the ship wheel and perhaps use the drapes we removed from the Merrick for a sail."

This was, perhaps, Ezra's second-longest speech to date. He looked a bit chagrined when he finally ran out of breath, and so Shelby smiled widely, one hand on his forearm to give it a pat of solidarity. "I think that sounds like the perfect plan," she said. "We can get started on it early next spring."

She saw herself out, pausing in the doorway to confirm his attendance at the progressive dinner the following day.

"Yes, ma'am, Ms. Shelby," he answered immediately, straightening his shoulders. "Just tell me what I can do to help."

She smiled at him and nodded before exiting the cottage with a pointless "You can start by just calling me Shelby, Ezra."

Chapter 29

Monday dawned clear, crisp, and bright, the sky a deep blue that Debbie, dropping by unacceptably early to share stats on the uptick of visits to the tourism website, claimed was unheard of in October. Over breakfast, she, Shelby, and the boys pored over the flurry of social media mentions the inn had garnered after the tour, which included plenty of favorable mentions of San Juan Island's talented artisan population.

"And after the progressive Thanksgiving thing, all the growers and cheese makers and stuff will be famous, too," Dillon pointed out, adding, "What *is* for dinner tonight, anyway?"

"What *isn't*?" Beth laughed, describing the menu while simultaneously burning her toast.

"We should tag Dad's firm on some of these," Alex suggested, noting an Instagram reel highlighting the Merrick's Victorian architecture. "They'll re-share, and I bet Portland is a good drive-to market for us. My media professor talks about that sort of thing."

"Young man, you have a positive knack for PR," Debbie crooned. "Come back and see us when you graduate from that fancy college of yours."

"Hear that, Dillon? I already have a job offer." Alex smirked.

"Congratulations, you get to live with your mom," Dillon shot back.

A half-eaten scone went flying. Luckily, Debbie's hair, teased high enough to risk being caught in the cross fire, came out unscathed.

As promised, Holly checked in right after lunch, having put the finishing touches on her winery decorations, and by 3 p.m., the San Juan Sisters had assembled at the Merrick, ready and willing to take orders. Adrienne's T-shirt of the day declared unequivocally, SORRY, GUYS. I'M GAY, making Shelby wonder whether the news of Alex and Dillon's arrival on the island had already circulated among the women.

All the formal linens for the dining room tables had been laundered and starched, and Jolene and Holly teamed up to dress each table for the guests who would arrive for the finale of the progressive dinner. Shelby trailed behind them with bundled silverware and napkins, adding the finishing touches, while in the kitchen, Dee and Alice filled heavy glass drink dispensers with water and tea, dodging Jasper expertly as he ran amok between the legs of the adults.

Shelby took several trips back and forth between the storage shed and the Merrick, first for more beeswax candles and then for the string of lights she'd wanted to drape over the Bay Bar. Everyone agreed her grape centerpieces would look great on the tables at the winery, adding to the rustic ambience. Holly had positively beamed upon being presented with them, which had been all that mattered to Shelby.

"They actually look better fired in that rustic kiln of yours," Dee contributed earnestly, surveying Shelby's work. "It reminds us that in art, and in life, we are all a work in progress."

Adrienne rolled her eyes. "What a load of crap. Shelby, you should petition in protest that you were denied entry into that co-op space."

Shelby waved her off while enjoying a rush of gratitude for all the San Juan Sisters. Beth had been right: She could continue to lean on people other than her and Josh, even while standing on her own two feet.

Shelby's newly hired housekeeping team arrived to sweep the last vestiges of incense ash from the corners of the hallway and guest rooms upstairs. The geriatric Mrs. Sanderson bustled from end to end of the Merrick with impressive energy, up and down the stairs, through the vestibule and back, her twentysomething assistant looking downright haggard and useless in comparison. Sandy appeared from Queen of

Tarts as if by magic, laden down with more pink bakery boxes filled with berry tarts and popovers, stashing them in whatever spaces she could find in the stuffed fridge like a hyper squirrel preparing for winter. By four, the entire place shone and twinkled and smelled great.

"Leave it to a group of women to get shit done," Beth noted with satisfaction.

"What am I, chopped liver?" Ezra asked with a stilted laugh, looking up from his task of untangling lights. His attempt, Shelby supposed with a swell of affection, at a vintage joke.

"Yeah, what about us?" Dillon agreed.

Shelby placed calls over to the Dancing Goat and Stone Soup to ensure everything was in order at her other progressive locations, then sent Alex and Dillon upstairs to their guest room to change. The sisterhood dispersed to get ready and, in Dee and Alice's case, make sure Jasper took a quick nap. He could attend the dinner, Alice had promised him, but the overnight was just for mamas.

Shelby turned in a circle in the bright and cheery Merrick dining room, taking stock. Thirty minutes later, she, too was showered and dressed, and squished between the boys in Beth's car, en route to the Dancing Goat. Ezra sat shotgun, his hands primly folded in his lap, and Beth and the boys talked over one another a mile a minute while Shelby fought a flutter of nerves. What if this dinner didn't go smoothly? What if her invites hadn't been printed and distributed soon enough? What if no one showed, despite their publicity?

The parking lot of the Dancing Goat was packed, however, and Beth shot a sidelong look at Shelby and smiled, knowing without having to be told that, as usual, she'd been second-guessing everything. Inside the cozy artisanal space, the appetizers circulated smoothly thanks to the professional catering team overseen by Anthony, who would shadow the progressive dinner from location to location. Debbie took Shelby under her wing immediately, working the room with her bubbling energy, hovering at Shelby's elbow to whisper names of prominent island business owners in her ear and introduce her to new faces. The

Friday Harbor mayor told Shelby around a mouthful of Gouda and jam that he looked forward to the Merrick once again being an asset to the island, and Rosemary invited her to bring around a stack of Merrick brochures before her next trade conference. The inn would be the focal point of her PowerPoint case study.

Over by the refrigerated dairy cases, Ezra had been cornered by a few curious souls, including Kurt from the paper, but he seemed more than capable of answering their inquiries about the new direction of the Merrick, despite his awkward social skills. To Shelby's surprise, she heard him mention the proposed children's garden and *Evergreen Lady* play structure to several potential donors, including Captain Mitchell and the president of Friday Harbor's only bank.

When the clock rolled around to six, Holly caught Shelby's eye and tapped at her wrist, and the entire party moved to San Juan Winery. Walking through the heavy barn door and into the tasting room, Shelby's jaw dropped and she let out one long *ohhh*. Holly had outdone herself. Heavy, autumnal swags adorned the exposed beams of the barn, each fragrant fir bough interspersed with berries, leaves, and what looked like dried figs and pomegranates. Tiny fairy lights twinkled in addition to the usual string of globe lights in the rafters, backlighting the winemaker herself, already at the helm behind the bar, in the ambient glow.

"What do you think?" she asked softly.

What did she *think*? She almost made a joke about fishing for compliments before noting how serious Holly looked, like Shelby's opinion meant . . . well, everything. "I think," she said boldly, "that I am the luckiest woman in the world, to have walked into this winery eight weeks ago."

Holly let out a soft, surprised laugh, and then actually blushed, the way Shelby was more prone to. She was saved from further embarrassment only by the tide of islanders coming through the doors with their own *ohhh*s and *ahhh*s.

Shelby suspected that, for many guests, this crab cake and white wine course at the barn would end up the highlight of their evening, and she didn't begrudge Holly this for a second. Everything was Instagrammable: not just the decor, but the food, the soft lighting, the generous pouring of wine . . . In fact, Holly had just sent Dan to retrieve another case from the storage area behind the crush pad, and Shelby made a mental note not to let her overlook this additional expense on the invoice she'd only vaguely agreed to produce.

As this course wound down, Shelby recruited Beth to stand on one of the barstools to give one of her room-silencing whistles, so she could announce the option of utilizing the island's small fleet of taxicabs, all of whom had been engaged for the evening to get them to their next stop. Piling into cabs and cars, they all made their way to Snug Harbor for Penn Cove oysters next, and then to Stone Soup, where the fireplace crackled and a piano tinkled and people clustered around tables of eight to ten for the restaurant's famous roasted corn fritters and smoked turkey.

Shelby thought she'd feel nerves again in anticipation of the final stop on the progressive dinner, but by the time they all turned down Merrick Lane, everyone was in a more-than-generous mood, well fed and well lubricated. She was happy to concede the need to showcase perfection in favor of enjoying the comfortable welcome this island extended. When she got her first glimpse of the inn peeking over the dip in the hill, lights cheerily aglow, the first thing she felt was contentment. The second thing she felt was home.

As host, Shelby resisted the urge to oversee the task of setting out cakes and pies, taking coffee orders, and turning on the gas under the kettle for those who wanted lavender tea. Leaving it all in Anthony's capable hands, she found a perch at the Bay Bar where she could observe the bustle of friends and guests. She let herself remember herself and Josh, just kids barely older than Alex, arriving on this island so long ago to taste their way through it, setting into motion all that came after.

Silently, she thanked him. For loving her, for wanting, always, what was best for her. She thanked *herself* for giving herself permission to seek what she needed, even before knowing if he could forgive her. For making that leap, for herself. For her future and the Merrick's future.

From her vantage point, she watched micro scenes play out before her: Adrienne chatting up the kayaking guide rumored to have just been dumped, Holly and Beth laughing about something by the window. Bloggers chatted with local artists, who pointed out with pride their wares on display. Kurt circulated the room, documenting it all for posterity. Dirty dessert dishes stacked up, and Jolene flitted from table to table, clearing them, even though Shelby and Anthony had hired a crew for this task.

Alex found her there, surveying the scene, and they watched as Dillon gave Jasper a piggyback ride around the circumference of the room, both of them, it seemed, on a sugar high from all the desserts. Shelby bumped her son's shoulder companionably. "Looks like you're losing your best friend to a preschooler."

He threw back his head and laughed while brushing his sandy hair out of his eyes, and in that moment, he looked and sounded so much like Josh, Shelby's chest ached. As if reading her mind, Alex followed her gaze around the dining room and said, "Dad would have been so stoked by all this."

Shelby braced for her brain to reject this idea, for guilt to seize her for hijacking his dream, for remorse to slide into the spaces still hollowed out in her, trying to heal. Instead, her answer came easily. "He sure would have been, wouldn't he?"

"You did great, Mom," Alex said. "Really amazing."

"Well, I didn't do it alone," she answered, looking back out at the sisters, at Ezra, at Holly and Beth.

"True," he said, and that single, simple word, *true*, that had been missing in Shelby's core for so long, which had proved so elusive and then so hard-won, floated up between them like air. Not even that.

Less than air. It dissipated in the cacophony of voices and music and tinkling of silverware.

Shelby squeezed Alex's shoulder, drawing him closer to her. "I'm glad you're here," she whispered. "And somewhere out there, I know Dad is glad, too."

"He'd be toasting your success right about now, if he were with us," Alex agreed, "leading the room into some theatrical speech."

"Always larger than life." Shelby smiled.

Alex straightened his shoulders, affecting his father's customary exuberance with a dramatic sweep of one long arm. "Welcome to the new Merrick Inn," he invited in a booming voice, managing to stay in character until trailing off into a fit of laughter.

Welcome, Shelby added silently, *to the rest of your life.*

Author's Note

While some locations depicted on San Juan Island are indeed real places, such as the lighthouse at Lime Kiln State Park and the San Juan Historical Society and Museum, others have come directly from my imagination, inspired by my time on-island. The Captain Merrick Inn is not a real place, as much as I wish it were, and while there is indeed a San Juan Vineyards, Holly's San Juan Winery is of my own creation. I do encourage readers to download the book club guide for *Now That I Know You by Heart* at https://amyhagstrom.com for a list of real-life San Juan Island restaurant and sightseeing recommendations from yours truly.

Acknowledgments

Every writer needs a supportive team, and I am extremely fortunate to have a long list of literary team members. At the top of this list is always my agent, Abby Saul of the Lark Group, the best champion, support person, and advocate I could ask for. An echoed thank-you goes to my entertainment/film agents, Alec Frankel and Debbie Deuble, at the Independent Artist Group. I love that they are always envisioning more for my books.

The support for my work continues with my Lake Union team, including my editor, Laura Van der Veer; developmental editor, Faith Black Ross; and the copyediting and proofreading team. Thank you for helping to polish this novel to a shine!

I would be lost without my faithful writing group, who has the hard task of always seeing my work at its most raw. To Kathleen Basi, Brian Katcher, Heidi Stallman, and Joseph Marshall, thank you from the bottom of my heart. You never let me get away with runaway sentences and always know when I need to move my plot along, and for this I'm forever grateful.

I was a travel writer before I became a novelist, and if that fact peeks through in this novel, it's due to the familiarization trips I was fortunate to take to the San Juan Islands during my career writing for regional and national magazines. I want to thank the San Juan Islands Visitors Bureau for its dedication to this special place in the world, and for doing such a good job of showcasing the archipelago's many treasures, including its many local artisans, growers, and makers.

It is also essential to me to acknowledge the Coast Salish and Straits Salish peoples, who have called what is now known as the San Juan Islands home since time immemorial. A heartfelt thank-you to the Lopez Island Historical Society and Museum, in particular, for the thorough materials it provides on Salish heritage, including oral tradition, fiber art, and the impacts of European colonialization. The Salish people's stories are not mine to tell, and as such, Jolene's depiction of Ayita is fictional. However, it was my intention to echo and honor the wisdom of the Salish oral tradition through Jolene, as well as to acknowledge the challenges inherent in passing stories such as these down to subsequent generations.

On a personal note, I want to acknowledge the grace given to me by Charlie Whitley while I wrote the earliest (and messiest) drafts of this novel. Having the creative freedom I needed was essential for me to tell the story I wanted to tell.

Last, but never least, I want to thank my immediate family for the continual support, which takes on many forms, from early reads to prioritizing my writing and lots of encouragement in between. These tasks fall most often to my wife, Erika Balbier, who is the best cheerleader a writer could ask for. I am also so appreciative of the support offered by my amazing young adult children: Nate, Claire, and Toby; my parents, Julie and Jerry Hagstrom; and all my extended family.

Book Club Questions

1. Shelby undergoes a personal transition in her life from the start to the end of the novel. Was physically relocating herself from Portland, Oregon, to the San Juan Islands essential to this transition? Why or why not? How else can individuals effect change? Bonus question: How much credit or blame should Josh get for Shelby's move and purchase of the Captain Merrick Inn?
2. The theme of identity lies at the heart of *Now That I Know You by Heart*, with Shelby in a bit of a crisis when we meet her. How do the people she encounters on San Juan Island, namely the San Juan Sisters, influence her on this journey?
3. Ezra Peterson's attempts to conjure his grandfather are very literal, and quite destructive. In what ways does Shelby hold tight to the past as well, and how does this practice affect her life in the present, as well as her relationship with Ezra?
4. Holly tells Shelby that sometimes "in the queer space, we have to . . . eventually leap, steeling ourselves to get burned." How did she show her vulnerability to Shelby throughout the novel? Was she wise to do so? Why or why not?
5. Why was Beth's approval and acceptance so important to

Shelby, even after she'd moved to the island? What role did their shared past play in their present dynamics and in Shelby's overall growth as a person?

6. In what ways was the greater San Juan Islands community essential to Shelby's success with the relaunch of the Captain Merrick Inn? Was this tight community ever a hindrance or roadblock?

About the Author

Photo © 2022 Erika Balbier

Amy Hagstrom is the author of *The Wild Between Us* and *Smoke Season*. She is a writer and editor with two decades of experience in the travel and outdoor industry. Amy has been recognized as an *O* Magazine Insider and was a columnist and feature writer at Travel Oregon, *US News & World Report*, and *HuffPost*. She holds a bachelor's degree in creative writing from Whitworth University. A lifelong outdoors enthusiast, she served as a volunteer EMT with her local county search and rescue unit before launching her travel writing career.

After raising three children in the Pacific Northwest, Amy traded the Cascade, Siskiyou, and Sierra Nevada Mountain ranges for the Berkshires, making her home in western Massachusetts with her wife. Visit her at https://amyhagstrom.com.